BIG BEN STRIKES
ELEVEN

BIG BEN STRIKES ELEVEN

DAVID MAGARSHACK

with an introduction by
MARTIN EDWARDS

This edition published 2023 by
The British Library
96 Euston Road
London NW1 2DB

Big Ben Strikes Eleven was first published in
1934 by Constable & Co., London.

Cataloguing in Publication Data
A catalogue record for this publication is
available from the British Library

ISBN 978 0 7123 5483 7
e-ISBN 978 0 7123 6856 8

Front cover image © London Metropolitan Archives

Text design and typesetting by Tetragon, London
Printed in England by TJ Books, Padstow, Cornwall

CONTENTS

INTRODUCTION

Big Ben Strikes Eleven, originally published in 1934, was the first of three detective novels written by a remarkable man who later earned renown as a translator. David Magarshack boldly gave the sub-title *A Murder Story for Grown-Up People* to the original printing of this story about the death of the rich and (naturally) unpleasant Sir Robert Boniface, who is found shot in his blue limousine. At first it seems possible that he committed suicide, although so far as the reader is concerned, the sub-title kills off that explanation for his death. We are introduced to a fairly narrow range of suspects, and the detective work is undertaken not by a brilliant amateur but by two Scotland Yard men, Superintendent Mooney and Inspector Beckett.

Dorothy L. Sayers gave the novel a warm reception in a review for the *Sunday Times*: "a very jolly book, with sound plot, some good characterisation, and everything handsome about it." She thought his sub-title meant "that the motives and behaviours of his characters are such as the adult mind can reasonably accept" and judged the novel to be the best of the week. *The Times* was equally enthusiastic: "A first rate detective story... all sound, quick and exciting."

The *Manchester Evening Chronicle* was also impressed: "A detective story that will rank amongst the finest of the year. The story is extremely complicated, but so skilfully is the material handled and so cleverly are the main points brought out that one never realises it while reading. Mr. Magarshack makes his characters all real and convincing. His psychology is as good as his deduction."

No doubt much encouraged, Magarshack quickly followed up his debut with *Death Cuts a Caper* in 1935. But it is one thing to write a good mystery novel, quite another to produce high-calibre crime fiction time and again. Sayers was less enthusiastic about the second book: "the creaking of the machinery is not sufficiently compensated by the undoubted cleverness of its morbid psychology." A third mystery, *Three Dead*, soon appeared in 1937, but then Magarshack abandoned crime writing and concentrated on the work that was to make his name.

In my introductions to British Library Crime Classics, I have often mentioned the help that I receive, sometimes from complete strangers, in working on this series. This novel offers a good illustration of the serendipitous way in which things can develop, often over a period of several years. While researching Peter Shaffer's *The Woman in the Wardrobe*, published in the series a few years ago, I had the pleasure of meeting Peter's brother Brian and sister-in-law Elinor. Elinor Shaffer, an eminent academic, introduced me to Professor Muireann Maguire of Exeter University, a fan of the series who asked if I might consider recommending the detective novels of David Magarshack to the British Library. Muireann in turn introduced me to Dr. Cathy McAteer, the leading expert on Magarshack's work, which she discusses in depth in *Translating Great Russian Literature: The Penguin Russian Classics*. I am indebted to Cathy and Muireann for the information and help they have kindly provided to me in order that I could compile a detailed account of Magarshack and his crime fiction. Without their encouragement and enthusiasm, I doubt this rare book would be making a fresh appearance in the twenty-first century.

David Magarshack was a Jewish intellectual, born in 1899 in Riga, now the capital of Latvia but then part of the Russian Empire. After the Russian Revolution, he feared that repressive regulations targeted at Jewish people would make it difficult for him to pursue his educational ambitions, and he moved to England in 1920. His arrival in the UK coincided with the tail-end of the so-called "Russian craze", that is, the Edwardian readership's fascination with Russian literature spanning 1885 to 1920.

Interestingly, various biographical details connect Dostoevsky and Magarshack. Both men, for instance, turned to writing as route in part as a response to financial pressures. For Dostoevsky, writing became a means for recovering gambling losses. For Magarshack, writing offered a potential route out of the "tight corner" (as he explained to the editor of the *Manchester Guardian*) in which he found himself at the end of the 1920s and throughout the 1930s. Financial need not only dictated the fast pace at which Dostoevsky and Magarshack both worked, but also resulted in less-than-standard rates of payment to which they each agreed; Magarshack agreed to a much-reduced rate of royalty for his Penguin translation of *Crime and Punishment* on the understanding that Penguin would proceed with high-volume print runs. Both men were helped by capable wives; Elsie Magarshack, a Yorkshire-born Cambridge graduate of English corrected and proof-read each of Magarshack's publications and continued to chase royalties and publicity after Magarshack's death in 1977. And both writers recognised the benefits of recycling previously successful literary formulae, applying them to their own works.

Magarshack was aware of the parallels. He said in his notes that a "good" translator must possess the ability to "crawl into the mind of his author", and it seems he made a conscious attempt to work in the Dostoevskian tradition when writing detective fiction. As Penguin's first translator of all the key works by Dostoevsky between 1951 and 1958 and Dostoevsky's first biographer in English, Magarshack owed much of his later literary success and reputation to the great Russian author. His three detective novels failed to provide Magarshack with the literary breakthrough he longed for, but they suggest a literary link with Dostoevsky as a crime writer. In her essay "Crime and Publishing: How Dostoevskii Changed the British Murder", Muireann Maguire acknowledges a critical reluctance to celebrate Dostoevsky specifically as a crime writer, pointing out that Leonid Grossman's description of *Crime and Punishment* as "a philosophical novel with a criminal setting" neatly emphasises the extent to which Dostoevsky's interest in crime has been perceived as playing second fiddle to his philosophy.

Magarshack's novels attempt to capture both the philosophical and the crime elements of Dostoevsky's writing. He recycles key themes such as overdue rent, murder, and close police surveillance; thus, Porfiry Petrovich finds new life in Inspector Beckett and Superintendent Mooney. As Cathy McAteer argues, for Magarshack, these motifs are reworked for a British readership. Magarshack also experiments with Dostoevskian philosophising, description, and characterisation, as in his exploration of genius in this novel. His musings about whether it is a burden or blessing for a person to have genius bestowed upon them and whether genius impacts upon an individual's actions are reminiscent of the self-obsessed narrative of Dostoevsky's Underground Man and of Raskolnikov, the protagonist of *Crime and Punishment*.

In this story, Magarshack's debt to Dostoevsky is evident, in the way he transposes Raskolnikov's imagined Napoleon to the culturally-modified context of British commerce: "Sir Robert had justly been called a Napoleon of Industry. The question was whether civilisation, which had made such tremendous strides since Napoleon on the perilous road of self-realisation, could survive another Napoleon?... the time was coming when the civilised world would have seriously to consider the alternative of either putting its Napoleons to death or of perishing by their swords."

Right from the start of this novel, there are echoes of Dostoevsky. The first sentence evokes, if distantly, the style and mood of the opening lines of *Crime and Punishment*. Dostoevsky gave distinctive voices to characters playing minor roles in his novels, and so did Magarshack. It is impressive that *Big Ben Strikes Eleven* was published only a decade after Magarshack graduated from University College, London, having arrived in the country with scarcely any English. After his third novel was published, however, he found that translation work was more remunerative. For all its merits, his fiction didn't yield the financial or reputational rewards he'd hoped for.

Magarshack was one of a large number of people better known for their achievements in other fields, who tried their hand at detective fiction during the "Golden Age of Murder" between the wars. Examples range from A. A. Milne and Billie Houston to Ronald Knox, J. C. Masterman, and C. P. Snow. They were drawn to the genre for a variety of reasons, including its perceived intellectual rigour and, no doubt, the prospect of commercial reward. Sustaining a career as a crime writer, however, presents serious challenges and is hardly a guarantee of easy money. Most of the dabblers fell by the wayside, at least so far as the genre is concerned. But their work is often interesting and enjoyable and Magarshack's debut novel certainly deserves this fresh life as a Crime Classic.

MARTIN EDWARDS

www.martinedwardsbooks.com

A NOTE FROM THE PUBLISHER

The original novels and short stories reprinted in the British Library Crime Classics series were written and published in a period ranging, for the most part, from the 1890s to the 1960s. There are many elements of these stories which continue to entertain modern readers; however, in some cases there are also uses of language, instances of stereotyping and some attitudes expressed by narrators or characters which may not be endorsed by the publishing standards of today. We acknowledge therefore that some elements in the works selected for reprinting may continue to make uncomfortable reading for some of our audience. With this series British Library Publishing aims to offer a new readership a chance to read some of the rare books of the British Library's collections in an affordable paperback format, to enjoy their merits and to look back into the world of the twentieth century as portrayed by its writers. It is not possible to separate these stories from the history of their writing and as such the following novel is presented as it was originally published with minor edits only, made for consistency of style and sense. We welcome feedback from our readers, which can be sent to the following address:

British Library Publishing
The British Library
96 Euston Road
London, NW1 2DB
United Kingdom

I

THE BODY IN THE CAR

THE DISCOVERY OF SIR ROBERT BONIFACE'S BODY ON THE FLOOR of his blue limousine was made quite accidentally on a sultry Friday evening towards the end of June. The car was drawn up by the side of the road leading into the Vale of Health, that curious jumble of a few dozen houses of different periods and in different stages of respectability, huddled together on the edge of a large pond in a hollow on Hampstead Heath. The large blue limousine failed to attract particular attention at first, because it is usual for cars to stop there in the evenings at all seasons of the year, and particularly on a hot summer evening, this being the most accessible spot on the Heath for couples out for an hour's undisturbed love-making in a car. Samuel Halstead, a small, lean, beady-eyed man with a yellow moustache, first noticed it on his return from his day's work at a quarter to seven. He had had a very busy day. Window-cleaning was an occupation which seldom kept one busy so late, but to-day was an exception. He had spent the morning and the afternoon on his usual rounds, working on the windows of half a dozen houses in the morning and on the windows of two more houses and of a public-house in the High Street in the afternoon. He got to work in earnest, however, soon after five o'clock on a very large house which had been occupied only recently. Mr. Halstead, being an old resident of Hampstead, had quite a large number of houses on whose custom he could rely at more or less frequent intervals, but the prospect of adding one of Hampstead's largest houses to his list of regular customers made him spend quite an hour and a half on the job. He passed the large blue limousine on his way back, but did not take much notice of it then.

About an hour later Halstead left his basement flat after a somewhat stormy scene with his wife and daughter and went to spend his usual evening at the public-house. His feelings were deeply hurt. His authority in his own home, never too strong, had been challenged this time in a way which required the application of a certain amount of persuasion by force. He was used to beating his wife occasionally, but this time it was his daughter Agnes who stood in need of chastisement. In the heat of the argument, his evening meal unfinished, he forgot the usual prudence which had kept him from asserting his authority over his daughter ever since she had grown too strong for him to manage. She was as headstrong as her mother, but not till that evening had she provoked him with so much impudence. He had forbidden her to engage herself as a model to Matt Caldwell, an artist who occupied a studio in the public-house in the Vale of Health. He had always disliked the man, whose bulk loomed so large over his own puny figure. He hated him for his loud assertiveness, his salacious jocularity and his great strength, and he despised him for his poverty and for the casualness with which he borrowed money from all and sundry, but he could not help touching his cap whenever he met him. Agnes was employed as a daily help at the public-house and of her intention to become Caldwell's model he had only learned from a few words exchanged between mother and daughter some days ago. He forbade it instantly. But not till that evening in June had he thought it necessary to suit his action to his word. He discovered too late that he was no match for Agnes...

With a feeling of great bitterness against fate for having made him so small and weak and his daughter so overtowering and strong, and displeased, besides, at his own recklessness in driving the argument to such an unprofitable length, Halstead merely glanced at the blue limousine, which was still standing on the same spot close to the gorse bushes and about three hundred yards from the front gate of No. 1, Highcroft Villas, whose basement he had occupied for over ten years. He went straight to the public-house. Never abstemious, Mr. Halstead found the large number of silver coins in his pocket that evening a great solace to his lacerated feelings. He did not stay long, however. For in his usual place at the bar, smoking his pipe, stood Matt Caldwell, the cause of his recent humiliation and, as he quite rightly surmised, the seducer of his daughter. Halstead, with the air of an injured man, barely replied to Caldwell's always hearty greetings. He gave his order, repeated it, and consumed his two pints in dead silence. When he emerged from the public-house about ten minutes later he had quite made up his mind to go straight home and bring his argument with Agnes and her mother to a more satisfactory conclusion. But at the gate he stopped to consider his best line of action. "What that girl wants," he muttered to himself, "is somebody to give her a darned good hiding!" The thought had occurred to him many times during the last quarter of an hour, as he reflected ruefully on his own attempt to chastise Agnes. And then, all at once, without any apparent reason the presence of the blue limousine burst into his consciousness...

He had first noticed it on his return from work. There was nothing extraordinary for a car to be standing at that particular spot even for a few hours, but now he had a queer feeling that he had noticed something unusual about the blue limousine when he had first passed it. And although, try as he might, he could not remember anything distinct about it, the inexplicable feeling persisted. The windows of the car were closed and there did not seem to be anyone inside it. There was nothing extraordinary in that, either. The occupants of the car might have gone off for a walk on the Heath. But whether it was that his courage had suddenly failed him and he preferred to find a pretext for postponing the resumption of the argument with his family, or that some mysterious foreboding of the fame which was to descend on him so soon stirred within his brain and drew him towards the blue limousine, the fact remained that Mr. Halstead quite forgot his original intention of restoring his badly shaken paternal authority and went straight towards the car.

It was exactly eight, for the clock of Christchurch, whose tall spire could be seen in the distance clear above the trees and houses, was striking the hour when Samuel Halstead crossed the road and made his way cautiously towards the empty limousine. He did not want to be embroiled in an angry quarrel with some surprised couple and, although there did not seem to be anyone in the car, he preferred to proceed with due regard to the demands of propriety. Another closed car had in the meantime drawn up behind the blue limousine, and Mr. Halstead could see the figures of a young man and a girl at the back. These, however, were too absorbed in their love-making to notice the workman with the yellow moustache standing on tiptoe and peering through the windows of the blue limousine, then, a few moments later, opening the door and looking inside. Almost immediately after, however, Halstead was knocking frantically at the windows of the second car. His face was ashen grey, his small beady eyes protruded and his moustache seemed to be moving up and down with an unnaturally comic effect. In his excitement, Halstead had lost all power of speech. At last he managed to emit a high squeaky sound and to point to the open door of the blue limousine. Exasperated at the stranger's intrusion at a time when nothing in the world, not even a real corpse a few yards away, seemed to matter, the young man jumped out of the car, pushed the window-cleaner unceremoniously aside and went straight to the car in front. A single glance at the floor of the car apparently satisfied him, for he closed the door, came back and spoke a few hurried words to the girl, who had in the meantime recovered from her rude awakening a few moments ago, told Halstead to wait for him and rushed off to fetch a policeman.

The little window-cleaner soon recovered his wits. An event of overwhelming importance had happened in his life. He was the first link in the chain which fate was even now forging for bringing to justice the perpetrator of the greatest crime against the laws of ordered society. But Halstead was chiefly occupied with the effect of the crime on his own future. The hopeless obscurity of his station in life, he now perceived, had come to an end. To-morrow the papers would be full of the account of his discovery of the murder on Hampstead Heath. His picture would be on the front pages of the morning, evening and Sunday newspapers. If Mr. Halstead had known the identity of the murdered man, he would hardly have survived the shock which the anticipation of his fame would have given him. He had always been of a very poor physique and his recent domestic upset had left him weak. The girl in the car watched him recover his composure and was surprised at the tone of authority which crept into his voice as he suddenly addressed her.

"Look here, Miss," he said, pointing to the blue limousine, "you'd better see no one don't come near this car till I come back. Nothing must be touched till then... Understand?"

The little man seemed to be gratified at the way the girl in the car had reacted to his words of command, (so unlike his own daughter whose lips always curled with contempt at the slightest order from him), and, satisfied that she was too frightened to undertake any unauthorised investigation of her own, he hurried off to the public-house.

The general consternation at the news he had brought gave Samuel Halstead his first taste of the exhilaration which bringers of important tidings, whether good or bad, experience. Even Matt Caldwell stopped his loud exchange of pleasantries with Mrs. Perkins, the charwoman who had looked after the gentlemen painters in the public-house for almost twenty years and whose knowledge of the ways of artists with women was encyclopædic. A few minutes later found the window-cleaner heading a procession to the place of the murder. On their arrival they found two policemen and the young man from the second car standing by the blue limousine; one of the policemen, a sergeant of forty with bushy eyebrows and a large, fleshy nose, was peering inside the car through the open door and flashing his torch at something on the floor.

"Shot through the head," he muttered, addressing no one in particular. "Bad business..." he shook his head slowly, and, to some remark from the younger policeman who was looking over his shoulder, he added: "No, we'd better not move him till the inspector comes..." After a close scrutiny of the inside of the car, he emerged to face the new arrivals. "Hello," he exclaimed, obviously surprised at the ill-assorted group of people headed by a small, ratty-looking man, "who have we here?"

The young man pointed out Halstead as the person who first discovered the body. The window-cleaner began to relate how he came to find it, when he was stopped by a suppressed oath from Matt Caldwell. The artist had been looking at the car first with doubt, then with growing recognition. At last he could not restrain himself any longer.

"I'm damned," he exclaimed, "if that's not old Boniface's car!"

"How do you know that?" the sergeant asked sharply.

There was an unmistakable note of alertness and even suspicion in his voice as he examined keenly the massive, bareheaded figure of the artist clad in loose, ill-fitting tweeds.

"Why…" Matt Caldwell hesitated for a moment, "I just recognised it… You see, I've been inside it a few times…"

"Who are you?" the sergeant asked. He had seen the artist many times on the Heath and had even spoken to him, but now in his official capacity his voice assumed a stern gruffness.

"My name's Matt Caldwell. I'm an artist. A painter of portraits. I live in the hotel there…" he pointed in the direction of the public-house. "I painted Sir Robert Boniface's portrait, but the old swine returned it to me. He didn't like it. It showed him up too much. And he wouldn't pay me for it, either, the bloody swine…" A few more choice oaths from the rich store of Matt Caldwell's vocabulary completed the sentence.

The sergeant kept his eyes steadily on Caldwell's face. The injustice the artist had suffered at Sir Robert's hands seemed to have moved him to a fit of uncontrollable anger. The sergeant seemed uncertain whether he should take advantage of it and ply Caldwell with more questions, or whether he should first see if the painter could identify the body. He decided on the second course.

"Do you know who's inside?" he asked quickly.

"No." Matt Caldwell recovered his temper as suddenly as he had lost it a moment ago. "Do you?"

"I've a shrewd idea who he is, but I'm not certain… I don't want to move the body till the inspector from Scotland Yard and the police doctor have seen it. But you could have a look at it through the door. You may be able to identify him…"

The sergeant opened the door of the blue limousine for Caldwell to look in.

"Be careful," he warned him. "Don't go leaving your finger-prints about…"

But Matt Caldwell only laughed.

"I shouldn't mind being accused of murdering the bloody old baronet," he said grinning. "I could have shot him myself any day."

There was really no need for the sergeant's warning, for the head of the shot man lay close to the door with its face downwards, almost touching the white rim of metal near the doorway. A glance at the glossy dome of Sir Robert's skull with the semicircle of carefully trimmed grey hair, was quite sufficient for Caldwell to identify him. He knew that short, thick neck too well.

There was a small patch of blood near the head of the shot man from the wound in his right temple. The painter bent over to examine the wound very carefully, as if to make sure that some idea that had struck him was right. Then he straightened up and cast a leisurely glance at the profile of the dead man's face, which was still quite ruddy, the large, fleshy ear, the lobe of which was already turning blue, and his thick lips. He seemed entirely satisfied with his inspection, for a smile of intense pleasure, almost joy, lit up his large open face. Nor did he try to conceal his feelings from the sergeant.

"It's the old boy all right," he declared, withdrawing his head from the car. "I know every line of his head, front and back." For a moment he regarded the stolid expression of the sergeant's face with amusement, then he bent over and whispered into his ear: "Believe me," he announced a little dramatically, "this is the happiest moment of my life!"

The sergeant did not speak. The murder of Sir Robert Boniface, the industrial and financial magnate of immense national and international power, was in itself an event of world significance, and the possibility that he might have been killed by that young fool of an artist in a squabble about an unpaid bill seemed so utterly grotesque. So trivial a motive for such a crime! And yet, the very unlikelihood of so paltry a motive for cutting short the life of a man of world influence made it appear extremely possible. In life it is the trivial that very often shapes history. The sergeant, who was of a philosophic turn of mind, a fact belied by his face which bore unmistakable signs of a kindly disposition towards a glass filled with the right kind of liquor, for a moment played with the idea of carrying on with the examination of Matt Caldwell before his superiors arrived, but a stern exclamation from the constable recalled him to his more immediate duties.

The small crowd of people round the blue limousine had meantime swelled to a large crowd, and from every corner of the Heath people could be seen running towards it. The news of a murder had spread like wildfire and it was evident to the sergeant that it would soon require a strong force of police to keep the crowd at a proper distance. The young constable could hardly manage it even now, and in another few minutes the mob of curious excited people would become quite unmanageable. The sergeant acted promptly. He blew his whistle a few times and ordered the constable to keep the crowd as far back as possible. His whistle brought the required reinforcements on the scene, but it also helped to increase the crowd which was now collecting on the surrounding slopes, threatening to block the access to the Vale of Health itself.

The cars with Chief Detective-Inspector Beckett of Scotland Yard and a number of plain-clothes men and the police doctor soon arrived, followed almost immediately by an ambulance. On learning from the sergeant who the murdered man was, Inspector Beckett, a tall man with a slightly stooping carriage and a very narrow, long face, whistled softly.

"How have you identified him? Have you found anything?" he asked, moving quickly towards the limousine.

"The licence on the car is made out in his name, sir, but…" and the sergeant gave a brief account of Matt Caldwell and his extraordinary behaviour.

"Caldwell? Which is Mr. Caldwell?" the inspector surveyed the group of people round the blue limousine questioningly.

"The tall gentleman, sir." The sergeant pointed to the artist, who now stood apart from the rest and was filling his pipe.

"Good evening, inspector. I'm at your service whenever you want me," Caldwell replied very genially, with a smile at the inspector's interest in him. He put the pipe into his mouth and was now trying to light it, striking one match after another till he succeeded in setting it properly alight. "There can be no doubt about the corpse, in there…" he said, pointing to the car. "It's Sir Robert Boniface, Bart., or, at least, it was a few hours ago." For a moment his face lost its composure and his lips were twisted with hatred. Mrs. Perkins, full-bosomed and dominating the small group of people which had accompanied Samuel Halstead from the public-house, must have expected him to burst out into a string of curses, for she made a sign to him as though warning him to be on his guard. Whether in response to that sign or simply because it was his nature to flare up at one moment and to subside at another, Caldwell recovered his equanimity almost immediately. "With your permission," he said to the inspector, "I shall leave you now…"

"I should like you to stay a little longer, if you don't mind, sir," Inspector Beckett replied, with sufficient insistence in his voice to leave Matt Caldwell in no doubt as to the necessity for complying with his request. The artist nodded. He did not seem to mind very much whether he went or stayed. "Who else knows anything about this?" the inspector asked, pointing vaguely to the car.

It was now Samuel Halstead's turn to come into his own. He had listened with amazement and ill-concealed chagrin to the unexpected developments which he could barely follow. The name of Sir Robert Boniface conveyed very little to him, except that to judge from the sergeant's, and now the inspector's face he must be a very important person indeed. What disturbed him, however, was that Matt Caldwell seemed to have suddenly leapt on to the middle of the stage and so unexpectedly become an object of interest to the police. It was not till later that he realised the full significance of this interest and his feelings changed accordingly. He now stepped forward and the sergeant introduced him as the person who first discovered the body.

"What's your name?" Inspector Beckett's voice suddenly became harsh and cold. "Samuel who? Halstead? Yes?..."

He listened for a few minutes to Mr. Halstead's somewhat confused account and then stopped him. "We shall hear your story later," he said and turned to the sergeant: "Anyone else?"

The sergeant pointed to the young man who went to fetch the police, whose name, address and the particulars of his connection with the discovery of the crime he read out of his notebook.

"All right!" Inspector Beckett threw a quick glance at the girl at the back of the second car and decided that the young couple could go at once. "We may want to get into touch with you again," he warned him, and he turned to the sergeant and told him to send everybody away who had nothing to do with the case. "Keep the crowd away! Keep them on the move!" was his last order before he addressed himself to the task of investigating the interior of the blue limousine.

The police doctor had already made a hurried examination of the body. Death, in his view, had taken place some two or three hours before. He would be able to say for certain after a more careful examination at the mortuary. Death was due to a wound in the right temple which must have been caused by a bullet fired from a very small pistol. He could not say from how far a distance the shot had been fired, although there seemed to be some signs of scorching. It was getting dark and he would have to decide all these points at a more convenient place with the help, maybe, of the Home Office pathologist. He therefore advised the removal of the body at once in the ambulance. Or would the inspector prefer to take a photograph of the body in the car?

The inspector seemed to hesitate, but after a careful examination of the position of the body he decided to allow the doctor to remove it in the ambulance.

"I can't see that a photograph would be of any use," he said, and then he turned to the sergeant: "You haven't found the gun, have you?"

"No, sir. I had a look round for it myself, but it doesn't seem to be in the car."

"Right. We shall have to examine the car more carefully later. Carry on, doctor."

It was not easy to get the body out of the car, but with the help of the two ambulance men and a policeman it was at last taken out and laid on the stretcher. Another examination was then made by the doctor, but with no definite results. A glance at the body was sufficient for the inspector to recognise the murdered man. He had never met him alive, but he had often seen photographs of him in the Press. The necessity for informing the Scotland Yard chiefs decided him to make haste and to get away the body at once. He emptied the dead man's pockets and made a note of their contents: a wallet filled with bank-notes, two letters, some loose change, a bundle of keys, a gold watch, a fountain pen, a small pocket diary (the inspector made a hasty examination of it, but most of its pages seemed to be blank), and an almost full gold cigarette-case.

When the ambulance with the mortal remains of Sir Robert Boniface had gone, the inspector turned his attention to the blue limousine. A thorough search failed to reveal anything material. There was no trace of the small pistol with which the crime must have been committed, nor of an ejected cartridge, a fact which definitely ruled out all likelihood of suicide. Judging from the position of the body in the car and from the fact that there were no marks of blood on the seat, Sir Robert Boniface must have been shot and his body thrown on the floor almost at one and the same time. The small quantity of blood which had soaked into the rug was now almost dried up, a fact which might confirm the doctor's conjecture about the time of the murder.

Between the back and the front seats of the large car the body would be quite invisible from the outside. The windows of the car had been tightly closed, which was in itself a very suspicious circumstance on such a hot day. It was little wonder, therefore, that the body had remained undetected for so long. The glass partition which divided the interior of the car from the chauffeur was quite intact and bore no marks of any struggle. Under the back seat in the right-hand corner of the car the inspector made his first find: it was a cigar which had been lighted, but hardly smoked. It must have fallen out of the murdered man's hand after he had been shot, Inspector Beckett conjectured, and it rather confirmed the impression that there had been no struggle or quarrel previous to the murder. There was a scorch mark in the rug where the lighted end of the cigar had lain.

It was odd, the inspector thought, that the cigar should have lain just there, for Sir Robert must have been sitting at the other side of the car when he was killed, since he was shot through the right temple, and the murderer must have sat just where the cigar had been found. It was also odd that among Sir Robert's belongings no cigar-case had been found, but although Sir Robert very likely preferred to smoke cigarettes, he might have accepted an occasional cigar. Had the man from whom he had taken the cigar murdered him or was the cigar lighted by the murderer?

All this was mere speculation at present. The examination of the interior of the blue limousine had so far failed to furnish any other positive clue. There was only the negative circumstance of the disappearance of the gun and the even less conclusive fact that there was nothing else found in the car.

Inspector Beckett wrapped up the cigar with great care and put it in his pocket. He then went to the front of the car. The chauffeur's seat had so far escaped investigation. There was, of course, the question of the whereabouts of the chauffeur during the murder. That, no doubt, could be easily established. Sir Robert was hardly likely to drive his own car unless he had good reasons to wish to be alone. Would the chauffeur be able to shed any light on these reasons? The inspector shook his head doubtfully, but the chauffeur's evidence might prove important all the same.

In the front of the car, however, a surprise awaited the inspector: on the floor under the seat next to the chauffeur's lay a woman's grey silk handkerchief. It was crumpled and had evidently been clasped tightly in the hands of the person who had dropped it. It was quite new and bore no laundry marks. This, at any rate, was something, the inspector reflected, spreading the handkerchief on the seat and flashing his torch on it. No, there were no marks on it, nor any initials. Still, it might prove a very valuable clue, and then again its presence in the car might have quite an innocent explanation.

"Quite an innocent explanation"—the tail end of the inspector's thoughts was no sooner translated into words than they took an entirely new turn. Who was the last person to drive the car? Was it Sir Robert Boniface or his murderer? If it was his murderer, then the crime might have been committed elsewhere. It was, therefore, important to establish when the car was first seen on Hampstead Heath and whether it had been seen anywhere else within the last three hours. And, in the first place, why was the car on Hampstead Heath at all?

Would the handkerchief lead to the explanation of these puzzling questions? The ownership of the handkerchief would, of course, have to be established, but, somehow, the inspector did not look with favour on the idea of associating a woman with the murder. Sir Robert was well over sixty, long past the age at which one might be suspected of being the victim of a crime of passion. Blackmail was, of course, more likely, but if Sir Robert was being blackmailed by a woman, why should he be killed? Wasn't it more likely that he should wish to get rid of the blackmailer than that the blackmailer should wish to get rid of the source of her income?

On the whole, Inspector Beckett did not know what to make of the presence of the handkerchief, but he anticipated unnecessary complications, not to mention the wild constructions which the Press reporters, if they got to know of it, might almost certainly put on the whole affair... The finding of the cigar and the handkerchief, he decided, must be kept a closely-guarded secret.

After having disposed of the handkerchief in another of his pockets, Inspector Beckett carefully examined the steering wheel for finger-prints, but with little success: neither the wheel, nor the self-starter, nor the hand-brake had any marks on them. The inspector decided to leave the car where it stood till next morning, when a more thorough examination for finger-prints and other evidence could be made as well as all the necessary photographs taken.

On emerging from the car, the inspector found the Press reporters already hot on the trail. He gave them a short statement on the murder, being careful not to give anything away that was of the least importance. There was, unfortunately, he said, no doubt at all about the identity of the murdered man, but that the reporters knew already: the news, in fact, had already been flashed round the world so that the next day people in every civilised country could read of the death by violence of Sir Robert Boniface, the famous captain of industry, the almost legendary figure of gigantic financial deals, the staunch upholder of capitalist ethics, the head of one of the biggest trusts in the world, the former member of the British Cabinet, the munificent supporter of the Fascist movement at home and abroad, and the bitter enemy of the Soviets.

"There's no doubt that it was murder?" The question had been asked simultaneously by about a dozen eager, excited newspaper-men.

"Not the slightest," the inspector assured them. "Sir Robert was shot dead in his car. There is no trace of the assassin's gun, but it has already been established that it must have been a very small pistol, most probably an automatic, and that the murderer either took it away with him or threw it away. We shall know that quite soon. The whole case is, of course, extremely puzzling and the police would be obliged if during the first few days, at any rate, the Press would not publish anything that might make the discovery of the murderer more difficult."

"Do you expect it to be a long job?"

But the inspector merely shrugged his shoulders. "It is impossible to tell till we know all the facts. Sir Robert's business interests or his political associations might have something to do with his murder. On the other hand, it might be an entirely private affair. Nothing has so far transpired to justify any theory."

"What has Mr. Caldwell, the painter, to do with it?"

"Mr. Caldwell?" The inspector turned to where the sergeant, together with the artist, was standing, surrounded by some of the detectives he had brought with him. It had just occurred to him that Matt Caldwell must be the painter whose exhibition last December had been vigorously denounced by a Sunday newspaper. It was very strange, if that was so, that Sir Robert Boniface should have ordered a portrait from him, but the inspector could, at any rate, understand why Sir Robert had sent it back. "Oh," he said, hastily, "Mr. Caldwell only identified the body. He seems to have known Sir Robert Boniface quite well... He painted a portrait of him..."

The reporters apparently found his explanation entirely satisfactory. After giving permission to take a few flashlight photographs for the Press, the inspector joined the group where the artist was standing. He apologised to Matt Caldwell for having kept him waiting so long. There was something, he said, he would like to ask him about, in view—he hesitated a moment—in view of his statement to the sergeant, but he did not think there was any particular hurry about it, at least not before he had reported to his chiefs at Scotland Yard. The police might want to take a detailed statement from him about his movements and so on, a mere matter of form, in which case they would get into touch with him, of course...

Matt Caldwell did not seem to have the slightest objection to making a statement about Sir Robert Boniface, but he doubted whether his statement about his own movements would be of any use to the police in tracing the cause of Sir Robert's death. And, for a reason which was known to himself alone, the artist grinned broadly.

"Just a matter of form." Inspector Beckett made a mental note of the artist's grin, but he smiled quite good-humouredly. His good-humoured smile was entirely disarming. It was intended to be so, and that was why it was so feared by those who knew what it meant. "Any fact, however apparently unconnected with the murder, might be of some use."

With that Matt Caldwell was allowed to go. Samuel Halstead, too, was dismissed after his brief statement about the finding of the body had been taken down. The inspector then gave orders to guard the blue limousine and made arrangements about the search for the missing weapon. The small pistol might have been thrown anywhere on Hampstead Heath, or even in one of the ponds, and it might take days before it was discovered. A large force of police was, however, to be employed in the search for the missing gun. The plain-clothes men were also instructed to find out whether anyone in the Vale of Health had witnessed the arrival of the blue limousine. It would also not be amiss, the inspector told his men, to keep an eye on that painter chap. Perhaps make discreet inquiries about him. No official surveillance, though. They'd have to put him through it to-morrow or the day after, but that the superintendent would probably want to take in hand. Anyway, it was going to be the devil of a job, and no doubt about it.

With this gloomy foreboding, Chief Detective-Inspector Beckett motored off to lay his report before his superior at Scotland Yard.

2

THE DEATH OF SIR ROBERT BONIFACE WOULD HAVE BEEN A front page event for Fleet Street, even if it had been due to natural causes, but the tragic end of the powerful industrial magnate had transformed it into a story which news editors dream about. Fleet Street acquitted itself nobly "in this hour of the nation's mourning for one of her most illustrious sons," to quote the first sentence of an obituary notice from, it is true, one of the more popular of the daily papers with positively the largest circulation in the world, which, as it stated a little lower down in the column, had had the great honour of "enlisting the services" of Sir Robert Boniface as chairman of its board of directors. It was, in fact, Sir Robert who, in his passion for the modern phase of huge commercial and industrial combines, had, among his other numerous amalgamations, brought off the greatest newspaper coup of the century by combining two outwardly thriving, though below the surface sorely tried, national newspapers into one super-national *Daily Courier-Tribune*. As usual, however, it was *The Times* which expressed most felicitously the opinion of the entire national Press. "Fleet Street," it observed in its news columns reserved for the most momentous events of the day, "was deeply shocked to learn of the assassination of one of the greatest industrial leaders of our age," and it went on to deprecate the panic on the New York Stock Exchange produced in certain important groups of shares, owing to an "unhappy" report as to the real cause of Sir Robert's death.

Of this, indeed, there could be no doubt whatever: Sir Robert Boniface had been murdered, brutally murdered in his car in broad daylight, "within a stone's throw (a journalistic licence, surely?) of Whitehall." The whole of the London Press was unanimous on this point. The fact of the disappearance of the gun with which the murder had been perpetrated was given great prominence in the headlines, together with the assurance of Lord Rollesborough, the Vice-Chairman of the Board of Directors of the Industrial Development Trust, the huge industrial and financial combine with which Sir Robert's name had been most prominently associated, and which he had brought into being, that the financial position of the numerous companies amalgamated in the Industrial Development Trust, Ltd., was absolutely sound and that their shareholders had not the slightest reason for any anxiety.

The passing of great men is usually an occasion for national stocktaking, and the career of Sir Robert Boniface provided a splendid opportunity for long surveys of the rapid development of trade and industry, not only in Great Britain but throughout the whole world, during the active years of Sir Robert's life. The obituaries which appeared in the newspapers on Saturday, June 24th, the day after the discovery of his body on Hampstead Heath, and on Sunday, June 25th, though written in different styles and for different readers, brought out in sharp outline the main facts of Sir Robert's career.

He was born in the slums of Southwark and educated in an elementary school. He began to earn his living at fourteen as a grocer's assistant. He rose to be a manager, while still in his twenties, in one of London's multiple stores, and was soon picked out by the managing director of his firm for an executive post, since when, as the writers of many obituaries so aptly expressed it, "he never looked back."

There was, perhaps, nothing that had distinguished Sir Robert's early career from the careers of other successful self-made men.

Where Sir Robert did strike out an entirely new line was in his utter disregard of the lines of demarcation between different industries. It was, of course, a piece of utter lunacy, he once declared in a much-quoted public speech, for industries depending on the same sources of supply to compete with each other and thus encourage the increase of economic waste, the most poisonous weed in the fields of modern industrial development.

Sir Robert Boniface, it was the almost unanimous verdict of the Press, was one of those rare industrial geniuses who not only thought in advance of his time, but also succeeded in putting his ideas into action. He, at any rate, acted on the principle that the industrial development of one country to the detriment of the rest of the world was no longer possible, but that the well-being of one country to-day depended on the well-being of every other country in the world.

The Industrial Development Trust, Ltd., the gigantic industrial and financial edifice erected by Sir Robert Boniface, was not confined to Great Britain, or to the British Empire. It had subsidiary companies, known under different names, in almost every country in the world, but its various aliases were merely intended as a sop to the strong nationalist sentiments which had sprung up in the world since the Great War. In reality it was one and the same concern which owned oilfields in Europe, Asia and America, coal and mineral mines in Great Britain, Germany, the United States, Australia and China, and tracts of forests and paper-mills in Canada, Norway and Finland. It also owned factories, multiple shops and distributing agencies of all kinds in almost every country in the world.

This gigantic structure was built up by Sir Robert Boniface in the course of thirty-five years. The materials used for its construction were not always of the best: there were times when it was necessary to use substitutes for the cement of finance and the granite of industry. But when these substitutes many a time threatened to bring the whole magnificent edifice down in ruins, under which not only the career of Sir Robert Boniface, but the lives of hundreds of thousands of human beings would be crushed, they were, very deftly, and assisted by a strong element of luck (for Sir Robert was obviously a favourite of the gods), removed, and stronger and more enduring stuff put in their place. Thus the awe-inspiring skyscraper of finance and industry was built up stone by stone almost single-handed by Sir Robert Boniface, to whose great courage and single-minded purpose it owed its being. But even when it reared its head over continents, Sir Robert was not satisfied. His was the life of a great adventurer and the thick of the battle was his element. The battlefield and not the bed was the place where he hoped in the end to find rest.

Sir Robert's great success was due to his clear perception of the economic laws of modern capitalism and to his steady application of these laws. The elimination of waste in industry became the guiding principle of his life and he carried out this principle to the uttermost. The creation of human waste which his industrial operations involved he regarded with the utmost indifference. He had the ingrained contempt of the self-made man for people who seemed unable to leave the rut. He had no patience with stick-in-the-muds, whether in industry or in politics. And he refused to regard unemployment as a problem demanding the interference of the State for its solution. To him it was not a problem at all; he did not see the unemployed as a mass, he regarded them as individuals, and as individuals he despised them.

The obituary writers, with very few exceptions, tactfully refrained from referring to a speech which Sir Robert Boniface had addressed to the members of the Institute of Advertisers, at a banquet given in his honour a few days before his tragic end. In that speech Sir Robert had offered the Government "a few brutal home-truths" on the subject of the right way to deal with the unemployed, the "social misfits," as he called them. The Press, on the whole, had dealt severely with Sir Robert on that occasion, and even that part of it which was under his direct control refrained from "splashing" his speech.

It was an extraordinary fact, that, while avid for power and eager for public recognition, Sir Robert Boniface had been a sorry failure as a politician. His obituaries considered that he was essentially "a leader of industry," "a man of action who was too impatient to put up with the give-and-take attitude of the successful politician." It was true that in the most gigantic of his business deals he "had hated compromise and had brooked no opposition," but it was quite false to assert that Sir Robert was "absolutely unaware of the wisdom of strategic retreats." He would not have reached that pinnacle of power, had he not known when it was necessary to give in and when he could safely ride roughshod over the wills of other men. Nor was it true to affirm, as the special correspondent of *The Daily Courier-Tribune* did, that "Sir Robert was not really interested in politics," and that "he despised the professional politician." The view expressed by an "independent" Sunday paper that "Sir Robert knew perfectly well that he was the real power behind the throne and that he did not in consequence care for the plums of office," was also quite wide of the mark. For the truth was that Sir Robert Boniface had tried hard to get into Parliament, that he had tried hard to obtain a seat on the Front Bench when he did get into it, that he had not abandoned politics when he resigned from the Cabinet after holding office for barely a year and when he finally turned his back upon Parliament, and that, up to the time of his death, he took an active part in the affairs of the Fascist movement and was one of the most prominent foes of the Soviet Union.

Active politics had undoubtedly a great attraction for Sir Robert Boniface, but there was little one could glean from his obituaries to explain his failure as a politician.

Nor did the miscellaneous obituary writers give much consideration to Sir Robert Boniface's personal character. These two important
omissions, however, were made good in an article written by Frank
Littlewood, the only nephew of the late Sir Robert, which appeared
in *The Call*, an obscure and little-read weekly sheet. Up to a very
short time before the death of his uncle, Frank Littlewood was one
of Sir Robert's private secretaries, and he had a unique opportunity
of studying the idiosyncrasies of the lamented magnate of industry at close range. It should, however, be pointed out in fairness to
the memory of Sir Robert Boniface that Frank Littlewood had left
his uncle's employment after a sharp quarrel, during which many
disagreeable words had been exchanged, and that that quarrel was
only one of many serious disagreements between the uncle and his
nephew.

Frank Littlewood's article bore the rather pretentious title of "The
Social Phenomenon of Sir Robert Boniface," and its main thesis was
concerned with Human Document versus Historic Myth. According
to Frank Littlewood, all great historic figures had during the latter
part of their lives been busy fabricating the myth which survived
them and passed into history as their true image. It was thus Sir
Robert Boniface's desire to pass into history as the Great Captain of
Industry, the Hundred Per Cent. Capitalist, the Irreconcilable Foe
of Socialism, the Ruthless Fighter for the Freedom of Individual
Enterprise. Actually, however, Sir Robert, his nephew contended,
did not care a button for any of the causes for which he had been
fighting. All Sir Robert really cared about was his own ego. All he
was really concerned with was the satisfaction of his own vanity. He
was incapable of appreciating anything that did not contribute to
the advancement of his own social and economic ambitions. He had
abandoned politics because the Prime Minister had told him plainly
that he was incapable of team work and that he was a disintegrating

influence in the Cabinet. (This was officially denied by the Prime Minister who let it be known, in an authoritative statement to the Press, that "there is not an atom of truth in a recent statement purporting to give the true reason for Sir Robert Boniface's resignation from the Cabinet," and he added that he was "painfully impressed by the string of abusive insinuations emanating from a source which is so close to the great public figure whose tragic death is so universally lamented.") He had refused the offer of a peerage, Frank Littlewood went on, because he could not tolerate to associate with peers whose lineage and social position was so obviously far above his. (The offer of a peerage was also officially denied.) He had no understanding of art, and his valuable collection of pictures had been bought for him by art dealers, to satisfy his desire to possess something no one else could. He had no understanding of literature and his vast library was acquired for the same reason as his art collection. He had no appreciation of music, and the series of concerts which had been organised under his patronage and whose losses he had met, had been given at the express wish of an intimate friend who was a great lover of music. He had no love for home life, whose virtues he had so often extolled in public, and he rarely spent an evening at home. He detested children, and his alliance with the anti-birth-control forces in the country was inspired by his belief in the imminence of another great war and by his conviction that to realise his dreams of industrial expansion such a war was eminently justified.

Sir Robert, Frank Littlewood admitted, was undoubtedly a man of genius, but could, he asked, civilisation afford such a genius? Every genius was no doubt self-centred, every genius was in the first place a sublime egotist, especially where his own work was concerned, but while civilisation could and should put up with the small annoyances and provocations of its men of genius for the great benefactions which they conferred on the whole human race, could it afford to tolerate a genius whose egotism was so all-embracing, whose appetite was so all-devouring, that he needed the whole of humanity to appease his hunger? Sir Robert had justly been called a Napoleon of Industry. The question was whether civilisation, which had made such tremendous strides since Napoleon on the perilous road of self-realisation, could survive another Napoleon? In his (Frank Littlewood's) submission, the time was coming when the civilised world would have seriously to consider the alternative of either putting its Napoleons to death or of perishing by their swords.

"Our Communist friends," Mr. Littlewood added in a parenthesis at the conclusion of his article, "would have us believe that men like Sir Robert Boniface are the sole products of capitalism. This is not true. Communism, and, indeed, any dictatorship, is a peculiarly fit medium for the culture of the Napoleonic breed. Under communism, Sir Robert would have soon grasped supreme power. His leanings towards Fascism were a natural part of his whole philosophy of life, determined by the 'ideological' substratum on which his whole moral code had been built up. But had Sir Robert been born and bred in the land of the Soviets, he would have applied his genius to the realisation of the ideals of the Red Revolution, he would have been a Red, instead of being a White, Blue, Black, or Brown Warrior..."

Frank Littlewood's article in *The Call* which appeared on Monday, June 26th, only two days after the murder of his uncle, was, as was perhaps to be expected, almost completely ignored by the rest of the Press. Only *The Daily Courier-Tribune* thought it necessary to publish a correction of "some of the glaring misstatements" about Sir Robert's career "which had found their way into a certain weekly." It also deplored "the baseless slanders," spread by a person who stood very near to Sir Robert, which were sure to deepen the sorrow of the wife and sister of the deceased, "the two brave ladies who are bearing their great loss with such indomitable courage."

The Communist *Daily Worker* reproduced with evident approval almost the whole of Frank Littlewood's article, but it took strong exception to its conclusion and went even so far as to inform its readers that it had learnt from a creditable source that the author of the article, who "was so obviously a social-fascist," had made his revelations owing to personal pique, and was not at all inspired by the desire to tell the truth.

No theories of the murder had so far been advanced by the criminologists employed by the daily papers. One of the special crime correspondents had, however, already at that early stage hinted at the likelihood of the emissaries of a certain power having had a hand in it. The suggestion had been thrown out in the vaguest of terms, but to make its meaning clear the paper printed in the same column a quotation, dug out from an old number of the *Pravda*, the organ of the Russian Communist Party, which, in an article purporting to expose Sir Robert Boniface's machinations against the Soviet Union, declared that *"there was only one way in which to deal with such enemies of the Proletariat."* The last sentence, needless to say, the paper had taken care to print in italics.

In their description of the murder, the Press reporters reproduced the facts as far as they were known to them with as few embellishments as possible. Theories about the time of the murder were numerous, but, as the police had withheld the medical evidence on that point, they were rather beside the mark, the general view being that Sir Robert must have been killed about an hour before his body had been found, that is to say, about seven o'clock, or a quarter of an hour after Samuel Halstead first passed the car. Photographs of the limousine figured large on the front page of the more popular papers. Halstead's picture, too, had made its appearance. The little window-cleaner had apparently shown great business acumen in capitalising his extraordinary experience. His account of the discovery of the body seemed to have varied in length and dramatic intensity according to the price the various papers had been willing to pay for their information. A Sunday newspaper, which must have been exceedingly generous, had even succeeded in getting a scoop out of his story, for it was the only paper to have recorded that on his way back home from work on Friday evening, Halstead had seen some-body at the steering wheel of the blue limousine. He was not sure who the person was, though he fancied it might have been a woman.

The newspaper story went on: "Asked why he thought it might have been a woman, Mr. Halstead again repeated that his recollection was very vague, because he had hardly glanced at the car at the time, for he was rather late that evening and in a hurry to return home. But he might have been vaguely surprised at not seeing a man at the wheel of the blue limousine, and from that feeling of surprise, which, strangely enough, was all he had definitely retained from his first glance at the car, he could only surmise that it must have been a woman he had seen…"

"Mr. Halstead," the reporter summed up, "had returned home about a quarter to seven, and if his vague impression of having seen a person at the wheel is at all to be trusted, the murderer must have had just about an hour in which to cover up his or her traces. But, of course," the reporter was careful to admit, "Mr. Halstead was so vague about the whole matter, that the possibility must not be excluded that he might have imagined it."

But this admission did not prevent the Sunday paper from making the best of its scoop, and in a headline printed in thick type across its front page, it asked boldly:

WAS SIR ROBERT BONIFACE
MURDERED BY A WOMAN?

3

SUPERINTENDENT MOONEY TAKES OVER

SUPERINTENDENT EDWARD F. MOONEY HAD JUST RETURNED TO his office from a conference with the Commissioner of Police and other heads of Scotland Yard. He had been summoned to London from his country cottage, where he had gone to spend a long week-end. He had arrived at Scotland Yard on Monday morning and had just had enough time to study the reports of the murder of Sir Robert Boniface, which he had found on his desk, and to send for the Press cuttings relating to that sensational event, when he was called over to the Commissioner's room.

At the conference with the Commissioner the larger aspects of the murder were discussed. The Cabinet, it appeared, was greatly perturbed at the consequences that the murder might have on the international Stock Market. Already it had been found impossible to stem the flood of wild rumours about the murder, and the report that Sir Robert Boniface had really committed suicide seemed to persist in spite of the denials by the police and the Press. So far as could be reliably gathered, the affairs of the chief companies under Sir Robert's control were in excellent order, although some of the Ministers had been given to understand that, had the murder taken place even as recently as three months ago, there would have been the devil of a mess. For Sir Robert liked to play for high stakes, and he did not always take his fellow-directors into his confidence. That was, of course, well known in financial circles at home and abroad, and the reaction of the New York Stock Exchange to the first report of the murder was symptomatic of the general feeling on the Stock Exchanges of the chief capitals of the world. Luckily, the murder had taken place on a Friday and a Stock Exchange panic in London could be averted.

But it was imperative that the police should get to work energetically on the case and produce results as speedily as possible; that was the view of the Cabinet conveyed to the Commissioner by the Home Secretary. What they wanted immediately was undeniable proof that it was not a case of suicide. The disappearance of the gun with which Sir Robert had been shot was, no doubt, sufficient proof, but it was not *complete* proof. The medical report, the Commissioner had to admit a little ruefully, had been rather disappointing, for it was the view of the Home Office pathologist that there was not sufficient evidence to show that the fatal wound could not have been self-inflicted, as the traces of burning round the hole showed that the gun had been fired at close range. Chief Detective-Inspector Beckett had certainly committed a blunder in not having the body photographed in the car, but that could not be helped now. His action in ordering the removal of the body to the mortuary was no doubt justified in the circumstances, but knowing who the murdered man was, he should have at once realised the importance of establishing beyond doubt the real cause of death. Still, it was perhaps unfair to blame him for failing fully to appreciate the international repercussions of the murder.

There was another ticklish aspect of the crime, and that concerned the suggestion, which had appeared in one of the papers, that the murder might have been committed from political motives. But the Commissioner was very sceptical about it. The Special Branch would naturally have to look into it (the Assistant Commissioner had already issued all the necessary instructions), and Mooney could be certain that if anything was discovered, he would at once be informed about it, but it was not that way the Communists worked. Sir Robert, the Commissioner inclined to the belief, had been killed either by some business associate or by someone from his own private circle. He was, he understood, a very difficult man to get on with. In the course of his amazing career, he must have made thousands of enemies. It was Mooney's task to find out which of them had killed him. But, above all, he would have to furnish the Cabinet as soon as possible with indubitable proof that a murder had been committed, proof which would convince not only public opinion at home, but would be sufficiently tangible to convince also the foreigner.

Back in his office, Mooney could not help smiling at the Cabinet's anxiety about getting indisputable evidence that a murder had been committed. It was certainly unfortunate that Beckett had failed to take a photograph of the body in the car, but, after all, if the authorities are to be suspected of a desire to hush up a suicide case by giving it out as a murder, would a photograph of the body in the car be more convincing than the disappearance of the revolver? It was impossible to stop rumour, especially if it was spread with some malicious intent. Anyway, the inquest should help to clear the point up.

Superintendent Mooney's first thought as he sat down at his desk was to have a talk with Beckett, but the inspector had gone out after an urgent call from the Hampstead police. Mooney left orders for Beckett to see him as soon as he came back. In the meantime he decided to go over the case item by item and to make a list of those points which required instant clearing up. So far as the gun was concerned, the efforts of the police to find it had been unsuccessful: the Heath had been combed and the ponds dragged, but without result. The search was still continuing, but it was almost certain that the murderer had taken the gun with him. The following questions wanted careful consideration. Mooney wrote them out on a sheet of paper:

(1) What is the evidence furnished by the car?
(2) What is the evidence furnished by the body?
(3) Why did Sir Robert go to the Vale of Health, or why was the car driven there?
(4) Does the evidence collected by the police already implicate any person in the murder?
(5) What light do the discovered clues throw on the circumstances of the murder?

(1) An examination of the car in daylight, Mooney noted, had failed to produce any more clues than those already found by Beckett on Friday night, except that the back of the car seemed to be rather badly scratched. The evidence of Sir Robert's chauffeur showed that the scratches, which Beckett thought might have been caused by backing into a fence of some kind, had not been there when he had cleaned the car last, and that was on Thursday evening. The chauffeur, who was brought down to the Vale of Health to examine the scratches, could not in any way account for them. The last time he had driven the car was on Friday morning. Sir Robert had dismissed him about twelve o'clock on Friday morning, and he had left the car outside Sir Robert's private office in Lownds Square. He was ordered to be ready at 7.30 to drive Sir Robert to a meeting that evening and he was naturally surprised at Sir Robert's absence at the appointed time. It was plain that the chauffeur was speaking the truth (his movements that day had been checked by the police and found to confirm his story).

But that was not all the chauffeur had to tell. He had made what Mooney considered an extraordinarily important statement which might help to trace at least some of Sir Robert's movements on Friday. Asked whether Sir Robert used often to drive himself, the chauffeur had replied that his employer used to drive his car himself about three or four times a week, mostly in the afternoons. This, it seemed, had been his habit for years. He was a keen motorist and, whenever he possibly could, he preferred driving himself. The first thing to establish, so far as the car was concerned, Mooney decided, was where Sir Robert spent his afternoons when he was away alone in his car. The next thing to find out was where the car had received the scratches.

"A broken fence…" the superintendent murmured doubtfully, trying to recall if there were any fences accessible to motorists on Hampstead Heath. He could not recall any, but he would have to make sure when he visited the Vale of Health after he had had his talk with Beckett.

(2) What was the evidence furnished by the body? Well, in the first place, there was the agreement of the police doctor and the Home Office pathologist as to the time the murder had been committed. Both agreed that it could not have taken place earlier than three and a half hours before the first examination had been made at 8.30 p.m., and not later than two hours before. The body, it seemed, was still warm when it was brought into the mortuary, which, of course, could be accounted for by the fact that it had lain in a closed car on a very hot day. But there was, further, the fact that *rigor mortis*, which usually sets in between three to six hours after death, had not set in till two hours after the finding of the body. The murder had, therefore, most likely been committed, if the medical evidence was to count for anything, somewhere about six o'clock.

The rest of the medical evidence seemed rather irrelevant. The presence of slight burning of the skin round the wound was really of no great consequence since Sir Robert had quite obviously been killed in the car and the murderer must have sat very close to him. Mooney was quite ready to agree with the Commissioner that, on the whole, the medical evidence was disappointing, but then, what exactly could you expect from it?

(3) A possible reason which Sir Robert might have had for going to the Vale of Health was easily suggested by the two letters found in his wallet by Beckett. One of those letters was from his sister, Mrs. Mary Littlewood, and the other from his nephew, Frank Littlewood. The Littlewoods lived in the Vale of Health in a house called Sycamore Cottage, and Sir Robert, it would appear, had consented to see his sister at her own urgent and, as was obvious from her letter, repeated request. This was confirmed by Mrs. Littlewood who had told the police that she had received a telephone call from Sir Robert's office at about eleven o'clock on Friday morning to tell her that her brother intended to see her at about six o'clock on the same day. It was not the baronet who had telephoned, but his confidential secretary, Miss Pritt, whom Mrs. Littlewood seemed to know quite well.

Nor was there any secret about Mrs. Littlewood's anxiety to see her brother. She was very upset by a violent quarrel which had taken place about four weeks ago between her son and her brother. The consequence of that quarrel was that Frank Littlewood had been dismissed by Sir Robert, one of whose private secretaries he had been for over two years, and his mother was now doing her best to patch up that quarrel. Sir Robert, Beckett pointed out in his report, had no direct descendants, and Frank Littlewood would, in the ordinary way, be his sole heir. The police had not yet had time to question Frank Littlewood, as he was not at home on Sunday afternoon when his mother had been interrogated, and he had not returned till after Beckett had gone back to write his report. (That, Superintendent Mooney thought, must account for Beckett's sudden departure from Scotland Yard.)

Frank Littlewood's letter, which was typed and dated June 20th, three days before the murder, Mooney re-read very carefully a few times. It was, to say the least, a very extraordinary letter from a nephew whose whole future depended so much on the good-will of his only uncle. It referred to something written or said to Frank Littlewood by Sir Robert Boniface, and it contained the veiled threat that, unless the uncle withdrew his statement and apologised to his nephew in writing, he (Frank Littlewood) would show Sir Robert a piece of publicity which would hardly be to the baronet's advantage.

From what he knew of Sir Robert, Mooney reflected, such a letter would hardly be likely to help to bring about a reconciliation between the two men, and Sir Robert must have kept his nephew's letter intending to show it to his mother with the object, no doubt, of justifying his action in dismissing Frank Littlewood.

It was not clear what Frank Littlewood had meant by the "piece of publicity" with which he threatened his uncle, but it must have been some revelation which the nephew, with his intimate knowledge of Sir Robert's character, knew would annoy his uncle.

Altogether, Mooney thought, putting the letters carefully away, a queer story, which would repay a thorough investigation, and he was a little displeased that Beckett was probably at this moment questioning Frank Littlewood; for he already apprehended that in Sir Robert's nephew he would find a highly-strung, nervous young man who would have to be handled with great care and psychological insight, a fact which Beckett, fine investigator though he was, might fail to appreciate. Still, the whole thing turned, so far as suspicion against Frank Littlewood was concerned, on his whereabouts on Friday afternoon and on whether his alibi was any good or not.

The evidence of the letters, except in so far as they established the fact that Sir Robert had intended to go and see his sister, and might thus explain the presence of the blue limousine in the Vale of Health, did not really come to much.

The letters did not establish the fact that Sir Robert intended to see his sister on Friday evening. The presence of the letters in Sir Robert's wallet might conceivably suggest that he had intended to discuss them with his sister, but there was nothing in Mrs. Littlewood's letter to indicate the time of the meeting. She had evidently left it entirely to her brother to decide when he would see her, and there was nothing surprising in that. Sir Robert's small pocket-diary, however (a very disappointing document, Mooney thought, after having gone through it a few times, for it seemed to record mostly his political meetings and threw very little light on his private affairs and none at all on the mysterious visits mentioned by his chauffeur), showed that he had intended to pay a visit to his sister on Saturday, June 24th. The meaning of the only entry for Saturday was unmistakable: "See Mary at six." For Friday, Mooney noticed there was also only one entry: "Speaking at A.S.U. (the Anti-Socialist Union, Sir Robert was going to address that day) at eight."

Sir Robert must have changed his mind about the day he had intended to see his sister. Was there any reason why he had changed his mind? His confidential secretary, Miss Pritt, might be able to explain that. Miss Pritt could, if she would, explain quite a good deal of Sir Robert's affairs, but would she be willing to do so? That, Mooney decided, he would have to find out for himself very soon.

If, however, Sir Robert had gone to see his sister as arranged over the telephone, then the medical evidence that he had been killed at about six o'clock coincided with the time of his intended visit. Sir Robert must, in that event, have arrived in the Vale of Health just about six o'clock and have met his murderer on the way to Sycamore Cottage.

So far as Mooney could see, that corresponded entirely with the evidence discovered by the police and, when he came to think of the two possible suspects, the eccentric artist and Sir Robert's nephew, an accidental meeting resulting in a quarrel and ending in murder was just what might have happened.

But against this theory, there was the extraordinary unanimity with which the people, living nearest to the place where the blue limousine had been found, had denied having heard anything at all out of the usual at the time when the murder was supposed to have been committed. But the quarrel and the shooting would have taken place inside a closed car, and not much of it could, in any case, be heard. What conflicted more seriously with this theory was that the police had so far failed to discover anyone who had seen the blue limousine before a quarter to seven and, according to the medical evidence, the murder must, at the latest, have been committed at half-past six.

It was at a quarter to seven that Samuel Halstead had seen the car for the first time, and the police investigation showed that shortly after that time the blue limousine had been seen by quite a number of people. It was true that the people who had passed the place where the car was abandoned, between five and a quarter to seven (a large number of people who were quite certain about the time had been interrogated by the police), did not say that the car was not there: what they said was that they did not see it. Might not the car have been there all the time without attracting attention? In the plan of the place where the blue limousine had been found, Inspector Beckett had been very careful to indicate that there was a footpath on only one side of the road which led into the Vale of Health and that it was a little above the level of the road and that the car was found not alongside but opposite that footpath. There must have been many more people who had used that footpath between five and a quarter to seven and someone might yet be found who had seen the blue limousine before a quarter to seven.

Still, Mooney had to admit that these two facts taken together weakened the theory that Sir Robert Boniface was killed at the place where his car had been found. The possibility that he was shot elsewhere, unlikely as it appeared at present, could not, therefore, be excluded.

(4) Coming to the question whether the evidence so far collected by the police already implicated any person in the murder of Sir Robert Boniface, Superintendent Mooney saw only two possibilities:

Sir Robert was killed either by Frank Littlewood, in which case the murder might have been premeditated, if not prearranged, since Frank Littlewood might have known of his uncle's intended visit to his mother. Or the murder was committed by the painter, Matt Caldwell, who had not only behaved strangely when the body had been discovered, but who also had been overheard by several people in the public-house where he lodged vowing that he would kill Sir Robert, not so much for refusing to pay for his portrait, as for insulting his art and for the general reason that he was a "bloody swine."

Caldwell, it was true, was one of those men who, in the words of Mrs. Perkins, his charwoman, "always talked wild," but his grievance against Sir Robert, according to Inspector Beckett who seemed to have collected a mass of evidence (most of it of little value) about Caldwell's ways, was genuine enough, and if a meeting between Caldwell and Sir Robert Boniface had taken place on Friday about six o'clock, murder might certainly have resulted.

It was not at all clear what Frank Littlewood's grievance against Sir Robert was. His mother could not give any coherent account of it. She did not seem to be confident herself that her son had no hand in her brother's murder. Besides, she was naturally grief-stricken and resented Beckett's personal questions. What was it Frank Littlewood

wanted Sir Robert to apologise for? Why had Sir Robert dismissed
his nephew? To these questions a proper answer would have to be
given before Frank Littlewood could be entirely freed from suspicion.

(5) There was, lastly, the question of the articles found in the car.
Mooney was not altogether inclined to accept Beckett's conclusions
about the cigar. His own theory so far, full of holes as he himself
admitted it to be, presupposed a murder following upon a quarrel.
Beckett, on the assumption that Sir Robert had lighted the cigar,
concluded that there had been no struggle or quarrel before he had
been shot. But that did not follow at all. Beckett must have been
taken in by the general tidiness inside the car, but then two men
could quarrel violently while sitting side by side in a car. Men might
quarrel and smoke at the same time. It was quite likely that at the
height of the quarrel with his murderer Sir Robert had lighted a cigar
just to indicate his final determination to stick by his decision, either,
if Caldwell was the person he was having an argument with, that he
would not pay a penny for a portrait which he considered an insult,
or, in the case of Frank Littlewood, that he did not care a damn for
his nephew's threats and would neither give the demanded apology
nor agree to reinstate him as his private secretary, or whatever it was
that Sir Robert refused to do. And that gesture might conceivably
have cost Sir Robert his life.

It was certainly odd that Sir Robert had no cigar-case on him.
He seemed to prefer to smoke cigarettes, but Beckett was probably
right in surmising that Sir Robert might have smoked an occasional
cigar. He was also right in thinking that if Sir Robert had been shot
through the right temple, he must have been sitting in the left-hand
corner of the car. It was, therefore, certainly curious how the cigar
could have rolled such a distance from where it must have fallen out
of Sir Robert's hand. But then the murderer might have inadvertently
pushed it there, although the fact that the rug in the car was only

burnt in the place where the cigar had been found, showed that it must have been pushed there almost as soon as it had fallen out of Sir Robert's hand.

As for the lady's silk handkerchief, Mooney really did not know how to fit it in with his theory. Sir Robert must have been driving the car the whole afternoon and there might have been a woman with him at some time or other before he had gone to the Vale of Health. Beckett, he noticed, purposely abstained from questioning the chauffeur about it, and the latter would hardly have known anything about it, anyhow. But Sir Robert's movements on Friday, Mooney told himself again and again, would have to be followed up carefully and then the mystery of the handkerchief would, no doubt, be easily cleared up.

This, then, was how Superintendent Mooney saw the position at present from a study of the reports on his desk. What he would have to find out at once was the whereabouts of Matt Caldwell and Frank Littlewood about the time of the murder of Sir Robert Boniface. (It would be necessary, incidentally, to find out what the relationship between Caldwell and Littlewood was. Did they know one another? Was there any possibility of a plot between them?) He would also have to find out why Sir Robert had changed his mind about seeing his sister on Saturday. Again, where did Sir Robert go in the afternoons when he used to drive himself? This might have no direct bearing on the murder, but it might help to piece together the daily routine of the millionaire baronet, for Sir Robert's movements on the day of his murder would have, of course, to be established and then those scratches on the back of the blue limousine would have to be explained.

Mooney did not know why, but those scratches worried him. He decided that he would himself examine them carefully, and he rang up the Hampstead police to make sure that the blue limousine, which was still standing where it had been found two days ago, should not be moved till he had seen it.

The case seemed quite simple so far. "A little too simple," the superintendent muttered, feeling suddenly a wave of pessimism coming over him. He knew too well how impressions created by the study of documents were apt suddenly to change entirely once one came face to face with the living people about whom documentary evidence conveyed so false an impression. In his practice of tracking down criminals he had also learnt that the unexpected was always round the corner, that a chance find which apparently had no connection with the investigation might in the end turn out to be the connecting link without which the whole collected evidence made no sense, and that a faulty alibi, or sometimes the entire absence of an alibi, was as little a sign of guilt as a fool-proof alibi was a sign of innocence.

Superintendent Mooney got up from his desk and went to the bookcase from which he took out a map of Hampstead Heath which he studied for some time, holding it out before him with his back to the window. His tall, spare figure was a little bent, his face with a long scar on the right cheek running almost perpendicularly from his jaw to his eye (a memento from a Turk's bayonet in Gallipoli) was set grimly as he picked out the places on the map. But while he was studying the map doubt was creeping in at the back of his mind. Somehow, he did not believe he would be able to satisfy the Commissioner's request to produce a satisfactory result speedily. The case appeared to be much too simple for his liking. His theory, when he came to think of it, was really untenable. Why should Sir Robert wish to discuss anything with Matt Caldwell or Frank Littlewood? Was he likely to waste his time on some fool discussion with an artist? Or would he really try to argue with Frank Littlewood, who had threatened to expose him in some way or another? Was Sir Robert, anyhow, a likely person to give in to threats, and especially when they came from his own nephew?

A knock at the door interrupted Mooney's thoughts. The newspaper cuttings he had asked for had been sent up. He sat down at his desk again. But before going through the cuttings he made another inquiry for Beckett. The inspector, however, had not come back yet.

The first thing that caught Mooney's attention was the headline in the Sunday newspaper: "Was Sir Robert Boniface Murdered by a Woman?" He read the report of the interview with Samuel Halstead very carefully, but the eagerness with which he took up the cutting died out by the time he had come to the end of it. Halstead would have to be examined again, but really the length a Sunday newspaper would go to to secure a stunt was astonishing. What was that mysterious feeling of surprise Halstead was making such a song about? He had said nothing about it to the police. Was he promised a big reward if he could remember something sensational and did he oblige the paper accordingly? Or had the window-cleaner just been drunk? Still, the human mind works in a very mysterious way, and there might really be something in Samuel Halstead's vague impression that he had seen somebody at the wheel of the car at least a quarter of an hour after Sir Robert had been murdered. And a woman, too. That silk handkerchief? Confound it all, was he, too, giving way to vague impressions and beginning to dream about things? He would have to see Halstead, anyway, Mooney decided. However preposterous this story about a woman at the wheel might sound, it must be probed to the bottom.

Mooney put aside the cutting with the stunt heading and turned to the still unread pile on his desk. He was disposing of one newspaper report after another with unusual speed, when suddenly his eye caught Frank Littlewood's article in *The Call* which had only been published that morning. There came a gleam of triumph in Mooney's grey eyes as he read the article avidly from column to column. It was just what he was looking for! He now understood the reference in Frank Littlewood's letter to the "piece of publicity." What Frank Littlewood was threatening his uncle with was neither more nor less than an exposure in the Press! Considering that he had been Sir Robert's private secretary for some years and was sure to know quite a lot about his affairs, a threat of that kind must have touched the old baronet to the quick. That article contained no disclosures of any sensational kind. It was merely introductory, no doubt, and yet there were one or two references that might be helpful. There was, for instance, that veiled reference to "an intimate friend" for whose delectation Sir Robert had organised a series of concerts. That might be worth looking into, especially if taken in conjunction with Sir Robert's mysterious afternoon visits. And, furthermore, there was that no less cryptic remark about the alternative civilisation would have to face of either putting its Napoleons to death or perishing by their swords. It was an unfortunate phrase, which could be interpreted in many ways. Taken literally, however, and in the light of what had happened so recently, it acquired a somewhat sinister character. What sort of man was Frank Littlewood? To judge by his article he was not a man who would put his words into action, but given also other motives would he be likely to fancy himself as civilisation's saviour?

Struck by a sudden thought, Mooney decided to ring up the editor of *The Call*. The information which he sought was readily given. As he suspected, Frank Littlewood's article had been sent in long before Sir Robert's death. It had lain on the editor's desk for nearly three weeks, and the editor had almost made up his mind to return it ("It was much too outspoken for our purpose," he told Mooney), when the murder of Sir Robert had made the subject and the writer of too topical an interest to be overlooked, and the article was rushed off to press on Saturday and got out just in time for the current week's number.

For the first time since he had taken over the case Mooney looked satisfied. Now, if Beckett did not turn up at once, he would go off to the Vale of Health without waiting for him. But Beckett did turn up. He also brought rather disconcerting news: Matt Caldwell had disappeared!

4

INSPECTOR BECKETT MAKES A FEW MORE DISCOVERIES

MATT CALDWELL HAD BEEN LAST SEEN IN THE VALE OF HEALTH on Sunday morning. Agnes Halstead, one of the maids at the public-house where he lodged, who had been his model for the last two weeks, had sat for him for about half an hour that morning, but Caldwell seemed to be unable to get on with his painting. He had clearly been greatly annoyed by something and, according to Agnes, he was continually swearing at the police. In the end he threw his brush at the picture and told her to dress and clear out. She saw him about half an hour later outside the public-house, dressed for hiking, in shorts, a rucksack on his back and carrying his painting tackle. She asked him where he was going and he told her he was fed up with the police sneaking round the place and that he had decided to go away into the country for a few days till that idiotic murder affair had blown over. His absence did not arouse any suspicion till the next morning, when the sergeant who had first questioned him made inquiries and found that the artist had cleared off without leaving any information as to where he had gone and for how long he intended to be away. Inspector Beckett was informed by telephone and he decided to go down himself at once to the Vale of Health. He did not learn any more about Caldwell's disappearance than was already known to the police, but he did learn enough about his whereabouts on Friday, the day of Sir Robert Boniface's murder, to wish the painter had not been allowed to give him the slip.

For there could hardly be any doubt that Matt Caldwell had spent the whole of the Friday afternoon in close proximity to the place where the blue limousine with Sir Robert's body inside it had been discovered. He was seen painting near the marshy ground by the Vale of Health pond about three o'clock in the afternoon and again at the same spot about two hours later. He then seemed to have moved up a little, for at about five he was seen sitting under some birch trees, with his back to the pond and quite near to the road, painting some seventeenth-century cottages. The exact time when Caldwell had been seen was difficult to establish, the two nursemaids and some boys who had given the information to the inspector being uncertain and even a little contradictory, but Beckett was satisfied that the painter had been there all right between three and seven o'clock on Friday afternoon. Both places where the artist had been seen painting were only about two minutes' walk from the spot where Sir Robert's car had been found. Caldwell came into the public-house about half-past seven. He had been up to his studio to put his painting materials away and he had remained in the public-house till Halstead's arrival with the news of the murder about half an hour later.

But that was not all. A still greater surprise awaited the inspector. He asked permission to look into Matt Caldwell's studio, and while there he noticed nothing suspicious till he idly opened a drawer in a table by the window. That drawer had attracted his attention because it was not altogether shut. On opening it, the inspector gave a gasp of surprise. For the drawer was in reality a little ammunition dump: it contained a large German army revolver, a large Browning, a small Webley and two small pistols. On examining the guns, the inspector found them all to be loaded, but none of them had been used for some time. These were not all the guns in the room: on the walls there hung two ancient flint pistols to which the inspector hardly paid any attention on entering the studio, but on examining them he found that they, too, were rammed tight with powder and shot. He then proceeded to make a thorough search of the studio with the sergeant who had accompanied him, and in one of the cupboards he found a large canvas riddled with bullets: it was the portrait of Sir Robert Boniface, still recognisable, but the face almost entirely in holes from the bullets fired quite unmistakably from an automatic pistol of the same calibre as that from which the fatal shot was fired that killed Sir Robert.

They found nothing else of any importance. The automatic pistol similar to that which must have been used by the murderer of Sir Robert Boniface the inspector could not find. But he concluded that if the artist had done the shooting, and the riddled portrait was, in his opinion, pretty conclusive proof, he must be carrying the pistol on him, unless he had disposed of it somehow.

The inspector then went back to the place where the blue limousine had been found and made another thorough search among the gorse bushes by the roadside. He could find nothing there, and he decided to return to Scotland Yard to report to Superintendent Mooney the new startling developments of the case. Instead of going back to the Hampstead Tube Station by the road, however, Beckett took the rough path leading to the top of the hill where a new block of flats had recently been erected. Half-way up the hill the path led past another clump of gorse bushes, and, prompted more by a sense of duty than by any real hope of finding anything else that morning, the inspector embarked on another careful investigation among the second clump of bushes, cursing the prickly leaves of the gorse against which he had already scratched his hands a few minutes ago. But here again a surprise awaited him, for almost in the middle of the confounded thicket of prickly branches he found what certainly looked like the spent cartridge from the bullet of the small automatic pistol which had put an end to Sir Robert Boniface's life.

Inspector Beckett emptied the arsenal he had discovered in Matt Caldwell's studio on Superintendent Mooney's desk together with the spent cartridge he had so providentially found that morning and the tiny bullet extracted from Sir Robert's skull which fitted it to a nicety. He also unwrapped a brown-paper parcel and produced the disfigured portrait of Sir Robert Boniface, which he displayed in eloquent silence before the superintendent.

Mooney had listened without interruption to Beckett's report. He now examined the holed canvas, spent some time in scrutinising the cartridge under a magnifying glass and toyed gingerly with the bullet before opening the conversation.

"Well, Beckett," he said at last, "you've certainly spent a very profitable morning. What do you propose to do now? Will you apply for a warrant for Caldwell's arrest?"

"I think so, sir. The portrait gives the whole show away."

"I'm not so sure," Mooney said smoothing his scarred cheek and regarding the inspector with an inscrutable smile. "It looks to me like a case of atavism. Caldwell must be rather a primitive brute."

"He's the murderer all right!" the inspector declared with great conviction, thinking of the artist's broad grin when he denied that his movements on Friday would help the police to trace the murderer. "I'm sure he had the automatic on him on Friday evening." And seeing that his conviction was not shared by his superior, he added: "Even if he had nothing to do with the murder, and the circumstantial evidence against him will take some disposing of, we can have him on a charge of being in possession of firearms without a licence."

"Quite." The superintendent looked gloomily at the collection of guns on his table. "H'm. I wonder what he wanted all these guns for?" he asked, looking a little bewildered at the inspector. "Was he a gun collector?"

"It's impossible to tell, sir. All I know is that he certainly had no licence for them. I have made sure of that. The people in the pub. did not seem to know he had all those guns. His charlady, Mrs. Perkins, denies having seen them before, although she must have opened that table drawer many a time. The key had been lost long before Caldwell moved in. I also questioned Agnes, the maid whom he has been painting, but she, too, denies having seen the guns."

"A conspiracy to obstruct the police in the carrying out of their duties?" Mooney asked, smiling at the puzzled expression on the inspector's face.

"Well, sir," Beckett returned his superior's smile, but he felt a little annoyed at the faint note of scepticism which he could detect in Mooney's voice, "I did warn them of the consequences of holding anything back that might help the police in the investigation of so serious a matter as murder, but after that I couldn't get a word out of either of them."

"Caldwell, then, seems to be quite popular in spite of his violent temper?"

"With the women."

"But not with the men?"

"Well, hardly, sir. There was that quarrel of his with Mr. Littlewood, who, it seems, had got him his commission to paint Sir Robert Boniface's portrait. Littlewood and Caldwell, I found out on Saturday, although I did not think it sufficiently important at the time to mention it in my report, had apparently been very good friends. They were seen very often together in the evenings and Caldwell was at one time quite a frequent visitor at Sycamore Cottage. But a few months ago their friendship came to an end, and since then they have not even been on speaking terms."

"Did you find out what was the cause of their estrangement?" Mooney asked eagerly.

"The chief reason, according to Mrs. Perkins, was Frank Littlewood's fiancée. A very pretty girl."

"Also according to Mrs. Perkins?"

"Yes, sir," Beckett replied with a smile. "I haven't met either Sir Robert's nephew or his fiancée yet. I called at Sycamore Cottage again this morning, though, and impressed upon Mrs. Littlewood the importance with which the police regarded her son's evidence. She told me she expected him to be back about seven o'clock and she promised to persuade him to stay at home the rest of the evening."

"In your report, inspector, you say she resented your questions on Saturday, and that she gave you the impression of not being sure herself that her son had nothing to do with the murder of Sir Robert. What exactly was it she said that gave you this impression?"

Beckett did not seem to be certain himself. "She said nothing, of course," he replied. "She was quite prostrate with grief and our first interview was a little painful. And yet I couldn't help feeling that she was afraid of something. There was fear in her eyes at the mere mention of her son's quarrel with her murdered brother. She was much calmer this morning, however, although I had Caldwell so much on my mind that I did not stop very long."

"But why should Mrs. Littlewood be so apprehensive? Does she think her son has something to hide from the police?"

The inspector could hardly be expected to enlighten his superior on this point. He simply did not know what to make of it.

"But to return to Caldwell..." The superintendent pursued his argument, taking up Sir Robert's ill-starred portrait and looking at it wonderingly. "Suppose it was he who killed Sir Robert. He must have realised, of course, the terrible risk he was running of being recognised by somebody who knew him either while he was still in the car with Sir Robert or when he was leaving his car?"

"He could not help that. Once inside the car he had to take his chance. I suppose after the murder he was careful to leave the car when no one was about."

"But," Mooney persisted, "if Caldwell is the murderer, the murder must have been committed in the Vale of Health and as the medical evidence shows conclusively that it took place no later than half-past six, how is it that no one saw the blue limousine before a quarter to seven. And, besides, why did no one notice the painter's paraphernalia apparently abandoned on the Heath for at least half an hour?"

"Someone may have seen the painter's things on the Heath," the inspector replied, with some hesitation, it is true, "but there's nothing unusual in an easel, a small canvas and a painter's stool being left for half an hour on the Heath. I, of course, made inquiries from the people living in the small cottages Caldwell had been seen painting, between five and seven o'clock, but I could not get any satisfaction from them."

"But, surely, if Caldwell was painting their own cottages!"

"Well, it certainly is a curious fact, sir, but people never see what is happening outside their own doors."

"Very well. But how do you account for the fact that the blue limousine wasn't seen much before seven o'clock? Would it have been possible for anyone to pass the car on the way to the Vale of Health without noticing it?"

The inspector shook his head rather despondently. "I'm afraid," he confessed, "that's very improbable. The road is really very narrow at that point and a large car like Sir Robert's blue limousine cannot be easily overlooked. I asked many people who passed the very spot where the car was found between six and a quarter to seven, and all of them deny having seen it. Of course, there is always the fact to be considered that people who are not interested in seeing a thing just don't see it, like the old ladies in the cottages Caldwell was painting."

"H'm. Y-yes…" Mooney seemed rather doubtful. After a brief lull in the conversation, "Still supposing," he went on, "that Caldwell is our man, why didn't he go straight back to his painting? Why should he walk up that hill to the block of new flats? He could, surely, have disposed of the cartridge, supposing he did want to dispose of it at once, on his way home by throwing it into the pond?"

"That's so," Beckett agreed. "On the other hand, he may not have realised at the time what he was doing. He may have just found himself walking up the hill, and, half-way up, he regained sufficient self-control to think of disposing of the cartridge."

"One more question, inspector," Mooney said, "and we shall leave Caldwell for the time being. Was it possible for him to have seen Sir Robert's car from the place where he sat painting the cottages?"

"He wouldn't be able to see the car where it was found, but he might have seen it on its way to the Vale of Health."

"But would he have recognised it?"

"He did seem to recognise it later."

"Yes. But isn't it rather extraordinary that he should admit that he did so, if he was the real murderer? Why should he be so anxious to draw suspicion on himself? Why didn't he dispose of the guns in his room? Why didn't he burn Sir Robert's portrait? Why, in heaven's name, should he want to get mixed up with the police at all? Why express his pleasure at Sir Robert's death? Why take the trouble to identify the body? A lot of nonsense is talked about a murderer's irresistible desire to revisit the place of his crime, but, surely, it is going a little too far to expect the murderer to take the police into his confidence about his pleasure on seeing the dead body of his victim?"

But here the inspector refused to follow his superior's reasoning. A man's soul had unplumbed depths and no one could tell what might be at the bottom. The blunders committed by criminals who wished to outwit the police, but in the end only succeeded in outwitting themselves, were well known to every experienced detective. What Caldwell might have intended was just to produce these doubts in the minds of the police. What Beckett said aloud, however, was: "Everything will be plain sailing, sir, once we get Caldwell."

"Will it?" Mooney questioned grimly, and he changed the subject abruptly: "What do you think of this?" he asked the inspector, handing him the cutting with Halstead's interview in the Sunday newspaper.

The inspector must have seen it before, for he made a wry face: "A lot of ballyhoo!" was his uncompromising opinion.

"But what about the handkerchief?"

"The handkerchief?" For a moment it seemed as if Beckett had quite forgotten his own find in the car. "I don't know what to make of it yet, sir," he said at last, "but I'm quite certain that it will be possible to explain its presence in the car quite—quite simply. Sir Robert's movements on Friday afternoon will, no doubt, provide the explanation."

"I'm coming to that in a moment, inspector," Mooney interjected, taking up Frank Littlewood's article from the pile of cuttings on his desk. "First of all I want you to read this and tell me what you think of it."

Beckett seemed at first appalled at having to go through four columns of small print, but, having complied with his superior's order, he readily admitted the justness of Mooney's inference about Frank Littlewood's intention to frighten his uncle by threatening to expose him in the Press. Sir Robert, he did not doubt, had quite a cupboardful of skeletons and his nephew had evidently caught a glimpse of one or two. As to the peroration about the modern Napoleons of industry, underlined by Mooney, he just thought it a lot of "journalistic twaddle," and he quite resolutely maintained that

fellows who expressed their bloodthirstiness in ink usually fainted
at the sight of blood.

"Which may or may not be true," Mooney commented, "but
which will not exempt Littlewood from the necessity of giving a
detailed account of his movements on Friday afternoon. But there is
one more point about this article which you seem to have overlooked,
inspector. What do you make of that reference to the intimate friend
of Sir Robert's who is apparently a great lover of music? If it was her
Sir Robert had been visiting regularly on several afternoons a week,
he may have been to see her also on the day of his murder. Is it too
far-fetched to suppose that the handkerchief you found belonged to
the same person, and, if so, can we be sure that she is not in some
way or another mixed up in Sir Robert's murder?"

"I've naturally considered the possibility of a woman being
involved in the murder," the inspector replied, a little apologetically
in view of his uncompromising opinion of Halstead's story, "but that
would presuppose, wouldn't it, that Sir Robert was murdered at a
different place from that where he was found and wouldn't it also
imply that the woman who killed him either on account of jealousy
or blackmail, drove him to the Vale of Health?"

"Not necessarily. But if anyone did drive the blue limousine
with Sir Robert's body to the Vale of Health, that person must have
known of Sir Robert's quarrel with his nephew and possibly also
that he intended to see his sister about it. For it is obvious that, on
this assumption, the murderer drove the car to the Vale of Health
for some purpose, and that purpose could only be to try to put the
blame for the murder on Frank Littlewood. And so, if we assume
that the murder took place outside the Vale of Health, we shall have
to examine carefully all the people who knew of Sir Robert's quarrel
with his nephew, and especially anyone who knew of his intended
visit to his sister. Who were they? There was Miss Pritt, of course,

who telephoned the message through to Mrs. Littlewood, but was there anyone else? Did Sir Robert's particular friend also know of it?"

"I suppose she may, if he was on very intimate terms with her and had seen her the same afternoon, but the fact that somebody else knew of Sir Robert's intention to visit his sister does not in itself make that person a suspect or even an accomplice to a suspect."

"Anyway, the case may turn out to be much more difficult than you think, and if I were you, inspector, I should not at present press any murder charge against Caldwell. You can apply for a warrant for his arrest by all means, but it would be best to limit the charge at present to his possession of firearms without a licence."

"Yes, sir." To the inspector it mattered little on what charge he could have Matt Caldwell, so long as he was authorised to take the usual steps for his detention.

Mooney rose from his desk. "You'd better collect these," he said, pointing to the guns and the canvas on his table. "I'll keep the cartridge and the bullet for the time being, as well as the cigar and the handkerchief. And, by the way, Beckett," he stopped the inspector as he was about to leave, "I shall want you to make the following inquiries for me: find out in which public park or open space in or around London a fence or railings was broken or in any way damaged by a car last Friday and you might also circulate among the Metropolitan Police a description of Sir Robert's car with the order to report at once to me if a car at all similar to the blue limousine was seen *anywhere* in the vicinity of Hampstead Heath between five and a quarter to seven last Friday afternoon. I shall see the Littlewoods myself as well as Miss Pritt and, perhaps, also Sir Robert's mysterious friend, if I can get on her track to-day."

Beckett smiled his good-humoured smile, the mask he always assumed to conceal what was in his mind. He knew that Mooney usually got what he wanted in the end and he had no doubt that he would find the lady in question, but would that bring the superintendent any nearer to finding the murderer of Sir Robert Boniface? He was quite certain that it would not, but one does not question the wisdom of one's superiors, and so he decided to get on with the Caldwell end of the search and leave the superintendent to his own devices.

5

SUPERINTENDENT MOONEY MEETS MISS PRITT

SUPERINTENDENT MOONEY CONSIDERED HIS PLAN OF ACTION over lunch. He decided to go to Lownds Square to see Sir Robert's confidential secretary, Miss Pritt, first, and pay a visit to Lady Boniface at Sir Robert's private residence next door to his office, and then to see Frank Littlewood in the evening. He had a call put through to Mrs. Littlewood to let her know when he was coming and of his desire to "have a chat" with her son. He also made arrangements for the postponement of the inquest on Sir Robert Boniface, and informed the Commissioner about the discovery of the cartridge. The news seemed to gratify the Commissioner, who thought that it would be best, perhaps, to let the Press have the story, as it considerably strengthened the evidence that Sir Robert had been murdered. The Press accordingly got the story and, for lack of anything else, made the most of it.

Mooney did not go to Lownds Square at once; for before everything else he wanted to have a look at the blue limousine. He took a constable with him and went up in his second-hand two-seater to Hampstead. He found the part on the Heath round the Vale of Health guarded by uniformed and plain-clothes police, who were still, it seemed, conducting a search for the missing gun. He was met by Inspector Marlow of the Hampstead police, who was in charge of the search, and who informed him that there were no fences anywhere on the Heath where cars could easily get.

Mooney found the blue limousine where it had been standing since Friday evening and examined the scratches on its back very carefully. Barbed wire, he thought, was the most likely cause. He next walked along the path by the side of the road leading into the Vale of Health, and he realised that Beckett was quite right in maintaining that it would be difficult for anybody to have passed the car on Friday evening without seeing it. He asked Inspector Marlow if anybody had yet been discovered to have seen the car between six and a quarter to seven on Friday, and was told that by now almost everybody living in the Vale of Health, as well as all the shopkeepers in Hampstead who might have been sending orders to the Vale of Health, had been examined by the police, but without any satisfactory result. After going across to where Caldwell had been seen painting on Friday afternoon, Mooney went back to the blue limousine, gave it a rapid look over and proceeded to the second gorse bush where Beckett had found the cartridge from the automatic pistol with which Sir Robert had probably been shot. Press photographers had just been taking pictures of the place, but, when Mooney went up to it, they had already gone and the only person near it was a policeman who had been stationed there by Beckett in the morning. The policeman pointed out to him the spot where the cartridge had been found almost in the middle of the bush.

"A beastly place to get it out from," Mooney commented, remembering Beckett's scratched hands. He was on the point of going back to his car when he noticed a small green piece of paper, half-covered with sand, which he at first took for a bit of a bus ticket, but when he picked it up he found it to be the half of a two-and-sixpenny cinema ticket.

It was not difficult to make out where the ticket had come from. The letters which could still be deciphered were: "—PIRE" and under it in smaller capitals the word "SQUARE," and across the number 68582.

"The 'Empire', Leicester Square, a two-and-sixpenny seat..."
Mooney muttered absent-mindedly and shoved, almost mechanically,
the remnant of the ticket into his pocket.

His car was waiting for him at the top of the hill. Before going
to Lownds Square, however, Mooney gave orders to remove the
blue limousine to Scotland Yard and to raise the siege of the Vale
of Health.

"It has occurred to me, inspector," he said to Marlow, "that we
might have a better chance of finding the gun if we withdrew the
police."

Without waiting to explain his meaning to the puzzled policeman, Mooney drove off.

No. 93, Lownds Square, was a grey-pillared Georgian house,
one of a row of similar houses which gave the square its character
of remoteness. It was almost sepulchrally quiet and the roar of the
traffic a few streets away came in a subdued, continuous throbbing in
which sounds lost their distinctness and were merged into a rhythmic
growl. It was curious, Mooney reflected, that from this quiet square
Sir Robert Boniface should have directed his gigantic operations, that
the large mergers, the mighty combines, the vast factories, the whole
stupendous organisation of modern industry and finance should
have been planned within the four walls of a Georgian mansion in
an old-world square which seemed so far removed from the feverish
activity of modern life.

Mooney was shown up to Miss Pritt's room almost immediately.
The first thing about Miss Pritt which he noticed was that she was
dressed entirely in grey: a grey flannel waistcoat, an embroidered
grey silk jumper, a grey skirt, grey stockings and grey shoes. It was,
no doubt, a colour she affected. His impression of Sir Robert's confidential secretary was that of a thoroughly efficient modern business-
woman. She was very tall and well built, between thirty-five and forty,

with decided features and silvery streaks in her black hair. She rose
to greet him and there was in her large dark eyes the unmistakable
expression of an anxious desire to be of use to him, which at once
made the superintendent feel very predisposed to her. There was, he
thought, a tremendous strength of character in this woman.

Miss Pritt sat before a huge desk in what must have been the ball-
room of the old house, now covered with a thick carpet. The desk
was piled high with documents and letters. A miniature telephone
exchange was on her left on a specially built low desk and during
their conversation they were continually interrupted by calls. Miss
Pritt answered the calls in a high, rather unpleasant voice, and she
seemed to be very careful not to say anything in his presence, for
she put many calls off by a blunt request to ring her up later as she
was very busy at the moment.

In spite of the favourable impression created by Miss Pritt's
disposition to be helpful, Mooney had all during their interview an
odd feeling of being carefully watched by her. At times he could not
help thinking that Miss Pritt was not really concerned with what
they were discussing, but that somewhere at the back of her mind a
completely different set of ideas occupied her, and that those ideas
were intimately connected with himself.

Miss Pritt did not waste her time in any preliminary talk, but asked
the superintendent to come straight to the purpose of his visit. Sir
Robert's sudden death, he would, of course, understand, had meant
an enormous amount of extra work for her, but she was only too
glad to be of any assistance to the police in anything that they might
wish to know that had any *direct* bearing on the shocking tragedy.

Mooney hastened to assure her that he did not contemplate any
exhaustive inquiry into Sir Robert's affairs (there appeared for a fraction of a second, he noticed, a faint ironic glint in Miss Pritt's eyes,
but it had vanished almost before he had become aware of it and

her face was again grave and full of the desire to help), he merely wished to find out a few facts about Sir Robert's movements on the day of his murder.

Miss Pritt seemed for a moment to be lost in thought, as if she was trying to remember all she knew of his engagements on that day. "In the morning..." she began.

"I'm really interested in Sir Robert's movements on Friday afternoon," Mooney put in hastily.

"Oh, in the afternoon?" Miss Pritt repeated with just a suggestion of snappiness in her voice and she regarded the superintendent very steadily for a little while. "I really couldn't tell you," she declared at last, "because as it happens I had taken that afternoon off myself and was not in the office. It is so difficult for business-women like myself to find time to do their shopping out of office hours and I always take off the afternoon of the fourth Friday of each month to do mine."

"Of course," Mooney gallantly assented, thinking at the same time of the thousands of business-women who could not dream of claiming such a privilege for themselves, "but have you no knowledge of his plans that afternoon?"

"Not that afternoon. I know Sir Robert intended to go to see his sister, Mrs. Littlewood, at six o'clock." At the mention of Mrs. Littlewood's name, Mooney observed, Miss Pritt's expression changed to one of grave concern that, somehow, did not impress him as entirely natural. For a moment he wanted to interrupt her with the question of why Sir Robert had changed his mind about seeing Mrs. Littlewood on Friday instead of on Saturday, but a feeling he could hardly understand himself prevented him and he decided not to mention the discrepancy between Sir Robert's diary and his telephone message. "But I really couldn't tell you what he intended to do before that," Miss Pritt went on, and, as if feeling that the detective was not convinced, she added: "You must realise, of course, that Sir Robert had such a multitude of engagements and that I was merely concerned with his business appointments."

"Was he seeing Mrs. Littlewood on business?"

"No. I don't think so," Miss Pritt replied, obviously nettled at his quick thrust, "but he asked me specially to give that message to Mrs. Littlewood, because he had an important board meeting in the morning and as he was going away on Saturday he was anxious to settle..." Miss Pritt stopped abruptly. "I don't know if you have already heard about Sir Robert's difficulty with Mr. Littlewood?" she asked him with that look of deep concern which Mooney had already observed at her first mention of Mrs. Littlewood's name.

"Well, yes... I have heard that there were certain disagreements between Sir Robert and his nephew," he admitted reluctantly, feeling that Miss Pritt was intentionally trying to get away from the subject of Sir Robert's engagements. "Do you happen to know where Sir Robert was going to on Saturday?" he asked, thinking that Sir Robert might have changed his mind about when he would see his sister owing to his journey and forgotten to alter his diary (which had no entry at all about his intended journey).

"I believe," she replied quite readily this time, "he was going to Ireland."

"On business?"

"I don't know." Miss Pritt again hesitated. "I don't think so," she said at last.

"Do you happen to know why Sir Robert was going to Ireland?"

But this question Miss Pritt blankly refused to answer. It was an entirely private matter, she explained, which only concerned Sir Robert. If the police wanted to know that they would have to address their questions to persons who had a more intimate knowledge of Sir Robert's private affairs than she had.

"Do you happen to know," he tried for the third time, "where Sir Robert usually spent his afternoons when he was driving his car alone?"

Miss Pritt evidently considered that rather a humorous question, for there was a cold ironic light in her eyes, but she merely remarked that Sir Robert very often had the car out alone.

"But to return to Friday," Mooney resumed. "Could you perhaps tell me when Sir Robert left his office on that afternoon?"

To his surprise Miss Pritt became quite communicative again.

"Sir Robert left his office," she informed him, "at exactly 2.30."

"Did anyone leave with him?"

"Yes," Miss Pritt informed him quite firmly: "I did!"

This time it was the superintendent who smiled. "I suppose," he said, "I'm right in assuming that Sir Robert offered you a lift to the shops you were visiting that afternoon?"

"You're quite right!" Miss Pritt assented. "He drove me to Harrods."

"And you didn't see him again that afternoon?"

"No."

"Tell me, Miss Pritt," Mooney went on, "were you sitting beside Sir Robert during that drive?"

"Yes. You see, you were not quite correct in suggesting that the reason Sir Robert drove me to Harrods was that he wanted to give me a lift. Not that he would not have offered me a lift if he had known I was going that way, but I am myself an enthusiastic motorist and could have taken my own car. On that particular occasion, however, he wanted to discuss some business matters with me. He was going away the next day and he wished to leave certain instructions."

"What was Sir Robert discussing with you on the way to Harrods?" Mooney asked with that tone of authority in his voice which rarely failed to produce the required answer.

The question and the tone with which it was put failed, however, to produce the desired result, although Miss Pritt was taken entirely by surprise. For one brief moment she seemed to have relaxed that steady intentness with which she had been anticipating his questions. There was no doubt that his last question, fired at random and without any particular reason, had upset her balance for however brief a period. Whatever the cause, Mooney had no doubt now that Miss Pritt was trying to conceal something important from him, something that she knew had a certain connection with the murder of Sir Robert. The telephone rang at that moment and a brief interval was sufficient to restore completely Miss Pritt's lost balance.

"I'm afraid," she replied, "I've nothing to add to what I told you a few moments ago. Our conversation was concerned entirely with business matters."

"But are you sure," Mooney ventured again, "that Sir Robert's murder had nothing to do with his business?"

This time Miss Pritt seemed to have completely lost patience with him and her eyes flashed angrily.

"I'm quite certain it hadn't!" she disposed of the matter finally in that sharp, unpleasant voice with which she disposed of the telephone calls.

"By the way," Mooney said casually, "was this the dress you were wearing on Friday?"

For a moment he thought he could again detect a certain unsteadiness in her eyes, but Miss Pritt was obviously well on her guard now. She wanted to know if she really had to reply to all these irrelevant questions? What had her dress to do with Sir Robert's murder? But Mooney soothed her scorn by assuring her that she need not reply to any of his questions if she did not want to, but that by his last question he was really trying to elucidate something that he had found very puzzling but that he now thought might have a very innocent explanation. Miss Pritt was evidently not convinced, but she was quite willing to let him have the information he sought: yes, she wore the same grey costume on Friday.

"In that case," Mooney said, smilingly producing the grey handkerchief found in the blue limousine, "this is probably your handkerchief."

Miss Pritt seemed distinctly bewildered as she took the handkerchief from him and spread it out before her.

"Where did you find it?" she asked. "I thought I'd dropped it in one of the shops I visited on Friday!"

"Oh, no. You didn't!" Mooney assured her. "You dropped it in Sir Robert's car. It was found there by the police."

There was another moment of distinct tension. Miss Pritt seemed to scrutinise the superintendent's face as if searching for an answer to a question which had been worrying her even before Mooney's arrival, but which she dared not put.

No, Mooney decided, it was not the handkerchief that was troubling her, it was something else. What could it be? Miss Pritt, he perceived, was not a person who was easily rattled, and yet once or twice she had been distinctly put out. He made up his mind that he would get to the bottom of it. When he went to see Miss Pritt he merely intended to clear up a few points about the relations between Sir Robert and Frank Littlewood and, if possible, find out Sir Robert's engagements on Friday afternoon. But something about Miss Pritt made him feel uneasy. She was undoubtedly hiding something from him. She was also feeling her way with great caution. Was it some document she was afraid Sir Robert might have had on him at the time of his murder? But whatever it was, Mooney was dead certain it had some close relation to Miss Pritt's own person and not to the Miss Pritt who was the confidential secretary of Sir Robert. In fact, the thought occurred to him for the first time now, what proportion was Miss Pritt, the confidential secretary, of that other woman who so obviously had a private existence of her own, who apparently set great store on her personal appearance, and who must have quite a number of interests outside her business life?

But there was not a suspicion of the thoughts that raced through Mooney's brain to be read on his face. Miss Pritt, who very soon completely regained her composure, assured him that she was certain that she had dropped the handkerchief during her shopping and she had even made inquiries about it. Not that it mattered much, she hastened to add, but she was always annoyed at losing any of her personal belongings, and women's clothes were so stupidly devised: not a place to put a handkerchief in! Miss Pritt opened her bag, which she had taken out of one of the drawers of her desk ("Also grey!" Mooney noted), and was about to put away the handkerchief when Mooney stopped her.

"If you don't mind," he said apologetically, but firmly, "I should like to keep it for a bit. I shall, of course, return it to you in due course."

Miss Pritt was unmistakably annoyed at not being allowed to keep her property, but she returned the handkerchief to Mooney with a show of good grace. He decided to ask her only one more personal question: how long had she been in Sir Robert's employment? But Miss Pritt evidently resented any kind of personal question, for it was with unconcealed reluctance that she informed him that she had been working with Sir Robert for over fifteen years.

On the subject of Frank Littlewood, however, Miss Pritt had not the slightest desire to be uncommunicative. What Mooney learnt from her about Sir Robert's nephew seemed to confirm his own impression that Frank Littlewood was a highly unbalanced young man. Miss Pritt, it was at once apparent, did not like him, although, as she was eager to point out, she had always tried to be just to him and in the frequent quarrels he had had with his uncle she had always tried to play the part of the peacemaker. She had even gone so far as to have a private talk with Mrs. Littlewood, although it was not really her business, in order to see if pressure could not be brought to bear on her employer's nephew to—well, to bring about some sort of reconciliation.

About the reason for those frequent quarrels Miss Pritt was vague. It was, Mooney gathered, chiefly a matter of temperament. Sir Robert, of course, had always been anxious to help his nephew to carve out his own career. He was himself a man who owed everything to his own exertions and he was naturally keen on seeing Frank Littlewood follow in his footsteps, by starting from the bottom and working his way up to the top. His engagement as Sir Robert's private secretary was not really to Sir Robert's liking: he had agreed to it merely because his wife, Lady Boniface, and his sister, Mrs. Littlewood, had for years begged him to give his nephew a good start. He had yielded at last, but his condition was that Frank Littlewood should use his time as his private secretary to get a good general idea of his business and then be transferred to one of his companies where he would have to sink or swim. Frank Littlewood's position was, therefore, really a temporary one and his salary, too, was not high. Sir Robert was not a hard man, Miss Pritt insisted, but he had his own conception of things and he prided himself on the way he stuck to his principles.

Miss Pritt did not conceal the fact that Sir Robert disliked his nephew (this dislike was fully reciprocated), but she also suspected that he could really not forgive himself for having yielded to his wife and sister and taken somebody into his private office who had a claim on him other than a purely business one.

"But what was Frank Littlewood's business before he entered his uncle's employment?" Mooney asked.

Miss Pritt was not sure, but she believed he had worked on a newspaper for some years. He was rather proud of being a journalist, and he was extreme in his views on politics. That was, of course, a further complication, but the real trouble between uncle and nephew started about a year ago when Sir Robert made the discovery that Frank Littlewood had gone through one of the private files in his office without his authority. Sir Robert had been away at that time and Frank Littlewood, of course, had no business to do it. As a matter of fact, the file was usually kept locked up and it was partly due to her own negligence, Miss Pritt regretfully confessed, that the thing had happened. Still, that did not excuse Littlewood who, in general, seemed to have taken his uncle's rather vague promise to let him get a general hang of his business a little too literally and, Miss Pritt thought, not without some ulterior motive, as was subsequently proved.

"Do you mean," Mooney interposed, "that Frank Littlewood was trying to find something which he could later use to obtain a hold over his uncle?"

But this interpretation of her words Miss Pritt was very quick to deny. She did not want to suggest anything of the kind, at least nothing definite. She naturally did not know what was in Littlewood's mind. She always tried to hold the scales evenly between uncle and nephew and, as she had already indicated, she was very anxious when the break did come, to smooth things over.

"Was Frank Littlewood anxious to get a job with Sir Robert?"

"I really can't say," Miss Pritt replied looking genuinely perplexed. "If he did, he certainly behaved very peculiarly."

"How do you mean?"

But at this moment they were interrupted in a manner that seemed rather unusual to Mooney, who suddenly became aware of a tall, thin man of forty-five with a bundle of papers in his hand who seemed to have appeared from nowhere and who was looking at him very intently. He had a long, white face and he wore pale horn-rimmed glasses. His hair was sandy and his eyebrows almost white. He had not knocked, and it was only when he was half-way across the thick-carpeted floor that Mooney noticed him. The man quickly averted his glance and walked up to Miss Pritt, to whom his appearance seemed to be unwelcome, for she frowned, her face lost all its affability and became hard, almost cruel. No less striking was the change in the appearance of the man with the bundle of papers. He blenched, his lips seemed to tremble and his hand went to his pale horn-rimmed glasses, which he began to adjust nervously. Not a word had passed between the two. Miss Pritt took the offered papers and the man vanished silently through the door by which Mooney had entered the room.

All this happened so suddenly and was over so quickly that Mooney had hardly time to take in the significance of the scene. Had the man been listening to their conversation? He must have known Miss Pritt had a visitor and, from the way he had scrutinised the superintendent, it was clear that he must also have known who the visitor was. His reaction to Miss Pritt's frown was also so odd, so strikingly out of keeping with his tall figure, that Mooney could not help smiling. Miss Pritt certainly knew how to inspire respect, though respect was perhaps too weak a description for the terrified state of the tall man with the horn-rimmed glasses. But what was even more odd was the way in which Miss Pritt completely ignored his intrusion. She turned to Mooney, again all affability and attention, and resumed the conversation from where it had been so unexpectedly broken off.

What she meant was, she explained, that Frank Littlewood did not seem very anxious to keep his job. He did not try to adapt himself to the necessary routine of office work. He was always punctual, and he worked hard, but he did not show sufficient understanding of his real position in the office. He seemed to have counted too much on his blood relationship to Sir Robert. He had even gone so far as to express the view that to be consistent, Sir Robert ought to let him take charge of some of the work, for he was his natural heir and, surely, inheritance was one of the main planks of a capitalist's social and political platform. He had not said it to Sir Robert, he had said it to Mr. Benjamin Fuller, the man who a moment ago had brought in some papers and who was the head of the publicity department of Sir Robert's private office. But, of course, such remarks could not be long kept from spreading abroad, and Sir Robert naturally considered his nephew's expectations as an impertinence.

Finally, there was the unfortunate affair of some shares which Frank Littlewood had bought and on which he had lost very heavily. It must have been a matter of some five thousand pounds. He had placed an order for the shares with Mr. Fuller who, Miss Pritt believed, had an occasional flutter on the Stock Exchange himself, and when, a short time after, the shares had dropped considerably in value, he could not meet his obligations. Instead of finding some private way in which to settle his debt, he went to Sir Robert, who was naturally very angry.

"But what did he expect Sir Robert to do?"

"I believe," Miss Pritt replied, with that ironic twinkle in her eyes which Mooney had noticed before, "that he wanted his uncle to make up for his loss. The shares, you see, belonged to one of Sir Robert's chief companies, and Mr. Littlewood seemed to think that Sir Robert was responsible for the fall in their value."

"Did Sir Robert pay?"

"He did." Miss Pritt's face became overcast for a moment, as if she did not want to go into all the details of that unpleasant event. "But Mr. Littlewood had to go, naturally."

"H'm." There was a pause during which Mooney seemed to be lost in thought, and Miss Pritt was watching him closely. "Was there any likelihood that Sir Robert might have been persuaded to re-engage his nephew's services?" he asked at last.

"I don't think so." Miss Pritt seemed to be quite certain about that.

"When was Mr. Littlewood dismissed?"

"On May 25th."

"Has he attempted to see his uncle at his office since his dismissal?"

"No. He was up here this morning, though. I didn't see him. But Mr. Fuller told me he merely wished to collect some things he had left. His departure was rather sudden, you see."

"You know, of course," Mooney continued, "that after Mr. Littlewood's dismissal a certain correspondence passed between him and Sir Robert?"

"Yes," she replied after a short pause, "I read the letters."

"What was it Mr. Littlewood wanted his uncle to apologise to him for?"

Miss Pritt seemed to consider her reply. She thought, she said at last, that during that last talk with his nephew Sir Robert was very outspoken about Mr. Littlewood's work. She could not tell him what exactly was said by either of them, but she knew that Sir Robert had been very dissatisfied with his nephew's work in the publicity department, and that Mr. Littlewood, who prided himself on his journalistic ability, was very resentful of criticism. There was, of course, the further fact that both men disliked each other and had had many disagreeable scenes before.

Mooney felt somehow dissatisfied with Miss Pritt's account. Again he gained the distinct impression that there was something she would not disclose to him. What were her relations with Littlewood, for instance? To judge from the way she treated that man Fuller, she must have tried to get the same measure of subservience from Sir Robert's nephew, but had she succeeded? From what he knew already about Littlewood, he was almost certain that she had not. And yet Miss Pritt was very careful to make him believe that she wished to bring about a reconciliation between the uncle and his nephew.

Mooney produced Frank Littlewood's article and watched Miss Pritt's reaction to it as she read it. She did not seem to have seen it before and, at first, her surprise was very great. She was evidently genuinely interested in what Frank Littlewood might have said, for she read the article through with great care. But she showed no sign of being apprehensive of any unpleasant disclosures, a fact which Mooney found a little disconcerting, for he had shown her the article with the idea of provoking her to an admission of fear at Frank Littlewood's intention of carrying out his threat to expose Sir Robert. There was obviously nothing in this article to trouble Miss Pritt, for when she finished it, she looked quite pleased, and she seemed especially pleased, Mooney noticed, with the underlined passage about the modern Napoleons of industry, for she smiled for the first and only time during the interview, although she tried to cover up her amusement by murmuring something about how deplorable it all was...

"There's one point in this article which is not clear to me and which you might be able to help me to clear up," Mooney said, making a last attempt to draw Miss Pritt into an explanation about Sir Robert's intimate friend. "I'm alluding to Mr. Littlewood's reference to the person for whom Sir Robert had organised concerts. It is absolutely essential that the police should trace Sir Robert's movements on the day of his murder and it is very possible that that friend of his saw him shortly before he was killed. Won't you tell me who it is?"

But Miss Pritt was not to be drawn. She was quite firm in her refusal to discuss Sir Robert's private life and she thought that that reference in the article was really scandalous. If the police wanted to find out the person's name, why didn't they go to Mr. Littlewood for it?

Mooney admitted the justness of the retort and, feeling that he was not likely to get anything more of importance out of her, he rose to bid Miss Pritt good-bye; but before going he asked her if she could tell him what Sir Robert usually smoked: cigars or cigarettes?

According to Miss Pritt, Sir Robert certainly preferred cigarettes to cigars, but he did quite often indulge in a cigar. Mooney asked her if she could produce any of Sir Robert's cigars. She seemed a little surprised at his request, but went out of the room through the door in the inner recess by which Fuller must have entered and returned with a box of cigars, which were not of the same brand as the cigar found in the car. That, of course, did not prove that the cigar found in the car was not one of Sir Robert's own.

Miss Pritt saw the superintendent out of her room and, before taking his leave, Mooney reminded her that he might want to see her again quite soon. She assured him with a faint trace of sarcasm in her voice that she would be glad to be of any assistance to him at any time he cared to call.

"I wonder..." Mooney muttered a little grimly as he was descending the wide staircase of the old Georgian mansion, for there was no doubt that the superintendent was disappointed with his interview. Miss Pritt had supplied him with a few very valuable facts, but he could not help feeling that she had kept back many more which might be even more valuable to him in solving the mystery of the murder of Sir Robert Boniface.

6

FRANK LITTLEWOOD TELLS HIS STORY

ALTHOUGH DISSATISFIED WITH THE RESULTS OF HIS INTERVIEW with Miss Pritt, Mooney had to admit that he had found at least two extremely valuable avenues for further exploration. He had, in the first place, established that Miss Pritt knew something which had some sort of relation to the murder. Was it some fact she did not want to disclose because it might have some connection with herself? Or was it that she did not want to involve some person, Frank Littlewood, for instance, more than he was involved already? He did not know, but he was absolutely certain Miss Pritt was concealing something which she knew might be of value to the police. His second impression was not so definite. It concerned, oddly enough, Miss Pritt's smile, her only smile during their interview, when she read that passage about the modern Napoleons. There was nothing malicious in that smile. In fact, however much Sir Robert's confidential secretary might have disliked Frank Littlewood—and Mooney was not sure that her dislike was so strong that she would actually rejoice at his being involved in a trial for life—that smile of hers had no reference to him. Of that Mooney was certain, although, if asked to explain his impression, he would not know what to say. Miss Pritt, he felt, must have thought Frank Littlewood's reference to the necessity of disposing of our modern Napoleons by violence a good joke, but what exactly was the joke about? That Mooney could not tell.

There was something else about Miss Pritt which had struck him as very peculiar, but till he saw the grief-stricken, pathetic little figure of Lady Boniface he could not make out what it was. When face to face with real distress, however, the total absence of any sign of sorrow in Miss Pritt forced itself for the first time upon his consciousness.

There could be no doubt that Sir Robert's death had been a great blow to his wife. The small, shrivelled, prematurely aged woman was heartbroken. She could hardly talk without bursting into tears. What did the world know of the real Sir Robert Boniface? What did they know of his early struggles, of his failures, of his great fight against terrible odds, of the days when privation stared them in the face, when he had not enough money to provide a decent home for her? What did the world care about those early days of hard trials, of want and even of hunger? It was she alone who had gone through it all with him, and it was she alone who knew the real extent of his triumphs. And, whatever else they might say about Sir Robert, she knew that he had always been a devoted husband to her. Even when his business interests had taken him away from her, he used to come back to her whenever there was real trouble. She had not seen him very much during the last years of his life. To her his great success was really a great tragedy, but she did not complain. His terrible death had atoned for all his transgressions against her. The world, she kept on repeating, did not know him; the world had fawned on him the hour of his triumph, but it would have turned against him again if he had fallen from the high place he had reached. The world knew no pity. The world knew no forgiveness. The world was full of envy, hatred and cruelty. It was to her alone Sir Robert had always turned when he was in trouble, and she knew that it would have been to her alone that he would have turned for consolation had he failed again.

To Mooney this continual harping on Sir Robert's return to seek consolation in the hour of his failure on the withered bosom of this shrivelled, pathetic little woman seemed rather morbid and he wondered how much Lady Boniface believed it herself. But there seemed to be some hidden message for him in her words, something which became more definite when she began to talk about her husband's powerful enemies, about the very bad time they had given him recently and about how certain she was that they must be triumphing over him now.

If, however, there was anything at all in her talk, she left it deliberately very vague, and Mooney could make nothing of it. Whether she was referring to Sir Robert's political or business enemies he also failed to find out. On the whole, he was inclined to dismiss Lady Boniface's vague suggestions as being due to her overwrought emotional state. She seemed to have not the slightest suspicion of her nephew, and she was genuinely puzzled at the inquiries Mooney was making about him. It seemed, however, that Miss Pritt had been right about Lady Boniface's part in securing the position of private secretary for Frank Littlewood. She had always been trying to persuade Sir Robert to give his only nephew a position with good prospects and she was really grieved that the two had failed to get on together.

On his return to the Vale of Health in the evening, Mooney found that his instructions about the withdrawal of the police had already been carried out. Except for a few policemen who kept moving on the still quite large crowds of curious onlookers at the place where the blue limousine had been found, the Heath had only its usual complement of uniformed and un-uniformed police.

Before calling on the Littlewoods, the superintendent decided to have a brief talk with Samuel Halstead, the window-cleaner, who was responsible for that extraordinary story in the Sunday newspaper. He found the entire Halstead family at supper, and there was no doubt at all that Agnes was put out by his call. She was a large, fat, round-faced, rather vulgar-looking girl of about twenty and she kept her cow-like eyes fixed on the superintendent all the time he was in their kitchen, as if she was anxious to find out what was really in his mind.

The little window-cleaner seemed to be very uncomfortable. He repeated the story of his discovery of the dead body in the blue limousine without adding, however, to what was already well known. About his revelation in the Sunday paper he seemed to be feeling rather uneasy. He insisted doggedly that there was something "funny" about the car when he had first passed it, but what it was he could not tell. The story about seeing a woman in the car was really half-suggested to him by the reporter, who offered all sorts of suggestions in order to stimulate his memory. But now, of course, he could see that he must have been mistaken.

Asked what had happened to change his views, Halstead looked frightened, squirmed uneasily in his seat and muttered something about the discoveries in the pub. that morning. But before he could make himself properly understood, his daughter Agnes rose like a fury from the table and, almost lifting her father out of the chair, began shaking him violently.

"You shut up, you dirty little rat!" she screamed at him, her face red and distorted with passion and her eyes streaming with tears.

Mooney left the little window-cleaner to restore his badly shaken paternal authority as best he could and addressed himself to the chief task of the day: his interview with Frank Littlewood.

He found that Sycamore Cottage was a little old brick house which took its name from a large sycamore tree growing beside it. His knock was answered at once by a young, extraordinarily pretty girl whose large, dark brown eyes looked up at him with silent entreaty and whose pale, troubled face showed up the redness of her full, finely-curved lips.

"Mr. Mooney of Scotland Yard?" she inquired a little breathlessly, still searching his face for some answer to the question in her mind: "What sort of man is this detective? Is he kind? Will he understand?"

Mooney seemed to have read her thoughts, for he smiled reassuringly at her: "You're a very sweet child," his eyes seemed to say, "and I shall help you all I can!"

She read his answer and smiled gratefully back again. In the few seconds they had been together a bond of understanding had been established between them. She had asked for his sympathy and friendship and he had responded instantly and promised them both to her.

"Will you come in," she said, brightening up all at once. "Frank is waiting for you inside. I'm June Gayford. I'm Frank's..." she stopped as if in search of the right word: "... future wife," she concluded very precisely and she smiled a little self-consciously at the description she had given of herself.

Mooney followed her into the drawing-room where Frank Littlewood, a pale, haggard-looking young man in his early twenties, with keen black eyes, a high forehead, and very sensitive features, was waiting for him evidently in a state of considerable agitation. Mrs. Littlewood, an elderly, sad-eyed woman whose extraordinary resemblance to the murdered baronet Mooney noticed at once, sat in an easy chair by the window. She seemed to be ill, for she could hardly stand up to greet him and she sank back into her chair obviously in pain.

"Mother is really ill," Frank Littlewood explained. "She should be in bed, but she insisted on being present at our talk..."

He spoke in an even, low, musical voice, but his lips trembled slightly, and his whole bearing showed that he was keyed up to a tremendous pitch of excitement. There certainly was something seriously wrong there, Mooney thought, as he sat down in the offered chair near the door and proceeded to explain the purpose of his visit.

He was at present engaged, Mooney said, on a preliminary investigation into the general facts surrounding the mystery of Sir Robert Boniface's death. Everything, of course, pointed to its being a case of murder, but until they had all the facts before them death from suicide or accident could not be excluded. In a case of that kind it was usual to make a thorough inquiry into all the circumstances, and everyone who had come into close touch with the deceased was, as a rule, interrogated with a view to elucidating every possible fact which might have a bearing on the ultimate purpose of the investigation. Now, it had come to the knowledge of the police that Sir Robert Boniface had intended to pay a visit to Mrs. Littlewood on the day when his body was found shot dead only a short distance from her house.

"I didn't know anything about it!" Frank Littlewood suddenly burst out passionately. "I swear I didn't know anything about it!"

"Frank," June Gayford implored him earnestly, "do be calm. Let Mr. Mooney explain what he wants you to tell him. You needn't anticipate his questions."

But it seemed difficult for Frank to control his excitement. He bit his lips impatiently and addressed himself to Mooney:

"Can't you cut the cackle," he almost shouted, "and let us know what it is you want?"

"Well, yes," Mooney replied, quite unruffled by the rudeness of the question and trying to calm the girl's obvious dismay at her sweetheart's outburst. "I want to know quite a number of things, but first of all I should like you to tell me what your relations with your uncle were."

"You know, of course, that he fired me?"

"Yes. I've already made certain inquiries at your uncle's office."

"Oh, so you've met Miss Pritt, have you? I hope you made a careful note of all the lies she told you!"

"Frank," Mrs. Littlewood's voice came weakly, but sternly, from the corner of the window, "I wish you'd listen to June. I wish you'd answer this gentleman's questions calmly and I wish you'd stop accusing people of telling lies before you've heard what they've said."

"I'd leave Frank alone now, Mrs. Littlewood," June Gayford's voice sounded unusually composed, though there was a clear note of resignation in it. "Let him do what he likes."

She got up from her chair and went across to the window where she knelt down at Mrs. Littlewood's feet and put her arms caressingly in the old woman's lap.

"You don't understand," Frank turned to the two women, still unable to curb his agitation, "you don't understand that unless Mr. Mooney knows everything it will be impossible for him to see things in their true light."

"Now," Mooney interposed firmly, "let's keep strictly to the point. If you don't mind I shall make a few notes of your replies to my questions, and I want you to understand that there is no obligation on your part either to reply to my questions or to make any statement. On the other hand, I must warn you that anything you say…"

"Might be used in evidence against me?" Frank completed the sentence defiantly. "Well, I don't mind. I have done nothing, and I don't care what you do with my statement!"

"Very well…" Mooney seemed almost as much resigned as the two women to let Frank Littlewood reply to his questions in his own way. "I want you to give me a detailed account of your experiences in your uncle's office and the reasons for the termination of your work as his private secretary."

"Private secretary!" Frank repeated scornfully, jumping up from his seat and facing the detective with flaming eyes. "Oh, cut that out!

I wasn't his private secretary. That was just the bluff he put over on his wife and my mother. He promised to give me a job as his private secretary and like a fool I accepted it. But there was no room in his office for another secretary. I found that out soon enough. There was only one person who mattered in that office and that person was Miss Pritt, and she was his secretary and everything else."

"What do you mean by 'and everything else'?"

"I mean what I say. Miss Pritt was everything in that office. He had first singled her out from the typists. That was a long time ago, fifteen years or more. Sir Robert Boniface had tasted power and he found it good. But he wanted something more than power. He wanted to taste the joy of controlling a human being entirely, of fashioning it to his own fancy, of training it to understand all the intricacies of his business and yet to remain faithful to him, compliant to his will. A man wouldn't have done for that. He couldn't trust a man not to want to strike out on his own after he had learnt the ropes. But a woman is different. There is much less danger of a woman's turning traitor and a woman is not only more loyal by nature than a man, she not only possesses less initiative than a man, her loyalty actually increases if she is treated roughly, if she is bullied by a man she has a great respect for, a man she idealises. Sir Robert had a deep, instinctive knowledge of human nature. He wouldn't have got on as he did if he hadn't. But he also had a very shrewd perception of his own shortcomings. He couldn't help being harsh, even brutal at times, and no man would have stood such treatment for long without revolting, unless, indeed, he was a rag, but Sir Robert had no use for rags, except for minor posts in his office. And so he wanted a woman for the most important post in his business, a woman of great capacity, of brains, of business ability; a woman who could control his staff in his name, a woman who would stand no nonsense except from him. But that woman must also owe everything to him. He must be her master and she must understand that, being her master, he claimed the right to cast her down to where she had started from, if at any time she showed the least sign of rebellion. Such a woman he found in Miss Pritt. He had raised her from the position of a typist earning three pounds a week to that of his own confidential secretary with a salary running into four figures. I think he was even contemplating making her secretary of the Industrial Development Trust. At least, that was the common talk of the office just before I left. Apart from their business relations, they had only one passion in common: their enthusiasm for motoring. Miss Pritt, it's true, was only Sir Robert Boniface's shadow, but she was contented with that position, for even in his shadow there was power and she, too, loves power. But an end comes to everything. The shadow has vanished from the earth and, I suppose, Miss Pritt will vanish with it, too! His sudden death must have shattered her dreams a bit…" Frank Littlewood concluded, not without a note of satisfaction in his voice.

This long, passionate outburst seemed to have been a little too much for him, for he sank back in his chair and brushed his hair wearily from his high forehead.

"You don't understand," he resumed almost at once with that ever-recurring phrase, raising his hand to stop some unspoken remark from the superintendent. "Miss Pritt hates me. That's why I said that whatever she told you about me must be lies. She hates me with a terrible, deadly hatred. She hates me because I gave her the greatest fright of her life. She always objected to having me at the office. That was really why Sir Robert would not give me a job. And the reason why Miss Pritt objected to my presence in the office was because she was afraid that I might discover things, and, having some access to Sir Robert which she could not control, might prevail on him to bring her to account, as she ought to be…" Frank brushed away some hardly audible objection from his mother impatiently. "She is a crook, I say," he cried defiantly, thumping the table, his eyes flaming passionately and his face of a deadly pallor, "she's a crook! Not in the colossal way in which Sir Robert was a crook. Only a man of real genius could disregard the moral code of humanity with such utter contempt and get away with it. Miss Pritt might have learnt dishonesty from Sir Robert, but she had not his genius. She was dishonest in a comparatively small way, she could forge a few entries involving a few thousand pounds to cover her losses on the Stock Exchange, she could forget to forward a big cheque, one among many, to some charity, and as any inquiries that might be made would have anyhow to come to her first, she could cover up her traces very cleverly, for, mind you, she's devilishly clever, although in a rather stupid way, if you understand what I mean."

"I think I do," Mooney said, taking this opportunity to bring Frank Littlewood down to earth, "but, tell me, have you any proof of Miss Pritt's dishonesty?"

"He hasn't any!" Mrs. Littlewood, who had tried to stop Frank ineffectively before, interposed in a shrill, defiant voice which left her exhausted for the rest of the evening. "He hasn't any!"

"Mother's right," turning to the superintendent Frank spoke quite calmly now, "I haven't any proofs, but if I had stayed at that office a little longer I should have had plenty. And that's why I was booted out!"

"But," the question was so obvious that Mooney wondered how it had not occurred to Frank himself, "don't you think Sir Robert would have found out long ago if there was any dishonesty of that sort?"

"Well, I don't say he didn't. He may have known perfectly well that Miss Pritt was not above forging. Neither was he. And so long as it was merely a matter of a few thousands a year he may not have minded. On the contrary, he may have been saving all this up for the day when he might wish to put Miss Pritt in her place. But, of course, it would have been quite a different thing if I had obtained real proof. So I had to go."

"Didn't you have rather frequent quarrels with Sir Robert?"

"Of course I did. But so did everybody else. Sir Robert quarrelled with everybody, and, having his own nephew on the staff, he naturally couldn't forgo the pleasure of having a jolly good bust up every now and then with one of his own family."

"I suppose you didn't exactly discourage him?" June Gayford asked a little wistfully, having really given up arguing with Frank, but still wishing to make him see that there was such a thing as fairness to the other man's point of view.

"No. I didn't!" Frank raised his voice suddenly but subsided almost as suddenly with a gesture of resignation: "I'm sick of it all," he said, speaking softly to himself, "I'm absolutely sick of it!"

There was a pause, during which June Gayford quite unexpectedly buried her head in Mrs. Littlewood's lap and began to cry silently. Her shoulders shook convulsively, the loop of brown hair, the colour of burnished copper, on the nape of her neck came undone, and the long, thick plait untwisted and fell down her back. She jumped to her feet almost immediately and began arranging her hair. She did not seem to be aware of her wet, tear-smudged face. It was clear she could not forgive herself for having collapsed in the presence of the stranger from Scotland Yard.

"I'm so sorry," she exclaimed appealing to Mooney for help, "I'm really very sorry..." And turning to Frank, she cried passionately: "Please forgive me, Frank. It came over me so suddenly I couldn't help it..." Without waiting for any reply, she again addressed Mooney: "Won't you have some coffee with us? It's ready, *please* don't refuse! I'll bring it in in a moment."

When she was gone, Mrs. Littlewood addressed her son with a

question which gave Mooney at least one clue to the extraordinary scene he had witnessed.

"Won't you tell us now," the old woman said in a clear, sharp whisper, "where you spent Friday afternoon and evening?"

"I can't. I tell you I can't!" Frank sprang to his feet and began pacing the room. "This isn't fair!" he said at last, stopping before his mother: "You've been trying to force it out of me for the last two days. I've told you, I knew nothing about the murder till I saw it in the evening papers at about ten o'clock. Then I hurried back home at once. I can't tell you where I was. I can't, because it would mean..." But he stopped without finishing the sentence and sat down in his chair again.

"But," Mooney pointed out quietly, "you will have to give the police an account of your movements on Friday. You could do it in writing and send it on to me. I shall have to check your statement, of course, but it needn't go any further."

"And what about the inquest? Will you be able to keep it out of the coroner's court as well?"

"I can't promise you that," Mooney had to admit. "You see," he explained, "we found two letters on Sir Robert: one from your mother asking him to call on her and another from you in which you threatened to expose him in the Press unless he offered you a written apology for some insult which..."

"It's quite true," Frank interrupted, "he said..."

"We'll come to that in a moment!" Mooney rapped out in a voice which demanded and received instant obedience. "What I'm pointing out to you now is that we shall have to produce these letters at the inquest and we have no power to prevent the coroner from asking any questions he pleases about them."

"I don't mind answering any questions about my relations with my uncle," Frank replied, evidently not heeding the superintendent's reference to the threat contained in his letter, "but if there's the slightest possibility of—of that coming out, I shan't say a word about it."

"Do I understand you to say that whatever you were doing on Friday afternoon had no connection whatever with Sir Robert?"

"None whatever. At least, that was his fault, too, the—" but Frank suppressed the uncomplimentary reference to his uncle.

"But was it anything that the police?…"

"No!" Frank almost shouted, evidently exasperated beyond endurance by Mooney's questions. "It was nothing that the police would take the slightest objection to. It was nothing that you would consider criminal, but it's something that might mean more than death to me, something that might…" He stopped abruptly, brushing away the hair from his forehead with a gesture of weary despair. "You won't understand," he said, "what's the use of my talking?"

"But what about the coroner and the coroner's jury?" Mrs. Littlewood asked in her clear, sharp whisper.

"I don't mind the coroner's court and jury, mother. I don't even mind being tried for a murder which I haven't committed. What have they got against me, anyway? Not enough evidence to hang a cat. Besides, I didn't know Uncle Robert was coming to see you. You purposely kept it a secret from me. You didn't care about the hell I went through in that office. It was nothing to you but my imagination. You wanted to force me to go back, and I shouldn't have been surprised if you had persuaded Uncle Robert to give me another chance. Even Miss Pritt might have agreed to let me come back, but on her conditions, no doubt. She would have soon got me cornered. She'd tried to do it twice already."

"You're referring to the private file and the shares?" Mooney asked.

"I can see Miss Pritt has already given you all the facts!" Frank exclaimed sarcastically. "But as I told you before, she's the biggest liar in the world!"

At this moment the door was opened and June Gayford brought in the coffee. There was no trace of her recent emotional breakdown on her face. She looked bright and refreshed. She smiled at everybody in the room, evidently trying to cheer things up, to be a real ray of sunshine on the stormy landscape. Her smile did produce the desired effect. It eased the tension in the room and it almost brightened Frank up. He got up and helped her with the coffee cups and squeezed her arm. They exchanged quick impulsive glances. To Mooney it seemed that it would be best, perhaps, if he went now and arranged to have a talk with Frank at his office the next morning. But when he made this proposal he found that both Frank and his fiancée preferred him to go on with his questions and finish it all that night. Frank Littlewood, indeed, was very outspoken about it.

"Much as I've enjoyed meeting you to-night, Mr. Mooney," he said, sitting down on the settee close to the young girl and putting his hand caressingly on her shoulder, "I should prefer not to see you again professionally, if I can help it."

He certainly was in a more reasonable frame of mind and for the rest of the interview he gave a coherent and quiet account of the "frame-up," as he called it, against him.

According to Frank Littlewood, he was first made aware of the existence of the private file in his uncle's office by Fuller, who certainly succeeded in exciting his curiosity about the "mysteries" that the file contained. But actually, when he examined it (it was, he asserted, left open on purpose so that he could examine it, although he admitted it was really not his business to do so), he found that it referred to something that had happened about ten years ago. The file contained the correspondence with a large City banking concern, which had since been absorbed by the Industrial Development Trust, and it was interesting because it showed Sir Robert's methods. Indeed, if the demands of that bank had not been fully met,

Sir Robert's career would have come to an untimely end and the
baronet would have had to serve a longish stretch in jail, for it was
nothing more nor less than a case of pure forgery on a large scale,
a somewhat desperate act which Sir Robert had been forced to take
"as a temporary expedient," as one of the letters in the file quaintly
put it. The particular transaction, which had forced Sir Robert to
make use of that "temporary expedient," however, had proved a
brilliant success and the company whose securities he had forged
had greatly benefited from it. To-day, the people who would have
suffered most from Sir Robert's forgery, if it had been discovered at
the time, would probably be the very people to wish to prevent the
true facts of that particular transaction from being brought to light.

There was, of course, no doubt, Frank Littlewood went on, that
the same thing, only perhaps on a much larger scale, had occurred
again and again. Three months ago there was a tremendous upheaval
at the office. Miss Pritt and Mr. Fuller were in the thick of it all, but
not another soul at the office knew anything about it, although, Frank
surmised, at the offices of the Industrial Development Trust quite a
number of people must have known what was happening. But the
storm seemed to have blown over all right, and as a special reward
for the services rendered by Miss Pritt to Sir Robert she was to be
appointed by him as secretary to the Trust. There seemed to have
been some hitch about that appointment, though, for Miss Pritt was
still Sir Robert's confidential secretary when that final scene with his
uncle about the shares had brought to an end Frank's engagement
as "private secretary" a month ago.

It was Fuller again, Frank declared, who had persuaded him to
have a "flutter" on the Stock Exchange. It was not for the first time
that he had been urged to buy some shares "without putting down
a penny," but, knowing nothing of the Stock Market, he refused to
have anything to do with it. That he had given in at last was merely

because he had all along been such a "mug" where Fuller was concerned. He really regarded him as his only friend at the office, little suspecting that he was being deceived and that Benjamin Fuller was really Miss Pritt's tool. He had, however, since learnt so many startling things about Fuller that he had come to the conclusion that his erstwhile friend was the biggest blackguard of them all. However, the fact remained that he had acted like an idiot about those shares. (This admission did not seem to weaken June Gayford's love, for she clung closer to him and put her hand over his reassuringly.)

It was Fuller who had transacted the whole business and it was Fuller who, about a fortnight later, had informed him that his first adventure on the Stock Market had been a costly failure, for the shares, which, by the way, were of one of Sir Robert's most important companies, had slumped heavily and, although he had not put down a penny for them, he was in debt to the tune of over five thousand pounds. Of course, the fact had staggered him. He had even tried to deny that he had ever said he would take so many, but Fuller produced his written note recording the number and character of the shares he had wished to buy and there could be no doubt about it at all.

He wasn't even now sure whether he was legally responsible for the loss on those shares, nor was he sure whether the whole transaction had ever been carried out, but at the time the only thought that occupied his mind was how to raise the necessary amount of money.

That, of course, he could not do, unless he had gone to the moneylenders and had mortgaged his very slender prospects of inheriting anything from his uncle's fortune, but he did not think that even the most optimistic of moneylenders, and they must all be a very optimistic lot, would have lent him anything on that score. His only resort was his uncle. After all, the shares belonged to him, in a way, and if they had slumped in value it was certainly due to his uncle's most recent adventure in high finance about which Miss Pritt and Mr. Fuller were so excited and which must have been well known to every stockbroker in the City. Anyway, he merely intended to ask his uncle for a loan, but when he was called over to Sir Robert's room, he found that not only had everything already been reported to him, but that everything had already been settled. His debt, he was informed, had been paid and his employment was terminated.

Needless to say, he was stupefied, and there occurred a rather vehement scene during which Sir Robert had to listen to what was perhaps the most outspoken analysis of his career made during his lifetime. Frank seemed to be rather proud to have been the author of that biographical sketch, which he had later committed to writing (Mooney nodded and pointed to his breast-pocket where the two pages from that week's issue of *The Call* reposed). What he seemed utterly incapable of swallowing was that his uncle should have been so mean as to tell him that he was "a rotten journalist," and that he did not know the first thing about publicity. That, Frank considered, was the unkindest cut of all. To be fired because of a plot, which was as transparent as it was contemptible, was quite bad enough at a time when the journalistic profession was so overcrowded and insecure, but, in addition, to be deprived, as it were, of one's character, to be told that one is no good at one's own job was, to Frank's mind, just a blatant case of adding insult to injury. Coming from a man who occupied so powerful a place in the journalistic world as Sir Robert, who was practically the owner of one of the largest popular dailies in England, such an insult demanded the most proper redress, namely, an apology in writing. Failing the receipt of such an apology, Frank was quite determined to expose the British "Trust King," to give Sir Robert his journalistic title. But, of course, Frank ruefully admitted, it was not easy to get any paper to accept an outspoken article about so powerful a person as Sir Robert, and even the editor of *The Call* had not published his article till Sir Robert's murder had provided him with a cheap sensation.

"Have you been to your uncle's office since May 25th?"

"Not till this morning. I had to collect a number of personal things. I left rather in a hurry," Frank smiled a little shamefacedly. "I hadn't been before because I was not very anxious to meet my uncle again. Not at his office certainly."

"You didn't consider your prospects of being Sir Robert's heir were very high," Mooney asked, turning back a few pages in his notebook, "but you seem to have made that claim to Mr. Fuller?"

Frank merely laughed. "I was joking," he said, "and that was the first time I realised that I must be careful about what I said to Fuller, for my remark was reported almost at once to Sir Robert, who gave a fine exhibition of a sturdy descendant of the good old bulldog breed which made England what it is, or rather was. He blustered and swore and called me a damned impertinent pup and worked himself up into a mighty passion till I thought he'd die of a stroke before finally disinheriting me, but he had plenty of time to alter his will if he ever thought of leaving me anything in it. In fact, he wrote me a letter last week on purpose to tell me that I needn't expect a penny from him."

"There's just one thing more I should like you to clear up," Mooney said, after consulting his notebook again, "and that is who was Sir Robert's intimate friend for whom, as you say in your article, he had been organising concerts?"

But Mooney had not counted on the effect of this question on Mrs. Littlewood, who had been listening listlessly and without any more interruptions to her son's story. The superintendent's question, however, seemed to be considered by the old lady as the last straw, for she rose angrily from her chair and, refusing the young girl's offer of assistance, she stalked out of the room, barely acknowledging Mooney's courtesy in opening the door for her.

"I'm afraid," Frank said smilingly, for he seemed to have quite cheered up by now, although it was plain that the dark cloud which had been hanging over him had not lifted, "that you, unwittingly no doubt, let out one of the best specimens of our family skeletons. My uncle was at heart an incorrigible sentimentalist where women were concerned. He was all for Home and Beauty. Unfortunately in his case the two were separated: at home he had his devoted wife, and beauty resided elsewhere. He was not promiscuous by nature and his only romantic adventure outside marriage he treasured almost as much as the sanctity of his home. There was, it's true, a little complication: the lady had a husband. However, that was very soon settled in the most amicable fashion. The husband was provided with a very good position and, so far as I know, he did not make his presence felt, except occasionally when his gambling on the Stock Exchange made a loan necessary. I don't believe there was any question of blackmail, although, seeing that the husband in question was my friend Mr. Benjamin Fuller, I should not be surprised if Sir Robert had to cash out rather heavily at times."

"Mr. Fuller?" Mooney asked, unable to disguise his astonishment. "But surely…"

"Not at all, I assure you," Frank replied, not a little amused by the effect of his disclosure on the detective. "There were no difficulties of any kind, so far as I know. You see, everything happened in the most natural way. Sir Robert first met Susan, that is Mrs. Fuller, about twenty years ago. That was long before he received his title and long before he moved into Lownds Square. The Fullers lived next door and the friendship came about in the most ordinary way. It is true, my aunt very soon refused to visit her next-door neighbours, but that difficulty was soon settled by the Fullers' moving to a different district. Benjamin, luckily, could be easily managed. He very soon, I believe, obtained consolation elsewhere, and at one period Mrs. Fuller and my uncle and Mr. Fuller and his particular friend used to spend quite a good deal of their free time together. But later, when Sir Robert's business interests became more involved and claimed more and more of his time, a more satisfactory arrangement was arrived at: Mr. Fuller was given a job in my uncle's private office and it was agreed that his wife should obtain a legal separation from him. He was henceforth to consider himself, as it were, divorced from his wife, without, it is true, enjoying the freedom of a really divorced man. For that serious disadvantage he was, no doubt, sufficiently compensated. Anyway, meeting Sir Robert almost every day in his business capacity he could, doubtless, raise any necessary loans without the threat of being dismissed. For, whether Fuller would have been able to secure a divorce or not after having been a consenting party to his wife's adultery for so many years, he could always have brought divorce proceedings, which would have been jolly awkward for Sir Robert, not only because of the very prominent position he occupied, but also, and chiefly, because of his well-known veneration of home life and his devotion to marriage as an institution and also, perhaps, to his wife as the person who had been through the mill with him and whose youth and happiness had been sacrificed on the altar of his success. Well, that's our most treasured family skeleton and, as you observed, my mother could not bear to have it displayed before a perfect stranger. Mother was always, of course, on the side of the angels in this affair and that's probably why she and Lady Boniface have been such great friends all these years."

"You are being horrid, Frank!" June Gayford suddenly burst out, getting up and moving away from him. "It's a disgraceful thing. I always told you I thought it was a disgraceful thing. Poor Lady Boniface."

"Why, what's wrong with Aunt Beatrice? I'm sure she stopped minding very soon!" But seeing the expression of distaste on June's face, Frank added rather hastily: "Of course, she may not have ever reconciled herself to Sir Robert's infidelity, she may just have got used to it. Anyway, isn't Sir Robert to be given credit for remaining faithful to his Susan for over twenty years? I must say I admire him for that. I must say I…"

"You couldn't remain faithful to one woman for so long?" June flared up scornfully.

"Darling," Frank suddenly looked very meek and heartbroken, "you know, I love you so. You know I'd do anything for you."

"Even be faithful to me for twenty years?"

"Darling," Frank was at her side at one bound and was holding her in his arms and looking anxiously into her eyes, "I'd kill myself for you…"

"I don't want you to kill yourself for me, Frank." June seemed to have suddenly relented and was being very sweet to him. "I want you to love me always… Only me… I couldn't bear the thought of your deceiving me!"

The scene was obviously getting too intimate for the presence of a third person. It was, Mooney thought, feeling a little moved himself (there was a strong sentimental streak in his nature which at times took most unexpected forms), quite certainly a moment when three was a crowd. He got up somewhat noisily, trying to recall the two lovers to the fact of his presence in the room.

"Well," he said to Frank, "that seems to be about all I wanted to find out from you, unless, of course, you're willing to reconsider your refusal to give me an account of your movements on Friday afternoon."

"Please, dear, do!" June Gayford implored, clinging to Frank and looking up beseechingly into his face.

But if she hoped that the warmth of her love-making had melted Frank's obstinate and perverse heart, her woman's instinct had led her very badly astray this time, for the effect of her entreaty was most unfortunate. Frank pushed her away from him, his face went deadly pale and there was an agonised look in his eyes. For some time he could not bring himself to say anything.

"I can't... I can't..." he murmured at last, looking like an animal at bay. "I've told you a hundred times I can't..." And then he exclaimed in a kind of hopeless despair: "Darling, I love you so. Please, don't ask me again!"

Mooney's last impression before leaving the drawing-room of Sycamore Cottage was the pale, almost expressionless face of June Gayford, her beautiful dark eyes full of tears, and her lips twitching like a child's who has been wrongfully punished and who is about to cry.

The superintendent decided to take a stroll on the Heath before returning to his car. He felt the need for fresh air. He had certainly succeeded in collecting a mass of valuable information during the first day of his investigation into the murder of Sir Robert Boniface. But this information was very contradictory in some parts and extremely unsatisfactory in others. He would have to sort it out very carefully to-morrow morning, but for the present he preferred to give his mind a rest. It was about eleven o'clock and the night was light, warm and still, the sky clear and full of stars. Mooney went up the short road to the Heath, past the entrance of the public-house where Matt Caldwell lodged and into the dark patch of the pine trees beyond. He stumbled a little against the exposed roots of the trees on the rising ground and was glad to be out on the gravelled road again, where the shadows of two cyclists had just vanished round the bend into the darkness.

The strong scent of the flowers of a large locust tree made him stop short and inhale the sweet, overpowering fragrance. The road at that place forked, a path branched off to the right and went steeply down, while the road itself continued to the left describing a wide circular bend. For a moment Mooney stood still watching the great expanse of the sky and the countless lights in the distance, with here and there a square of red light, where the vast enormity of London lay sprawling in dark outline.

He decided to take the steep path on the right, but he was sorry almost immediately that he had done so, for the path was very rough, rising suddenly and then again descending, broken up with deep ruts, holes, and cracks in the ground into which he kept on stumbling. He was glad to emerge again at last on the smooth gravelled road which led to the bridge across the Viaduct Pond. He stopped on the bridge, leant against the wide stone parapet and watched for some time the white, ghostly outlines of two swans moving noiselessly below among the leaves of yellow water-lilies.

Mooney was aroused from his contemplation of the swans by the noise of somebody hurrying past and, on turning round sharply, he caught a glimpse of a tall, thin man with a long, white face and pale horn-rimmed glasses walking away rapidly towards the rough path he had come down himself only a few minutes ago. It was Benjamin Fuller. There could be no doubt about it: a single glance at the man even in the half-darkness of the summer night was enough for Mooney to recognise him. He set off in pursuit, but in his anxiety to overtake Fuller he forgot his recent experience of that path and soon stumbled and fell full-length and barked his shins rather badly on some sharp stone. The rest of the way to the Vale of Health the superintendent completed very slowly, walking painfully. There was no sign of Fuller, but he was told by a constable whom he found by the closed doors of the public-house that a man replying to his description had passed a few minutes ago on the path leading past the Vale of Health pond.

What was Fuller doing on Hampstead Heath at that time of night? The question kept on recurring to Mooney as he drove back in his car to Scotland Yard.

7

INSPECTOR BECKETT SAT IN THE LEATHER CHAIR BY MOONEY'S desk and listened attentively to the brief account of the superintendent's interviews with Miss Pritt and Frank Littlewood. He was absorbed in thought and occasionally he would drum his fingers on Mooney's desk. The inspector was not happy. He had spent the whole of Monday afternoon and Tuesday morning in scouring the countryside round London for Matt Caldwell. He had not been entirely unsuccessful, for he had traced the painter to Godalming where he had had some refreshments at a teashop on Sunday evening, but, although it was now two o'clock on Tuesday, not a trace of the painter could be found. It annoyed the inspector that he had allowed Caldwell to disappear on Sunday, but it annoyed him even more that, having got on the track of so conspicuous a figure, he had lost it so completely. He had tried to keep his inquiries secret, but now he was afraid that he would have to enlist the aid of the Press and even the wireless to help him to find the missing painter, and he hated the thought of the unnecessary publicity which such a step would inevitably involve.

The case against Frank Littlewood, Beckett admitted to himself, had been considerably strengthened by the evidence collected by the superintendent. It was very strange that Littlewood should refuse point-blank to give an account of his movements on Friday. The inspector failed to see why Mooney seemed to hesitate about taking

Sir Robert's nephew to Scotland Yard and interrogating him there: away from his womenfolk he might be willing to give the police at least a starting-point from where the inquiries about his whereabouts on Friday could be begun. There was sufficient evidence against him to justify such a step. But, there again, the disappearance of Caldwell was an unnecessary complication. The painter would have to be found and he would have to give a thoroughly satisfactory account of himself, for the evidence against him, as the inspector saw it, was really overwhelming.

Altogether, it was already quite a perplexing case, and why Mooney wished to drag in that Benjamin Fuller, against whom there was not really a shred of evidence, Beckett could not understand. After all, why shouldn't he be on Hampstead Heath late last night? And what was the case against Fuller, if, indeed, one could go so far as to formulate a case against him at all? His wife had been the mistress of Sir Robert Boniface and he was said to have received certain irregular payments in addition to his regular salary. But that might just be slander! So far as they knew he might have received nothing from Sir Robert except his salary. The inspector, somehow, could not help regarding Fuller as the injured party, and he was not at all sure that he had given up his wife as complacently as Frank Littlewood had implied. In his experience, or rather in his judgment, for in matters of conjugal relations the inspector had definite views, it was usually the woman and not the man who took the first wrong step. Anyway, why the superintendent should have thought it necessary to order a thorough search of the Viaduct Pond after that meeting of his with Fuller, Beckett could not grasp. Nor was Mooney quite able to explain it. It was just that he had a vague feeling of uneasiness which he wished to throw off.

Beckett had great faith in Mooney's powers of unravelling the most puzzling crimes, but even after watching him achieve brilliant results in cases which were given up as hopeless by the most experienced detectives, he still held that his superior's belief in the importance of vague, indefinite impressions as a guide to action was very exaggerated. He could not understand Mooney's technique: it was like the scent of a dog, or even something which depended so much on a sixth sense as to be utterly beyond him. What, for instance, was the use of picking up a bit of a cinema ticket near the gorse bush where the cartridge was found? When he asked him that, Mooney had laughed. Just an odd fancy! Another addition to the large collection of mysterious odds and ends with which he filled albums, just to keep himself amused during the holidays! But that bit of a ticket wasn't even a mystery. A child could have guessed where it had come from. Yet Mooney actually wanted him to find out from the management of "The Empire" cinema, Leicester Square, at what time approximately it had been issued. What were the chances that a person who had committed the murder at about six o'clock had gone to a cinema a few hours earlier? A million to one!

The two inquiries Mooney had asked him to make yesterday had drawn blanks, or almost so. No definite report that the blue limousine had been seen anywhere near Hampstead Heath could be obtained. There were hundreds of blue limousines of that make on the streets and no policeman was likely to memorise the numbers of passing cars. As for the broken fence or railings in a London park, there was only one case reported and that in Richmond Park, where a wooden fence with barbed wire seemed to have been broken either on Friday or Saturday by a car backing into it. It was rather a secluded part of the Park, and the broken fence was only discovered after the Scotland Yard inquiry had come through.

Richmond Park? Well, well. Beckett could not help smiling to see the disappointment on Mooney's face. Even if the murder had not taken place in the Vale of Health, Richmond Park was, so far as the evidence in their possession went, a little off the map. What were the chances of its having been committed there? Not even a million to one.

The thing was utterly preposterous and Mooney had admitted it, and yet he had given orders for the broken fence to be left in the condition in which it had been found. Another manifestation of his "technique": when, Mooney generalised, a thing appeared to you utterly preposterous there must be something in it. If the thing had really been impossible, it would not have provoked comment! That was the explanation Beckett had got and that was why he was rapping out popular tunes on Mooney's desk. When words failed or were inadvisable, the inspector preferred to give vent to his feelings in that way.

"Well, inspector," Mooney said, regarding the somewhat solemn face of his subordinate with kindly amusement, "what's our programme now?"

"I shall get that b— of a painter, sir," Beckett exclaimed with a touch of ferocity in his voice, his somewhat unorthodox language in the presence of his superior being, no doubt, explained by the depth of his feelings.

"Very good. I shall take up the Fuller end."

"A dead end, I'm afraid, sir!" Beckett declared with stolid conviction.

"Maybe. Anyway, I'm going to see Mrs. Fuller first, although I shall probably have to get her address from her husband."

"Why not try the telephone directory first, sir?"

"A brilliant idea. Let's see. Here we are. Fuller, Mrs. Susan, 42, Conway Avenue, Chiswick. Inspector, you're a second Sherlock! I hope, though, it *is* the lady we want."

"Sure to be, sir, considering her relations with Sir Robert."

"Quite. But, of course, you can never be sure with millionaires. They might install private telephone lines for their lady friends!"

At that moment the telephone on the superintendent's desk rang.

"Who?" Mooney rapped out incredulously. "Why, of course, show her up at once!" Beckett looked up expectantly. "Inspector," Mooney said, "I shall give you three guesses."

"It isn't Mrs. Fuller, by any chance, is it, sir?" Beckett ventured on a guess.

"Inspector," the superintendent said in despair, "I'm evidently fated to play Dr. Watson to your Sherlock Holmes. Perhaps you can also tell me why the lady is calling on me?"

"That I can't do, sir."

"You surprise me!" Mooney shook his head deprecatingly. "Anyway, you'd better be off now. And if you don't get that wretched painter by the end of the week—"

"By the end of the week?" Beckett looked at his superior with wide-open eyes. "I shall have him by to-morrow at the very latest, sir!" he said with dead conviction.

At that moment a discreet knock at the door announced the arrival of Mrs. Susan Fuller.

Mrs. Fuller was an elegantly dressed woman of forty-five. She was of middle height. She wore a small, neat hat with a suggestion of a veil. Her face was still very pretty and it was skilfully made up. Her eyes were blue and intelligent. She was slim and graceful. In the distance she might even now have passed for a young girl of twenty. Her maturity, however, did not detract from her charm. Mooney quite appreciated now why Sir Robert had stuck to his Susan for over twenty years. She satisfied perfectly the second part of what Frank Littlewood had quaintly characterised as Sir Robert's conception of "Home and Beauty." Mooney, though, was a little surprised to see that she was not dressed in black. She wore a light beige dress with everything else to match. But she seemed to have a harassed, almost frightened look in her blue eyes, although she kept her feelings well under control. Mooney showed her to the comfortable leather chair (Inspector Beckett having discreetly vanished), and sat down at his desk.

"You've come to see me in connection with Sir Robert Boniface's murder?" he asked.

"Yes," she replied almost inaudibly, and she closed her lips tightly and gave a firm nod, as if she wished to confirm it to herself.

"What sort of statement do you want to make?"

"I came to tell you who murdered Sir Robert!" she said simply, sitting up a little stiffly in her chair and crossing her hands in her lap.

The superintendent regarded her for a moment in silence. She was very collected, unnaturally quiet, her blue eyes looking straight at him with hardly a tremor of an eyelid.

"I shall save you any preliminary introduction," Mooney said. "You were Sir Robert's mistress, the undivorced wife of Benjamin Fuller employed by Sir Robert Boniface as the head of his publicity department. It was you Sir Robert used to visit regularly about three or four times a week and it was with you that he spent some part, at any rate, of the afternoon of last Friday, the day when his body was found on Hampstead Heath in his blue limousine."

If Mrs. Fuller was surprised at Mooney's knowledge of the circumstances of her life, she did not show it. She still did not turn her eyes away from his face (the long scar on his right cheek seemed to fascinate her), and her voice was strangely unemotional, though very soft and a little husky.

"Yes," she said, still with that strange emphatic nod.

"And you say you know who killed Sir Robert?"

"Yes." She nodded. "My husband killed Sir Robert."

"Your husband?" Mooney's face assumed a stern, impenetrable expression. "How do you know that?"

"Mr. Fuller had an appointment to meet Sir Robert at six o'clock on Friday evening. Sir Robert and I were leaving for Ireland on Saturday night. We got to know that Mr. Fuller had intended to have us shadowed by his solicitor because he wanted to take divorce proceedings against me. He had been threatening Sir Robert with divorce proceedings for some time. Sir Robert had arranged to meet my husband, for he was anxious to prevail on him to drop these proceedings. Sir Robert would, of course, have been willing to make it worth his while, as he had done before when my husband threatened to divorce me. Only it seems that this time my husband was serious about his intentions. You see, he had met somebody he was anxious to marry."

"Did Mr. Fuller see Sir Robert at six o'clock?"

"Yes. He told me so himself. He came to see me on Sunday. He said he was determined to carry on with the divorce proceedings even now, as he thought he had sufficient evidence to procure a divorce. I told him that he could have no evidence that would legally entitle him to a divorce, as he was a consenting party to my relations with Sir Robert. But he said he could, even if he had to go back fifteen years for it, and he added that during his talk with Sir Robert on Friday evening an arrangement for an undefended divorce action had been reached between them. But I knew that it couldn't be true."

She finished almost inaudibly and gave that curious nod of her head, a mixture of petulance and firm resolve, as if she was fully aware of the dreadful implication of her words, but was determined to go through with it.

"You mean," Mooney said in his slow, deliberate way, "that Sir Robert would never have agreed to an undefended action?"

"No. Never."

"But he couldn't have stopped your husband from filing a divorce petition?"

"No. But, you see, the very fact that my husband was so anxious to get an undefended action showed that he was perfectly aware of the difficulties he would experience in getting a divorce. Sir Robert said so again and again on Friday. But even if my husband did file a petition, Sir Robert was determined to fight him in the courts. He was not going to be browbeaten by my husband to agree to an arrangement which he had consistently refused for so many years. He didn't really believe, though, that my husband wanted to marry again. He thought it was merely another attempt on his part to extract a large sum of money."

"And you think your husband was in earnest about marrying again?"

"I don't know. He may have been. I really hardly know my husband. Even when I first met Sir Robert we had already stopped living as man and wife, and we had been married then only about two years."

"You are quite certain that Sir Robert couldn't have agreed to an undefended action?"

"Quite certain." She nodded with great decision.

"And you..." Mooney paused as if in search for the right word, "you *suggest* that during his interview with Sir Robert your husband shot him dead. But why? Would they have been likely to quarrel so violently?"

"Yes. Sir Robert was quite certain to fly into a passion. He was convinced that my husband was only holding out for a large sum, and he resented my husband's refusal to come to a reasonable settlement."

"But even if they had quarrelled, why should your husband have killed Sir Robert? They must have had arguments about the same subject before without any fatal results!"

"It was different this time!" Mrs. Fuller declared quite decisively. "First of all my husband seemed quite determined to get a divorce. He seemed to have met somebody he was genuinely fond of, and she," her voice suddenly became hard, "she wanted to be married."

Susan Fuller turned her head away and was for a time silent, absorbed in a thought which must have given her pain, for her face was set and she closed her mouth tightly, as if wishing to suppress some emotion which threatened to overcome her. Was she sorry, Mooney wondered, she had not been firm about marrying Sir Robert at a time when marriage was not quite out of the question?

"He told me so on Sunday," Mrs. Fuller resumed again as suddenly as she had broken off. "He seemed very excited, almost hysterical, because even now that Sir Robert was out of the way, he couldn't take a divorce action against me unless I was willing to provide him with evidence."

"And was there any other motive to make your husband wish Sir Robert out of the way?"

Mrs. Fuller hesitated a little before answering. She was evidently very uneasy about what she was going to say. "Sir Robert," she began uncertainly, "was not only quite determined to refuse Mr. Fuller's request for an undefended divorce action, but he also intended to tell him that unless he agreed to some reasonable settlement he would have to get some other employment."

"Isn't it," Mooney asked quickly, for the question had been troubling him, "isn't it extraordinary that your husband should have for so many years occupied an important position in Sir Robert's office?"

But, like Frank Littlewood, Mrs. Fuller apparently did not think it at all extraordinary. Sir Robert, she explained, found Mr. Fuller's services very valuable. Mr. Fuller had occupied quite a good position before Sir Robert had asked him to join his staff. That was many years after the arrangement between them had been amicably agreed to.

Mr. Fuller had no particular feelings about Sir Robert or herself. They had seriously gone into the question of divorce long before Sir Robert had come into their lives. Mr. Fuller had held out for some time before he finally accepted Sir Robert's offer, but after that their business relations seemed to have been quite correct, perhaps not in every respect, for Mr. Fuller rather took advantage of his position later on and got Sir Robert to settle some of his debts, but, then, Sir Robert's intentions in offering Mr. Fuller a job on his staff were not quite disinterested. He had thought that by making Mr. Fuller dependent on him he would be able to insure against any possibility of a divorce action.

Sir Robert, Mooney gathered, had regarded the whole transaction from an entirely business point of view, and if Mr. Fuller persisted in breaking his part of the bargain, then the deal was off and Benjamin Fuller would have to pay the penalty of his folly. That was the position as outlined by Sir Robert to Mrs. Fuller during his visit on Friday afternoon.

Mrs. Fuller, however, did not think it was quite right to go so far as to deprive her husband of his job. It was not, in her view, playing the game, and Sir Robert had quite a heated argument with her about that. But Sir Robert was very obstinate, and when he had left her, she was uneasy about the outcome of the whole thing. When the terrible news of Sir Robert's murder had reached her, she was not immediately certain in her mind that it was her husband who had killed him. Her strong suspicion, however, was confirmed when Mr. Fuller, whom, by the way, she had not seen for years, came to see her on Sunday and behaved in a most extraordinary manner and told her the lie about Sir Robert's having agreed to an undefended divorce suit.

This Mooney gathered, after he had questioned Mrs. Fuller very pertinaciously for about a quarter of an hour. He had also found out that Fuller had a flat in Marlborough Road and that it was very unlikely that Sir Robert should have agreed to discuss their position in the flat. He was fond of having conferences in his large car and what, according to Mrs. Fuller, must have happened, was that Sir Robert had asked Fuller to talk things over in his car and, in order not to attract attention, they had driven to some place on Hampstead Heath.

"When did Sir Robert visit you on Friday?"

"At three o'clock," Mrs. Fuller, who had suddenly grown to look very tired, repeated quite inaudibly, so that only her lips could be seen moving: "At three o'clock."

Mooney bethought himself of the decanter of brandy he kept in his room and Mrs. Fuller accepted his offer of a glass of brandy and soda very gratefully.

"I'm afraid, Mrs. Fuller," Mooney said, "I shall have to ask you a few more questions. You realise, of course, the gravity of the charge you are making against your husband?"

"Yes," she replied nodding, and she added: "I want to go through with it!"

"Right." Mooney paused a little, then he proceeded: "How long did Sir Robert stay with you?"

"He didn't stay long. At most only an hour. He had two important business appointments to attend to before seeing my husband."

"Do you know whom he was having the business conferences with?"

"No." Mrs. Fuller was quite definite. "We never discussed business," she explained. "This was an arrangement we made at the very beginning of our life together, and Sir Robert was most particular about it. He always forgot all his business cares when he came to see me. At least, that's what he used to say. But I knew, of course, that he had been very troubled about something lately. And on top of it all there was Mr. Fuller's sudden decision to take divorce proceedings. Sir Robert was really furious about it, because he thought that

Mr. Fuller, who knew he had serious business worries, was taking advantage of it in order to extort a high price from him, but..."

"But you don't think so?"

"I don't know. Only I thought it would perhaps be best if we did have it settled once and for all. It could have been arranged without letting Lady Boniface know anything about it. And, after all, now that Sir Robert was no longer in the Cabinet, it wouldn't have mattered much. But, of course, Sir Robert wouldn't hear of it at all. He thought divorce proceedings would ruin all our happiness. And we were happy together!" Mrs. Fuller suddenly raised her voice, which was very clear and musical: "We were very happy together," she repeated with great emphasis as if challenging the whole world to deny it. "And, after all," she added as an afterthought, "isn't happiness everything in the world? Everything in the world!" And she nodded emphatically, as if she was not really quite sure herself and she had to convince that silent questioner within her who kept on worrying her incessantly.

"What was the object of your going to Ireland together?"

"To Ireland?" Mrs. Fuller repeated, as if roused from some deep reverie. "Oh, yes. Just for a short holiday. Sir Robert had been rather worried over some business matters. I've told you that. And his two conferences on Friday were just to wind up all his recent difficulties. After that he wanted to go away somewhere, and as we'd already been to Ireland a long time ago, when Sir Robert was not so rich, and liked it very much, we decided to go there together again."

"When was it you decided on your Irish holiday?"

Mrs. Fuller could not remember exactly the time when they had first discussed their proposed holiday, but it must have been quite two or three months ago.

"Oh, no." Mooney explained his question. "I mean when did Sir Robert make his final arrangements for going to Ireland? Buy tickets, order a cabin, engage rooms and so on."

Mrs. Fuller looked rather puzzled. She seemed to wonder why Mooney wanted all this information about the Irish trip which had never come off and the thought of which was evidently very painful to her.

"I can't say exactly," she repeated, without concealing her unwillingness to answer, "I should think about a fortnight or three weeks ago."

"So it wasn't a sudden decision?"

"No, not at all."

"What time were you leaving for Ireland on Saturday?"

"I believe…" Mrs. Fuller began, then she suddenly burst out: "Is that important at all?"

"I'm afraid it is," Mooney assured her very earnestly, "or I should not have asked you."

"Well…" Mrs. Fuller did not seem at all convinced, but she gave the required information: "We were to leave in the evening on the 8.45 train from Euston."

"Do you know," Mooney persisted with his irrelevant questions, "whether Sir Robert had any other engagements on Saturday evening?"

"Yes. He was going to see his sister at about six o'clock, I believe. It was rather a bother, because it was so near the time of our train. And it was the last train, too. But it seems Sir Robert had quite made up his mind to see his sister. He wanted to settle something finally. It must have been some troublesome family matter, because he was very angry about it. And Sir Robert was never angry about business matters."

"You don't know at all what it was he wanted to see his sister about?" Mooney inquired incredulously.

"No," she replied firmly. "Sir Robert never discussed his family or his business with me." And she shut her mouth tightly and shook her head.

"Did Sir Robert change his mind about seeing his sister on Saturday?"

Again Mrs. Fuller looked very puzzled and uneasy. "No," she replied, "at least, he didn't tell me anything about it."

"You're quite sure, then, that it was your husband and not his sister that Sir Robert intended to see at six o'clock on Friday?"

"I'm quite certain!"

"Would you be surprised to hear that Sir Robert had telephoned to his sister on Friday morning, fixing an appointment with her at six o'clock on that day?"

"Indeed I should!" Mrs. Fuller replied, her uneasiness suddenly flaring up to anger. She seemed to be quite a different woman, all her former restraint had gone, her eyes blazed and two red spots appeared on her cheeks.

"When he saw you at three o'clock on Friday, Sir Robert discussed his visit to Mr. Fuller with you?"

"He certainly did!"

"And your impression was that he intended to see your husband at six o'clock on that day?"

"It isn't a question of my impression! I know that he was going to see him. Besides, Mr. Fuller told me himself that Sir Robert had been to see him."

"And you're convinced that it was your husband who killed Sir Robert?"

"Yes. I know it was!" Mrs. Fuller had relapsed into her former state of dull inertia. She nodded as if in reply to that silent questioner within her own mind, who seemed to have been repeating Mooney's questions like some mocking echo.

"Tell me, Mrs. Fuller," Mooney finally asked her, "what impelled you to come here? Why do you want to incriminate your husband? Do you hate him so much?"

"He killed Sir Robert!" she replied in a dull monotone, looking straight before her with unseeing eyes. And as if in reply to some unuttered objection from Mooney, she went on: "I know it. I tell you I know it!"

"Do you hate your husband?" Mooney insisted on a reply to his last question.

"No!"

Mrs. Fuller smiled a little disconsolately. That Scotland Yard man's mind was running along such conventional lines. Did she hate Fuller? Why should she hate him? She merely wanted to see justice done. Sir Robert would have wished her to see justice done. She could see him standing by that mantelpiece now. His eye stern and his jaw set. He always had such a combative expression when he wanted to be obeyed, and she admired it in him: he was a real fighter! He wanted his murderer brought to justice. Law and order must be upheld. The State must not flinch from inflicting severe punishment on those of its citizens who had broken its laws and threatened its order. Fuller had killed Sir Robert, hadn't he? But she didn't hate him for that. After all, it was merely a single act occupying but a fraction of the time he had been hanging like a nightmare over her life. It is true that act had shattered her happiness and her whole life lay in ruins, smashed with such savage senselessness. She might have married Sir Robert one day. She had always wanted it, and she was ready to wait. Couldn't Fuller have waited, too? He had talked to her on Sunday as if she alone was responsible for messing up his life. That wasn't true. He had agreed to everything. He knew what he was doing. And during that meeting on Sunday she had realised as never before what a complete stranger Fuller was to her. And yet he was always in her thoughts, he was always lurking in some dark recess of her mind, destroying her happiness, poisoning all her joy. And now he wanted to marry again. He had destroyed her happiness, but he wanted to marry again and was angry with her for refusing to help him! What claim had he on her help? And yet she did not hate him. She saw that what had happened was, somehow, appropriate. She had been expecting something of the kind.

"Oh, no," she repeated softly, but decisively, and she murmured rather vaguely as if wondering at some inexplicable act of fate: "He's quite a stranger to me!"

Mooney saw Mrs. Fuller into the lift. He had told her that he would have to see her again and take down her evidence in the presence of witnesses. A certain formality would be necessary, but at present he preferred to leave it rather informal till he had made some inquiries. She nodded mutely. Of course, she was ready to go through with it.

Mooney returned to his room looking far from pleased. He stopped at the window, gazing idly at the traffic on the embankment and on the empty hulk of some sea-going ship making her way upstream with her funnel lowered and her masts dismantled, a red patch of paint on her side, to be broken up at some up-river wharf. That ship reminded him of the woman he had just shown out of the room. She, too, had left an impression of a bare, dismantled hulk with that mark of an assassin's gun as a sign of her tragic destiny. She did not hate her husband. Well, her motive in coming to Scotland Yard was not really very important, but her story was!

What bothered Mooney, however, was how Sir Robert thought he could be in two places at the same time. If Mrs. Fuller's story was right, then he was determined to see Fuller at six o'clock on Friday to try to prevail on him to drop the divorce proceedings. But he had asked Miss Pritt on Friday morning to arrange an appointment with his sister at the same time. There was no doubt that he had first intended to see Mrs. Littlewood on Saturday. That left him with quite a good margin of time for catching the 8.45 train at Euston even if he had intended to have a long talk with his sister. But he probably must have thought that half an hour at most would be sufficient to say what he had to say.

Why, then, did Sir Robert change his mind? He might, of course, have thought of some more pressing engagement for Saturday. His pocket diary was very unsatisfactory in this respect: it seemed to record nothing but his unimportant engagements. For Friday there was only one entry about the meeting he was to have addressed at eight o'clock. Not a word about the much more important business conferences in the morning and in the afternoon! For Saturday there was only the entry recording his intended visit to Mrs. Littlewood. If he had changed his mind about that, why hadn't he also changed his entry in the diary? But, then, pocket diaries seem to exist to be neglected. Again, he might have decided to keep Saturday afternoon free from all engagements. It was obvious that Mrs. Fuller did not like the idea of Sir Robert's rushing off to see his sister barely two hours before their train was due to leave Euston.

But why should Sir Robert decide to see his sister at the time he had previously arranged to see Fuller at his flat in Marlborough Road? Did he decide not to see Fuller after all? Why, then, did he discuss the Fuller interview with Mrs. Fuller only two hours before?

Suppose that he did see Fuller at the appointed hour. What could have happened was that, being very busy that morning, his mind occupied with the important board meeting, he had just made a slip, six o'clock being rather an important hour for him that day, and mentioned six o'clock instead of seven o'clock to Miss Pritt for his interview with Mrs. Littlewood. Perhaps he had thought of taking Fuller to Hampstead Heath as a rather convenient place where they could have their talk out, and the idea that he might as well kill two birds with one stone and settle the two rather disagreeable interviews in one evening had commended itself to him. That, at any rate, would

explain the fact that the blue limousine had not been seen in the Vale
of Health before a quarter to seven, for Sir Robert might have had
his talk with Fuller at some other place and then driven himself or
been driven by Fuller, who most probably knew of his intended visit
to Mrs. Littlewood, to the place where the car had later been found.
Miss Pritt very likely did not know that Sir Robert had an engagement
for six o'clock on Friday, for Sir Robert seemed to be very particular
about keeping his private affairs out of his business.

There was, of course, the fact that at eight o'clock on Friday, Sir
Robert was addressing the Anti-Socialist Union and he would, surely,
want some sort of a meal in between. But he might have thought of
having a meal at his sister's, although that did not seem very likely.
That was certainly a difficulty, but not insurmountable.

The Fuller theory, Mooney had to admit, was a much more satisfactory theory than the one he had formed after the first study of
the reports of the murder yesterday morning. It, of course, had one
serious flaw: it depended on an entirely negative supposition, namely,
that Sir Robert had made a mistake about the time he wished to see
Mrs. Littlewood, but such a slip might easily have occurred, especially
as Sir Robert had so many important matters to attend to that day.
But even that theory did not preclude the possibility that the murder
had been committed by someone else. It added another suspect to
the two who had already been engaging the attention of the police.
Fuller certainly had a stronger motive and a better opportunity
for committing the murder than either Frank Littlewood or Matt
Caldwell, and his behaviour on Hampstead Heath by the Viaduct
Pond last night had also been very suspicious. He must have noticed
the superintendent on the bridge and made a dash to get away. If
Fuller was merely taking a stroll on Hampstead Heath, why did he
sheer off like that on recognising the detective? Again, that stealthy
entry of his into Miss Pritt's room while Mooney was there was very

extraordinary. Fuller quite evidently wanted to get a good view of the visitor from Scotland Yard, so that he might recognise him later.

Mooney's thoughts were interrupted by the ringing of the telephone. Inspector Marlow of the Hampstead police was speaking: the search of the Viaduct Pond ordered by the superintendent a few hours ago had yielded the most important discovery yet made by the police: a small automatic pistol with one bullet missing was found in about two feet of water. So far as Marlow could tell, it must be the gun with which Sir Robert Boniface had been murdered. Chief Detective-Inspector Beckett had also examined it and he was at present making inquiries. He would be at Scotland Yard in about half an hour, and he wanted the superintendent to wait for his arrival.

Mooney replaced the receiver only to pick it up at once to make arrangements for the detention of Benjamin Fuller for questioning.

8

THE FINDING OF THE SMALL AUTOMATIC PISTOL IN THE VIADUCT Pond had an unexpected sequel, unexpected, that is, to Mooney, but not to Inspector Beckett.

Half an hour after the message of the latest discovery had reached Mooney, the inspector was sitting in the leather chair at the side of the superintendent's desk and he was enjoying the satisfaction of having completely turned the tables on his superior. The gun lay on the desk before them: a little toy automatic that could easily be concealed even in the palm of a woman's hand. A very dangerous toy, as poor Sir Robert Boniface had learnt to his cost. The spent cartridge and the bullet extracted from Sir Robert's skull lay beside it. There could be no doubt that it was the identical gun that was fired by Sir Robert's murderer. Only one bullet had been fired from it, the other eleven were still in the magazine. It was made of beautifully polished steel and it shone with a dull blue light. The inspector enjoyed the sight of it. It had been the cause of intense pleasure to him. Even now as he regarded the rather gloomy face of the superintendent, it made him feel happy. Theories were all right, but what a crime investigator needed most was sound commonsense!

Informed of the important find in the Viaduct Pond, Inspector Beckett, who had been trying unsuccessfully to find out from Agnes whether she knew of the whereabouts of Matt Caldwell (the girl was slow-witted, but very cunning, and quite obviously infatuated with the artist), rushed off at once to the Hampstead Police Station where Marlow had taken it. He went back to the Vale of Health, however, with the gun in his pocket, and, as he entered the public-house, he almost collided with Mrs. Perkins, Matt Caldwell's large-hearted charwoman. Mrs. Perkins regarded the inspector with cautious and rather hostile eyes, but her feeling changed when he invited her to have one with him. Having established a certain communion of interests, it was not difficult for him to gain the goodwill of that excellent woman, who had mothered a score of artists, darned their socks, tidied their rooms, watched their progress from obscurity to the walls of the Tate Gallery, and been a wise counsellor to them in their troubles with her own sex. The inspector waited patiently for the most propitious moment, and then produced the automatic pistol. Mrs. Perkins seemed to have recognised it at once.

"I wondered," she exclaimed, "why you 'adn't found it last time you searched 'is rooms!"

It was now too late to withhold any information from that "sly sarpint" from Scotland Yard, and Mrs. Perkins had to confess that she had seen the small automatic pistol in Caldwell's rooms many times, that one day she had even picked it up and was examining it rather awkwardly, when Caldwell saw her and made a big row about it as the gun, he explained to her, was dangerous and fully loaded. The inspector took down her statement and warned her a second time, but now with full justification, of the consequences of trying to withhold important information from the police. There could, indeed, be no doubt at all that the automatic pistol belonged to Caldwell. Mrs. Perkins said that the last time she had seen the gun was about three months ago. The painter must have hidden it away from her after he had found her playing about with it.

The inspector next went to the Viaduct Pond and had the exact spot pointed out to him where it had been found. It was almost immediately under the bridge at the least accessible part of the pond and the inspector was quite satisfied that in the first perfunctory search of the pond the police had made (it was rather distant from the place where the blue limousine had been found and the police did not consider it a very likely place for the missing gun), it might easily have escaped discovery. Besides, the whole pond was thickly covered with yellow water-lilies, and it was a wonder the police had succeeded in finding the gun at all. He considered that it was not at all unlikely that the person who had thrown the gun into the Viaduct Pond knew perfectly well that it would be the devil of a job to find it there, in fact there were a hundred chances to one that it would never be found at all. It was, he considered, really a piece of pure luck.

A piece of pure luck! But what could Mooney make of it? The superintendent sat gloomily at his desk thinking of his last night's adventure. Where on earth was Fuller, as he was coming down that rough path to the Viaduct Pond? The bridge was then quite empty. He was sure of that. Fuller must have come from the other side of it. But in that case he wouldn't have been able to throw the gun in, for Mooney did not hear any splash. He might have done it before, of course, then taken a stroll round to steady his nerves and come back on his way home. He would have to walk back that way. Then he must have noticed the superintendent and shied off rapidly up that rough path.

The gun? Mooney had examined it. But how could the gun, which undoubtedly belonged to Caldwell, have got to Fuller? It might possibly have been given by Caldwell to Frank Littlewood, but how could Fuller have got hold of it? Mooney made up his mind quickly: Matt Caldwell must be found as soon as possible. The Press, the wireless, anything!

Inspector Beckett rose well satisfied from the chair. His tall, stooping figure towered over the desk, his long, narrow face was full of confidence: he had already taken every step and, as he had already assured the superintendent a few hours ago, he would have that painter lad by to-morrow at the latest. But before he went he also received instructions to give the story of the finding of the gun to the Press without mentioning, however, who its owner was.

Mooney went out to have tea and on his return to his office at half-past five, he found Fuller, a detective-inspector and a sergeant, who had accompanied him from his office to Scotland Yard, waiting for him. Fuller seemed to be rather frightened, his white face was drawn, his lips trembled, and he stammered badly. If the identification of the gun had for a moment upset the superintendent's plan of action, the scared look Fuller gave him as he entered the room confirmed him in his belief that there was something in his second theory after all.

Mooney began by explaining that certain information with a direct bearing on the murder of Sir Robert Boniface had come into the possession of the police, which made a detailed statement from Fuller necessary. He had to give him the usual warning that whatever he said would be used in evidence, but he hoped that Fuller would realise that, by telling the whole truth about his relations with Sir Robert, he would be more likely to help the police and himself than by trying to cover up facts from a perhaps mistaken desire to shield his late employer's reputation. Inspector Ransome would take down his depositions.

It was plain that what made Fuller feel so ill at ease was his ignorance of what the police had already discovered about his relations with Sir Robert Boniface. But the scared look in his eyes signified more than that, Mooney felt quite sure about it. Was Fuller afraid that the police might have discovered some fact which would implicate him in the murder? That was the most essential thing to find out.

After a few introductory questions to establish the facts of identity, age and so on, Mooney asked Fuller whether he was taking divorce proceedings against his wife and whether he was intending to cite Sir Robert Boniface as co-respondent?

"Y-yes," Fuller stammered, evidently believing that to reply in monosyllables would be the best course for him to adopt before the superintendent showed his hand more clearly.

"Did Sir Robert know that you were taking these proceedings?"

Fuller shot a furtive glance from under his white eyelashes and adjusted his pale horn-rimmed glasses with unsteady hands: "I believe he d-did," he said slowly, blinking, his almost invisible eyelashes making him look like some strange bird.

"How did he get to know it?"

"I-I t-told him so m-myself."

"You told him so yourself? But surely that was a very unwise thing to do before you had all your evidence?"

"I had already s-s-sufficient e-evidence, a-anyhow."

"But if you had sufficient evidence, why did you instruct your solicitor to follow Sir Robert and your wife to Ireland?"

Fuller again shot a quick glance at the superintendent. It was obvious the police knew much more than he thought. "I th-thought," he said in his painful stutter, "that I sh-should w-w-want more recent e-evidence."

"Did you tell Sir Robert you were instructing your solicitor to have him and your wife followed to Ireland?"

For a moment Fuller seemed to be in doubt what to say. Then he must have made up his mind to make a clean breast of his matrimonial troubles. "Y-yes," he replied.

"But, surely, this was a very extraordinary course to adopt! Didn't it occur to you that Sir Robert might have cancelled his intended trip and left you high and dry, with no proper evidence to go to court on and no possibility of ever getting such evidence?"

"N-no!" Fuller said firmly. "You s-say that because you d-don't kn-know Sir Robert. It w-w-wouldn't have made any difference to him if he had a s-squad of solicitors following him to Ireland. If he d-decided to go there he w-w-would go there."

"But he was afraid of divorce proceedings, wasn't he?"

"N-no." Fuller was quite firm about that, too. "He w-wasn't. He w-wouldn't hear of divorce p-proceedings b-because he d-didn't think that I ought to take them, but he wasn't afraid of them. He thought it was a b-breach of my a-agreement not t-t-to take any action in court, our a-agreement to settle our differences amicably."

"Did you enter into any such agreement?"

"Y-yes. A l-l-long time ago. After I had b-been separated from my w-w-wife for some t-time."

"Why did you enter into such an agreement? What did you get out of it?"

"It w-w-wasn't my suggestion. It was Sir R-Robert who m-made that s-suggestion. At that t-time he w-wouldn't agree to a divorce because it w-would have ruined his career p-politically. He w-wanted to be a Ca-Cabinet minister. I w-was a f-f-fool to have agreed, I admit that now."

"Why did you agree?"

"I…" Fuller seemed to have stuck hopelessly over some word and gave up his attempt to reply.

"You got something very substantial out of your agreement with Sir Robert, didn't you?"

"Y-yes," Fuller admitted.

"Your so-called agreement with Sir Robert was, then, just a cold-blooded attempt on your part to exploit your unfortunate matrimonial situation for some substantial pecuniary advantage?"

"No!" Fuller almost shouted. Mooney's suggestion seemed to be sincerely resented by him. He became very agitated, his white face flushed, and his hands trembled as he kept on adjusting his pale horn-rimmed glasses. "I m-must explain. I m-must explain," he repeated, evidently trying to control his agitation and to speak calmly: "It isn't true to s-say that I c-consented to this agreement from the f-first. I didn't c-c-consent to anything. I didn't consent to my wife's relations w-with Sir R-Robert at f-first, either. I t-t-told you w-we w-were not really separated. Wh-when we first made the ac-ac-acquaintance of Sir Robert we still lived to-together as m-man and w-w-wife. I m-mean n-not really as man and wife, b-but w-we still shared one b-bedroom. My w-wife w-wanted a divorce, but I w-wouldn't agree. I still b-believed we could settle our d-differences. Wh-when my w-wife and Sir Robert became f-f-friends, she naturally t-took his view and dropped her talk about divorce. But I objected very strongly to her relations with Sir Robert. I often t-told him so myself. I w-wanted my life straightened out, I b-believed my wife w-would come round to my point of view in the end. B-b-but Sir Robert and my w-wife t-tried to get me into a false position. They t-tried all sorts of plots to c-compromise me, or at least to m-make it appear that I was a c-consenting p-p-party to their relations. I have rather a w-weak character. I—I admit it. I w-was quite dominated by my w-wife and she, in the end, b-b-brought me over to her p-point of view."

"You mean your wife persuaded you to make that agreement with Sir Robert?"

"Y-yes. My w-w-wife and Sir Robert."

"But hadn't you already obtained certain favours from Sir Robert?"

"Y-yes. He helped me out of some f-financial scrapes."

"That was before you entered into that agreement with Sir Robert?"

"Y-yes. But at that time I didn't realise that he w-was merely trying to m-make me de-dependent on him."

"And since that agreement with Sir Robert he helped you financially quite a number of times?"

"W-w-well... Not t-too many times. You s-see, our agreement w-was that I w-w-would refrain from t-taking divorce p-proceedings and Sir Robert w-w-would finance my Stock Exchange transactions wh-whenever necessary, which he continued to d-do. But I didn't always lose. I more often m-m-made quite a lot of m-money."

"But when called on to finance your transactions, Sir Robert had to cash out pretty heavily?"

"N-not always."

"Sometimes?"

"Y-yes."

"And you didn't see anything extraordinary in that?"

"N-no. That is, I sh-shouldn't have thought of it myself. But Sir Robert and my w-wife..."

"Quite," Mooney interrupted. "Tell me, was it also Sir Robert's suggestion that you should join his staff?"

"Y-yes. Cer-certainly. I didn't w-want to hear of it for a long time. I had qu-quite a good p-position with an important b-business firm. But I w-was again p-persuaded against my w-will."

"And when working for Sir Robert you still went on gambling on the Stock Exchange?"

"I w-wasn't gambling," Fuller corrected firmly, "I was merely investing my m-money in what I b-believed to be p-profitable stock. Everybody does it."

"You mean other people in your office were also doing it?"

"Y-yes." Fuller's face lit up suddenly, as if he had for the first time got hold of something which might explain his action in a convincing, straightforward way. "You see, at the office w-we've got advance information about the Stock M-Market. That, I admit, w-was a c-consideration that w-weighed with me wh-when I ac-accepted Sir Robert's offer. Certain departmental heads at our office at t-times c-consult me about their investments. Even M-Miss P-Pritt, who's the head of our office, p-plays quite heavily on the Stock Market, and she's always g-glad to know my views. And Sir Robert's nephew, Mr. Frank Littlewood, also l-lost quite a packet some time ago."

"I shall want to ask you a few questions about Mr. Frank Littlewood a little later," Mooney said, and he noticed that this promise seemed for some reason or other to gratify Fuller. "Now I want to get your own position quite straight. You've admitted so far that owing to some kind of agreement with Sir Robert..."

"He c-called it a g-g-gentleman's agreement," Fuller put in.

"... you had refrained so far from taking any divorce proceedings against your wife," Mooney went on, not heeding the interruption, "and Sir Robert had paid your losses, sometimes very heavy losses, which you incurred on the Stock Exchange in spite of your advance information on the condition of the market."

"That is s-s-s-so," Fuller agreed rather gloomily.

"Very well. Now, didn't any disagreements arise between you and Sir Robert at any time about the settlement of your losses? I mean, you said that Sir Robert always paid your losses, and I accept your statement, but didn't he at times show a certain reluctance in meeting them?"

"Very rarely."

"But once or twice he did object?"

"Y-yes. He thought I was rather f-foolish about certain shares, and he didn't want, he said, to p-pay for my folly as that w-wouldn't t-teach me to be w-wiser in the future."

"And did you or did you not apply pressure to Sir Robert on those occasions by threatening him with divorce proceedings unless he paid up?"

But Fuller would not admit so much. All he would say was that he regarded Sir Robert's refusal to settle his unfortunate transactions on the Stock Exchange as a breach of their agreement and merely warned Sir Robert of the consequences of such a breach.

"Are you very much in debt now?" Mooney shot out the question in his usual quick-firing fashion, but to his surprise it made very little impression on Fuller, who replied very firmly that he was not.

"No? But you told me yourself only a moment ago that Mr. Littlewood lost quite a packet over some recent transaction. Didn't you lose anything over it?"

"No." Fuller was very firm about it. "I m-merely," he explained, "gave Mr. Littlewood certain advice about some shares. He was f-free to t-take it or l-leave it. I p-personally didn't buy any of those shares. B-but I admit," he added, "that my judgment was wrong."

"So your divorce proceedings have now nothing at all to do with any financial difficulties?"

"N-no." On this point Fuller was adamant. "You c-can examine my banking account, if you w-wish," he said.

"And the reason for your divorce proceedings is that…"

"I w-want to m-marry again," Fuller said with great emphasis.

And in reply to further questions he explained that the lady he intended to marry (she was a widow and a woman of strong character, a point which Fuller made quite clear), insisted on his getting an immediate divorce. She said that he had allowed matters to drift too far, and that if he did not take a strong stand now and seek a dissolution of his marriage, which had never been anything of a marriage, anyhow, she would refuse to have anything to do with him. She had refused to wait till Sir Robert was in a more tractable frame of mind. He had, of course, made it clear to her that in his case the difficulties of getting a divorce were very great and that unless he persuaded Sir Robert and his wife to agree to an undefended action, he might not be able to get a divorce at all. But she thought, and in that he was in agreement with her, that when Sir Robert realised that he was in earnest, he would agree to an undefended action, as such an action would be much less likely to arouse public interest and might, indeed, pass over without any publicity at all. He realised only too well, of course, that Sir Robert might prove very awkward and he would be likely even to misconstrue his intentions, but he was determined to "straighten his life out" once and for all.

And, in answer to a question from Mooney, he explained that he had considered the possibility of being compelled to give up his present situation, although, he admitted, he would not willingly have done so. But no threat of dismissal, if Sir Robert ever intended to use such a threat, would have deterred him from filing his petition for divorce. He had not made it all clear to Sir Robert, he had merely intimated very firmly his wish to end that "gentleman's agreement" he had entered into with him against his own wish. But Sir Robert, very naturally perhaps, had pointed out that if he had known that at any time Fuller intended to go back on that settlement, he would not have made it, and that now that he had carried out his part of the bargain, he would not on any account agree to be a party to an unde-fended action. He had had, Fuller stated, one or two more talks with Sir Robert, but without effect. Then he told Sir Robert that he had engaged a solicitor to prepare his petition and that he had instructed him to get all the evidence necessary for a successful action. He knew, of course, that Sir Robert's first reaction to that would be to fly into a violent temper, but he was glad to have it all over and settled. He thought he could detect a certain hesitancy in Sir Robert's attitude when he had mentioned the solicitor, and he hoped that at that talk which Sir Robert had agreed to have with him at six o'clock on Friday, he would be able to prevail on him to agree to an undefended action, in spite of his seemingly firm refusal even to discuss it.

But, unfortunately, things had turned out rather differently. Sir Robert's murder had upset all his calculations. It was now impossible for him to get any fresh evidence of misconduct and the old evidence that he could get, apart from its dating back to about fifteen years ago, was capable, he was very much afraid, of being seriously misinterpreted, as, rather unfortunately, he himself and a girl friend of his had been at the same seaside hotel with Sir Robert and his wife at that time and had even signed the hotel register together. The fact that Sir Robert and his wife wished to share the same bedroom came rather as a shock to him, for it was the first time that he realised what the relationship between Mrs. Fuller and Sir Robert Boniface was. But, as his girl friend was willing to comfort him for his enforced loneliness, he did not protest very much. Now, looking back upon it all, he realised that he had then acted foolishly and he even believed that Sir Robert and his wife had prepared everything beforehand so as to compromise him, for they had encouraged his liaison with that girl. The whole thing was, of course, exceedingly lamentable. He admitted it now, but the fact remained that his only hope of a successful divorce action depended on the circumstance that Sir Robert and Mrs. Fuller had spent a night together at that hotel, and that if the judge got to know that he, too, had misconducted himself on the same night and at the same hotel, and that he and the co-respondent and Mrs. Fuller and his girl friend had had supper together and generally had gone about everywhere together, he might not quite believe that he had put up a fight for his marital rights and had yielded only to pressure. It was a situation which was rather apt to be misconstrued by people who did not realise the hold Mrs. Fuller and Sir Robert had, at that time and a long time after, exercised over him. But that was the position. He was now in the devil of a fix, and if Mrs. Fuller did not agree to help him he was afraid that his chances of getting a divorce were very slender indeed.

Mooney did not interrupt Fuller's halting, but on the whole convincing, narrative. But Fuller's pains to make him believe that Sir Robert's death had spoilt his chances of ever getting a divorce put him on his guard again.

The whole theory that Fuller had committed the murder was based on the assumption that, whether it was premeditated or not, it was committed during or immediately after a violent quarrel when reason played a subordinate rôle. The motives for such a violent quarrel were there, and, considering Sir Robert's well-known temper, the likelihood that such a quarrel had taken place was quite feasible. The fact that Fuller was absolutely in earnest this time about obtaining a divorce would, of course, not only have precipitated the quarrel, but would also have provided another strong motive for the crime; for once Fuller had realised that Sir Robert was ready to fight him in the courts, he might, in the heat of the dispute and feeling absolutely defeated by the man who had deprived him of his wife and had generally "messed up" his life, have yielded to the impulse to murder Sir Robert.

"What was the result of your talk with Sir Robert on Friday?" Mooney asked, after Fuller had a little recovered from his long speech, with surprise in his voice that Fuller had made no mention of it.

"M-my t-t-talk with Sir Robert on F-Friday?" Fuller repeated, looking at Mooney rather bewildered and that scared expression coming back into his eyes.

"Yes. At six o'clock on Friday. Didn't you say he was coming to see you at that time?"

"Oh, y-yes. B-but he d-didn't t-t-turn up. I w-waited for him t-till s-s-seven, b-but he didn't c-c-come."

"Didn't Sir Robert let you know that he had changed his mind? Didn't he ring through to say that he would not be able to keep the appointment?"

"N-no." Fuller denied it emphatically.

"But didn't you think it strange that Sir Robert should change his mind without letting you know? He'd seen you at the office in the morning, hadn't he?"

"It w-was rather strange," Fuller admitted, "b-but it didn't surprise m-me in the least. He m-might have thought that by not t-turning up he would be more likely to influence m-me, or he m-might have decided to let me c-carry on with the action. In either case he w-wouldn't have thought it necessary to inform m-me. He'd have w-w-waited till I approached him."

"But," Mooney said slowly, fixing Fuller with his gaze, and he could see that Fuller fully anticipated the question, "why did you tell your wife that you did meet Sir Robert at six o'clock as arranged and that as a result of that meeting Sir Robert agreed to an undefended divorce action?"

"I—I…" Fuller's lower jaw dropped, and for some time he seemed unable to control the convulsive attack of stammering which made speech impossible, "I told her a lie!" he suddenly brought himself to say with unusual distinctness, and there was something in his voice which made him sound entirely convincing. "I told her a lie! I knew that she r-r-respected Sir R-Robert's judgment and ac-accepted his decisions w-w-without criticism. I knew that she herself w-would have w-welcomed a divorce, and, as everything depended on her now, I thought that by telling her this lie, I w-w-would obtain her c-consent. B-but I c-could see at once that she didn't believe me and that she even s-suspected me of ha-hav-hav…" Fuller again lost his speech in a fit of stammering.

"… having murdered Sir Robert?" Mooney finished the sentence for him.

"Y-yes," Fuller assented, and there was no doubt that he was afraid of such a suspicion.

"You say that you spent the time between six and seven o'clock of Friday at your flat waiting for Sir Robert? Could anybody confirm that?"

But Fuller could not provide any satisfactory alibi for that time. He lived in a service flat and he did not employ any servants of his own. He left his office at five-thirty and went straight home. It took him about twenty minutes to get home and the commissionaire at the door might or might not have seen him when he arrived. He had a hasty meal from the store of food he had in his flat, as he had no time for a proper meal. He then waited for a whole hour, and the only proof he had of being at home at that time was that he had his wireless on without break and that the broadcast programme might have been overheard by some neighbours above or below the flat. At seven o'clock he had given up all hope of Sir Robert's arrival, but he waited another quarter of an hour to make quite sure. He then rang up Mrs. Tracey, the lady he intended to marry, as she was anxious to know the result of his conversation with Sir Robert. Mrs. Tracey was naturally very disappointed that Sir Robert had not turned up, as she fancied that he would have come round to Fuller's point of view. Fuller arranged to see Mrs. Tracey the same evening and he met her at Baker Street Station, but, again, when he left his flat to keep that appointment he met no one who could identify him. He and Mrs. Tracey then went to Madame Tussaud's cinema where they stopped till almost the end of the programme. On coming out of the cinema he saw the newspaper poster with the announcement of the murder of an ex-Cabinet minister. He bought the paper and his shock was very great when he learnt that it was Sir Robert who had been murdered; he realised then that he might have to give up all hope of ever getting a divorce.

It was then and there that he decided to go to see Mrs. Fuller to demand that she should release him from that unnatural bond with which the two of them had been chained to each other for nearly twenty years. He was so anxious to settle everything with Mrs. Fuller that he would have gone to see her on Saturday, but Mrs. Tracey persuaded him to wait till Sunday as Mrs. Fuller would hardly have welcomed discussion so soon after Sir Robert's death. Now Fuller was sorry he had gone even so soon as Sunday, for he believed that if he had waited a fortnight, or even a month, Mrs. Fuller might have proved more tractable. As it was, her blank refusal to help him to get his divorce, even if he himself supplied her with evidence for a successful action against him, had simply staggered him. He lost his head and made an ass of himself and, as his wife assumed that he had seen Sir Robert on Friday, he told her the lie about Sir Robert's having kept the appointment with him and of his consent to release him.

"Let us go back a little," Mooney said, after he had been provided with Mrs. Tracey's private address and had made arrangements for checking Fuller's statement as far as she was concerned at once. "Could you tell me exactly when Sir Robert met your last request for a settlement of your losses on the Stock Exchange?"

Fuller remembered it quite well: that was about the end of November. It was usually paid to him by cheque from Sir Robert's personal account, and the whole transaction was absolutely private. He was quite certain that no one at the office, for instance, not even Miss Pritt, knew anything about it. The cheque would, of course, be crossed and be paid into his own account where it could be easily traced.

"Did you already know Mrs. Tracey?"

"Y-yes."

"When did you first meet her?"

"I m-met her during a M-Mediterranean cruise ab-b-bout a year ago."

"Had you already thought of marrying her in November?"

"N-no." Fuller was quite definite about it: their friendship had, of course, taken a certain course about that time, but the thought of marriage had not yet occurred to him.

"Or to her?"

But Fuller did not grasp the superintendent's meaning. He admitted, however, that it was Mrs. Tracey who insisted on marriage. He fell in entirely with her wish as he had always desired to "straighten his life out" and live decently in his own home with a wife and children. As soon as Mrs. Tracey and he had decided to marry, he took steps to acquaint Sir Robert with the changed circumstances. The first time he had spoken to him about it was in April, about the end of April.

"Only at the end of April?" Mooney asked, a little surprised. "Didn't you decide to marry earlier than that?"

"Y-yes," Fuller replied. "We decided about Christmas. Only, owing to b-business reasons, I d-didn't think it was advisable to b-broach the subject to Sir Robert earlier. Even in April the situation w-w-was not q-quite propitious for a t-t-talk with Sir Robert, b-but Mrs. T-Tracey insisted that I s-should get on with my divorce."

Mooney was a little curious to know what these business troubles he had so often heard about were, but Fuller was even more reluctant to speak about them than Miss Pritt. He hardly knew himself what the trouble really was, except that it was quite impossible to approach Sir Robert even on routine office matters without provoking some sort of disagreeable scene.

But about Frank Littlewood, as Mooney had already observed, Fuller was very outspoken and even anxious to impart information. According to him, Frank Littlewood's attitude towards Sir Robert and his position in the political and business world was entirely deplorable. Had he not been so closely related to Sir Robert, he would have been dismissed long ago. It wasn't that his political views were rather advanced. It didn't matter, after all, what your political views were, so long as you were careful to keep them out of business. But Frank Littlewood was not able to keep his views to himself. He would obtrude them all over the place. He would talk to Fuller about them, although he was certainly not encouraged to do so, and he would invariably drag in Sir Robert and his immense business interests to justify his point of view.

Frank Littlewood was especially keen on getting some private information about his uncle's affairs, as he always suspected some sensational revelations. About a year ago he went even so far as to ransack a private file in Sir Robert's own office which had been left open by mistake, although Fuller had warned him of the consequences. Besides, in his personal references to Sir Robert, he was always very offensive and since, as Fuller regretfully admitted, he knew about Sir Robert's relations with Mrs. Fuller, he quite wrongly assumed that Fuller would be likely to share his views about Sir Robert's public position and kept on reviling his uncle in Fuller's presence, making the latter regret he had ever allowed any confidential talk to pass between them. Frank Littlewood had, besides, quite an exaggerated idea of his own talents and was resentful of the slightest criticism. That was chiefly the reason why Miss Pritt had disliked him so much. This dislike was deepened by a few personal scenes between them, during which Frank Littlewood had even challenged Miss Pritt's authority in the office, and, being quite incapable of taking a detached view of his own position, owing, no doubt, to the fact that he was closely related to Sir Robert (this was a point Fuller stressed again and again), he began even to hint quite transparently that Miss Pritt was in some way or other remiss in her duties, although he never made his meaning quite clear. He had always been, Fuller regretted to admit, rather rude about Miss Pritt. Such a position couldn't, of course, last without a definite break between Sir Robert and his nephew occurring sooner or later, especially as the two did so obviously dislike each other.

Fuller was sorry, however, that the cause of Frank Littlewood's dismissal was that unfortunate transaction for which he had quite unwittingly been responsible. Frank Littlewood, according to him, was always anxious to get rich quickly. He did not blame him for that, except that he had always noticed that people with very advanced views somehow resented having to work hard for a living, and wished to get rich quickly, so as to be able to be independent of the sordid money-making game which they so condemned; although what else they would themselves be able to do with their money when they got it but invest it in some lucrative business enterprise, he, Fuller, did not know. Anyway, Frank Littlewood was eager to make money, and the modest salary his uncle paid him only increased his desire in that direction. He had consulted Fuller about the purchase of some shares of one of the more important of his uncle's companies, as the thought of being a shareholder in one of Sir Robert's companies rather appealed to him. Fuller had given him his opinion for as much as it was worth, and had even gone so far as to buy the shares for him. That Frank Littlewood should buy shares on spec, did not strike Fuller as in any way reprehensible, but that he should be such a bad loser surprised him and (Fuller here took off his pale horn-rimmed glasses and gave them a good polish), even shocked him in a way, for it seemed that Frank Littlewood did not quite appreciate that he was solely responsible for the unfortunate transaction. The result of it all was rather startling, but not unexpected. Fuller personally was very sorry for Frank Littlewood who, according to him, was in many respects a very promising young man, though hopelessly conceited and rather inexperienced in the ways of the world. He was particularly sorry that Frank Littlewood could not get on with his uncle and that their mutual dislike should have had such a tragic sequel.

Asked at once what he meant by his last remark, Fuller got excited and inarticulate and, after a good deal of stuttering, he assured the superintendent that the remark had escaped him against his will and that he was merely referring to the extraordinary fact that Sir

Robert should have been killed so near to where Frank Littlewood lived. Of course, the fact that Sir Robert had arranged to see Mrs. Littlewood on Friday was liable to quite unfortunate deductions, but the police must have looked into everything by now. And he hastened to explain that he had first heard of Sir Robert's intended visit to Mrs. Littlewood on Monday morning from Miss Pritt, and that it was only then that he had realised that Sir Robert had definitely changed his mind about keeping his appointment with him and had decided to see his sister instead. He met Frank Littlewood on Monday when the latter came up to the office to take some of his belongings away and he was struck by his peculiar behaviour: Frank Littlewood would hardly speak to him and he seemed very upset by something, but, Fuller hastily put in, he supposed the death of a near relative was upsetting even if you disliked him.

Mooney again let Fuller speak without interruption. His stammer was not so bad when he was allowed to speak freely and, besides, it was obvious that Fuller was anxious to explain away something which he dare not mention himself and Mooney hoped that it might escape him when he wasn't so much on his guard. But the unexpected and startling hint which Fuller allowed himself against Frank Littlewood made a distinctly bad impression on the superintendent. Fuller was the first person he had interrogated in connection with the death of Sir Robert Boniface who had tried to implicate Frank Littlewood in the murder of his uncle. However much he seemed to have tried to explain away his remark about the tragic sequel of the mutual dislike Sir Robert and his nephew had towards each other, Mooney felt that that remark was not at all unprepared, but, on the contrary, had been carefully considered and put in with a casualness that was, in itself, suspicious.

But why should Fuller go out of his way to accuse Frank Littlewood, however vaguely, of the murder of Sir Robert? Well, if his second theory was right and Fuller was the real murderer, who had purposely taken the blue limousine to the Vale of Health in order to cast suspicion on Frank Littlewood, then his more direct hint to-day could be easily explained. And again the question what Fuller had been doing at the Viaduct Pond last night began to worry the superintendent. Fuller did not know that the police had found the automatic pistol with which Sir Robert had been killed. Would he express any astonishment at being shown the gun?

Fuller's behaviour during the last quarter of an hour of his questioning at Scotland Yard strengthened Mooney's suspicions.

For at the mention of the Viaduct Pond Fuller's excitement returned and that scared look came back to his eyes. He began adjusting his glasses with trembling hands, his stutter became very painful and troublesome, and there could be not the slightest doubt that he was feeling very uncomfortable indeed.

At first he wouldn't admit having been near the Viaduct Pond, although he did confess that he had taken a stroll on Hampstead Heath on Monday evening, just to have a look at the place of the recent tragic occurrence. But when Mooney described to him the exact position of the Viaduct Pond, Fuller admitted that he might have passed the place as his stroll had really taken him all over the Heath. He denied emphatically having seen Mooney on the bridge and his white face turned deadly pale when it was suggested to him that when he saw the superintendent he beat a hasty retreat from the Viaduct Pond.

But, although Fuller's eyes narrowed with fear when Mooney produced the small automatic pistol and asked him if he had ever seen it before, he recovered his self-possession sufficiently to remember his right to refuse to answer questions which, as he put it, had nothing to do with him. To his great relief Mooney let him go after warning him to hold himself in readiness for further questioning.

To Mooney this sudden collapse of Fuller could have only one meaning, but he realised that so far he had no real evidence against him. His alibi, such as it was, would have to be carefully investigated.

Fuller's story, Mooney had to admit, was quite convincing up to a point. But even where it did sound most convincing, as, for instance, in that part of it which concerned his desire to get a divorce, it was not without a flaw. Thus, at the very beginning, Fuller insisted that he had sufficient evidence to get a judgment in his favour, but later on he confessed that that evidence was not only very old, going back fifteen years, but it was almost worthless, so that he now had no hope of getting a divorce unless Mrs. Fuller consented to help him, rather an illegal proceeding which might, in itself, lose him his action. Then there was his assertion that he had entered Sir Robert's service against his will, but almost in the same breath Fuller confessed that the consideration that at Sir Robert's private office he would be able to obtain "advance" information about the movement of Stock Market prices had weighed with him considerably in accepting Sir Robert's offer. His account of Frank Littlewood's unhappy experience at his uncle's office was altogether too glib, too thought out, too fluent to have come naturally in answer to an unexpected question. No, Fuller must have anticipated that he would be questioned about Frank Littlewood, and his veiled (and not very veiled, either) attempt to throw the guilt of the murder on Sir Robert's nephew was also part of a thought-out plan.

Mooney distrusted most of all Fuller's assumed concern about Frank Littlewood's dismissal. That affair of the shares was a very tricky business and he wouldn't be surprised if Miss Pritt hadn't had a hand in it, too, as Frank Littlewood claimed.

There was, indeed, no doubt in Mooney's mind that both Fuller and Miss Pritt considered Frank Littlewood's presence at Sir Robert's private office a nuisance, and that either of them would have given much to be rid of him. Whether they had actually conspired to bring about his dismissal, he could not say for certain, but he would not be in the least surprised if that proved to be the case.

However, he was most concerned with Fuller now, and if he could prove that the gun, at the sight of which Fuller had blenched so ostensibly, had really been thrown into the pond by him, the case against Fuller would be almost complete, in his mind, at any rate. But until he could prove that and until he could prove how the gun, which must once have belonged to Caldwell, had got to Fuller, he could not overlook the other two possibilities that Sir Robert Boniface had been killed either by Littlewood or by Caldwell, or even some as yet totally unforeseen possibility that he had been killed by somebody else.

Before going home on Tuesday night, Mooney thought it would be as well to summarise the motives of the three suspects and to reconstruct the murder as each might have committed it:

THE CASE AGAINST BENJAMIN FULLER

Fuller's motives for committing the murder were the strongest and his defence the weakest of the three. He confessed to have demanded Sir Robert Boniface's consent to an undefended divorce action, which the baronet consistently refused to consider. Fuller, however, wanted to be married again and he was quite in earnest about it. He knew that Mrs. Fuller was almost as anxious as he was to be free again. The only obstacle to his freedom was Sir Robert.

Fuller was expecting Sir Robert to arrive at his flat at six o'clock. He had just sufficient time to have a hasty meal and to put on the wireless. He was anxious, however, that no one who knew him should see him either leave his flat or enter the blue limousine. He, therefore, left the block of flats by a side door and went out to meet Sir Robert some distance away. He signalled to Sir Robert to stop and they went off together to Hampstead Heath to thrash out their difficulties. Sir Robert, as Fuller might have foreseen, flew into a temper at the very mention of an undefended divorce action, but his attempt to browbeat the husband of his mistress, who had hitherto proved himself tractable to such treatment, failed. Fuller refused to be persuaded and Sir Robert, in the end, told him to bring his action and be damned! So far as he was concerned, the discussion was over. He lit a cigar and prepared himself for a quiet smoke to soothe his somewhat frayed temper.

But Fuller found that as a result of his talk with Sir Robert Boniface he had lost everything: his chance of re-marriage, his chance of getting his Stock Exchange losses paid in future (for by accepting his challenge to fight a divorce action, Sir Robert would probably consider their "gentleman's agreement" at an end even if Fuller refrained from filing a petition), and, possibly, also his chance of retaining his job—had all gone! By killing Sir Robert he would at least save his job and possibly his chance of marrying again. Fuller, therefore, shot Sir Robert.

His next steps were not difficult to reconstruct. Fuller must have learnt from Sir Robert that he intended to see Mrs. Littlewood the same evening. He thought that he could easily put the police on a wrong scent by throwing suspicion on Frank Littlewood, whom he must certainly have hated. He, therefore, drove the blue limousine with Sir Robert's body to the Vale of Health, where he arrived just a few minutes, perhaps, before Samuel Halstead saw it for the first time at a quarter to seven. He then left the car unobserved, disposed of the cartridge and kept the gun, which he hoped to get rid of at a more convenient opportunity.

On Monday night he visited the Vale of Health again and, seeing it entirely free from police, he threw the gun into the Viaduct Pond and went straight on. When he turned back he suddenly noticed on the bridge the superintendent whom he had seen already in Miss Pritt's room (a wise precaution that, which had turned out a little differently from what he intended) and made off at a run, but not before he had been recognised.

The only serious difficulty about the case against Fuller was the gun. Where did Fuller get hold of Matt Caldwell's gun? Once that was clearly established, the case against him was complete.

THE CASE AGAINST FRANK LITTLEWOOD

The whole case against Frank Littlewood is built up entirely on his recent quarrel with Sir Robert Boniface and the threats of exposure contained in his letter to his uncle. There was obviously no other motive, for Frank Littlewood himself realised quite well that his prospects of inheriting his uncle's fortune were extremely slender, and the idea that he might have killed his uncle because he considered him to be a threat to civilisation was too improbable to be seriously considered.

Frank Littlewood alleged that he did not know that his mother wished to see Sir Robert, nor that Sir Robert had arranged to talk things over with her at six (or seven) o'clock on Friday. But he might have been on his way home when his uncle arrived in the Vale of Health. Suppose, again, that Sir Robert did see Fuller at six and that Fuller was a liar, though not a murderer. Sir Robert might then have arrived in the Vale of Health about half-past six. Frank Littlewood saw him, realised that he had come to see his mother, and resented the fact that his mother was carrying on negotiations with his uncle behind his back. He accosted his uncle, who invited him inside the car to discuss their differences. The threat of exposure must have bothered Sir Robert even if the private file his nephew had examined was rather ancient. During the discussion Frank Littlewood shot his uncle; either because he had received no satisfaction to his demand for an apology, or because he was incensed at something his uncle had said. Frank must have been in a state of great excitement to have done it, and it was surprising that he had left no clues of any kind behind him. After leaving the car he disposed of the cartridge and, perhaps, also of the gun, and disappeared for another three hours to work off his excitement.

(The time the murder had taken place would have to be postponed to between six-thirty and seven o'clock in Frank Littlewood's as well as in Matt Caldwell's case, which conflicted somewhat with the medical evidence, though not, of course, very seriously.)

The case against Frank Littlewood sounded really improbable, but people were known to have killed their relatives in the heat of a quarrel; and, unless Frank Littlewood changed his mind and supplied a good alibi, he might be in for some serious trouble. It was, of course, unfortunate for him that neither his mother nor his fiancée should show absolute confidence in his innocence.

Here, again, it would have to be established how Frank Littlewood got hold of Matt Caldwell's gun.

THE CASE AGAINST MATT CALDWELL

The case against Matt Caldwell is really the simplest of all.

The artist had undoubtedly a serious and apparently justified grudge against Sir Robert Boniface. He was painting on the Heath, only a few paces from where the blue limousine was found, all the afternoon till at least seven o'clock. If he did see Sir Robert's car, he was almost certain to have gone over and accosted the baronet. Suppose this was what had actually happened. Wishing to avoid a brawl in the road, Sir Robert invited Matt Caldwell into his car, where a violent quarrel took place and the artist shot the baronet with his own gun. He then left the car, went up the hill to the block of flats, disposed of the cartridge by throwing it into the second gorse bush and got rid of the gun before the police began their search. He returned to the public-house, waited there for the discovery of the body and joined the window-cleaner and the crowd of other people who proceeded all together to the place where the car had been abandoned. There Caldwell engaged in conversation first with the sergeant and then with Inspector Beckett, and obliged the police by identifying the body. He was in a state of great elation and behaved very queerly. On Sunday, however, he decided to disappear till the affair blew over.

There was no difficulty in the case against Caldwell so far as the gun was concerned. It was his own and he most probably carried it about on him. Neither could the testimony of Sir Robert Boniface's portrait be overlooked, especially as the holes in it were certainly caused by bullets from the automatic pistol that killed Sir Robert. Caldwell had no alibi. The only fact which must be explained was why, fearing they would be discovered, he didn't dispose of his guns and of the portrait.

In none of the three cases, Mooney reflected, did the scratches at the back of the blue limousine or the returned half of the cinema ticket, which he had picked up by the second gorse bush, count for anything. But then, Sir Robert might have damaged the back of his car anywhere between four and six o'clock on Friday. As for the cinema ticket, Mooney himself never really thought anything of it.

9

MATT CALDWELL GOES ON A HIKE

MATT CALDWELL LEFT THE VALE OF HEALTH ON SUNDAY IN search of quiet. The Heath was overrun with police and the public-house was full of gossips. It was too hot to remain in his studio, and a long tramp through the lanes and by-ways of Surrey was what he desired most.

As it happened, his tramp through Surrey also enabled him to fulfil an engagement made some months ago during his last exhibition at the Leicester Galleries. That exhibition had been a financial failure. Only a few pictures had been sold. But among those who had bought them was a Mrs. Helen Thurston, whom he had not met, but who had written to him from her Surrey home and who was anxious that he should paint a portrait of "a dear friend" of hers. Matt Caldwell had no idea who that "dear friend" might be, and from his experience of wealthy women he would not have been surprised if it turned out to be a pekinese. Anyhow, he was not at the time free to accept the commission as he was still busy painting the portrait of Sir Robert Boniface, but he did acknowledge Mrs. Thurston's letter and promised to pay a call on her some time to discuss her proposal. He was not certain even now that he would call on Mrs. Thurston, but, as he was going on a hike, he thought he might as well visit the part of the country where she lived, especially as it was only a day's walk from Hindhead.

There was nothing, anyway, to keep him in London. His work had not made much progress lately. He had lost his enthusiasm. The fact was he had counted too much on a fat cheque from Sir Robert Boniface to compensate him for the long period of straitened circumstances since his exhibition. He could hardly afford a tube of paint now and he had to fall back on a lump like Agnes for a model. Agnes had got on his nerves badly. He hated his models to be infatuated with him, and there was, besides, a strong possessive instinct in Agnes, which, combined with her stupidity, simply appalled him. He cursed himself for ever having desired that girl and for having, in a weak moment, agreed to paint her. What had driven him to do it was, of course, his inability to afford a model; but Agnes was no good as a model, she got fatigued very quickly, she had no time to pose for him, she whimpered when he swore, and she insisted on obtruding her personal relationship with him, of which he was beginning to get tired.

Matt Caldwell was a man of powerful instincts. When he desired a thing he went straight for it and, if it was a woman, he was usually successful. But, except for his art, he had never yet stuck to anything for long, and least of all to a woman. And yet somewhere in his huge frame there was a persistent longing for romance, for an adventure that did not leave a bitter taste in one's mouth when it was all over, for a parting that was as full of wonder as a first meeting.

He had thought that June Gayford possessed that fine spirit of the real adventurer. Her smile when he met her first was refreshing, like a cool drink from a spring on a hot summer day, her dark brown eyes so clear and candid and yet also so challenging, and she had wit that added edge to romance, but she was one of his great disillusionments. She had hurt his vanity very badly, she had laughed at his approaches, she completely ignored the sincerity of his sudden passionate avowal, and she refused to visit his studio again. She did more: she told Frank Littlewood about that rather disconcerting scene and he had had to fling that damned journalist out of his rooms.

June Gayford was really much more than a disillusionment, she was a complete failure. She, like the others, left a bad taste in his mouth, a reminder of that devilish possessive instinct in women which was so abhorrent to him.

Matt Caldwell was a sentimentalist, but he wished to keep sentiment unsullied by possessiveness, in the same way as he wished to keep his art unsullied by money values. When Sir Robert Boniface had sent back his portrait with a curt note that he was not going to pay for such rubbish, Matt Caldwell swore and banged his fist against the wall with such force that he nearly dislocated his wrist. But it was not the loss of the money that had hurt him at that moment, although he had been planning for days how he was going to spend it and was waiting impatiently for the arrival of the cheque. It was the insult to his art. What did that fool of a millionaire know about painting? Why, his art gallery, of which he was so proud and on which he must have spent thousands of pounds, did not contain anything as good as this portrait of a modern privateer, a corsair of industry, if his nephew's account of him was to be trusted, and there was no doubt that Frank Littlewood was right in that!

Matt Caldwell had fathomed Sir Robert Boniface's soul. It was in his portrait, and he did not wonder that Sir Robert was appalled to see it. It was Satan, a demon of darkness, a ruthless despoiler, a man to whom possession and power was everything. You could see it in his eyes, in his thick lips, in the whole cast of his face, in the hard, ruthless lines round his mouth, in the domineering slant of his nose! And yet to Sir Robert it was rubbish. A work of art—rubbish!

Holding the canvas before him, the artist had laughed as he thought of the neat gallery Sir Robert so proudly showed him round, on his first visit to Lownds Square, so beautifully kept with all the comfortable priceless pictures on the walls, madonnas, saints, eighteenth-century ladies, landscapes, large canvases and small, nothing to trouble one as one gazed from one picture to another. And that smell of wax polish which gave the place the real public gallery touch! Ah, yes, a few moderns, a seascape by a royal academician, a nude by a lady associate, a still life from the walls of Burlington House and two portraits of Sir Robert Boniface himself, one in evening dress and another in some sort of uniform, painted on large canvases, bearing the signatures of men famous in the fashionable world of art—dead, absolutely dead! But so very comfortable: Sir Robert, the great magnate, the patron of the arts, the munificent donor of a number of art treasures to the nation, the organiser of cheap classical concerts for the masses, the sturdy defender of the constitution—there he was, beaming benevolently from the wall!

But no, Matt Caldwell felt he was not being entirely just: there was a portrait in that gallery, a single portrait, which had attracted his attention at once. It was a portrait of Lady Boniface, a small, shrivelled woman sitting stiffly in a chair, her hair and dress beautifully tidy, but her face and hands disturbingly tragic, uneven, scarred by life! A shadow passed over the face of Sir Robert as he, too, stopped before the portrait of the old lady. It wasn't quite a successful picture of his wife, he told the young untidy giant of a painter whose large feet left such ungainly marks on the polished floor of the millionaire's gallery, but it was the only portrait she had agreed to sit for, so he had left it there.

But why had Sir Robert Boniface agreed to sit for a painter whose reputation did not quite square with his own conceptions of art? Why did he waste his precious time in the company of this ultra-modern artist whose paintings merely provoked a few "stunt" notices in the Press?

Matt Caldwell had never asked himself that question, but Sir Robert had, for he had felt uneasy at the thought that he might have made a mistake about that young painter, that his "modern" portrait might not be worth the publicity that it would get. When the portrait was finished he said nothing. He had left it on the easel in his study in front of the desk where he had been posing. But that very evening he spent an hour by himself examining it closely. At first a feeling of uneasiness crept over him, then the feeling changed into something more definite, into terror and disgust. It was not his face at all! It was a crude, distorted mask!

A sudden hatred flared up in the old man's heart as he came to the realisation that it was his true face that the artist had painted, a face that he had hidden from the world and from himself, a face he was afraid to look at. For a moment he felt like slashing the portrait with a knife, but his good sense asserted itself. Why should he get excited over some immature work of an artist who could not make a decent living by his art? It was not art, it was rubbish! He'd have it sent back and let that painter starve! That would teach him to paint indecent pictures!

It was rubbish, was it? Matt Caldwell crumpled Sir Robert Boniface's note in his hand which still ached from that blow against the wall. He'd show that rapacious old swine that he did not care a hoot for his money. There, against the fireplace! He stepped back and began firing at Sir Robert's portrait from a small automatic pistol which he took out of his pocket, and he gave a loud whoop of joy as he hit the millionaire in the eye. He emptied the whole magazine and for the next few days he used the portrait as a target for his shooting practice very early in the mornings in a retired spot on the Heath. Then he got sick of the whole beastly business and shoved the ruined canvas into a cupboard.

It was a very hot morning, and Matt Caldwell felt tired when he emerged from the underground at Waterloo. The station was deserted, it being now about half-past one, and if he hoped for a companion on his hike he was sorely disappointed. There was in him a strong yearning for the companionship of women and the thought that he might be able to pick up some girl willing to spend a few hours in his company was always present in his mind. He was not always, however, out for conquests, a talk was to him quite often more appealing than any intimate companionship, but it was rarely that he could find anyone who would wish to make his acquaintance in that unconventional way who was worth talking to. This fact was rather a sore point with Matt Caldwell, and it was the only serious complaint he really had to make against the existing system of society, to whose other social characteristics he remained indifferent. There was too little companionship in the world for him, too little direct, straightforward intercourse between people, too much of the clannishness and empty politeness so characteristic of large modern cities.

At heart Matt Caldwell was rather clannish himself and rather lonely and reserved, which perhaps explained the sudden fits of raging temper to which he was subject. His nature was moulded very unevenly, it had its deep valleys and its high peaks, and the midway path that he usually trod was very narrow and unsteady; if he met any obstruction on his way he had either to climb some height to circumvent it or to lower himself to some deep valley and spend days in climbing back again.

It was in one of these deep valleys that Matt Caldwell's spirit was languishing when he took the train to Guildford. An empty train, an empty carriage. He threw his rucksack and his painting tackle on the empty seat and sat down opposite to read the paper he had bought at the station. His face for a moment took on an expression of derision as he read through the account of Sir Robert Boniface's murder. He was surprised to see not only himself mentioned as the one who had been the first to give assistance to the police, but also the fact recorded that he had recently painted a portrait of the murdered millionaire.

As he finished reading, his face lit up with that intense joy which first aroused Inspector Beckett's suspicions on Friday evening; but it soon recovered the gloomy, dissatisfied expression which it had worn the whole morning.

There was nothing in the paper that he did not know already, and, anyway, it wasn't of Sir Robert that he was thinking. He wanted to shake all that excitement off. It was, he realised, morbid. He was a fool to have destroyed that portrait, for now that its owner was dead he no longer felt any hostility to it. It was a work of art, abstract, eternal. But the work of art was destroyed, it did not even live any longer in his soul. It was folly to give way to one's emotions to such an unreasonable extent, almost madness, and that depression was a result of it. He wished he could meet somebody who would lift him out of his despair, who would make him forget his folly and his crime, for to destroy a work of art was a crime for which his conscience was only now beginning to torment him. The world was well rid of a man like Sir Robert Boniface, but not of his portrait!

Matt Caldwell left Guildford station and made his way to the bridge over the Wey. He intended to walk along the river-bank to Godalming and from there to pay his call on Mrs. Thurston and then continue his hike through little-frequented country walks to Hindhead. The path along the riverside was crowded on that Sunday afternoon, but he soon left the crowd behind him and followed a hardly visible path across meadows which were parched with the drought and over stiles which were ramshackle, keeping all the way very close to the river-bank. That parched grass was just like himself, all dried up and useless. He had gone to the country in the hope of finding comfort in nature, but nature herself was comfortless, nature herself was thirsty. The crimson heads of sorrel had turned brown, their seeds had dried up and dispersed and their reddish-brown stalks looked so forlorn with the few seed-cases still hanging precariously from them.

He passed several old mouldering wooden sluice-gates through which the water was pouring in a foaming stream. The river was rising perceptibly higher and higher, and the water in the sluices was pressing with great force against the old wooden gates. He had walked along the same river-bank six or seven years ago in the company of a fellow artist, a man of his own age who had since married and gone into business and was dealing in pictures on a small scale, and he remembered that the path he was following did not continue very far and that he had to cross the river at some point or else lose his way in a marsh. He had just passed a sluice which was built a little stronger than the others he had left behind and he decided to go back and see if he could not cross the river over the flood-gates. It was with great difficulty that he did so, but on continuing on the other bank for about an hour he found that he must have crossed too soon, for the path ended abruptly and a thick hedge, running to the very bank of the river, prevented his further progress. He had to go back and recross the river and his detour took him more than two hours, which only increased his irritation and angered him, for he wanted to be well out of Godalming before he settled down for the night at a village where he had stayed before.

He did not lose his way again, but it was rather late when, sore-footed and tired, he reached Godalming. He decided to have a meal before he continued on his hike. The café he entered turned out to be of the pseudo-Tudor style, with coats of mail standing in the corners, warming-pans hanging on the walls under the oak-beamed ceiling and a huge brick fireplace. Everything there was so spotlessly clean: the white table-cloths, the "period" dresses of the waitresses and even the home-made cakes. Every piece of brass and copper in the room showed marks of hard, painstaking polish.

Matt Caldwell must have presented a very untidy appearance after his long walk, for the people in the café eyed him with a certain curiosity. The place made him feel even dirtier than he was and he detested the whole spick-and-span pretentiousness of it. But for a small, dilapidated, dark-green two-seater car in front of it, he wouldn't have gone in! But that car, he reflected (mistakenly, as it very soon appeared), probably belonged to someone who dared not enter the café.

But once in, he took little notice of anybody. He chose a corner table, threw his rucksack and painting tackle on the floor and prepared to enjoy his meal. It was after he had finished tea, when he was beginning to feel a pleasant sensation of great comfort, to which rest and the meal had largely contributed, that he began to pay attention to the people around him. It was then that he became aware of a young girl of a type that had always irritated him in some obscure, uneasy way. He first noticed her when she passed his table to fetch some small parcel from the dilapidated two-seater (the artist, who did not at all take to the girl, could not help approving her choice of a car which, at any rate, fitted in with the landscape, if it did not fit in with her expensive clothes). She was having tea with a tall, blond young man, an officer, no doubt, meticulously groomed, clean shaven, his suit new and perfectly cut. The girl's fiancé, to all appearances, although Matt Caldwell noticed with malicious satisfaction that the pair did not seem to be on very friendly terms at the moment. The young man looked quite crestfallen when he accepted the small parcel from his companion and he had a lot to say, while the girl hardly spoke at all.

Matt Caldwell could not help admiring the beauty of the young girl's strong, healthy body, but what he disliked about her and what made him feel so irritated as he watched her from his corner of the room was the air of inaccessibility which was implied in her bearing and her expression generally. Her air of inaccessibility, however, was not a pose and that was the reason why Matt Caldwell disliked it so deeply. It was not altogether haughtiness, though there was more than a touch of that in her beautiful mouth and finely-shaped nose. It was not dignity, though her poise was certainly dignified. It was rather a certain aloofness touched with disdain, an indefinable feeling that she was standing on a pedestal, to be adored but not to be approached too close, to be admired but not to be touched. A certain coldness, too, in her eyes and derision on her lips, as she noticed the painter's attention and returned his glance, which made him wince.

"The blasted virgin!" he muttered through his breath.

Matt Caldwell paid his bill and left the café, put out of humour by that girl's look of cold disdain and trying to shake off the feeling of deep resentment and irritation which surged up within him when he caught her glance and found himself overawed by it. Poor devil, the artist thought of the officer, as he climbed the steps cut in the face of a high hill and left Godalming behind or rather below him, he must have a damn difficult, not to say exasperating, job to woo a girl like that, with her haughty mien and touch-me-not stare!

He felt a little out of breath as he reached the top of the hill, but he did not stop to recover and went straight on, wishing to get off the motor road as soon as possible. His country walk had not turned out at all as he wished. He had desired an adventure that would lift him out of his depression, that would give him back his enthusiasm, his pleasure in his work. But he had only succeeded in losing his way over parched fields and now he must again have missed his direction, for he could not find the path which was to have taken him through a park into a village where he intended to stop. He had spent about twenty minutes in an endeavour to find it, he had crossed the road twice and had almost given up hope, when all at once he saw the path he was looking for on the other side of the road, or at least a path which was uncommonly like it. He made a sudden dart across the road and he did not notice the small, dilapidated, dark-green two-seater which he had left standing outside the café and which was coming straight at him. He was too late to jump quite clear and was thrown on the ground and dragged by his rucksack some distance before the car stopped. He was not badly hurt, but he was bruised all over and he felt an acute pain in his right shoulder as he was trying to raise himself from the ground. His first impulse was to get up and make short work of the motorist who had knocked him down. But he was too late for that, because the motorist herself (it was the girl he had seen in the café in the company of the officer) had jumped out in a frenzy no less homicidal than his, and, without waiting for him to get up, had caught him by his right shoulder and began shaking it vigorously.

"What the hell do you mean by running across the road like that?" she shouted, without letting go of his right shoulder.

Matt Caldwell tore himself away from her with a cry of rage and pain, but as he turned to face her he fell back in amazement and stared at the girl without being able to say a word. It was not the way she had addressed him that rendered him speechless, for the language she used was not unfamiliar to him; it was that such frenzied speech should come from her, that goddess who seemed so aloof and cold on her pedestal, that staggered him and entirely robbed him of speech. She was no less beautiful now she was angry than before, and no less haughty, nor any less dignified. She seemed to have recognised him, another fact that surprised the painter, for he did not think she would remember him and he thought it even less likely that she would show that she did remember him.

"Are you hurt?" she asked, stepping back a little and regarding him frigidly, with lifted head and a curl of disdain on her lips, her sudden anger still visible in her distended nostrils and in her eyes.

"No!" Matt Caldwell bawled at the top of his voice, lurching forward in a spasm of blind fury sharpened by the pain he was suffering, and by a sudden hatred of the girl.

But he must have been more hurt than he had realised, for he suddenly collapsed on the road at her feet, stunned by the unbearable pain in his right shoulder.

"I'll give you a lift in my car," the girl said, helping the artist to raise himself from the ground and supporting him as he stood swaying in the road, dazed and angry. "Where are you going?"

Her voice had not lost its frigidity nor that hostility with which she had first addressed him, but she helped to undo his rucksack and picked up his painting tackle and led him to her car, the back of which she opened to throw in his belongings.

"You'd better sit in the front," she said, "it's more comfortable." And as, hardly realising what he was doing, he allowed himself to be placed in her car, she again repeated her question: "Where are you going?"

But Matt Caldwell could only wave his left hand vaguely and mutter something about a village whose name he had forgotten.

"Oh, you're hiking, are you?" she said, starting her car and setting off without any more questions about his destination. "You're an artist?" she asked after a short pause during which neither she nor Matt Caldwell had even glanced at each other, and when he had grunted an affirmative, she remarked with the same detached air: "I don't believe you've shaved to-day."

Matt Caldwell passed his left hand across his chin. That blasted virgin was right! He had forgotten to shave that morning. It was certainly curious he should not have noticed anything unusual about his face all day. Still, what business was that of hers?

"I am an artist," he said stolidly. "Why should I shave?"

She either did not hear him or did not think his idiotic remark required any comment, for she kept on driving without paying any more attention to him. She seemed to be taking him some distance, and at last he turned painfully in his seat and asked her where she was going to.

"I suppose," she replied, "I'd better take you back with me, though personally," she added scornfully, "I'd rather bung you out on the road than take you along with me. A man like you who throws himself in front of a car doesn't deserve any help!"

"I don't want to go home with you, I'm sure," he replied. "I've had quite enough of you, I don't want to know your parents!"

"I'm not taking you to my parents," she said with icy scorn, as if the very suggestion that she would think of taking him to her parents was an unheard-of impertinence on his part, "I'm taking you to some friends I'm staying with."

"I don't want to know your friends, either!" Matt Caldwell exclaimed with sudden fury, and he tried to lift himself up, but he fell back with a suppressed oath on his lips. "Set me down anywhere, do you hear? At some hotel or pub.," he shouted.

"Who'd take such a vagabond in?" she asked with that intolerable scorn in her voice, slightly turning her face in his direction. "You'd better stop fussing," she added, as he again tried to raise himself out of his seat, "it doesn't suit you."

"You blasted virgin!" Matt Caldwell bawled at the top of his voice, "will you stop your —— car and set me down at once?"

"I am not a virgin," the girl replied with great dignity, in her precise, icy, contemptuous, exasperating voice, "and I'm not going to be talked to by you in that language!"

"I don't suppose that pukka sahib you were having tea with talks to you in such language!" he exclaimed with savage fury in his voice.

"He does not!" the girl replied, reddening slightly.

"Caught her this time," Matt Caldwell muttered to himself triumphantly. "The iceberg's melting."

But the girl again either did not hear him or was indifferent to what he was saying. She drove on for another few minutes before addressing him: "I'd better tell you," she said in her cold, indifferent voice, "why I'm taking you to my friends. I want to use you as an experiment. One of the friends I'm staying with, or rather who's staying as the other guest of my friend, is a healer. His name is Dr. Adams. He's not really a doctor, he's called doctor just out of courtesy. This you won't understand, but never mind. Dr. Adams is a healer. He heals every kind of illness by his special powers, sprains included. But for about a year his healing powers seem to have quite left him, and he has spent the last nine or ten months in writing detective stories. Some days ago, however, he felt that his old powers were coming back to him, and my friend is very excited about it. Unfortunately neither she nor I require at present any assistance from Dr. Adams, and we shan't know about the result of any of his distant cases for several weeks. I think he's a fraud and I told him so. But, of course, my friend believes in him and so do scores of others. I'm going to use you as an experiment. If your sprained shoulder does not improve after one or two applications of his healing powers, it'll be just bad luck!"

"I shouldn't be surprised," Matt Caldwell said with cold fury, "if you didn't run me down on purpose to provide yourself with somebody to experiment on."

"I'm wondering myself," the girl replied with great frankness, "but I'm not quite sure. The thought might have occurred to me subconsciously, though, and I suppose I acted on impulse. You looked such a common tramp and a few days in bed with good food and proper attention wouldn't have done a tramp any real harm. Of course, I was careful not to hurt you very badly, but naturally I couldn't be sure. That's probably why I flew into such a temper."

"Don't try to apologise," Matt Caldwell said sarcastically. But the car bumped rather badly then, and he was thrown against the side with great force, his sprained shoulder giving him excruciating pain, which made him bite his lips to suppress a cry. The girl must have noticed that he was in great pain, for she stopped the car and put a few cushions round him.

"Now you're a real invalid," she said, looking at him with an encouraging smile and talking to him as one does to a rather naughty child. "You will behave nicely to my friends, won't you? We shall make you awfully comfortable. And, by the way, we'd better get introduced to each other. My name is Marjorie, Marjorie Trevor."

Matt Caldwell liked Marjorie's smile. It added charm to her fine head and it softened the cold dignity of her bearing. He also felt a sudden admiration for her, a feeling which had come over him the first time he saw her in the café, but it failed to exasperate him now. She was, anyhow, a girl who was quite a match for him, a girl who would take some taming! It was certainly a piece of damned impudence to knock him down for the sake of some healing experiment and then turn on him for having run into her car, but, on the whole, he was not sorry it had happened, though he was still feeling uneasy in her company, afraid that some unexpected thrust from her might rouse his antagonism.

"Next time you want to knock someone down for the sake of enlarging the practice of your friend, the quack doctor," he said with a wry smile, "don't hit him in the shoulder, get his leg or something which is not so inseparable a part of him."

"Oh, you mustn't call Dr. Adams a quack," she warned him earnestly. "He's a very charming man and I'm sure you'll like him, though I hope you won't use your foul language in his presence. You'll shock him terribly. You can use it to Helen, though, she'll adore it." And, after she had re-started the car, she asked him again for his name. "Matt Caldwell?" she repeated, and he was pleased to see that she regarded him with a new interest. "I've seen some of your pictures," she said. "I went with Helen to your exhibition at the Leicester Galleries last December. Helen, by the way, bought one of them. She's very keen on getting you to paint Dr. Adams. Didn't she write to you about it?"

Matt Caldwell couldn't help laughing sardonically. "So your friend is Mrs. Helen Thurston and her 'dear friend' the celebrated quack doctor! Well, I'm damned!" he said with great deliberation, but without surprise, for the adventure on the road had robbed him of all capacity for surprise. He was overcome by a dull feeling of exasperation with himself for having ever thought of paying his promised visit. He'd rather paint a pekinese than a quack! If only he had known what his commission was likely to be, he wouldn't have chosen that part of Surrey for his hike! He would have gone straight to Hindhead!" Would it surprise you to know," he asked bitterly, for a sudden jolt sent a sharp pain through his shoulder and re-awakened his anger, "that I was going to honour your friend with a visit to-morrow? But I don't suppose that would have made you drive any more carefully!"

"Oh, but I was driving very carefully!" she retorted. "You really must understand," she added, turning to him with a cold, mocking light in her eyes, "that I'm not interested in you or your engagements, but I'm very much interested in your sprained shoulder and that's why I'm taking you to my friends!"

But in reply Matt Caldwell merely swore viciously under his breath. "If I had known," he said, after a brief pause, "that it was the quack doctor your friend wanted me to paint, I should have spared you the trouble of running me down. Quacks offend against truth and as an artist I cannot object to them too strongly. Old Boniface, who loved money more than his soul, was at least sound about quacks. He had a healthy contempt for them and for those who employed them. He was always ridiculing Lord Rollesborough, one of the directors of his companies, who seems to be entirely in the hands of some quack doctor. That doesn't help him to restore the confidence of the shareholders of his companies, though. His lordship seems to be in such a stew that he's giving interviews to the papers trying to cover up the truth!"

It was not clear what Matt Caldwell meant by his last remark, but he said it with such feeling that to him it must have had some definite meaning. Marjorie Trevor, who had been listening to him with little interest, turned to him quickly at the mention of Lord Rollesborough's name.

"Why," she said, "but Lord Rollesborough is one of the greatest admirers of Dr. Adams!" And she added scornfully: "You may love truth as an artist, but it seems to me you still have to learn not to attack anybody you really don't know anything about!"

But here again a sudden jolt made the painter wince with pain, and he bit his lips and didn't reply.

"I shall drive more slowly," Marjorie Trevor remarked, an unexpected note of tenderness breaking into her voice, "we're not very far now."

It was quite true: they were not far. In another ten minutes Marjorie Trevor turned into a wide gravel road, passed through a wrought-iron gate and came up a long drive to a spacious house built on the top of a hill with a fine open view of the countryside below it. They were met by a slim, olive-skinned woman of forty with large ear-rings and heavy gold bracelets, wearing a long wine-red dress and a black embroidered shawl over her shoulders. She seemed to be waiting for Marjorie and the sight of the large unkempt man in the car rather startled her.

"This is Mrs. Thurston," Marjorie Trevor said to Matt Caldwell as she jumped out of the car and ran towards her friend. "You've always wanted to meet Mr. Matt Caldwell, the painter, Helen," she said. "I ran into him on my way back from Godalming and brought him with me. He was on his way here!"

"You didn't knock him down, Marjorie?" Mrs. Thurston asked with an expression of dismay on her small, sensitive face.

"Oh, no!" Matt Caldwell broke into the conversation in a voice full of sarcasm. "It was just a series of accidents. Miss Trevor was on the lookout for a tramp who would benefit from a week in bed and I happened to come along looking uncommonly like one and being rather in a hurry to cross the road!"

"How terrible!" Mrs. Thurston exclaimed, but not, Matt Caldwell noticed, without a certain note of gratification in her voice that a patient, on whom Dr. Adams's healing powers could be tested, had turned up at her very door. "I hope you're not badly hurt. I'd better call Parker to help you to your room."

But the assistance of the butler was not really needed. Matt Caldwell heaved himself out of the car and stood up, a somewhat shaken giant, in shorts, an open shirt, with a bristling beard. He seemed a little dazed by the quite unexpected surroundings in which he found himself.

At that moment a small, mild-looking, grey-haired man of about fifty-five, with keen light-grey eyes, a pale furrowed face and long, finely-shaped hands came out by one of the French windows of the house and went hurriedly to the group by the car. Mrs. Thurston introduced him to Matt Caldwell as her "dear friend," Dr. Adams, whose portrait she hoped he would agree to paint. She told Dr. Adams about the accident in which Marjorie and the painter had been involved, but the healer did not propose, as Matt Caldwell feared, to lay his hands on the invalid. He merely expressed his consternation at the painter's unfortunate experience and his hope that a night's rest might make him fit again.

"I could, of course," he said mildly, "invoke my powers, but I fear it would not be much good."

Mrs. Thurston, however, was of a quite different opinion and hoped Dr. Adams would help Mr. Caldwell to get well quickly.

"Matt Caldwell!" Dr. Adams repeated the name with emphatic deliberation. "Didn't you paint a portrait of Sir Robert Boniface?" Matt Caldwell grunted an affirmative and Dr. Adams looked for some reason very pleased. "Dear me," he said, "how very interesting. I saw your name mentioned in some of to-day's papers as one of those who identified the body of Sir Robert Boniface. Now, I'm very interested in this murder, merely as an amateur criminologist, you understand, a writer of murder stories, I should rather say…" And without observing the scowl which appeared on Matt Caldwell's face at the mention of Sir Robert Boniface, Dr. Adams expressed the hope that the painter would be able to supply him with a few more facts to substantiate a very interesting theory he had formed of the murder.

At that moment Parker appeared and, to the discomfiture of Matt Caldwell who regarded him with keen disrelish, lent his arm to help the bruised and aching painter to his room.

"Don't forget to provide Mr. Caldwell with soap and a razor, Parker!" Marjorie Trevor, who had lighted a cigarette, called after the butler in her cold, precise way, as the painter entered the house. And Matt Caldwell winced at the contemptuous note in her voice.

DR. ADAMS PROPOUNDS A STARTLING THEORY

MATT CALDWELL SPENT THE REST OF SUNDAY AND THE WHOLE of Monday in bed. Marjorie Trevor's promise that he would be made very comfortable hardly described the sort of motherly attention he received from Mrs. Helen Thurston. His hostess could not have looked after her own son with greater care. She went out of her way to provide for all his needs and she sent up a little library of light novels to amuse him. Among the books, though, Matt found a neatly-bound volume on "Spiritual Healing" by Dr. Adams, which Mrs. Thurston must have sent up just on chance of adding a neophyte to Dr. Adams's large circle of disciples; for even the most confirmed unbelievers, among whom she clearly perceived the painter belonged, saw the light of faith sometimes, and especially after they had benefited from the healer's powers.

There were, indeed, no salves of any kind among the things sent up to the painter's room, and it was at least doubtful whether Matt's right shoulder would have felt so much better on Tuesday morning had not Parker, whom the bruised and shaken artist soon learnt to value as his true friend, stolen into his room at night and asked permission to massage his shoulder and to apply an ointment which seemed to justify completely the butler's opinion of its marvellous curative properties. Matt appreciated Parker's help all the more as he realised that Mrs. Thurston would not be likely to pass over such a misdemeanour on the part of her butler without some drastic reprisal. Parker had intimated that he wished his part in the artist's cure to remain strictly secret, and Matt gave him his firm assurance that he would respect his wish.

Dr. Adams had not shown up at all on Monday, and Matt was grateful to him for that. He was beginning to think that the healer was not really so bad as he imagined him to be. But Marjorie did not come up, either, although she did send word that she was waiting impatiently for the outcome of her experiment and that she hoped he would soon get better. Mrs. Thurston, however, came up a few times and inquired anxiously how he was getting on. There could be no doubt that the result of Marjorie Trevor's experiment was awaited with suspense by the two women, at any rate, and, after having accepted the soothing ministrations of the butler, the painter was beginning to feel rather an impostor.

It was Matt's intention on retiring to his room on Sunday night to take leave of his hostess and her friends at the first opportunity. He would find some excuse for refusing to paint Dr. Adams's portrait. But on Tuesday morning his mind seemed to have undergone an unexpected and, he thought, an alarming change. Was it the kindness with which Mrs. Thurston had overwhelmed him or his desire to see a little more of Marjorie Trevor which accounted for his strong unwillingness to resume his hike as soon as possible? The second possibility somehow filled Matt with unknown dread, and yet there could be no doubt that he wished to see Marjorie Trevor. He did not even catch sight of her from his window on Monday, although he got out of bed a few times to look out for her, in spite of the pain in his shoulder. He spent the whole of Tuesday morning in his room at the express wish of Mrs. Thurston, who came up again to see him when he was having breakfast and informed him that Dr. Adams, who had been away in town last night, had promised her to invoke his powers on his behalf again on Monday. But while he was lying on the couch

by the open window and reading one of the novels Mrs. Thurston
had sent up, he caught himself many a time looking out in the vain
hope of seeing the girl with "the touch-me-not stare" who had run
him down on the road for some crazy experiment and whom he hated
with a fierce hatred all the time she was driving him. Every time he
caught himself looking out for Marjorie Trevor on the lawn in front
of the house or on the winding drive and the gravel road beyond, he
swore with a kind of desperate intensity, but when he did catch sight
of her emerging on horseback, quite unexpectedly and for a fleeting
moment, and disappearing on some path that was hidden from him
by trees, he jumped up from the couch with such suddenness that
the blood rushed from his head and he felt a dizziness come over
him. He rang furiously for the butler and asked for a drink. When
Parker reappeared with the brandy, he had recovered sufficiently to
explain to himself his sudden attack of dizziness as a consequence
of his accident, which seemed to have shaken him up more seriously
than he had thought. But his heart did not jump so violently without
cause, although what that cause was he refused to admit to himself.

When he came down in the afternoon, Matt found Mrs. Thurston
sitting in the shade of a tree and reading a voluminous French novel.
She regarded him apprehensively and asked him if he felt strong
enough to be up as she had heard from Parker about his faintness
in the morning. It was evident that Mrs. Thurston was very anxious
that his cure should be absolutely complete, and it was while she
was inquiring about his shoulder and listening with unconcealed
delight to his assurances that his pain had almost entirely gone, that
Marjorie Trevor joined them. She, too, seemed to be glad to hear of
his recovery, although, watching her very closely, Matt caught a look
of suspicion in her eyes as he demonstrated the ease with which he
could move his right arm. He was on his guard now, and the fact that
he had to be on his guard in the presence of Marjorie Trevor rather

alarmed him, but he did not suspect anything unusual when the girl offered to show him the rose garden at the back of the house. She even offered to support him with her arm and the frankness with which she did it appealed very strongly to him.

It was only when they were entirely by themselves in the shrubbery that Matt realised that Marjorie Trevor had tricked him: her frankness was but a mask to lull his suspicions. It was, indeed, with utter amazement that he perceived the suddenness with which the friendly, almost benevolent expression on her face changed into that of an angry, infuriated goddess. She did not even think it necessary to explain her anger; she just turned on him and, without asking his permission, bared his right shoulder, pulling his open shirt down his arm, and examined it closely. As if not satisfied with the testimony of her eyes, she punched his shoulder vigorously a few times, and, as he failed to exhibit any signs of pain, she passed her hand over it suspiciously.

"I thought so," she exclaimed in her usual scornful tone, softened now, however, by a touch of good-humoured banter, "you've been deceiving Helen! You're a fraud! I take the trouble to knock you down in order to test Dr. Adams's healing powers and you spoil everything by using some stuff on your shoulder. I shall have to drop you from an aeroplane next time!"

But Matt did not seem to hear a word she was saying, and there was something in his eyes that silenced her. She watched his pale, drawn, passionate face as if fascinated, then she turned away and disappeared quickly. He did not follow her. He remained in the same place for some time almost stupefied by the power of his passion and appalled by the strange feeling of helplessness which Marjorie Trevor's presence seemed to produce in him. He had never experienced anything like it before. He had never stood in helpless stupor before a woman he desired. But Marjorie Trevor seemed not only to have tamed him; she inspired an overpowering fear in him, as if he realised that for once in his life he had met a woman who might assert her possessive instincts over him without meeting any resistance. He passed his hand over his bared right shoulder, then he buttoned his shirt. He seemed at last to have regained some of his old assurance. "She hasn't got me yet," he muttered with savage determination in his voice.

He found Mrs. Thurston still where he had left her, reading her French novel and looking very cool and serene in the shade of the trees. She lifted her small, olive-skinned face as he approached, and there seemed for a moment to be a suspicion of some hidden under-standing in her eyes, as if she had sensed something of what was passing in his mind. But there was nothing in her voice to suggest that she had guessed his feeling for Marjorie Trevor. She proposed to take him for a walk round the grounds, and as they were cross-ing the lawn she broached the subject of Dr. Adams's portrait. Matt found himself discussing all the particulars of Dr. Adams's future sittings. He agreed to Mrs. Thurston's suggestion that he should do the painting at her house. There was no haggling over terms: Mrs. Thurston accepted the first figure he mentioned.

When the discussion came to an end, Mrs. Thurston pointed out several famous beauty spots to the painter. There was a wood quite near with a small stream running through it, which seemed to be only a mile away and formed part of Mrs. Thurston's estate. It was a wood, it seemed, that Marjorie Trevor was very fond of, a place, Mrs. Thurston told him, not, he thought, without a certain malicious purpose, where Marjorie liked to take her beaux.

Her beaux? The word sounded odd to him, but, if Mrs. Thurston thought she would be able to get any sign of jealousy from him, she was mistaken, for he did not seem to take the slightest notice when she told him the name of the wood: Boggerhanger Wood!

On their way back, Mrs. Thurston again expressed her gratification at his quite "miraculous" recovery. (Mrs. Thurston seemed to put so much meaning in the word "miraculous," that Caldwell looked apprehensively at her, but Marjorie must have kept his secret.) Dr. Adams, she went on, was very anxious to discuss the murder of Sir Robert Boniface with him, as he had formed some kind of a theory about it. He had spent some time in collecting all the facts about that terrible and quite inexplicable murder, and he was sure that the painter, who was so providentially sent to test his powers of healing, would be very valuable in helping him to elucidate a few important points.

Matt did not seem to like the idea at all, and Mrs. Thurston felt she ought to apologise for Dr. Adams, who, since his powers of healing had so suddenly, and, she was now convinced, temporarily, left him, had been writing very clever murder stories, and the psychology of crime, Matt gathered, had always had a great fascination for him.

When they returned to the house Parker was already busying himself with the tea, which was laid in the middle of the lawn, where there was a table, protected from the sun by a large orange umbrella, and four garden chairs. Marjorie Trevor was sitting by the table with Dr. Adams. She was smoking and looked as inaccessible and cold as ever, showing no trace of her outburst in the rose garden. She took hardly any notice of the painter's arrival, and seemed entirely absorbed in the antics of a large bull-pup, who was snuffling and fussing excitedly about the table. He was thrusting his great ugly head between everybody's legs, climbing up for morsels of bread, rushing off suddenly in pursuit of some bird, rolling over ecstatically on the grass, and generally giving an exhibition of utter imbecility and universal affection.

Dr. Adams got up to greet Matt Caldwell, whom he said he was glad to see looking so well. There was, indeed, no doubt about the doctor's gratification, but there was no mention of his supposed part in bringing about the artist's recovery. The quiet manners of Dr. Adams, his kindliness, his undoubted honesty, and the utter absence of the self-assertiveness of the charlatan, made a very favourable impression on the painter. Dr. Adams apologised for not having gone up to see how he was getting on. He had been called away suddenly on Monday morning to visit a patient in London and he had had to spend the night there. But now that they had met again he would like to have a talk with him about the murder of Sir Robert Boniface, which he considered a sensational event in many respects.

It was a subject that seemed to have fascinated the doctor, who again expressed his hope that Matt Caldwell would be able to supply him with some more data, without which, it seemed, he could not construct his theory at all satisfactorily. But Matt's willingness to supply the required data did not seem to be very great, a fact which, for some reason or other, made Marjorie Trevor sit up and take a keen interest in Dr. Adams's theory.

It was only after they had had tea, and after the too enthusiastic bull-pup had been taken away by Parker, that Dr. Adams really got going. To his mind, he said, the police were always too crude in their search for a motive in a crime like murder. They always assumed that the murderer was moved by some strong human passion, like love, jealousy, hatred, greed, and was always out for some very tangible advantage which he might derive from the crime. But the human mind was much more subtle than that, and human ambitions much more complex. History was, of course, full of murders or attempts at murders committed from entirely disinterested motives. All these murders were committed by people who were inspired by the noblest sentiments, such as the love of liberty, the hatred of tyranny, patriotism and the like. What, after all, was war itself but wholesale murder, committed from motives which the majority of mankind still found to be highly admirable and worthy to be inculcated in the minds of children?

He felt convinced that although the murder of Sir Robert Boniface had not been committed from a disinterested motive of that sort, neither had it been committed from a motive which was entirely personal.

The idea had occurred to Dr. Adams before he had gone to London for a reason which he wished to keep back for the time being. But while in London he had been attracted by the poster of a weekly paper with the rather odd title of *The Call*, a paper he had never seen before, which advertised an article on Sir Robert Boniface written by his nephew, a certain Frank Littlewood (Marjorie, who watched Matt like a cat who waits for the slightest movement of a mouse in order to pounce on it, noticed that the painter's face assumed a hard, unfriendly expression at the mention of the name of Frank Littlewood). Sir Robert's nephew, oddly enough, seemed to hold that murder might be committed from the purely idealist consideration that the elimination of men of such great power as his uncle was necessary for the sake of saving civilisation from the worse crime of being driven to disaster by them.

Dr. Adams merely mentioned that in passing, for he could not for a moment conceive that a murder of such a nature could be committed in England, a country which was happily free from the extreme passions which characterised the social and political life of the rest of the world. The circumstances of Sir Robert's murder, as published in the papers, did not warrant the assumption of that highly idealistic kind of disinterested motive for the murder, either. For the characteristic feature of such a crime was that it usually took place in the open, in a crowded street, during a parade, at a public conference, and so on. Sir Robert, he had noticed in one of the papers, was to have addressed a meeting of the Anti-Socialist

Union on the evening he was murdered, and he could not help feeling that, if there had been such a wrong-headed idealist at large in England, who would have contemplated murdering Sir Robert because he wanted to save humanity from the consequences of his great and indiscriminate power, he would have attempted to shoot him at that widely-advertised meeting of the Anti-Socialist Union. For it was only by such a public assassination that the murderer could have proclaimed his faith to the whole world, and without such a proclamation of his motives the murder was senseless.

"But," Marjorie Trevor interrupted, "couldn't the murderer have found another way of proclaiming his motives? Couldn't he, for instance, use the Press to declare his motives without at the same time confessing to the crime?"

"How could he do that, my dear?" Dr. Adams protested. "Oh," he suddenly grasped her meaning, "you're referring to the article in *The Call*? But, my dear, you can't suppose the murder was committed by Sir Robert's nephew? It would be an unnatural sort of murder which would involve all sorts of different motives of a highly personal character. I don't say that such motives could not have existed, but that's the business of the police to find out. I'm not at present interested in a theory that the crime was committed from motives which are so outspokenly personal..."

"But, Dr. Adams," Marjorie insisted firmly, evidently unimpressed by a theory which overlooked personal motives, "if Sir Robert Boniface *was* killed from highly personal motives, isn't it rather a waste of time to discuss a theory which is based on pure conjecture?"

"My dear," Dr. Adams spoke rather reprovingly, a fact, Matt noticed, which made little impression on her, "we don't know anything at present. Sir Robert might have been killed by somebody who came across him by sheer accident. If I am at present interested in a theory which transcends personal motives, it is because I know of a certain important circumstance which concerns Sir Robert's position on the Board of Directors of the Industrial Development Trust, of which he was chairman, and that is what forms the basis for my assumption as to the motive of the crime. I heard about it a few weeks ago, but it is only now, of course, that..."

"I am sorry to interrupt you again, doctor," Marjorie said (she was intent on discovering what there was between Matt Caldwell and Frank Littlewood, and she was not going to allow any of Dr. Adams's theories to interfere with her own curiosity), "but I'm rather interested in the idea that Sir Robert's nephew might have been his murderer. I believe," here she turned to Matt and seemed to enjoy the uneasy, almost ferocious look he gave her, "Mr. Caldwell knows Sir Robert's nephew. You do know him, don't you?"

But if Matt had been afraid that some fact of his relationship with Frank Littlewood would come out, he seemed now to have overcome his fear completely. Oh, yes, he replied firmly, he knew Frank Littlewood very well indeed, and he did not for a moment believe that he had committed the murder. He was too introspective a chap to do anything of the sort.

"Ah," Mrs. Thurston reminded him brightly, "don't forget Hamlet."

"Hamlet be damned!" Matt Caldwell suddenly flared up, but he collected himself in time and apologised to Mrs. Thurston. "What I mean is," he explained, "that I know that Frank Littlewood did not commit the murder. I know he couldn't have committed the murder."

"You mean," Mrs. Thurston said eagerly, for she was anxious to show that she was not at all offended by his rudeness, "that you and Sir Robert's nephew were somewhere together at the time the murder was committed?"

"No. Not at all." Matt seemed somehow appalled at her suggestion. "I simply mean that knowing him, or at least having known him, as I did, I don't believe that he was capable of committing such a crime."

"But you may be mistaken all the same," Marjorie insisted, that contemptuous note which so infuriated him creeping into her voice. "You wouldn't have thought me capable of murder, would you? And yet I nearly committed a murder this very afternoon. At least, I felt like committing one!"

"My dear Marjorie," Mrs. Thurston reproved her young friend with a significant glance, having put a rather romantic construction on the scene in the rose garden which she had guessed had occurred between Matt and Marjorie, "I'm sure Mr. Caldwell has a good reason for his assumption."

"No doubt," Dr. Adams, who had been listening to the conversation with a humorous twinkle in his light-grey eyes, intervened hastily, "Mr. Caldwell also has his own theory about Sir Robert's murder?"

"You bet I have!" Matt burst out suddenly, with quite unexpected passion. "You see," he added, a little lamely, taking himself firmly in hand, "I also know a rather significant circumstance which I believe has hitherto escaped the notice of the police."

"Dear me," said Dr. Adams, "that is very interesting. And what is your theory?"

"My theory is," Matt replied firmly, "that Sir Robert Boniface committed suicide!"

"Indeed?" Dr. Adams really seemed interested now. "And how do you explain the fact that the police failed to find the gun in the car?"

"I don't explain it," Matt rather startlingly replied, "because I don't know how to explain it. And what's more, I don't care what the explanation is. The police may be concealing the gun, or somebody might have discovered the body before…" He stuck for a moment as if in search of some word.

"You mean," Dr. Adams came to his help, "before it was discovered by Samuel Halstead, the window-cleaner?"

The fact that at the mention of Samuel Halstead's name, Matt flushed a deep crimson, did not escape Marjorie's notice. She made a mental note of it. In that struggle for possession which she knew was impending between her and the painter, the names of Frank Littlewood and Samuel Halstead, she instinctively felt, would be of importance. She guessed rightly that it was from her that Matt was anxious to conceal those two names, and she half-guessed the reason why he was so anxious to conceal them.

"Yes," Matt Caldwell replied, feeling his face going crimson and unable to prevent it. "You see, the Heath is usually overrun with boys to whom the possession of a real gun would be like the realisation of a dream. Boys are usually very inquisitive and are likely to peer into a closed car. Suppose such a boy had opened the door of Sir Robert's car and had seen the body and a beautiful automatic pistol lying beside it. Would he be likely to inform the police and lose the pistol? Not a bit of it! What he would do, at least that's what I should have done when I was a lad, would be to snatch the pistol and let somebody else discover the body and inform the police."

"But," Dr. Adams could hardly wait for Matt to finish, so eager was he to ask his question, "how do you know the crime was committed with a small automatic pistol? I could find no mention of it in the Press, and I have made a very thorough collection of cuttings about the murder from all the London newspapers!"

"Because," Matt exclaimed passionately, as though moved by some deep elemental force, "it was my pistol that killed Sir Robert Boniface!"

"Your pistol?…"

The cry came from Marjorie Trevor. It was a strange anguished cry, which burst out suddenly and unexpectedly and seemed to betray some secret feeling of which she herself was only vaguely, uneasily conscious. The effect of her cry on Matt was instantaneous. In a flash its meaning became clear to him and the conviction that Marjorie Trevor loved him filled him with intense happiness. If it had not been for the two strangers on the lawn, he would have rushed to Marjorie and caught her in his arms. He would have gone over to her even now, had not a sudden realisation of the embarrassment her own confession might have on her checked his impulse.

The realisation of the significance of the deep feeling of terror which had, with such overwhelming suddenness, forced that anguished cry from her, even before the thought that Matt Caldwell might have killed Sir Robert Boniface had been clearly formed in her brain, threw Marjorie into a momentary confusion. But she recovered her self-possession almost immediately and regained her cold, unapproachable air: the war between them was not over! The involuntary cry which was wrung out of her in spite of herself, was but a declaration of it. She had made a false step in letting him guess her true feelings, but it would be he who would have to pay dearly for it!

Mrs. Thurston, too, had not missed the true significance of Marjorie's cry, but in her it had merely provoked a deep feeling of uneasiness and fear. She was now sorry she had insisted that Matt Caldwell should stay at her house. She disapproved entirely of this sudden and quite unreasonable affair between Marjorie and the artist, for she felt instinctively that it might mean great unhappiness for the girl. The thought that it might also mean torment and tragedy for Matt Caldwell did not bother her. She felt she really hated that big, dishevelled artist, who had no understanding of the quieter beauties of human intercourse, who lacked completely the refinements of feeling and the graces of behaviour, and whose passion was a flame that burned itself out and left nothing but a heap of ashes behind!

Dr. Adams was the only one in this group of four who seemed to have missed the significance of Marjorie Trevor's question, for to him the implication of Matt Caldwell's announcement was so completely unexpected and disconcerting, that he merely re-echoed the girl's exclamation.

"What do you mean," he asked, "by saying it was your pistol?"

"It was my own pistol!" Matt repeated, completely unaware of the interpretation given to his statement. He spoke with a trembling note of exultation in his voice, and he addressed himself almost exclusively to Marjorie. "I knew it at once as soon as I saw his body in the car. I knew it because I sent him the pistol. He had commissioned me to paint his portrait. I worked on it for months. It was my best work. I put everything I had in me into it! It satisfied me as no other work of mine had ever satisfied me. I looked at it and I felt I was a real artist, that I had attained perfection for the first time in my life! But to Sir Robert it was an insult, a libel, an offence! It showed him to himself as he really was, a man who enjoyed power not because it might be an agency for good, but because it was in itself good, a man who, in order to increase his own power, would not hesitate to plunge the world into a war, a man to whom the happiness of an individual human being did not count for anything, a man without an understanding of art, poetry or music, who liked to figure as a patron of the arts because it gratified his devilish vanity! He hated my portrait of him, and I do not blame him for that. I take it as a compliment. But Sir Robert did not destroy his portrait, he did not hide it away. His satanic power to divine what was most ignoble in human nature and play upon it, dictated another course of action to him. He sent it back to me with a curt note telling me that he did not intend to pay me for 'such rubbish!' He knew such a note would infuriate me, not only because of the insult it contained to my art, but perhaps even more because of the implication that my art could be bought for money. I used to have talks with him about it, and he thought I was a damned fool to talk such nonsense. But that was his point of view. To me my art is priceless! I sell my pictures because I must exist somehow, but I would as soon give them away! I—" Matt paused, but not for effect. He seemed genuinely stricken with remorse. "I destroyed that picture. It was my best work, and I destroyed it with my own hands. I couldn't look at the portrait without wishing to shoot at it. I put it against the fireplace in my studio and holed it with bullets. I kept on at it for days, till I reduced it to a rag. I didn't answer Sir Robert's letter for some weeks, and then it occurred to me that the best thing would be to reply to him in the way he was likely to appreciate. I sent him my small automatic pistol with a short note telling him to blow his brains out! He knew the meaning of my message as well as I knew the meaning of his. Many a time in his career a bullet must have seemed the only way out of his difficulties. Such a time was sure to come again. I felt it when I was painting him. I knew his end would be violent and I knew that his pride would dictate to him the only exit which was left to him. He took my advice. Sir Robert Boniface committed suicide!"

"How horrible!" Mrs. Thurston exclaimed, addressing herself apparently mainly to Marjorie. "I think this really is horrible!"

But whether Marjorie Trevor did or did not share her friend's opinion of Matt Caldwell's action, it was impossible to say. Once or twice, indeed, she knit her brows as if disapproving of the intense feeling the portrait incident had produced in the artist and she even glanced at him quickly a few times as though anxious to confirm an opinion she had only just formed of him. But she would not betray her thoughts to anybody, and perhaps least of all to Helen, whose hostility to Matt she was beginning to suspect and whose desire to protect her against what her friend would call an unwise step she deeply resented.

But though outwardly calm and detached, she followed Matt Caldwell's speech with a deep emotional disquiet. She was afraid of herself, for that anguished cry of hers made her realise for the first time in her life that she was not any longer her own mistress. Something stronger than herself was impelling her to act in a way which roused her fierce resistance. But she was even more afraid of the mysteries of Matt's mind. She could understand his desire to tell Sir Robert Boniface to blow his brains out and she could even appreciate the act of sending the pistol to the baronet, but she was amazed at the passion which had moved him to destroy Sir Robert's portrait, the best work he himself admitted he had ever done, and she was terrified at the length of time his passion had obsessed him! And yet she felt also a strange thrill at the thought of entering alone among those dark mysteries, of mastering the untamed spirit of Matt Caldwell!

But Dr. Adams, who, when Matt began to speak, appeared to be listening with considerable apprehension, heard the end of the artist's confession with unconcealed delight. He dissociated himself from Mrs. Thurston's attitude towards Matt Caldwell's story, and he reproved her chaffingly for not taking account of the licence allowed the artistic temperament. Sir Robert's action in sending back the portrait and refusing to pay for it was, of course, utterly deplorable and Mr. Caldwell's indignation was quite justified.

The question of the pistol troubled him a little, but, as he presently explained, he clearly perceived that it was easy for Matt Caldwell to have made a mistake. It was evident that the painter had a real grievance against Sir Robert, and he liked to think that the millionaire who had insulted him so deeply had used his pistol for the purpose for which he had sent it to him.

But the murder might have been committed by another automatic pistol of a similar calibre! There must be hundreds of such pistols

about. And again it might have been committed with a quite different pistol, for surely a glance at a wound is not sufficient to identify
the gun with which it has been inflicted, even for a connoisseur of
guns like Matt Caldwell!

The fact of the disappearance of the gun, Dr. Adams considered
as established. The painter's explanation had not convinced him, he
said. He did not believe in the existence of boys who would grab
a pistol from a dead body and run away with it. Such a thing was
utterly incredible. Nor would the police be likely to conceal such
vital evidence as the finding of the gun near the body of the shot
baronet. Besides, and that Mr. Caldwell might not have known, he had
been informed from a source which was quite unimpeachable that
so far as the financial stability of the Industrial Development Trust
was concerned, Sir Robert Boniface had nothing to worry about.
Of course, he could easily understand why Mr. Caldwell favoured
the theory of suicide, and he could also appreciate, although hardly
sympathise with, the painter's unusual behaviour in destroying the
portrait and sending the gun to Sir Robert. Still, in his belief, the fact
remained that Sir Robert Boniface had been murdered.

Sir Robert Boniface was murdered, Dr. Adams repeated firmly,
as if disposing once and for all of Matt Caldwell's arguments, but
the question was, why was Sir Robert Boniface murdered, and who
murdered him?

"A piece of information which came to me from a very reliable
source," Dr. Adams said, addressing himself mostly to the painter,
who listened with little interest, for he adhered stubbornly to his
own theory of suicide, "has served as the basis of my theory. I shan't
mention names. I do not think it is necessary. I will merely say that I
received my information from a close friend of mine who occupies a
highly important position on the board of directors of the Industrial
Development Trust. Sir Robert Boniface had the controlling voice

in all the transactions of the Trust, and his private office in Lownds Square was its real headquarters in spite of the imposing building which houses the offices of the Trust in Leadenhall Street. Such a position of unlimited control naturally tended to create a state of constant tension between the board of directors and its chairman. The fact that Sir Robert was very jealous of any interference with his decisions and very often failed to take the directors into his confidence about highly important transactions, involving the fate of many companies and even endangering the existence of the Trust itself, did not help to bring about a satisfactory understanding between him and the directors. Matters had come to a head a few times in the course of the last five years, but it was only about three or four months ago that Sir Robert was definitely faced with an ultimatum from the board of directors who demanded either his resignation or his consent to a considerable curtailment of his powers, and the transference of the headquarters of the Trust from Lownds Square to Leadenhall Street. What gave the directors finally the power to break Sir Robert's resistance, I do not know. I can merely surmise that he must have been engaged in a rather difficult and dangerous scheme and must have committed an indiscretion which gave the board of directors a strong hold over him.

"If this were all the information I had received," Dr. Adams went on, "I should be inclined to favour Mr. Caldwell's theory of suicide, for, in the case of a man like Sir Robert Boniface, who enjoyed what really amounted to dictatorial powers and who suddenly found himself brought to his knees by a board of directors whom he regarded practically as his employees, suicide as a way of saving his pride might be preferable to surrender. But it seems that Sir Robert had agreed to accept the proposal of the board of directors to submit in future to their control, and his only condition seems to have been that his confidential secretary, a woman of great ability, I understand, should be given an executive post with the Trust. This condition the directors agreed to accept..."

"I don't see what this has to do with Sir Robert's murder!" Marjorie, who seemed to have given all her attention to Dr. Adams's account, interrupted him with an air of finality in her voice.

"I suggest," Dr. Adams said slowly, "that Sir Robert was murdered by a person who knew all about his recent troubles with the board of directors, who knew of the reason why he accepted the board's ultimatum and who was dissatisfied with the decision that his confidential secretary should have been given an executive position with the Trust. Why should such a person wish to murder Sir Robert? Well, in the first place, because he might think that Sir Robert was still capable of regaining his old position. Indeed, I happen to know that the appointment of Sir Robert's confidential secretary to an executive position on the Trust was the subject of a keen controversy among the directors, a number of whom regarded this merely as another way of assuring Sir Robert the complete control over the Trust's affairs, which they were determined he should not get. Although I don't know the nature of Sir Robert's indiscretion, I do know that quite a number of people who are in close touch with the Industrial Development Trust, among whom, by the way, is also my informant, stood to lose a fortune if Sir Robert's last scheme, which was bound to fail, had come off. The murderer of Sir Robert might have been one of these people."

"It isn't your friend, by any chance?" Matt asked with unconcealed sarcasm. Dr. Adams's theory struck him as quite off the mark, and he could not understand why he should be so much in earnest about it.

"Certainly not!" Dr. Adams replied firmly, though perhaps a little too emphatically. "But let me explain my theory: suppose there was a person who, as I have just said, knew all about the struggle between

Sir Robert and his board of directors, and who stood to lose every-thing owing to that scheme of his. Suppose also that this person was quite convinced that if Sir Robert ever regained full control over the Trust's affairs, he would again run the risk of losing all his fortune, and that he was also convinced that Sir Robert had not really changed his mind about sharing his power with the board of directors, but that he was determined to regain complete control with the help of his confidential secretary. Was it not possible that this person might have had a heated argument with Sir Robert and have killed him, so as to make certain that neither his own nor anybody else's money should be again endangered? Of course, there might have been a number of other motives, also, mind you, not necessarily entirely personal, either, such as the murderer's conviction that Sir Robert's day was passed, that he had done all he could and that, since he would not retire voluntarily, and since his future activities could only bring disaster, he was better out of the way…"

"But," Mrs. Thurston, who had been waiting all the time for the opportunity of asking a question, interrupted her "dear friend," "you said, Dr. Adams, that Sir Robert's indiscretion gave the board of directors the opportunity to force him to agree to their way. Couldn't your supposed murderer have always held the threat of disclosing that indiscretion if Sir Robert did not stick to his bargain?"

"Hardly, my dear," Dr. Adams replied, "because, you see, that indiscretion, whatever it was, could not be disclosed without harm-ing, and very seriously harming, the interests of the Industrial Development Trust. The board of directors, by their discovery of Sir Robert's imprudence, could, in their collective capacity, exert a great moral pressure on him, and, as you know, they succeeded in weakening his control. But there was never any question of disclosing Sir Robert's indiscretion to the world at large, as such a disclosure might have been disastrous to the interests of the Trust!"

"And have landed some of them in jail?" Matt interrupted sarcastically.

"I shouldn't go as far as that myself," Dr. Adams answered with a merry gleam in his eyes, "but business secrets certainly do not improve by being dragged into the light of day!"

"I cannot help feeling, Dr. Adams," Marjorie declared very firmly, tossing her beautiful head rather majestically and looking straight at the doctor, "that your supposed murderer is one of the directors of the Industrial Development Trust, and that you yourself have more than a shrewd suspicion who he is!"

"Not at all, my dear," the healer replied again a little too promptly, but his confusion did not make his denial very convincing. "It's just a theory of mine which I only formulated clearly to myself to-day, and," he added with one of his kindly smiles, "even now it is not so very clear to me, except that it explains in a very convincing way a fact which has also been puzzling Mr. Caldwell, namely the disappearance of the gun. If the murderer of Sir Robert Boniface had no connection whatever with the Industrial Development Trust, then it must have occurred to him that the best way of diverting suspicion from himself would be to leave the gun in the car and thus create the impression that Sir Robert had committed suicide. But to anybody connected with the Trust, such an idea would never have occurred, for the simple reason that the suicide of Sir Robert Boniface would have meant financial disaster to the holders of shares in any of the companies under his control. If my theory is right, and the murderer of Sir Robert was a man whose whole social position depended on the welfare of the Trust, then his first thought after he had shot Sir Robert would have been to make sure that the gun was not left near the body."

"But surely the ownership of the gun could be established by the police?" Marjorie Trevor asked.

"Well, of course, in that case…" Dr. Adams rose without completing his sentence. The discussion was apparently at an end so far as he was concerned.

But Mrs. Thurston, who was watching every movement of Dr. Adams with eyes full of devotion, seemed still dissatisfied.

"But," she exclaimed, "you've forgotten to ask Mr. Caldwell for the additional data which you thought he might be able to supply you with!"

"Dear me," Dr. Adams said, smiling a little confusedly, "this shows you how little qualified I am to solve murder mysteries in real life, doesn't it? Well, yes," he turned to Matt, "I did want to ask you, Mr. Caldwell, if you could supply me with a few facts which have not got into the papers. I wondered if you could tell me whether the police found anything in Sir Robert's car? Any clues, for instance?"

"No," Matt said, trying to recall the facts of Friday evening to his mind. "I went to the place where the car was found with a number of other people, and I was able to identify the body of Sir Robert. I was rather unconventional about it, I'm afraid. I don't remember noticing anything in the car. The body was, of course, lying on the floor and I couldn't see much really."

"Wouldn't he have remained on the seat if he had shot himself?" Marjorie asked quickly.

"I don't think so. It all depends whether he was sitting down or standing up when he did it. If he was standing up he would undoubtedly have fallen on the floor," Matt replied, turning to her eagerly, but his eagerness met with no response, for she seemed to be as aloof as ever.

"But you were there when the police searched the car?" Dr. Adams persisted in his questioning.

"Yes. As a matter of fact," Matt explained, "I had to wait quite a long time, till they took away the body and till the Scotland Yard inspector went through the car and talked to the reporters."

"And you're sure the police did not find anything?"

"Well, I…" Matt hesitated as if he were trying to recall all the circumstances of that evening.

"A cigar, or anything?" Dr. Adams seemed to throw out the suggestion at random.

"A cigar?" Matt repeated, rather puzzled. "I don't think so. At least, I don't know."

"Oh, well…" Dr. Adams smiled apologetically, as if he was sorry to have bothered the painter about the clues. "It's really just my curiosity, you know. A writer of detective stories is always looking for clues."

He rose, beaming good-naturedly at the painter, and expressed his wish to go inside the house to finish some writing. Mrs. Helen Thurston also got up. She looked a little undecided, as if uncertain whether she could leave the artist alone with Marjorie Trevor.

"I'm afraid," she said to Matt, "I can't offer you any amusement. I haven't any wireless. I hate the constant din it makes. You can't help putting on the wretched thing once you've got it. You'll find quite a nice gramophone in the blue drawing-room, though, if you'd like some music. Or would you prefer to stay outside?"

"I think we will, Helen," Marjorie said in her firm, determined voice. And after Mrs. Thurston had disappeared into the house, she said to Matt: "Helen's a dear soul, only she's a little too motherly sometimes. By the way," she asked him, "don't you think Dr. Adams is a big fraud? Not such a *big* fraud as you are, but almost up to your standard."

"I don't know," Matt replied. He distrusted her conversational tone and hated the lightness with which she seemed to rush from one subject to another.

"I mean," she explained a little severely, "that Dr. Adams knows a jolly sight more about that theory of his than he wishes to let us suppose."

"Oh, his theory?" Matt scoffed. "It's pretty far-fetched."

"Not as far-fetched as yours is, anyway," Marjorie declared with great firmness. "By the way," she said suddenly in the same lighthearted tone of voice, "I don't think I showed you round the rose garden, after all. Shall we have a look at it now?"

Matt rose stiffly, a scowl on his face, feeling rather helpless and suspecting some sudden storm to break at any moment. They walked off to the rose garden.

I I

MARJORIE TREVOR PROPOSES A SHOOTING MATCH

ROSE GARDENS WERE EVIDENTLY UNLUCKY PLACES FOR MATT, for his second walk with Marjorie under the pink and crimson rose pergolas of Mrs. Helen Thurston's beautiful garden merely increased his unhappiness. His only wish while Dr. Adams was speaking had been to be left alone with her, but now that she was walking by his side in the solitude of the garden he found that her nearness to him made him feel utterly helpless and strangely uneasy, as if he mistrusted his own power over her, and was afraid, lest, by losing control over his passion, he might commit some stupid blunder and wound her pride. For he realised very keenly that the one thing Marjorie would never forgive him would be an injury to her pride.

And yet in addition to that dread of losing Marjorie he was conscious of quite a different and, to him, entirely new feeling of wishing to protect her from any pain, from any unhappiness. It was a feeling that at first he could hardly explain to himself, for tenderness was foreign to his nature. He was a brute and he prided himself on being a brute. He was big and strong, but not, like most big, strong men, given to sentimentalising over women. When a woman pleased him he went for her; and if she were not accessible he cursed and went his way. When a woman had ceased to please him, he left her, and if she ran after him, he shut his door on her. It mattered little to him that he gave pain, that he was the cause of suffering. Quite often, indeed, he took pleasure in giving pain, as when he shouted at and cursed Agnes and saw her crawling back to him like a whimpering, beaten bitch.

But now the desire to protect Marjorie from anything that might give her pain burnt like an upright flame in his heart. A flame that somehow chastened him, although at the same time he feared that his nature might betray him into an outburst of blind passion which would shrivel up their love before it had taken root. For he knew that she, too, loved him. She had confessed it to him herself by her sudden cry of anguish when he told them that the gun was his; but he was sorry now he had been so clumsy in making that statement, for her involuntary avowal had now driven her to the other extreme. She was chatty, she mocked him, she chose a subject that she must have known he had had quite enough of for to-day and for the rest of his life, and, while talking about the murder of Sir Robert Boniface, she was waiting for an opportunity to overwhelm him by some question which he felt instinctively she was keeping back till he was least ready for it.

Was she so blind? Didn't she realise that she was playing with a wild animal who was capable of throwing off the conventions of civilised intercourse and asserting his will over her? Or was she doing it on purpose? Was she only playing with him, leading him on, exasperating him, because it pleased her to watch him bend his will to her pleasure? What if she bent it a little too far, and it snapped back and wounded her? Ah, she would jump back just in time, would she? Well, if she enjoyed that sort of sport, she would have to take the consequences even if it hurt him more than it hurt her!

But Marjorie seemed quite unaware of the thoughts that were torturing Matt Caldwell. If she realised that she was walking on the edge of a smoking volcano, she seemed to enjoy its nearness, for she looked quite unconcerned. Watching them from a distance, one would get the impression of a very attentive hostess, charming, dignified and indifferent, taking a rather morose, clumsy, taciturn guest round her beautiful garden and doing her best to divert him, without, however, succeeding in interesting him much. But that impression would vanish at a closer view. For even on the cool and composed face of the tall, beautiful girl it was possible to discern a deep disquiet, an awareness of some hidden danger, a desire to provoke it and a fear that she might be misjudging its strength.

Marjorie talked about the murder of Sir Robert Boniface. She discussed Dr. Adams's theory and she tried to guess who his informant might be. She was quite sure that Dr. Adams had not told them everything he knew, and she did not believe his denial that his patient, who was quite obviously Lord Rollesborough, had no connection with the person he suspected of having committed the murder. Dr. Adams must have stumbled across a very interesting piece of information and she disapproved of his concealing it from them after he had gone to such lengths of taking them into his confidence. She was especially intrigued by Dr. Adams's question about the cigar. What did he mean by it?

Then she suddenly picked up the thread about Frank Littlewood which Matt Caldwell's story of Sir Robert's portrait had left hanging in the air. Why did Matt talk as if Sir Robert's nephew was no longer his friend? Had they quarrelled over something and wouldn't be friends again? It was strange how women had a reputation for quarrelsomeness, whereas it was really men who quarrelled in all earnestness and refused to be reconciled.

She watched Matt intently and the mute, speechless way in which he tried to evade her curiosity only confirmed her first impression that the artist wished to conceal something from her and that he did not in the least welcome her inquisitiveness about Frank Littlewood. There could be no mistaking Matt's dislike of Sir Robert's nephew and Marjorie was set upon finding out the cause of it.

"I know what it is," she said suddenly, "you quarrelled about some girl!"

Matt's face flushed, not because she had guessed the reason of his quarrel with Frank Littlewood, but because he could not even now forgive June Gayford for having made a fool of him.

It was in reply to Marjorie's question that he threw out his first challenge to her after their somewhat unconventional meeting on Sunday. Was she very interested, he asked, in his affairs with women?

He expected her to flare up and to deny with that disdainful air of hers that his relations with women were any concern of hers. But to his surprise she said quite simply that she was very interested indeed. She was wondering how often he changed his mistresses and whether some were sorry to leave him.

Matt cast a long, apprehensive glance at her. There was not a sign of any perturbation on her face. If she was jealous, she certainly showed not the slightest trace of it, but Matt Caldwell had already learnt to distrust her calm, for it was when she was most composed and detached and dignified that a passionate outburst was to be expected.

"I'm afraid," he said, assuming the same lighthearted tone in which she spoke, "you're not quite right about Frank Littlewood. It wasn't I who quarrelled with him. It was he who made an ass of himself over some girl, as you so rightly guessed."

"Ah," she taunted him, "thus spake the conquering male!"

"Not at all," he was somehow terrified that she should have misinterpreted him. "I wasn't the conqueror. I was the one who was spurned."

"Oh, really," she said slowly, as if the significance of his admission had not occurred to her at once. Then, when she did guess, she laughed outright. "I see, you were trying to break up a happy family!"

And again he mistrusted the lighthearted way she was taking it. Her laughter certainly had an edge to it, a suggestion that she was glad that he did burn his fingers, but there was no trace of disapproval or reproach in it, and he felt rather alarmed.

"You're wrong again," he said, still giving the impression that he was merely engaging in a piece of chit-chat that was of no moment to either of them. "Frank Littlewood is not married yet."

She glanced quickly at him. "What's her name?" she asked, and her question was so unexpected that Matt couldn't for a moment make out whom she was referring to.

"June," he replied, and she guessed from the tone of his voice that it sounded rather disagreeable to him, for she smiled a little maliciously.

"June," she repeated slowly, "what a lovely name!" They came to a little fountain playing on top of a small heap of rough stones in the middle of a water-lily pool, and Marjorie sat down on the grass at its edge. Matt stood before her, a little undecided, resentful of what he considered the cheap way in which she was trying to exasperate him, in a fashion, too, which was so truly womanish and which he, somehow, did not expect from her. She must have guessed his thought, for he noticed an angry spark in her eyes.

"Why don't you sit down?" she asked, and, as he seemed still undecided, she got up quickly, intending to continue on their walk, but Matt stood in her way, silent and passionate, and, as a few hours earlier, she seemed to be spellbound by the power of his desire.

"Marjorie," he suddenly broke the silence and he spoke in a thick, strangled voice, "I love you. I love you as I never loved any other woman." But his words seemed to fail him. She stood before him, as inaccessible as ever, her lips parted in that tantalising, mocking, disdainful smile, not at all abashed by his confession, but rather amused by something.

Matt turned and strode away from her. He did not want to see her again. What was it that made him feel such a fool in her presence? He did not care now. He was suddenly aware of his mistake in speaking at all. The whole thing was impossible. She did not care a damn for him. That was quite clear to him now, but what angered him was the way he had been taken in. Lord, if they hadn't been in that blasted garden, among those overhanging climbers and the lily-pool, if they had been somewhere away from that smug gentility, where she seemed to fit so perfectly, and where he did not belong at all!

And what, anyway, could be the end of it, even if she did love him and was only exasperating him, making him pay for having betrayed her feelings at the tea-table? They'd marry, and then, when their love had come to an end, as end it must, they'd only hate each other. They'd go their ways with nothing but regret for their folly in thinking that two such utterly dissimilar natures could yoke their lives to each other without each pulling in a different direction? He, the vagabond, as she herself had called him, and she, the lady of the manor, rooted in the soil, bred to fill a high place in the scheme of ordered society, and breed others to fill the same place? What could be the issue of their marriage? She would try to tame him, to make a thoroughly respectable painter out of him, to fit him into her scheme of things!

No! The whole thing was impossible. He'd better go at once. After all, he wasn't very keen on painting Dr. Adams and it did not matter much if Mrs. Thurston did feel piqued that he should repay her hospitality by departing in so brusque a fashion. On the contrary, the fact that she looked with disfavour on his love for Marjorie had not escaped him. She'd probably be jolly glad to be rid of him!

But under all that angry splutter of thoughts that swarmed and jostled through his mind as he was leaving the rose garden, there stood out the one idea that filled him with savage fury: he had run away from her! He was afraid, then, of hurting her sensibilities. He was afraid of losing her by committing some *faux pas*! Then he was a damned sentimentalist, after all! He loved her, but he had not the courage to take her. She filled him with dread, with terror. What must she be thinking of him now?

To hell with it all! What did he care what she was thinking of him? He was clearing out! He was leaving her in possession of the field. He had lost the battle, and he was glad to have lost it!

Matt reached his room without encountering anybody. His rucksack and his painting tackle were downstairs and he could easily get them without being noticed. He merely wished to write a note to Mrs. Thurston and hand it to Parker. Then he would leave. But before he had even prepared to sit down at the bureau in his room to write his letter, the door opened and Marjorie came in.

There was a moment of great passion in their first embrace, a moment of agonised suspense in their first kiss, a moment of entire surrender, of annihilation of their two separate selves, a thrilling ecstasy that deprived them of speech, and made words unnecessary.

Their love now seemed to both of them so inevitable that the short time they had known each other appeared to lengthen into years of intimate knowledge, which went back to a dimly apprehended past where instinct and emotion were the common way of life. Their reason still warned them against too facile an assumption that their love had smoothed out all the unevenness in their characters; they were quite aware of the coming storms, of possible shipwreck, of tragedy, even, overwhelming them with the suddenness of an air accident, swift, cruel and senseless. But their adventure was worth any risk, even death itself was not too high a price to pay for it.

"Of course I love you," Marjorie was saying as she lay close beside him on the couch from which he had started with such suddenness to catch a glimpse of her in the morning. "Of course, I am quite madly, quite fatuously in love with you, Matt!" She was looking into his eyes with a smile entirely different from her usual aloof, disdainful smile which so exasperated him, for while it was still mocking, it was also very intimate and sent a thrill through him like some warm caress. "And I couldn't let you run away from me, could I? But why did you want to run away from me, Matt? Are you so afraid of me?"

But he laughed and kissed her lips and face, and stroked her bare arms with great tenderness. Oh no, he assured her, he was not afraid of her. It was the civilised tidiness of that rose garden that clashed so incongruously with the wild passion in his heart. He felt like striding through that lily-pool with her in his arms and carrying her off to some wood, miles away from people. But there weren't such woods, and the lily-pool was not to be desecrated, for she herself stood there like the goddess of that beautiful garden, forbidding it, holding him back, as beautiful and as cold as a piece of fine marble. That was why he ran away. He was not afraid, but he felt like some intruder, unwanted and out of place.

She didn't altogether believe him, but she listened to him with rapt animation, as if every word of his brought him nearer to her, and she returned his caresses with passionate intensity, as if she wished to assure him that his impression of her as cold and inaccessible was quite false. She, too, had a wild, savage passion in her heart, only she could mostly subdue it, for she had in her an even greater desire: the desire to rule and to command, the desire to keep her head, without which it was impossible either to rule or to command.

Genius, Marjorie felt, was the finest flower in creation, but, like every other flower, it had to be carefully nurtured, the tree on which it grew must be ruthlessly pruned, its bud must be protected against any attack, no canker must be allowed to work its insidious way into its heart. Marjorie knew Matt was a genius, but at present he was wild and undisciplined, he had not sufficient control over his passions, his heart was full of dark desires, some of which leapt out with uncontrolled force and wrought irreparable destruction, like that hatred of Sir Robert Boniface which made him destroy the portrait he himself had thought the best work he had ever done. Genius must be tamed, or it burnt itself out before coming to full fruition. It was true that the process of taming had its great risks. But risks had to be taken, and if Matt's genius was only on the surface, why, she would rather have him a Royal Academician than a pavement artist!

Did Matt guess her thoughts? Was that why sudden terror assailed him even when he held her so close to him, when he kissed her mouth and felt her body responding to the pressure of his? Was that why he really wanted to run away from her? He had boasted that she had not got him yet, but was he sure that he would be able to resist her design to fit him into her scheme of things? He would have a jolly good fight for it, anyway! Yes, he would show her that he had plenty of fight in him! She had caught him and held him fast, but if necessary he would break away. To hell with her! Even if she had hooked herself into his heart, he would tear her out, if he had to!

Women had an uncanny power. They would get him in the end, if he didn't look out. But he had so far laughed at their possessiveness. He had eluded their grasp and he had not hesitated to be cruel even to himself in order to keep free from their sense of ownership. In the presence of Marjorie, however, he seemed to falter, his will was confounded, his passion triumphed.

But love was not eternal, it was really the most short-lived of passions, and if it were isolated from innumerable other desires and associations in the same way as a microbe was isolated from millions of other microbes, it would pass away even quicker than it usually did. He had so far succeeded in isolating it, though here and there, as in the case of Agnes, for instance, he had not had the courage to put an end to it at once, with the result that he had been cruel to her and even came to enjoy his own cruelty. But then, these affairs of his could hardly be compared with that sudden fire which Marjorie had lighted in his heart. He was quite truthful when he told her that he had never loved any other woman as he loved her. Would he be able to isolate this love of his, too, or was it too pervading, too deadly a disease to which he would succumb inevitably?

The sound of a distant gong tore Marjorie away from Matt. She got up from the couch so suddenly that at first he could not understand the reason. Then he laughed loudly, sarcastically.

"Ah," he said, sitting up and watching Marjorie put her crumpled dress in order, "the call of the gong must not be disobeyed. You might be in bed with your lover, but the social function of dinner is holier than love. We must not offend against that!"

"Don't be so stupid, Matt," Marjorie replied, going back to him and putting her arms round his neck, "you know we're awfully late. I shall have to go to my room and change, and you, too," here she took a strand of his hair and pulled it across his face, "would be better for a wash."

But before leaving him she asked suddenly: "Are you a good shot, Matt? I shoot jolly well myself. Let's see one day who can shoot straighter? I've been wondering quite a lot about it."

And she kissed him on his lips and let him read the thought in her eyes: "Yes," she said softly, still holding his head between her arms, "I've been wondering whether I shall ever want to shoot you, Matt… I love you so much, and you don't know me really… Perhaps, if you knew me, you would have run away, after all."

12

INSPECTOR BECKETT MAKES AN ARREST

Mrs. helen thurston did not show any sign that she suspected the reason which made Marjorie and Matt so late for dinner. She was talking to Dr. Adams about something which seemed to interest the doctor very much, when Matt came in and was followed almost immediately by Marjorie. Dr. Adams turned to the painter and told him with a note of triumph in his voice that the evening papers, which had only just arrived from London, reported the finding of the revolver with which Sir Robert was killed. He was trying to find out from Mrs. Thurston where the Viaduct Pond was, but she did not seem to be very sure about it.

"The Viaduct Pond?" Matt repeated in surprise. "Why, what has that to do with it?"

"It was in the Viaduct Pond," Dr. Adams replied, "that the small automatic pistol was found this afternoon. I knew," he went on, "that the pistol would turn up somewhere near the place where the body of Sir Robert was found. It confirms my theory that the murderer was afraid to leave the pistol in the car because he was afraid that it might spread the notion that Sir Robert had committed suicide."

"And by the way," Mrs. Thurston said, "the police seem very anxious to interview you, Mr. Caldwell. There's a description of you in the papers. They seem to have been looking for you for two days. They want you to supply them with some information about the murder."

"Me?" It was difficult to say whether Matt looked more annoyed by the news that the police wished to interview him, or by the fact that the gun had been found in the Viaduct Pond. "I know," he explained, "because the inspector told me to keep myself in readiness for an interrogation. I don't know why. It seems to be in the regulations. You see, I helped them to identify the body." Mrs. Thurston seemed to watch him rather significantly and there was no doubt that he was quite unmistakably irritated that the police should have published a description of him in the papers. "I shall have to get into touch with them to-morrow, I suppose."

"Let them wait another day," Marjorie said firmly, looking angrily at Mrs. Thurston, whom she suspected of trying to get rid of the painter. "I want to take Mr. Caldwell for a run in my car to-morrow."

"But, Marjorie," Mrs. Thurston pleaded with her, "if the police publish an appeal they must be very anxious to get into touch with Mr. Caldwell... Of course," she turned to Matt, "you could telephone to Scotland Yard from here to-night and arrange for an appointment later, or at least find out what it is they want you for."

But Marjorie would not hear of it. The police had already waited two days, and they could surely wait another day. Mr. Caldwell could not tell them anything of importance, anyway. She was quite determined to spend the day in the country with him to-morrow, and she did not want it to be spoilt by that stupid murder.

Marjorie's anger only confirmed Mrs. Thurston's worst suspicions. She was hurt by Marjorie's hostility very much, and by that majestic air of hers which seemed to sit so naturally on her brow!

Mrs. Thurston was very attached to Marjorie. Although more than fifteen years older than her friend, she always felt like her contemporary in everything; but, in that affair between Marjorie and the painter, Mrs. Thurston certainly felt more like her mother than her friend. She knew Marjorie well and she could see that she was throwing herself away on that painter. But she decided that for the time being the best policy was to leave well alone. The thing might blow over, for she was shrewd enough to see that Marjorie and Matt would find it difficult to get over the first days of their friendship without some serious disagreement which might be the end of the whole love affair.

Mrs. Thurston's shrewd guess nearly became a reality the very next morning, for Marjorie and Matt had a violent quarrel almost as soon as they set out on their day's motoring in her dilapidated two-seater. The cause of their quarrel was Marjorie's proposal that before going on to Hindhead, as they had decided the evening before, they should spend a few hours in a wood she loved very much. It was called Boggerhanger Wood and it was part of her friend's estate. But Matt, to whom the queer name of the wood brought at once to mind Mrs. Thurston's words the previous afternoon, flew into a vile temper and swore that he would never go to a place where she had taken his predecessors.

Marjorie, who had almost immediately guessed the source of his information, inquired what he implied exactly by the use of that silly word? Was he jealous of her previous lovers? What had her past to do with her present proposal to spend the morning in a wood she was particularly fond of? Was he so mean as to envy her her old associations?

But Matt persisted in his refusal to go to Boggerhanger Wood. Of course he was jealous. He didn't dream of denying it: he was jealous of her past, present and future which did not belong to him. But as he couldn't help the past, he would at least do nothing to bring it back to his mind. And as Marjorie flew into a rage and asked him hotly what he wished to insinuate, Matt referred to the blond officer he had seen her with in Godalming and asked her what he was to her. Marjorie laughed, having suddenly and ominously regained her composure: Bunny, she said, was a friend of her childhood and was

Matt jealous of her playmates? She asked him in turn if she was right in supposing that he had involved himself in some sordid affair with the daughter of a window-cleaner? Matt resented her uncanny way of looking into his mind and reading his thoughts and he asked her sarcastically if she thought that a window-cleaner's daughter was any worse than the daughter of a duchess? But Marjorie merely said that, having picked him up from the gutter, she was quite resigned to see him go back to it again.

Their quarrel had now reached a stage where words meant little and where the desire to inflict pain had obsessed them both in a blind, insensate way. Matt's wish to protect Marjorie from pain, which had overwhelmed him with such strength during their walk in the rose garden and which had made him realise how very different his love for her was from anything he had ever felt, was perhaps even stronger now when he lashed out in bitter words against her than when he was careful not to offend her, for his dread of hurting her pride kept him instinctively from saying anything that might mean the end of their love. Marjorie, on the contrary, did not seem to be restrained by any such considerations, and the fury of her onslaught was all the more effective because she was able to keep her composure and take careful aim before delivering her shot.

Matt felt exasperated at the unfairness of her attack and he reflected with bitterness that women did not know how to fight clean. Even now she seemed intent on taking him to Boggerhanger Wood; and in the end he consented. He was mad with rage, but he consented, for what else could he do?

On the way to Boggerhanger Wood, Marjorie made Matt apologise to her for his insinuation about his "predecessors," and she told him all about the officer he had seen her with at Godalming.

It was all Helen's fault, and she would never have thought that Helen was capable of making that cheap sneer about her. She had always liked Boggerhanger Wood. It had such a lovely stream where, as a child, she used to play, looking out for the dark shadows of the trout darting mysteriously in its clear, but deep waters. Of course, she had taken Bunny there very often. He had known her as a child and he was always very much in love with her. For a time she thought that she also loved him, and in a very childish way they had been very happy. Yes, they had kept that childish attachment to each other even when she had decided to become Bunny's mistress.

Bunny was quite incorrigible. He was still in love with her and he asked her to marry him regularly about once every three months. But she had sent him away for good now. She saw him for the last time at Godalming and, as a sign of final parting, she returned to him the presents he had given her. It was not fair to keep him hanging about round her like some lovesick gallant. Besides, she was not faithful to him in the same way that she would have been faithful to him if she had intended to marry him. If she loved a man sufficiently to marry him, she would love him sufficiently to remain faithful to him. It was that that had made Bunny so utterly wretched, and she admitted that it was not fair to have kept him tied to her for so long. She was very much aware of having treated Bunny quite abominably, but it was her childish attachment to him which she was so reluctant to do without.

Marjorie was clearly trying hard to make up for their quarrel, and Matt, though still furious and swearing under his breath that he would wring Bunny's neck if he ever came near her again with his blasted proposals, suddenly realised that his ill-feeling towards Boggerhanger Wood had gone completely and that his love for Marjorie was too great to allow the past to disturb it for long. Lying by the trout stream in the shadow of a clump of tall elms, they let the hours pass, till Marjorie suddenly remembered that she had to get to a garage to have a small repair done to her car, and that it was, anyway, time they started for Hindhead.

While they were waiting for the car to be attended to, Matt suddenly remembered that his tobacco pouch was empty and, as they were just outside a village, he went in search of a tobacconist's, Marjorie telling him to get her a packet of her favourite cigarettes. The village seemed to be deserted on that hot June morning and Matt found some difficulty in discovering a tobacconist's shop. And so he was glad when he sighted a policeman on a bicycle pedalling leisurely down the street and wiping his perspiring neck with a large red handkerchief. Matt stopped him to ask if he could direct him to the tobacconist's.

The behaviour of that policeman was certainly very odd. At first he looked at Matt as if he had been some strange wonder, then, instead of volunteering the required information, he asked the artist his name. As Matt objected to his uncalled-for curiosity and refused to disclose his identity, the policeman asked if he was hiking and, on being told that he was motoring, an apprehensive look appeared in the policeman's eyes and he enquired very persistently what his destination was, and seemed suspicious, even after Matt had repeated several times that he was going to Hindhead.

To Matt, who had almost forgotten that the police in London were trying to get in touch with him, this interrogation appeared rather unusual, but he gave the policeman all the information he required and was at last told where the tobacconist's shop was. It was, in fact, just opposite, a little cottage with a weather-stained signboard, the local stores which was also the post office. It seemed queer to Matt that he should have overlooked that shop, but the behaviour of the policeman seemed to him even queerer, for when he turned round to thank him, the policeman was already off on his bicycle, pedalling furiously, his broad back and perspiring neck bent over the handlebars.

The ways of the country constabulary were little known to Matt, but he thought the behaviour of the policeman on the bicycle so strange that he told Marjorie about him, though she did not seem to think much of it at the time. They set off for Hindhead in a rather leisurely fashion and had lunch at a roadside tea-house. But about a mile from Hindhead Marjorie's dilapidated two-seater gave a fierce growl and stopped dead. After repeated attempts to start the engine, Marjorie got out and lifted the bonnet, but her efforts seemed to be unavailing. She knew very little about a car's engine, and Matt knew even less, and the only thing for them to do was either to ask a passing motorist for help, or to walk to the next garage and summon expert assistance. They decided on the second course, as there were very few motorists on the road at that time of day, and Matt set off towards Hindhead.

It was a blazing hot day and Matt found the walk bareheaded to Hindhead rather trying, there being hardly any shade on the road whose surface had melted and become sticky, which made walking even more difficult. He was approaching the Devil's Punch Bowl when he noticed a number of policemen a few yards in front of him. There seemed to be a police cordon thrown across the road, although why the police should choose the hottest hour of a June day to trap motorists was a complete mystery to Matt. On approaching the cordon he was stopped gruffly by an inspector of police who asked his name.

The inspector had a black mole under his right eye, and to Matt all the insolent aggressiveness of the police officer seemed to be concentrated in that black mole. He resented the inspector's tone, but he resented even more that an innocuous pedestrian should be molested by questions about his identity. He did not reply to the inspector's question, and merely said that he was anxious to get to the nearest garage as a car a friend and he were travelling in had broken down. The inspector did not seem to be in the least impressed by the plight of his friend. All he wanted to know was Matt's name and he repeated his question even more gruffly than before. Matt conceived a strong dislike for the inspector, but by that time he was completely surrounded by police, and he thought the best way of bringing speedy help to Marjorie was to comply with the officer's request and satisfy his curiosity. But his name seemed to produce a strange commotion among the police. The inspector glared at him in a most ferocious manner, his black mole appearing to be more aggressive than ever, and he repeated his name, asking him to confirm that he was Matt Caldwell, an artist, domiciled in the Vale of Health, Hampstead, London. By this time Matt was beginning to be really infuriated and, instead of expressing surprise at the policeman's knowledge of his London address or confirming his identity for a second time, he asked the inspector what the hell he thought he was doing, stopping people on a hot day and pestering them with stupid questions. To his astonishment the only reply elicited by his protest was that the inspector produced a warrant for his arrest and told him that he expected him to accompany the police to London at once.

It did not occur to Matt to ask to examine the warrant, or to demand why it had been issued. The only thought in his mind was that half a mile away Marjorie was sitting in the blazing sun in her car, waiting for him to return with help from the nearest garage. He therefore promptly refused to accompany the inspector anywhere before he had been to a garage and arranged for assistance to be sent to his friend. But the inspector merely winked to the policemen and Matt found himself seized from behind by half a dozen hands and pushed towards a waiting car.

This action made the artist lose his temper completely. He lurched forward, freed himself from the grasp of the policemen and hit out at the inspector with his huge fist. He aimed a stunning blow at the inspector's black mole, which represented to him all that he found objectionable in the man, and, having knocked him down, he made a dash towards Hindhead village, pursued by the policemen, who were blowing their whistles frantically. Half-way up the bend of the road, however, Matt perceived half a dozen more policemen, headed by another inspector, running towards him, and, having found the road thus blocked on both sides, he prepared for battle.

It was again the inspector who was the first to receive a smashing blow from Matt's fist. He fell to the ground, but in another moment Matt was surrounded by a dozen policemen, and for the next few minutes he was hitting out blindly, warding off blows that were raining on him from all sides. He had even succeeded in breaking through the attacking force. He was now standing close to the Devil's Punch Bowl, at the very edge of that gorge overgrown with brushwood and bracken, and the first policeman who approached him he sent hurtling down its side. But he was again surrounded and he stumbled, and, before he could get up, he was thrown to the ground and stunned with a truncheon.

When Matt recovered consciousness, he was sitting between two policemen in a closed car which was proceeding very swiftly towards London, followed by another car in which the rest of the somewhat disarrayed forces he had fought so fearlessly only a short time ago was accommodated. The inspector with the black mole who had stopped him on the road sat facing him, his right eye closed from the blow he had received from the artist. Matt tried to lift his hand to his bandaged and aching head, but his wrists seemed to be fastened to something. He looked down, blinking, his head still stunned from the blow with the truncheon, and saw that he was handcuffed to the two men on either side of him. This seemed to enrage him, for he suddenly lifted his huge bulk from the seat, wishing to shake off the two men, but he was set upon by them and by the two other men who were sitting on either side of the inspector, and after a short scuffle he was forced to sit down again. The inspector made no attempt to address him. He merely watched him stonily with his single open eye in which Matt, could he have read the message in it, would have seen a gallows already erected for him, and the hangman ready with the noose.

But Matt merely felt dazed. The only thought in his mind was of Marjorie sitting in her car in the blazing sun, waiting for him. All that time she was waiting for him. What would she think of his sudden disappearance? There was, so far as he could remember, not a single witness of the extraordinary scene on the road beside the Devil's Punch Bowl. She wouldn't be able to find out what had happened to him.

A sharp pain shot through the numbed brain of Matt Caldwell. If he hadn't been shackled to the two men beside him, he would have made another attempt to break away and get to Marjorie somehow. The bloody swine! Twelve to one and no reason given. No reason given? Painfully he tried to recollect the scene again. Yes, the inspector did say something about a warrant for his arrest. A warrant for his arrest. No, he couldn't think it out at all. He'd better see what happened next.

What happened next was that Matt's injury to the head was dressed by a police surgeon and that he was then taken into a room in Scotland Yard, where he saw two men, one of whom he recognised at once as the inspector who had spoken to him in the Vale of Health after he had identified the body of Sir Robert Boniface. The other seemed to be the inspector's superior, a tall, spare man, with a long scar on the right cheek, who watched him keenly, but left everything to the inspector.

Inspector Beckett, having given the usual warning, at first read out the charge against Matt Caldwell, for which the warrant for his arrest had been issued, to which was now appended another charge of criminal assault on the police.

The artist, whose hands were now free and whose brain was more or less clear, seemed troubled about something and paid little attention to either of the two charges. The first he admitted. He had no licence to own firearms. He had always collected guns. He had a passion for them. It was his hobby. He didn't see what the police wanted to search his rooms for, but he had never concealed his guns from anybody. If they wanted to charge him for having guns in his possession without a licence, they were welcome to do so. As for the assault on the police, it was all that damned inspector's fault. He had told him that a friend of his was waiting for him in a broken-down car and he had merely asked to be allowed to get a mechanic to go to the place where his friend was waiting for him.

But Inspector Beckett interrupted him and would not let him proceed with his explanation. He wanted a straight answer to his question: did he or did he not assault the police while in execution of their duties? Matt, however, was quite firm about it: he assaulted nobody, he merely defended himself against an unwarranted attack by the police.

"All right," Inspector Beckett let the question drop, "the magistrate will have to decide that!"

He waited for a moment, then he asked Matt to explain why he had disappeared from the Vale of Health on Sunday morning, to which the artist merely returned a blank stare. He refused to admit that he had disappeared from the Vale of Health. He knew the police wished to take a statement from him, but as he had nothing much to say and as the police did not seem to be very anxious about his statement, for they could have found him at home on Saturday if they really believed that he had anything important to tell them, he just thought he'd go away on a hike for a few days. Unfortunately he was run over by a car on Sunday night and spent the whole of Monday and most of Tuesday in bed.

"Run over by a car, eh?" Beckett asked suspiciously. "Are you sure you were not trying to evade the police? Why did you say to Agnes Halstead that you were 'sick of the police sneaking round the Vale of Health'?"

"Well," Matt replied, "I certainly was sick of the police. They got on my nerves. I dislike police in crowds!"

"You certainly do. You've shown that to-day. But can you prove that you were involved in an accident?"

"Yes. I can tell you the name of the owner of the house where I stayed. It's Mrs. Helen Thurston. I was taken there by the lady who ran over me." Matt nearly went on to tell them that he had been run over while he was actually on his way to Mrs. Thurston's house, but he thought it would be best not to mention that fact. For he perceived that while coincidences of that kind are accepted, after the first shock of surprise, as quite natural by those whom they involve, they might appear somewhat improbable to the police, who already seemed to doubt his statement, and, perhaps, all the more so since he couldn't, however much he tried, remember Mrs. Thurston's address. "I really can't remember it!" he assured the inspector again and again. "It's gone clean out of my head. But you could easily trace it. Mrs. Thurston owns an estate in that part of the country. I'm telling you I can't remember where it is!" he repeated irritably. "It's somewhere in Surrey..."

"Maybe in Sussex or in Hampshire?" Beckett threw in. "Well," he said, disposing of the subject, "we shall have to check it. I suppose if such a lady really exists we shall have no difficulty in finding her. At any rate, that would explain why we couldn't get hold of you earlier." And paying little attention to the indignant remonstrances of the painter, who seemed to resent deeply the doubt cast on his statement by the inspector, Beckett asked him to give a detailed account of his movements on Friday afternoon. "You'd better think carefully before you say anything," he warned him.

But there was no need for Matt to think carefully, because it was impossible for him to give a detailed account of his movements on Friday, for the simple reason that he had hardly moved at all. He spent the whole afternoon painting quite close to the place where Sir Robert Boniface's car was discovered and all he could do was to confirm the evidence collected by Beckett. He had no watch on him, for he had pawned it some time ago, and he was very hazy about the time when he started painting on the Heath by the Vale of Health pond. He was even surprised to hear that the police were so thorough in their investigations and knew that he had moved up to paint some cottages about five o'clock. The fact was, he explained, that he was very dissatisfied with his work. He felt very restless and he couldn't do anything for long.

"And you were painting those cottages from five to about half-past seven?" Beckett asked.

"But I've told you already," Matt replied irritably, "that I had no watch on me and couldn't tell the time. I didn't care what time it was, anyway. It made no difference to me."

"Well, let's leave the time for the present. What I want to find out is whether you remained in the same place all the time till you packed up your things and went back to the public-house or did you move anywhere else that afternoon?"

"I did not!" Matt replied emphatically.

"But, of course, you can't prove it? You could, for all we know, have gone across to the place where Sir Robert Boniface's car was found at about, say, a quarter-past six or later?"

"And have shot Sir Robert?" Matt inquired grinning, for he had suddenly grasped the meaning of Beckett's anxiety about his movements on Friday.

"Quite so. And shot Sir Robert."

"Well…" Matt seemed to think it over. "Of course, I could," he said at last, "and if I had known that Sir Robert was there at the time I most probably would have gone across…"

"And shot him?"

"Well, no. I shouldn't have shot him. I should most probably have told him what I thought of him."

"Why wouldn't you have shot him?"

"Because," Matt replied coolly, "I had no gun on me that afternoon, and, if you really want to know, because I didn't think it was necessary that *I* should shoot him."

"Who else did you expect to shoot Sir Robert?"

"I expected Sir Robert to shoot himself!" Matt replied, to the utter astonishment of both the inspector and the superintendent.

"You expected Sir Robert to shoot himself?" Inspector Beckett repeated, staring at the artist in angry bewilderment at his reckless assertion. "Why should Sir Robert want to shoot himself?"

"There might have been lots of reasons why he should want to shoot himself," Matt replied a little vaguely.

"There might be lots of reasons why anyone should want to shoot himself!" Inspector Beckett said with a note of severity in his voice, as if wishing to convey to the artist that he was not in the mood to discuss wild assertions at present. "The fact remains that Sir Robert was murdered."

"But Sir Robert was not murdered," Matt said with great conviction. "Sir Robert committed suicide!"

"Committed suicide?" Inspector Beckett whispered in blank bewilderment.

"Yes." Matt pierced the inspector with a look of utter contempt: the stupidity of the police was really amazing! "Sir Robert shot himself," he said, "with my own gun which I sent him for that purpose!"

A ray of sudden understanding lit up the long, narrow face of the inspector. "I see it now!" he exclaimed. "You read in the papers about the finding of your gun in the Viaduct Pond and realising that the game was up you concocted that story about a suicide! It's a very thin story, let me tell you! A story that will convince neither judge nor jury."

"I knew Sir Robert had shot himself with my gun long before you discovered it in the pond," Matt asserted with cold contempt. "I knew it as soon as I saw his body in the car. At the time I thought the gun was in the car, but when I saw in the papers that no gun had been found I thought that the police were either keeping it dark on purpose or that somebody might have discovered the body before Samuel Halstead and stolen the gun."

"Well, you know now that the gun was neither hidden by the police nor stolen. Could you, perhaps, explain how it got into the Viaduct Pond?"

But that the artist could not do. All he surmised was that the person who had stolen the gun must have got frightened by the great publicity the murder of Sir Robert Boniface had received and disposed of the gun by throwing it into the Viaduct Pond. When shown the gun he identified it at once as the one which, he was careful to say, had belonged to him before he sent it to Sir Robert.

To Inspector Beckett the whole story of Sir Robert's suicide was so transparently invented to provide Matt Caldwell with some means of defence, that it merely confirmed the conviction he had held since the artist's disappearance on Sunday, that it was by him that Sir Robert had been shot. Even as a means of defence the suicide theory, Beckett perceived, was very weak and it must have been invented by Caldwell on the spur of the moment, when he had learnt about the finding of his gun, and his sudden arrest had not allowed him sufficient time to think it out properly.

The case, so far as the inspector was concerned, was complete: the finding and the identification of the small automatic pistol with which Sir Robert had been shot, and the admission of Caldwell that he had been shot with his gun, provided the important piece of real evidence which, together with the ample circumstantial evidence, such as Caldwell's threats to kill Sir Robert and his proximity to the place where the blue limousine was found, made the whole case against Caldwell almost impregnable. Not to mention the artist's fight with the police after the warrant for his arrest had been shown to him, which, taken with the rest, was really nothing else but an attempt at escape.

After all, the police had no proof at all that Caldwell had been knocked down nor that there was any broken-down car at all. It was all part of Caldwell's story, and might be just as much an invention as his story about the gun. The only snag that Beckett could see was the artist's assertion that he had sent the gun to Sir Robert, but this Caldwell must have thought the best part of his story, for the likelihood of disproving it might naturally be rather difficult, since the recipient of the alleged gift was dead. But then, it was not for the police to disprove anything, it was for the accused to prove that he had actually sent his gun to Sir Robert.

The only thing, therefore, that remained to be done, in Inspector Beckett's view, was to charge Caldwell formally with the murder of Sir Robert Boniface and let justice take its usual course.

It was with more than displeasure, therefore, that Inspector Beckett perceived that Superintendent Mooney was about to question the prisoner. In spite of the complete fairness with which the superintendent seemed to have taken the evident collapse of his own theories about the murderer of Sir Robert Boniface, Beckett could not help feeling that his superior was hardly the man to confess his own defeat without, at least, the show of a fight. And in some obscure way the inspector, notwithstanding the fact that it seemed to him quite impossible that Caldwell should get off now, felt uneasy about any unexpected developments which might in some way delay the bringing to justice of the murderer. There was also, of course, the purely personal consideration that, in a big case like the murder of Sir Robert Boniface, weighed rather more than usual with the inspector and made him eager to bring it to an end as soon as possible.

He did not want to blow his own trumpet, but it was he, after all, who had made all the most important discoveries and it was he who had collected all the evidence against Caldwell and, although the inspector knew that Mooney was the last man on earth to stand in the way of his promotion, he suspected that he might wish to delay the actual charge against the artist; and he was quite right.

"You say," Mooney addressed Matt Caldwell, "that you sent your gun to Sir Robert with an invitation to shoot himself. What prompted you to this unusual action?"

And after listening to Matt's excited story about Sir Robert's return of his portrait and the artist's reasons for thinking that Sir Robert might very probably wish to end his career by blowing his brains out (a supposition which sounded so utterly improbable to Inspector Beckett that he could not help grunting his disapproval that such wild surmises should be put on record), the superintendent made a most careful note of all the circumstances of the alleged dispatch of the gun to Sir Robert. The actual date when he sent off the gun to the baronet, the artist could not give. It was, he remembered, about two months ago, on a Monday, about a week after the return of the portrait, or perhaps a fortnight. He addressed it to Sir Robert's private residence in Lownds Square. He had no proof that he had sent it as he had destroyed the post office receipt, but, he supposed, the Hampstead Post Office must have some record of his dispatch, as he had taken care to register it.

"You registered it, then?" Mooney repeated, looking rather pleased. "But, of course," he added with a smile, "you didn't disclose the contents of the parcel to the post office authorities, did you?"

"No," Matt replied smirking. "I meant it to be a secret between Sir Robert and me!"

"So that for all we know," Inspector Beckett interjected, "the parcel you sent to Sir Robert might have contained anything!"

But Matt entirely disregarded Beckett's interjection. What, anyway, did the inspector mean by it? What else could he have sent to Sir Robert but a loaded pistol?

"It must have been rather a heavy parcel," Mooney observed mildly, "and it must have cost you quite a lot of money to register it?"

"Quite," Matt agreed, looking for some reason very pleased with himself. "I had to pawn my watch to get the money."

"We shall check all that, of course..." Mooney said, turning to Beckett. "Now," he addressed the prisoner again, "tell us what happened to Sir Robert's portrait?"

But Matt, although he did not know about the finding of the riddled canvas in his room, did not conceal the fate of Sir Robert's portrait, a fact which, however, made no impression on Inspector Beckett, who naturally assumed that Caldwell was not such a simpleton as he would like to appear and that he must have guessed that the police had found the portrait in his studio and knew that it was best to make no secret about it.

"When did you first think of destroying the portrait by shooting at it?" Inspector Beckett asked quickly with an emphasis on "shooting."

"Why," Matt did not hesitate with his reply, "as soon as I got it back."

"And when was that?"

"It must have been..." Matt hesitated, then as the inspector's intention to trap him dawned on him, he added with a grin: "just about a week or a fortnight before I sent my gun to Sir Robert..."

"And did Sir Robert's portrait come back by post?" Mooney asked, and on being told that it had not, but that it had been sent back by Sir

Robert's chauffeur, he merely remarked casually to Beckett: "Another thing to be checked…"

That would have brought to an end Matt's interrogation were it not for the fact that the Special Branch had detained on suspicion a Russian citizen who was in London *en route* for Moscow. The Russian in question had arrived from South Africa where he had spent some time as an agent of the Third International. That much was quite clearly established. The Russian, whom Mooney had also interrogated, confessed to having visited a certain house in the Vale of Health on Friday evening when Sir Robert had been murdered. He had gone to the Vale of Health at the invitation of the Hampstead branch of the Friends of Soviet Russia Association to discuss arrangements for a meeting which he was asked to address. He had left the house at about half-past seven and, although he must have passed the place where the blue limousine had been found, he denied having seen the car. He was a very voluble chap, a Jew, with the characteristic brazenness of his race, and he threatened the British Government with all sorts of trouble if he was not released at once. The Russian Embassy had taken up the matter and the Foreign Office did not seem to be very pleased about the whole thing, for the relations with Soviet Russia were particularly delicate at that moment and the arrest of an emissary of the Soviet on suspicion of being involved in the murder of Sir Robert Boniface threatened to become a serious hindrance to the establishment of a calmer atmosphere between the two countries. The fact that Sir Robert Boniface had almost certainly been killed with Caldwell's gun did not seem sufficient to the Special Branch to warrant the release of the Russian, till it had also been established that Matt Caldwell had nothing to do with the Third International and could not, therefore, have supplied the gun to the arrested Russian.

Mooney, consequently, asked the artist if he had any connections with the Communist Party and the unfeigned look of surprise in

Matt Caldwell's eyes would have been sufficient to satisfy the superintendent that he was not a Communist and knew nothing about the Third International. But Matt went even farther than that and dissociated himself from any political movement, red, pink, blue or any other shade or colour.

As Inspector Beckett suspected, Mooney would not agree to a formal charge of murder being made at present against Matt Caldwell, who was taken to prison after his statement had been read out to him and the necessary signatures affixed. Matt, of course, realised the seriousness of his position, but he did not seem to worry about that very much. He would not hear of engaging any solicitor to act for him, as he thought he could conduct his case before the magistrate himself. Asked whether he had any friends he would like to get into touch with, the artist merely gave a mirthless laugh.

"Well, Inspector," Mooney addressed his subordinate, whose wounded feelings he was anxious to soothe, "that's certainly a good day's work. We've got Caldwell now, and he won't escape us this time, not for the next six months, at least."

But Inspector Beckett's feelings were not to be soothed by any commendations from his superior. Although it was half-past six already he decided to get the permission of the Post Office authorities to check the artist's statement about sending his gun to Sir Robert and then go to the Hampstead Post Office to examine their records. He took with him the superintendent's blessings.

I3

MARJORIE GOES TO MATT'S RESCUE

SUPERINTENDENT MOONEY REMAINED SITTING SOMEWHAT DIS-
consolately at his desk. It seemed to him that Matt Caldwell did
not do himself any good by advancing his theory of suicide. Artists,
he thought, were, of course, notorious for their egotism, and the
idea that Sir Robert Boniface should have committed suicide with
the gun he had sent him might have appealed to Caldwell's imagination as an act of retribution for the destruction of the portrait,
for which he, curiously enough, also blamed Sir Robert. But while
Mooney appreciated the fact that such an idea was quite in keeping
with Caldwell's character, the suicide theory was also very much
what one would expect from a man of the same character who,
after having killed Sir Robert Boniface in circumstances which he
realised would eventually throw a strong suspicion on him, worked
out his defence in accordance with what psychologists would call
the mechanism of wish fulfilment.

The proof of the artist's innocence now depended entirely on the
evidence of the gun. There was nothing to prove absolutely that the
registered parcel he claimed to have sent to Sir Robert contained the
gun, and Beckett was right in emphasising that point, but it supplied
at least some concrete fact on which the artist's innocence could be
built up. Besides, the weight of the gun could be ascertained and
if it corresponded with the weight of the registered parcel sent to
Sir Robert Boniface from the Hampstead Post Office, then it could

be assumed quite reasonably that the artist did send the gun to Sir Robert. If that could only be proved satisfactorily, it would also narrow down the search for the real murderer. For, if Sir Robert had received the gun, the question arose into whose possession it had subsequently fallen and how.

Frank Littlewood seemed to Mooney the most likely person among the suspects to have got possession of the gun, for it was he who had introduced the artist to his uncle, and the latter was almost certain to have spoken to him about Caldwell's unusual gift, if only for the sake of taunting him with the eccentricity of his friends. Sir Robert might even have given the gun to his nephew with the injunction to take it back to Caldwell, in which case the artist might, after all, still be the murderer.

But was it also likely that Fuller might have got possession of the gun? Mooney could not forget the collapse of Fuller when he was shown the small automatic pistol found in the Viaduct Pond, nor that it was only after he had been shown the gun that Fuller blankly refused to answer any more questions.

Everything, therefore, depended at present on the results of the investigation undertaken by Inspector Beckett. If Caldwell sent a parcel by registered post to Sir Robert Boniface, then the further adventures of that parcel would have to be thoroughly followed up!

It was because he hoped to receive a message from Beckett within an hour or two, that Superintendent Mooney was still in his office when Marjorie Trevor arrived at Scotland Yard at about seven o'clock that Wednesday evening and asked to see the officer who was in charge of the investigations into the murder of Sir Robert Boniface, as she had important evidence which might lead to the arrest of the murderer.

Marjorie had waited in her broken-down car till the failure of Matt to return began to worry her. Then she got a lift in a passing car to the nearest garage from where a mechanic was dispatched to fetch her own car. At the garage she was told of the fight between the artist and a dozen policemen on the road beside the Devil's Punch Bowl. There seemed, unknown to Caldwell, to have been quite a number of witnesses of that epic struggle between the forces of the law and the giant artist, and the stories which had reached the garage had assumed a somewhat fantastic character. To Marjorie, however, the essential facts were clear enough.

She knew that the police were anxious to interview Matt, but it was only now that it occurred to her that the announcement in the paper which looked so innocuous had a much more serious implication. Matt's incident with the village policeman, which she thought he had exaggerated, she now perceived to be the cause of the trap set for him by the police on the road to Hindhead. But the police would not have behaved in the way they did unless they had a warrant for Matt's arrest. Why should they want to arrest him? Marjorie did not know about the finding of the guns in Matt's studio, and the only reason she could think of for the artist's arrest was that the police wanted him for the murder of Sir Robert Boniface. So the automatic pistol found in the Viaduct Pond was Matt's pistol!

Again, as when Matt had exclaimed in his passionate outburst at the tea-table yesterday that it was his gun that had killed Sir Robert, sudden fear took hold of Marjorie. She could see now that she was wrong in having dismissed her fear so lightheartedly, and yet she knew in her heart that Matt had not committed murder. She felt sorry now she had not let him communicate with Scotland Yard last night, for she realised that after his fight with the police the suspicion against him would be greatly strengthened. She decided to go to London at once and she telephoned to Mrs. Thurston to let her know of her decision. She brushed away her friend's objections impatiently: she loved Matt Caldwell and she would do all in her power to get him out of the mess into which he had got himself. She had plenty of money and even if she had to spend it all to secure Matt's release she would not hesitate to do so!

Marjorie had to wait some time for her car to be repaired, but she just managed to get to her solicitors in time to instruct them to take up Matt's case. She then had a meal at her club and during the meal the thought occurred to her again that, while there was precious little in Matt's theory of suicide, there was something more in Dr. Adams's theory than the facts so far disclosed by the healer would lead one to believe.

She was quite certain that Dr. Adams had purposely concealed something from them, and then she suddenly remembered his question about the cigar. There was no doubt that Dr. Adams wanted to know if the police had found a cigar in Sir Robert's car. But why a cigar? That Marjorie did not know. But what if the police had found a cigar, couldn't she put them on the track of the real murderer by telling them about Dr. Adams's theory and about her suspicions that Dr. Adams might know who the murderer of Sir Robert Boniface was? Dr. Adams had certainly gathered quite a surprising amount of secret information about the Industrial Development Trust and the struggle for power between Sir Robert and its board of directors! She might, of course, be hopelessly mistaken, but, then, Matt's position was so desperate that she had to do something, even if that something turned out to be of little help in the end.

Marjorie decided to go at once to Scotland Yard in spite of the lateness of the hour. She found Mooney anxious to hear what she had to say and she could see at once that he was immensely impressed by her presence. The superintendent seemed glad to hear that the story about the broken-down car was true and that Matt Caldwell's account of his accident on Sunday evening was also quite accurate. He did not, however, disguise the fact that Matt's position was serious and that, unless something turned up to explain how it happened that Sir Robert Boniface had been killed with the artist's gun, nothing could prevent his facing a trial for murder.

The assault on the police was another circumstance that increased the odds against Matt Caldwell. Mooney smiled approvingly when Marjorie told him that she had already instructed her solicitors to appear for Matt's defence in the magistrate's court to-morrow and he even intimated that her presence in the court might conceivably induce the magistrate to take a more lenient view of the artist's assault on the police, although he did not think that Matt Caldwell would be able to get off without a term of imprisonment as well as a heavy fine for being found in possession of firearms without a licence, for which the warrant for his arrest had really been issued.

The information that the warrant for Matt's arrest had not been issued for murder seemed to have cheered Marjorie up quite a lot and the superintendent, who could not at first make out Marjorie's great interest in Matt's fate, began to suspect that it was more than mere sympathy for a friend which had induced that beautiful and dignified girl to come to see him.

Marjorie's exposition of Dr. Adams's theory interested Mooney rather more than could be guessed from his courteously attentive face as he listened to his visitor. He could not forget the vivid impression he had got from his interview with Miss Pritt that the confidential secretary of Sir Robert Boniface was trying to conceal something from him and he also remembered that when he had asked her if she was sure that Sir Robert's murder had nothing to do with his business affairs, she was much too emphatic in her denial.

Was it merely her loyalty (and, according to Frank Littlewood, it was her loyalty that had made Sir Robert choose her for his confidential secretary), which made Miss Pritt so reluctant to disclose Sir Robert's surrender to an ultimatum from the board of directors of the Industrial Development Trust, or was there something else besides?

Then there was the other vivid impression he had carried away from that interview. There was that curious smile of hers when she read the passage in Frank Littlewood's article about the necessity for disposing of the modern Napoleons of industry by violence. Subconsciously that smile of Miss Pritt's had worried the superintendent during the two days that had elapsed since his interview with her. He could not help feeling that she had found that passage a good joke. And still the question obtruded itself whenever he thought of it: what exactly was the joke about? But now, Mooney believed, he could guess the meaning of Miss Pritt's smile: she must have been amused at the crudity of Frank Littlewood's mind in conceiving that violence was the only way of bringing industrial Napoleons to their knees.

There was, he reflected, no real heroism about the Napoleons themselves. Their realism, without which their victories would be impossible, forced them to compromise with defeat when it became absolutely inevitable, in the same way as Napoleon himself had surrendered to the English after Waterloo instead of dying a hero's death on the field of battle. There was no heroic strain in Sir Robert Boniface, but the question was whether he had already reached the stage where defeat seemed inevitable to him, or was he still in that Napoleonic frame of mind when defeat was merely a prelude to further victories?

According to Dr. Adams's theory, the supposed murderer of Sir Robert seemed to have been convinced that Sir Robert's defeat was not final, that it was merely in the nature of a temporary compromise and that his insistence that his confidential secretary should be given an important executive position with the Trust was a proof that he intended to regain complete control of the Trust's affairs. That, of course, might have been the case and Sir Robert must have been well aware that certain of the directors of the Industrial Development Trust were his bitter opponents, for from whom else would Lady Boniface have learnt about the powerful enemies of her husband who, as she had told Mooney, had given him a very bad time recently and who also, according to her, were triumphing over him now? Was Lady Boniface also suggesting that Sir Robert might have been killed by a director of the Industrial Development Trust? Had she a vague idea of the situation that had led Dr. Adams to expound his theory with such conviction?

The fact on which Dr. Adams's theory was also founded, namely, the supposition that Sir Robert was engaged "in difficult and dangerous deals," a euphemistic expression of the healer which Marjorie could not forget, was also known to Mooney. Frank Littlewood was quite outspoken about it and the contents of the secret file, which he had examined without the authority of his uncle, were, at least, typical of Sir Robert's methods. But all that was not enough to substantiate Dr. Adams's theory that the murderer of Sir Robert Boniface was a person who feared to lose his money if Sir Robert regained control over the Trust, and who was not only concerned about his own money, but also about the fortunes of his fellow-directors and the thousands of people whose savings depended on the prosperity of the companies combined in the Industrial Development Trust.

Besides, there was the question of the gun with which Sir Robert had been killed. Dr. Adams's theory implied that the murderer, whose whole social position depended on the sound financial condition of the Trust, would be very careful not to leave the gun near the body. That was all very well, but it took no account of the very important fact that the gun had been identified. If Dr. Adams had known the history of the gun, he would not be so cocksure about his theory!

Although Mooney did not betray his thoughts to Marjorie Trevor, for he did not want to cause her undue pain by disposing of a theory on which she seemed to count so much for getting Caldwell out of his trouble, the girl guessed that the Scotland Yard chief was not very much impressed by Dr. Adams's theory. That did not surprise her, for she herself felt sceptical about it. She merely hoped to get him sufficiently interested to start some new investigation which might lead to new disclosures. That was why she tried her last trump card.

"Was there a cigar found near the body of Sir Robert Boniface?" she asked, without any preliminary introduction of the subject.

The mention of the cigar certainly gave the superintendent a jolt.

"What do you know about a cigar?" he asked her quickly, his interest evidently aroused.

"I know nothing about it," Marjorie replied, feeling suddenly elated that her last trump had not let her down, "but I'm sure Dr. Adams does…" And she told the superintendent that Dr. Adams had asked Matt Caldwell with suspicious casualness whether the police had found a cigar near the body of Sir Robert Boniface and that his eagerness to find out any more facts about the murder had cooled when he discovered that the artist knew nothing about a cigar.

"Who is Dr. Adams," Mooney asked after a pause during which he seemed to be weighing in his mind the importance of the latest bit of information, "and how does he come to have obtained all that highly confidential information about the affairs of the Industrial Development Trust?"

Dr. Adams, Marjorie explained, was a healer and enjoyed a high reputation for his powers among a small circle of very rich people. He was an entirely honourable man and he believed in his powers of healing as firmly as his very devoted patients. Recently, indeed, when he thought that his powers were leaving him he abandoned most of his patients, although he could easily have kept them, retaining only a few whom he treated for nervous disorders by a special method of his own, which seemed to be some sort of combination of psychoanalysis and the confessional. His patients had a firm faith in him and she did not doubt that their trust in his absolute reliability was entirely justified. She was not at all surprised that some of his patients should consult him about their business affairs and trust him with their business secrets. The question was whether Dr. Adams would agree to disclose what he really knew about the cigar and who his informant was, but she thought that, if he realised the great importance attached to his information, he might be persuaded to reveal all he knew to the police.

Personally, Marjorie went on, she suspected Dr. Adams's informant to be Lord Rollesborough, the Vice-Chairman of the Industrial Development Trust, who was one of his most devoted patients. Her impression was, indeed, that Dr. Adams definitely suspected Lord Rollesborough to have had a hand in the murder. But that, of course, was merely a speculation of hers, the truth of which Dr. Adams had emphatically denied.

"Lord Rollesborough?" Mooney asked, and for a moment he appeared to be lost in thought. "Well," he said at last, "if Lord Rollesborough knows anything about it, I should probably have found it out very soon, for I was intending to pay him a visit, anyway. I may even try to see him to-morrow!" And he thanked Marjorie for having come to see him and he assured her that he would make the fullest possible use of her information and would again communicate with her if he thought it necessary to consult Dr. Adams.

But the girl did not seem to be satisfied. If he did not object, she said, she would herself try to find out from Dr. Adams what he really knew about the murder and, if she was successful, she would let him know at once.

The superintendent consented. But there was apparently something else Marjorie was keen on finding out, for she still sat in the leather chair beside the superintendent's desk, cold and inaccessible, so perfectly well bred that Mooney wondered if he was not, after all, mistaken about the more intimate nature of her relations with Caldwell. He was astonished at the sudden change that came over her with her next question, which she seemed to be unable to keep back any longer.

"Was Mr. Caldwell," she asked, "very hurt in his fight with the police?"

Matt Caldwell, Mooney reflected, remembering the mirthless laugh the artist had given when asked if he had any friends he would like to inform about his arrest, certainly did not deserve the love of such a queen among women as Marjorie Trevor, but then, as Inspector Beckett had observed, it was just men like him who were popular with women. And when he gave Marjorie his assurance that the artist had come off much better than he deserved, the superintendent could not suppress a twinge of regret at the sheer injustice that men like Matt Caldwell should be able to exert so strong an attraction on women like Marjorie Trevor.

Marjorie must have guessed his thoughts (she was rather good at guessing thoughts), for she smiled a little enigmatically as she left Mooney's room, a smile which Mooney, who seemed to attach particular importance to smiles, could not make out.

14

THE EVIDENCE OF THE GUN

THE TELEPHONE CALL FROM INSPECTOR BECKETT CAME
through at last: the registered packet sent by Matt Caldwell
to Sir Robert Boniface had been traced. The evidence of the weight
of the packet had also occurred to Beckett, and, so far as that was
concerned, he supposed the packet might have contained the gun all
right. Beckett, who was speaking from the Hampstead Police Station,
did not seem very optimistic about being able to trace the movements
of the gun after it had been delivered at the private residence of the
murdered baronet, but it was obvious that that was the only place
from which to start the inquiries.

Beckett's surmise proved quite justified. Lady Boniface, he
reported to Mooney on the afternoon of the next day, knew nothing
at all about the gun, and the servants were all ignorant of its arrival.
But, then, Sir Robert, as a rule, opened his own private correspondence and he might have concealed the contents of Caldwell's packet
from everybody in his own home for fear that Lady Boniface, for
whose peace of mind he seemed to have been very anxious, might
be worried about it. Sir Robert's chauffeur remembered quite well
taking the portrait back to the Vale of Health and it was, as Caldwell
had surmised, ten days after that that the heavy registered parcel had
been sent off to Lownds Square from the Hampstead Post Office.

Beckett had also gone next door to Sir Robert's private office,
intending to make inquiries from Sir Robert's confidential secretary,

but Miss Pritt was not in. There was nothing unusual in that, for, as the morning's papers informed everyone who might be interested in the piece of news, Miss Pritt had been appointed secretary to the Industrial Development Trust, a fact, Mooney thought, which would probably greatly upset Frank Littlewood. There was nothing to be done but to wait till Miss Pritt was available for interrogation, although she might, of course, know nothing at all about the gun.

In the meantime Inspector Beckett was due to appear in the police court to give evidence about Matt Caldwell. Mooney told him of his visitor of last night. There seemed, in fact, no reason at all to doubt Caldwell's statement about his whereabouts since Sunday night, and in Mooney's view it would perhaps be advisable not to press the charges against him too much, although he did not doubt that the evidence of the two police inspectors who had been assaulted by the artist would make the magistrate take a serious view of the affray. It was quite clear, however, that the artist had not tried to evade arrest. He must have been merely annoyed at being prevented from securing assistance for his stranded friend.

But Beckett did not view the matter in quite so favourable a light, and Mooney could see that the new discoveries about the gun were not entirely to his subordinate's taste.

Left to himself, Mooney reviewed the latest developments. The visit of Marjorie Trevor had produced at least one valuable piece of information which, if it did nothing else, might help to piece together the events of the day on which Sir Robert Boniface came face to face with his murderer. According to Mrs. Fuller, Sir Robert had two important business conferences before his intended interview with her husband at six o'clock. If the cigar did not belong to Sir Robert, he might have accepted it at one of those conferences. Suppose that one of the conferences was with Lord Rollesborough and that it was the earl who had given the cigar to Sir Robert. Sir Robert's most natural action would be to light it. The fact that it had been thrown down almost immediately could, in that case, be explained by supposing that it was Lord Rollesborough who had committed the murder. That would account for Dr. Adams's anxiety.

But was it probable that Lord Rollesborough had known that Sir Robert was going to see his sister at six or seven o'clock the same evening and that he had taken the blue limousine to the Vale of Health to divert suspicion from himself? Sir Robert was not a very communicative person and he certainly seemed to keep his private affairs quite apart from his business. Who was most likely to have known about his disagreements with his nephew and, at the same time, to have also been connected with him in a business way? The only two persons Mooney could think of who conformed to those two requirements were Benjamin Fuller and Miss Pritt. And they also undoubtedly had a grudge against Frank Littlewood and might, therefore, be inclined, if they found themselves in a tight corner and were anxious to divert the suspicion of the police, to throw the guilt on Sir Robert's nephew. Lord Rollesborough was hardly likely to have harboured any ill-feeling against Frank Littlewood, and it was very improbable that he would know anything about the trouble between the uncle and the nephew.

Now, what were the most recent developments so far as Fuller was concerned? Mrs. Tracey, the widow whom he intended to marry, confirmed Fuller's evidence that he had rung her up at about a quarter-past seven and had told her that Sir Robert had failed to turn up to discuss the divorce proceedings with him. He had then met her at about half-past seven at Baker Street Station and they had gone together to Madame Tussaud's cinema. It was quite true that it was Mrs. Tracey who had persuaded Fuller to wait till at least Sunday before going to see Mrs. Fuller. The telephone call to Mrs. Tracey at about a quarter-past seven had also been checked.

But that did not prove that Fuller might not have committed the murder between six o'clock and half-past six. He was seen entering through the main entrance to his flat at ten to six, but so far as his whereabouts between six o'clock and a quarter-past seven were concerned nothing definite could be established. Fuller claimed that he had stayed in his flat all that time and the only proof he had adduced that he was at home was that he had had his wireless going without break from six to seven o'clock. The evidence of Fuller's neighbours confirmed the fact that the wireless was going rather loudly in Fuller's flat at the specified time. But it also established without a shadow of doubt that that was quite an unusual occurrence which had even given rise to certain surprise among the neighbours. Fuller could, at any time, have left the block of flats quite unobserved if he had used the back or side entrances. Fuller's only alibi was, therefore, his wireless, but that was really not much good to him.

So far as Frank Littlewood's movements on Friday were concerned, nothing of any real value could be established. He still refused to say anything, and his obstinacy was beginning to irritate Mooney, who had become almost convinced of his innocence after Fuller's attempt to implicate him in the murder of his uncle. From his mother and fiancée his usual movements for the day could be more or less reconstructed: he spent most of the day at the Reading Room of the British Museum. He also often went to his club (a small, one-roomed affair founded by a rather extremist group of Socialists), where he spent an hour or so after tea and he was back home usually at seven o'clock.

On the Friday of June 23rd Frank Littlewood kept more or less to his routine so far as the Reading Room of the British Museum was concerned. He had certainly been there in the morning when he had handed in some slips for books and, according to one of the assistants who received and returned the slips and who remembered Frank

Littlewood quite well, he had returned the books and presumably left the Reading Room at about three o'clock. He had not been to his club that day, and his movements between three o'clock, when he must have left the British Museum, and ten o'clock, when he came back to Sycamore Cottage, could not be traced.

The cinema ticket, the returned half of which the superintendent had picked up near the second gorse bush where the cartridge had been found by Inspector Beckett, it had been established, was issued somewhere between three and five o'clock on Friday afternoon. It was, of course, quite impossible for the cashier to remember any of the people who might have bought the ticket and a description of Frank Littlewood brought nothing back to her mind. It might have been mere chance that the ticket was found just by the second gorse bush. As Mooney, however, made a rule never to part with anything he had picked up while investigating a case, he still kept the torn piece of the cinema ticket.

There remained that rather disagreeable matter of the arrested agent of the Third International to dispose of; for the chief of the Special Branch, a general of somewhat rough and ready methods, refused to be convinced of Matt Caldwell's *bona fide* until he had interrogated him himself, and Mooney smiled as he thought of the meeting between the artist and the general and the spicy language that might pass between the two.

It was about five o'clock that Beckett rang up from the police court. Matt Caldwell seemed to have come off exceedingly lightly: he only got six weeks for his savage assault on the police, and the heavy fine imposed on him by the magistrate for being in possession of firearms without a licence was paid at once by his solicitors, a fact which rather staggered the inspector. Matt Caldwell bore himself exceedingly well in the dock. All his moroseness of the day before had gone and he seemed to be exuding goodwill and reasonableness, which must have made a very good impression on the magistrate. Another thing that must have influenced the magistrate to take so lenient a view of the whole matter was the evidence of the girl with whom the artist had been travelling. Beckett could not conceal the fact that had he sat on the bench that afternoon he would also have been charmed by Marjorie Trevor, but, perhaps, "charmed" was not enough to convey what he felt, impressed and charmed he should have said.

The magistrate had certainly fallen under her spell. Her story of the accident, in which Matt Caldwell had been involved on Sunday night, and of the shock from which she was sure he was still suffering and which, she believed, accounted for his action when confronted with a dozen policemen on his way to a garage to procure assistance for her, almost secured the artist's acquittal. At least, that was what Beckett feared, especially when the magistrate commented severely on the extraordinary fact that a whole squad of policemen should have been sent to arrest one man, and a sick man, too, for an offence which was, after all, not so serious. However, the law was the law, and Matt Caldwell was quite safe for the next six weeks.

Beckett was now on his way back to Lownds Square to resume his inquiries about the gun, and, while he was thus engaged, Mooney made up his mind to go down to Richmond Park to have a look at the barbed wire fence which had been damaged by a car either last Friday or Saturday.

Inspector Beckett was right when he thought that Mooney was very disappointed that the scratched back of the blue limousine had brought nothing to light to help to trace Sir Robert Boniface's movements on the day of his murder. For what should Sir Robert have been doing in Richmond Park? And yet Mooney did not want to dismiss anything, however improbable it might seem even to him, without investigation. He had wanted to see that broken fence in Richmond

Park all the time, and now that he had an afternoon to spare he went down in his car to have a look at it himself.

On the way to Richmond, Mooney again thought of Dr. Adams's theory. But what interested him now was the doctor's revelation about Sir Robert's business troubles. What, according to Dr. Adams, were the points at issue between Sir Robert and at least some of the directors of the Industrial Development Trust? Sir Robert had accepted the ultimatum of the board of directors, but the board, too, had made a concession: Miss Pritt was to be appointed to an executive post on the Trust. Dr. Adams seemed to have suggested that several directors were against that appointment; but if the opposition to Miss Pritt's appointment was at all strong, it was strange that she should have been made secretary to the Trust after the death of Sir Robert, when, one would suppose, there was no longer any obligation on the part of the directors to honour an agreement which they did not entirely approve.

Or was Miss Pritt so really indispensable, after all? But that Mooney could not believe.

The examination of the damaged fence in Richmond Park did not yield any particular results, except to convince the superintendent that it *might* have caused the scratches on the back of the blue limousine. But, as Inspector Beckett had so wisely remarked, Richmond Park was rather off the map! And yet, suppose the murder was committed there between five-thirty and six! It was an ideal spot for such a crime. A revolver shot would not have attracted the slightest attention, nor would any violent quarrel have been overheard. It was far from the main motor roads in the Park, quite far from any frequented road, in fact. The car which had damaged the fence must have come from a narrow winding road which branched off the main road a long distance away.

The question which occurred to Mooney at once and which seemed also to have puzzled the keeper whom he found at the damaged fence, was why the fence had been damaged at all? There was a long, smooth stretch of grass between the fence and the road and even if a car had stopped facing the fence there was plenty of room in which to reverse and turn back on to the road. The fence, however, must have been damaged by a large car backing into it. There could be no doubt about that, either. And that was even more extraordinary, for unless driven by a very inexperienced or very excited person there was no reason at all why any car should have backed into the fence.

But if Sir Robert Boniface had been murdered there on Friday, his murderer must have taken the blue limousine across the whole of London to the Vale of Health! How long would it have taken him to do that? At least between half and three-quarters of an hour. If Sir Robert had been killed before six o'clock, then his murderer could have brought the car to the Vale of Health in time to allow him to disappear before Samuel Halstead first noticed the blue limousine at a quarter to seven. And if the murderer wanted to bring the car to the Vale of Health in order to throw the blame for the murder on someone else, and that person could only be Frank Littlewood, he might also have thought of the time Littlewood was most likely to be on his way home so that he could be supposed to have met Sir Robert and killed him. But Frank Littlewood usually returned home at seven o'clock. In that case the murderer would be very anxious to bring the blue limousine to the Vale of Health well before seven o'clock! But if he had killed Sir Robert a little later than he had calculated, just after six o'clock, for instance, then he might have been in a great hurry to start and, in his hurry, he might have mistaken his gears, and, on releasing his clutch, moved backward instead of forward, and in this way have knocked down the fence. The fact that he had later passed through the whole length of London unobserved did not worry Mooney. Between six and seven the streets are always very crowded and, although that might have detained the blue limousine on its way to the Vale of Health (another reason for making the murderer anxious to start in a great hurry), it would also have prevented it from being particularly observed.

Mooney drew a long breath. It might work out all right, but, again, was it likely that it was Lord Rollesborough who had thought it all out? Or was it a choice between the two persons who certainly bore a grudge against Frank Littlewood? It couldn't have been Fuller, for he was seen entering his flat about ten to six. Was it Miss Pritt? She had certainly left a clue behind her, the grey silk handkerchief! And now that he came to think of it, it was hardly likely that she should have dropped it while Sir Robert had driven her to Harrods, for Sir Robert must surely have noticed it and picked it up. Miss Pritt's behaviour when he had shown her the handkerchief also struck him now as very suspicious. She was too eager to put it back into her bag! Yes. Now that he thought of it, he had to admit that he had dismissed the clue of the handkerchief a little too thoughtlessly.

But why should Miss Pritt wish to kill Sir Robert? She of all people seemed to be the most unlikely person to wish the baronet's death. And, above all, why should the murder have been committed in Richmond Park? Mooney looked at the broken fence with undisguised disappointment: if he had ever been let down by a clue, that certainly was the biggest let-down of his career!

Mooney was not in a hurry to go back to Scotland Yard. Having gone so far, he stayed in Richmond Park a little longer and made careful inquiries about the car that must have backed into the barbed wire fence. But hundreds of cars of all descriptions pass in and out of Richmond Park at that time of day and Mooney could get no satisfactory information of any kind.

It was rather late when the superintendent returned to Scotland Yard and he found that in his absence an important visit and a telephone call had been made on him. The visit was from Benjamin Fuller, who came with his solicitor intending to make a statement to Mooney about something he would on no account disclose to anybody. He had waited for almost an hour and he promised to come back next morning. He seemed very excited and he kept on adjusting his pale horn-rimmed spectacles so often that he got on the nerves of the inspector in the waiting-room. Mooney at once rang up Fuller's flat, but he could get no reply. The 'phone call was from Marjorie Trevor. She rang up from the country, probably from her friend's place, and she promised to ring up again the same evening.

Inspector Beckett seemed to have been again unlucky, for he could not find Miss Pritt at Lownds Square nor at the offices of the Industrial Development Trust in Leadenhall Street. He left a note to tell Mooney that he had made an appointment to see her next morning at twelve o'clock.

While Mooney was reading Beckett's note the telephone rang. It was Marjorie Trevor, who appeared to be very disappointed, for Dr. Adams had refused point-blank to tell her what he knew about the cigar and who his informant was. He seemed to be very upset when she told him that she had been to Scotland Yard and, mild-mannered though he was, he could not help showing his great displeasure with her. But she had gathered from her friend, Mrs. Thurston, that Dr. Adams had visited the Earl of Rollesborough, the former Vice-Chairman and now the Chairman of the Industrial Development Trust, on Monday, and she seemed now quite convinced that the earl was Dr. Adams's informant. If the superintendent, as he had told her, went to interview Lord Rollesborough, she wanted him to bear that in mind, but she asked him on no account to mention Dr. Adams as that would be very unfair to him.

Mooney promised, and he congratulated her on the result of Matt Caldwell's trial, but it seemed that Marjorie Trevor thought

six weeks almost as bad as six months. She was very worried about
the gun and, although he could not entirely reassure her, he did
tell her about the registered packet which the artist had sent to Sir
Robert Boniface and that it was quite probable that that packet
contained the gun, but, of course, what the police wanted was
proof positive and not mere suppositions. Still, if she would leave
him her telephone number, he hoped to be able to let her have
better news very soon.

Mooney put down the receiver and took down *Who's Who*. He
had seen the Earl of Rollesborough's name mentioned in the papers
as the likely successor to Sir Robert Boniface, but he did not know
that he had already been chosen Chairman of the Trust. But when
Mooney came to the end of the column in *Who's Who*, giving the
pedigree, titles, country estates, business interests, favourite sports
and hobbies of the Earl of Rollesborough, he gave a gasp of surprise, for one of the earl's London residences was in Richmond:
Steep Meadows, a beautiful eighteenth-century mansion, situated
in five acres of woodland only half an hour's run from the centre of
London. A hurried consultation with the Richmond police produced
the information that Steep Meadows was only five minutes' walk
from the North Gates of Richmond Park and, Mooney conjectured,
only three minutes in a car from the broken barbed wire fence.

Events, the superintendent felt, were beginning to move rapidly,
but an even greater surprise awaited him next morning, Friday, June
30th, exactly one week after the discovery of the blue limousine with
Sir Robert Boniface's body in it. He had been in his office for only
half an hour when the arrival of Benjamin Fuller was announced.
Fuller was again accompanied by his solicitor, a stolid, grey-haired,
red-cheeked lawyer with a massive face and a protruding jaw. He
looked very pale, his yellow eyebrows and white eyelashes were made
even more conspicuous by his reddened eyelids. It was evident that he

had spent a sleepless night, but he seemed to keep himself well under control, having, no doubt, taken something to steady his nerves.

The statement Fuller came to make concerned Matt Caldwell's gun. It was he who had thrown it into the Viaduct Pond on Monday night! When, the very next day, he was taken to Scotland Yard he made up his mind to confess everything, and he would have done it if Mooney had asked him about the gun at the very beginning of his questioning, but he had had to go through the very painful examination about his relations with Sir Robert Boniface and about the appointment with Sir Robert at six o'clock on Friday, which the baronet had failed to keep, and he realised that the police suspected him of having committed the murder. All that had naturally increased his nervousness to such a pitch that he could not trust himself with what he said. And it was while he was in that state of nervous prostration that the superintendent had confronted him with the gun! He felt that his only safety lay in refusing to answer any more questions. But, of course, he did not intend to conceal from the police what he knew about the gun.

Mooney, who already knew from experience that it was best to let Fuller get on with his statement without interruption, in spite of obvious contradictions and repetitions, listened in silence. The presence of the solicitor must have given Fuller the necessary assurance, for he spoke without being troubled by his stammer very much, and he glanced at his solicitor again and again as if seeking his support.

Fuller, it seemed, knew quite a lot about the gun. He had first seen it in Sir Robert's private room about two or three months ago. Sir Robert, it appeared, was not at all anxious to conceal Matt Caldwell's gift nor the reason why he had received it. He seemed to have been greatly amused by it and he rather liked the little gun, which he regarded as some neat little toy. He showed it to everybody, although Miss Pritt, who was also in the room when Fuller was shown it, was quite obviously displeased and did not approve of Sir Robert's amusement.

Fuller mentioned that fact in view of what had happened later. He had not seen the gun again till last Monday morning. He had already told the superintendent that Frank Littlewood came into the office on Monday morning to take some of his things away. Littlewood had his own small room where he used to work and where he kept all sorts of things, many of which had nothing to do with his work at the office. He took advantage of the fact that he was a near relation of Sir Robert Boniface and he used his room at the office as a sort of private office of his own. His dismissal, however, had been so unexpected and he had had such a violent scene with his uncle and was so utterly disgusted and upset, that he left the office at once without going into his room and did not come near it again till last Monday. He spent about an hour there, collecting his books and sorting out his notes, articles and letters and, leaving his room in a state of great disorder, he went away without seeing anybody.

It was after he had gone that Miss Pritt rang through to Fuller and asked him to go into Frank Littlewood's room and see whether there was anything of importance that he would like to keep for future office use. Fuller went and tried to sort out some of the stuff Frank Littlewood had left lying about on his desk and in the drawers, and it was while he was thus engaged that he came across Sir Robert's gun in the bottom drawer of Littlewood's desk. He, of course, recognised it at once and went immediately to Miss Pritt, to whom he reported the find.

Miss Pritt seemed to have been the first to grasp the awful significance of it all. At her request Fuller opened the gun and they saw that one bullet had been fired from it. It was then quite plain to both of them that it was Frank Littlewood who had killed Sir Robert. But Miss Pritt disliked the idea of being involved as a witness in a murder trial which had nothing to do either with her position in the office or with Sir Robert's business. The accidental finding of the gun in Frank Littlewood's room would have meant quite an unnecessary amount of trouble for her, at a time, too, when she could least afford it. But, on the other hand, they could not take upon themselves the responsibility of being an accessory to such a crime by concealing from the police so vital a piece of evidence as the gun with which the murder had been committed. What could they do? After discussing the matter in all its aspects, they decided at last that it would be best if they disposed of the gun in such a way that it could be found by the police somewhere near the place where the crime was committed. The police would then find the gun and draw their own conclusions.

The only difficulty was that by Monday the police must have already made a thorough search for the missing gun and, as it was also very probable that Frank Littlewood was under the supervision of the police, it was necessary to dispose of the gun in a place where it could have lain undetected since Saturday at least. Fuller, who knew the Heath pretty well, then suggested the Viaduct Pond, which would have to be dragged thoroughly several times before so small a gun could be found. Of course, even then they had realised that they might be running a certain risk, but, after all, the whole thing had been thrust on them by Frank Littlewood and they had nothing whatever to do with it!

With that rather feeble remark Fuller finished his statement. Mooney then again produced the gun and let him identify it. There was a short pause during which Fuller quite obviously prepared himself for the ordeal of questioning. The first few questions about the time when Frank Littlewood had called at the office on Monday and how long he had stayed there, Fuller answered quite steadily. It seemed that before going to the room that had been his, Frank Littlewood came into Fuller's office to inquire if anything in his room had been touched, and that he was told that his room had remained just as he had left it. Altogether he must have been at the office for about an hour. He came in at about half-past ten and Miss Pritt had rung up at half-past eleven.

"Was there anybody else in the room when you found the gun?"

"No."

"So you really have no proof that it was Frank Littlewood who left the gun?"

But this question seemed to have bewildered Fuller, who looked for help to his solicitor.

"I mean," Mooney explained, "that anybody might have left the gun in Frank Littlewood's room?"

"B-b-but," Fuller stammered, "who c-could have left it there?"

"You don't know the exact time at which Frank Littlewood left the office?"

"No."

"For all you know, he might have been away for some time before you went into his room?"

But Fuller did not think that that was at all likely. Miss Pritt had rung through to him as soon as Frank Littlewood had left.

"How did Miss Pritt know that Frank Littlewood had called?"

"I t-told her," Fuller replied without flinching.

"Did Miss Pritt tell somebody to watch Frank Littlewood's room and to let her know when he went?"

"I c-can't say."

"And, of course," Mooney said with deliberation, "anyone might have entered Frank Littlewood's room after he left."

"I d-don't know wh-what you mean!" Fuller declared stolidly, but it was clear from the desperate look he threw at his solicitor that the superintendent's implication had not come as a surprise to him.

"I think you know perfectly well what I mean," Mooney said. "I mean it might have been you who took the gun to Frank Littlewood's room!"

But here Fuller's solicitor intervened very firmly. There was nothing in his client's statement, he said, that would warrant such a suggestion from the superintendent. He therefore wished to repudiate very emphatically the implication contained in the superintendent's words. His client had come voluntarily and made a statement, the grave consequences of which to himself he fully realised, but that merely showed his desire to be helpful. He needn't have come...

"Well," Mooney interrupted, "I'm not so sure of that, either. The fact that the police are making inquiries about Sir Robert's gun must be pretty well known by now, and it might have occurred to your client that sooner or later the circumstance that he had thrown the gun into the Viaduct Pond would become known to the police. Why," he asked, turning to Fuller, "didn't you come with your statement earlier? It didn't take you three days to recover your nerve?"

But in spite of Fuller's assurance that since his interrogation on Tuesday he had intended all along to tell the police all he knew about the gun, Mooney did not believe him. He let Fuller go, however, with the warning that he might soon want to see him again.

The importance of Fuller's second statement was self-evident. For one thing it cleared Matt Caldwell entirely of any connection with the crime and, incidentally, it also made the Russian's release quite certain, unless the Special Branch took it into its head to insist on proof that none of the other suspects had any connection with the Third International.

Mooney got into touch with Inspector Beckett and was lucky to get him before he went to see Miss Pritt. Beckett took in the new position without betraying any surprise and without showing any signs of disappointment. The registered packet sent by Matt Caldwell to Sir Robert had already shaken his strong suspicion of the artist, for which, as Mooney admitted, he had seemed to have full justification. Beckett agreed with his superior that it was very unlikely that Fuller would have come out with his confession had he not got to know that the police were making inquiries about Sir Robert's gun.

Fuller, certainly, had a much stronger motive for killing Sir Robert than Frank Littlewood, and if it came to a choice between the two, Mooney would not hesitate whom to arrest for murder, but, as things stood at present, it was necessary to establish Frank Littlewood's innocence first. Frank Littlewood must be induced to reveal his movements on Friday afternoon.

But before dealing with Littlewood, Mooney decided to go down to see Miss Pritt himself. There were quite a number of things he wanted to ask her, apart from the circumstances of the finding of the gun.

Beckett, to whom Mooney gave a brief account of Dr. Adams's theory and of his own attempted reconstruction of the crime on the supposition that it had taken place in Richmond Park, did not know what to make of it at present. He thought Lord Rollesborough was quite likely to have been one of the persons Sir Robert might have seen on Friday, and if the cigar did belong to him...

But the inspector just gave it up. He smiled his good-humoured smile, his natural camouflage whenever he was anxious to conceal what was at the back of his mind. So far as he could see, it was just a toss-up between Fuller and Frank Littlewood, and he thought that they would be able to get their man very soon now. Evidently the shock which Matt Caldwell's entire elimination had given the inspector was greater than he would like to show, for he seemed strangely subdued.

Mooney instructed Beckett to get hold of Frank Littlewood at once and bring him to Scotland Yard for questioning. He also instructed him to go down to Sycamore Cottage and find out from Mrs. Littlewood the exact conversation she had had with Miss Pritt over the telephone on Friday morning and whether they had been in touch since.

Before going to see Miss Pritt, Mooney rang up Marjorie Trevor and told her the good news about Matt Caldwell.

15

IT WAS CURIOUS, MOONEY THOUGHT, AS HE STARTED IN HIS CAR for Lownds Square, how every time he considered the possibility that the blue limousine had been purposely taken to the Vale of Health in order to throw the guilt for the murder of Sir Robert Boniface on Frank Littlewood, he came up against the same two persons who, he knew, had reason to hate Sir Robert's nephew. But in the matter of the small automatic pistol with which Sir Robert had been killed there was for the first time direct proof of association between those two persons. How far that association was a mere matter of chance, the superintendent did not know. If Frank Littlewood had killed his uncle, then there might not be anything remarkable in two of his enemies coming to the same conclusion after receiving what they must have believed to be conclusive evidence of his guilt. But why should they have been so eager to dispose of the gun in so extraordinary a way? Mooney did not believe that Miss Pritt was solely concerned about the trouble the finding of the gun in Frank Littlewood's room might give her. She had let herself in for more trouble now.

There was another thing that seemed extraordinary to Mooney as he tried to recall every circumstance of his first meeting with Miss Pritt. It was her anxiety to appear to be very concerned about Frank Littlewood. At that time Miss Pritt was, according to Fuller, already convinced that Frank Littlewood had murdered his uncle, but, unlike Fuller, she was very careful to say nothing which would implicate him in the murder. And yet there was no doubt that she disliked Frank Littlewood very much. Even Fuller thought it necessary to make that clear in his depositions. Indeed, according to him, Miss Pritt had had good reason for her dislike, for Frank Littlewood had openly challenged her authority and had even questioned her honesty. That was, of course, quite true. Frank Littlewood himself admitted as much.

And although Mooney had no reason to suspect Miss Pritt of having killed Sir Robert Boniface, for, as he had already said to himself in Richmond Park, she was the last person on earth to wish Sir Robert's death, she seemed to have been the only person who was in communication with Frank Littlewood's mother on the morning of the murder and was, therefore, able to find out when he would be likely to return home that night.

The thought of Frank Littlewood's mother brought back to Mooney's mind her striking resemblance to the murdered baronet, and the tragic sorrow of that sad-eyed woman whose only son was under such strong suspicion of having murdered her only brother. The feeling of irritation with Frank Littlewood for keeping his mother and his fiancée in such suspense returned to the superintendent, especially when he thought of June Gayford and that bond of mutual understanding which had been established between them at their first meeting in the hall of Sycamore Cottage.

"A sweet girl…" Mooney murmured to himself, strangely moved by the recollection of June's sudden emotional collapse and her impassioned appeal to her fiancé for forgiveness. And he also recalled that very intimate moment between Frank Littlewood and June Gayford when the girl demanded scornfully if he would remain faithful to her for twenty years! She couldn't bear the thought of his unfaithfulness! And as the superintendent saw June Gayford again, pale-faced and her beautiful lips twitching like a child's at the violent repulse her last entreaty had received from her fiancé when she asked him to tell her where he had been on Friday, a vague thought began to stir in his brain and suddenly a possible explanation of Frank Littlewood's strange behaviour occurred to him.

Mooney had to stop for some time at Hyde Park Corner to let the traffic pass, and when he was free to move again his attention was absorbed in admiring the skill with which a woman driver in a small jade-green hat in front of him was manœuvring her way through the heavy traffic down Knightsbridge. The car she was driving was a green, long-bodied, open four-seater, and the fineness with which she gauged the distance between her car and the bus in front of her, the promptitude with which she accelerated at the right moment to pass it, the precision with which she signalled to the traffic behind her, and the whole cool efficiency of her driving was remarkable. "That woman has a cool brain and a steady hand!" Mooney said to himself as he followed her the whole length of Knightsbridge and even farther to Lownds Square, for the woman in the green car seemed to be going in the same direction as he. Indeed, she stopped at 93, Lownds Square, and it was only after Mooney, too, had stopped that he recognised her. It was Miss Pritt, who was evidently hurrying to keep her appointment with Inspector Beckett.

Miss Pritt did not disguise her surprise at seeing the superintendent instead of the inspector, but she collected herself almost instantly and there was in her eyes that steady, cold watchfulness which he had already observed during his first interview with her. Miss Pritt wore a jade-green coat and everything about her, including her handbag and the silk handkerchief in the breast pocket of her coat, was of the same colour. Indeed, Mooney could not help feeling that Miss Pritt's rig-out, which was quite new, was specially bought to correspond with the colour of her car which also seemed to be quite new. But green certainly became her, and he was quick to see that she appreciated his unspoken approval. While on the way to her office, the long, carpeted room on the first floor of the Georgian mansion, he congratulated her on her appointment to the secretary-ship of the Industrial Development Trust. To his astonishment she flushed and for a moment looked quite foolishly pleased. Her new position, the superintendent could not help thinking, must indeed be the realisation of dearly cherished dreams, if his off-hand con-gratulation provoked her to that momentary betrayal of her feelings!

Miss Pritt excused herself for a moment and, while she was away, Mooney glanced idly round the room, which had undergone a change since his last visit on Monday. Miss Pritt's desk, which had been piled high with documents and letters, was quite clear now, some of the office furniture had been removed, and altogether the room bore unmistakable signs of desertion. Miss Pritt, it was plain, was already transferring her office to the headquarters of the Industrial Development Trust in Leadenhall Street. She let Mooney wait quite a considerable time and he had no doubt that she was having a talk with Benjamin Fuller. When she came back, he could see that he was right. Indeed, she did not wait for him to begin, but started at once to give her version of the finding of the gun.

It corresponded almost word for word with Fuller's version, except that, according to Miss Pritt, the whole suggestion for dis-posing of the gun by throwing it away somewhere on Hampstead Heath came from Fuller, who also, of his own accord, undertook to get rid of it. She confessed, however, that the finding of the gun in Frank Littlewood's room had surprised her, for she could not understand what Frank Littlewood thought to gain by leaving the gun in his former office, unless his real intention was to replace the gun in Sir Robert's desk from which he had got it. Being prevented from doing that by the locked door, he must have hoped that, during the removal of the entire private office of Sir Robert Boniface to the headquarters of the Industrial Development Trust, his desk might easily have been confused with several other identical desks and, if the gun was eventually discovered, it would be difficult to prove that it had come from his desk.

The reason did not seem to be at all convincing to Mooney, for more often than not desks bore the mark of the persons who worked at them as unmistakably as though they had names engraved on them. He had himself been trying to think of some reason why Frank Littlewood (had he been guilty) should have left the gun in a drawer of his desk where it could easily be discovered and had given up the attempt to find any satisfactory explanation. That, in fact, was why he so strongly suspected Fuller's story.

"It did not surprise you to get such convincing proof that Mr. Littlewood shot Sir Robert?" Mooney asked, watching Miss Pritt's face keenly.

But it did not betray any signs of hesitancy. The fact that Sir Robert's car was found in the Vale of Health, she replied, had already convinced her that Mr. Littlewood had shot his uncle.

That simple statement, somehow, took the superintendent by surprise. He expected Miss Pritt to keep up, as during their first interview, the pretence that she felt aggrieved at the tragic outcome of the disagreement between Sir Robert and his nephew. But whether it was that Fuller's confession of the finding of the gun made no such protestations from her any more necessary, or that, being no longer Sir Robert's confidential secretary, she did not think that now she need be particularly diplomatic about Sir Robert's family affairs, Miss Pritt certainly made no attempt to conceal her conviction that Frank Littlewood had murdered Sir Robert. The only regret she expressed was that Mrs. Littlewood should have to go through such a double ordeal as the death of her brother and the trial for murder of her son.

It seemed to Mooney that Miss Pritt was a little too precipitous in expressing her sympathy with Mrs. Littlewood for her son's trial for murder, but in the circumstances her anticipation was perhaps not surprising. What was surprising, however, was Miss Pritt's unrestrained attack on Frank Littlewood. She repeated her accusation against him that he was entirely unbalanced and untrustworthy. She had no doubt now that he had ransacked Sir Robert's private file in order to blackmail his uncle. It was, indeed, surprising that Sir Robert had put up with his nephew's presence at his office for so long. It was, when everything was considered, very generous of him to have settled his nephew's enormous debt, but Frank Littlewood seemed to have made up his mind to use every method to extract more money from his uncle. His threat to expose Sir Robert in the Press was, in fact, quite indistinguishable from blackmail. Sir Robert himself had told him so in one of his last letters to him. Sir Robert, in Miss Pritt's view, had shown extraordinary forbearance and she had no doubt that but for his sister he would have dealt with his nephew in the only proper way.

Although Miss Pritt did not betray any personal dislike of Frank Littlewood, there was in her eyes a light of intense hostility, a flame which suddenly shot out and was quickly covered up, but which was sufficient to reveal in an instant the bitter hatred she felt towards Sir Robert's nephew. Frank Littlewood, Mooney thought, was right, then. Miss Pritt did hate him. But why had she taken so much pains to conceal her true feelings? Why had she misled him during the first interview with her on Monday? Why had she changed her front so suddenly and become so outspoken now? And, above all, why should she still hate Frank Littlewood?

To these questions the superintendent could find no satisfactory reply. He could merely surmise that Frank Littlewood's ideas about her were known to Miss Pritt and that she must also have been perfectly well aware of the accusations he was making against her. Coming from so near a relative of her late employer, could not those accusations, in spite of the fact that they were not based on any tangible evidence, be held by her ill-wishers, of whom she must have quite a large number, to represent the confidential opinion of Sir Robert Boniface?

Mooney quite appreciated the harm that Frank Littlewood could do to Miss Pritt by talking about her in the way he did. But, then, why should Miss Pritt not seek the expedient which she thought Sir Robert should have taken against his nephew? She could always bring an action for slander against him, unless, of course, there was something in what Frank Littlewood alleged against her!

But Miss Pritt must have felt that her outspoken opinion of Frank Littlewood contrasted too strongly with her reticence about him on Monday, for she thought it necessary to add the explanation that, as long as the police did not suspect Frank Littlewood, she did not want to be the one to implicate him; but now that he himself had furnished proof of his guilt, she did not see why she should not be quite candid about him. To which Mooney merely said that, so far as he was concerned, he was not at all convinced that Frank Littlewood had left Sir Robert's gun in his room on Monday morning and that before he made up his mind definitely he would like to examine the rooms which Sir Robert and his nephew had occupied. For a moment Miss Pritt's face expressed incredulity, but she got up very readily and complied with his request.

Sir Robert's room was on the first floor, next door to Miss Pritt's room. It was a little smaller, but much better proportioned, with large windows looking out on a well-kept lawn which adjoined the garden of Sir Robert's home next door. The two houses joined on to one another and one of the doors of Sir Robert's office led into the study of his private residence. Again, as in Miss Pritt's room, there were signs of removal, but the huge desk in the middle of the room still remained where it had always stood. It was empty but for a photograph of Lady Boniface and another of Sir Robert himself in hunting-coat and breeches, crop and peaked cap, his small, stout figure squeezed into the tightly-fitting clothes.

Miss Pritt pointed out to Mooney a small drawer in which Sir Robert had kept the gun sent to him by Matt Caldwell. On the subject of that gift she merely expressed her disapproval of Sir Robert's action in allowing himself to be painted by an artist who was obviously as mentally unbalanced as his nephew. At that time, however, Sir Robert seemed to have been on quite friendly relations with his nephew (this was the first time Mooney heard that Sir Robert had ever been on good terms with Frank Littlewood), but his portrait must have been very bad or else he wouldn't have returned it, for Sir Robert was very scrupulous in meeting his obligations and he was well known as a connoisseur of art.

On Miss Pritt's face indignation and perplexity were blended with telling effect: her opinion of Matt Caldwell's standing as an artist was that his art was so obviously outside the canons of good taste that she found it impossible to reconcile that fact with Sir Robert's commissioning a portrait from him. But Mooney was not interested in Sir Robert's artistic tastes. What he wished to establish was whether it was possible for Frank Littlewood to have entered his uncle's room and have taken the gun without being observed. That Miss Pritt decidedly confirmed; and she reminded the superintendent that Frank Littlewood had spent about an hour in his uncle's room examining a confidential file without any interruption.

"But," Mooney said, quite plainly unimpressed, "couldn't anybody else have gone into Sir Robert's room and taken the gun without being observed?" And he further wished to know whether Sir Robert wasn't likely to have missed the gun, for it must have been in Frank

Littlewood's possession at least a month, since he was dismissed on
May 25th.

But Miss Pritt did not think that Sir Robert would be likely to
miss his gun. It was only the first few days after he had received it
that he seemed pleased with it, but after that he just kept it in his
drawer. She admitted, however, that the gun could have been taken
by somebody else, but what was the use of making such utterly obvious suggestions, she asked, when the person who had taken the gun
must have been the one who had brought it back?

Mooney did not stop to reply to that question. He merely asked to
be shown Frank Littlewood's room. It was on the next floor, next door
to Fuller's room. It was quite small and the desk near the window
occupied almost the whole of its breadth. The bottom drawer was
divided into compartments, and it was in the back compartment that
Fuller alleged that he had found the gun. Mooney asked Miss Pritt to
invite Fuller in to show him himself how he had found it. Fuller could
not supply any more information, but it was certainly illuminating
to watch his behaviour in Miss Pritt's presence. He dared not open
his mouth without first glancing nervously at her. He stuttered, he
adjusted his spectacles, he ran round her like a faithful, but thrashed,
dog, and he hardly glanced at the superintendent. He had, indeed,
nothing to add to what he had already told Mooney at Scotland
Yard two hours ago, except that Frank Littlewood's desk was full of
all sorts of papers, mostly carbon copies of used up manuscripts of
articles and reports, which were of no use to anybody and which
Frank Littlewood must have been too lazy to throw out. The gun,
too, was concealed under some loose typewritten sheets.

Mooney tried to establish the exact time of Frank Littlewood's
departure, but couldn't get either Miss Pritt or Fuller to admit that
they knew when Frank Littlewood had left his office. Miss Pritt did
tell him, however, that she had rung through to the porter downstairs

and that it was from him that she had learnt that Frank Littlewood had left the building. Mooney insisted on questioning the porter, who gave him the quite surprising information that Frank Littlewood had left by eleven, that he had stayed, therefore, not longer than half an hour in his room and not, as Fuller suggested, about an hour.

"So far as I can see," Mooney summed up his impressions after his return to Miss Pritt's room, "anybody could have entered Frank Littlewood's room between eleven and half-past eleven and put the gun in the bottom drawer."

"Could you perhaps also suggest who you think is the most likely person to have done so?" Miss Pritt asked with a touch of sarcasm in her voice, looking at Mooney as though she could not conceal her astonishment that Scotland Yard should provide a career for him.

"I don't know," Mooney replied, passing his hand over the scar on his right cheek and playing up to her estimate of him. Again, as during his first meeting with Miss Pritt, he had the odd sensation that he was in the presence of two different people, one carrying on the conversation with him and the other weighing him up in her mind with silent, deadly precision. "But I'm determined to find out, even if I have to get every person in this office to prove an alibi."

There seemed to be a mocking light in Miss Pritt's eyes as she transfixed him with her comprehending glance: "You'd better start with me," she said, "for I shall be very busy all next week and you may find it difficult to get hold of me."

Mooney assured her that Scotland Yard did not usually find it difficult to interview even the busiest of people if there was sufficient cause for troubling them, and he proceeded to take notes of Miss Pritt's alibi.

The fact that last Friday was Miss Pritt's monthly shopping day did not make it more difficult to trace her movements than if she had stayed in her office the whole afternoon. Indeed, Miss Pritt seemed to be a very methodical person, a fact to which, no doubt, she owed her great business success, for she supplied the superintendent with a most detailed account not only of the shops she had visited, but also of the purchases she had made in each and, what was perhaps more to the point, of the exact time she had entered and left each shop.

It was apparently a rule with Miss Pritt never to waste time even while shopping, and she planned her shopping expeditions with the same precision as she drove her car. Precision, in fact, was her watchword, regarded by her in the same way as truth or punctuality are said to be regarded by many successful men and women in every generation.

As she had already told Mooney, she left the office together with Sir Robert at exactly two-thirty. Sir Robert drove her to Harrods where she stayed till three-fifteen. She then called at His Master's Voice's in Oxford Street and bought a few records. That was between half-past three and a quarter to four. Her next call was at Liberty's in Regent Street where she arrived just before four o'clock, for she did not take a bus, but walked there. She spent about half an hour at Liberty's and then took a bus to Swan and Edgar's in Piccadilly Circus, where she stayed only about a quarter of an hour as she wanted to make only a few trifling purchases.

Her purchases, Mooney thought, did not seem to occupy her very long, but then, as a business woman, she must have known her own mind pretty well before going to a shop. Of course, he suggested innocently, it would not be easy to check her movements so far, because all the shops she had visited were very crowded at all hours of the day and, unless she remembered the assistants who served her or could give him some other particulars which would enable him to trace her purchases, he was afraid that her shopping would not be of great use in proving an alibi.

But Miss Pritt scouted his suggestion and again she could not help showing her surprise at his slowness of perception. Did he think she would be carrying about all her parcels with her? As a matter of fact, the only parcel she did carry about was the one containing the records she had bought in Oxford Street. The rest she, of course, had forwarded to her place in Bloomsbury, where she occupied two rooms in a club for business and professional women.

Mooney laughed a little self-consciously. It was, he admitted, stupid of him not to have thought of that.

After her visit to Swan and Edgar's, Miss Pritt continued, she went to the pictures. What cinema? Oh, "The Empire" in Leicester Square, and Miss Pritt observed him keenly, that second self of hers, which had been watching him all the time with relentless intensity, having suddenly taken possession of the other personality which had been replying to his questions with that anxious air of wishing to be helpful, so well remembered by the superintendent from his first visit. But Mooney showed no sign that he regarded her cinema visit as anything out of the ordinary and his somewhat facetious remark that he thought that it was only the tired business man who frequented cinemas in the afternoons and that business women were much too conscientious to spend their free time in that way, seemed to have reassured her.

It was about ten minutes to five when she purchased her ticket, Miss Pritt said. She remembered it quite well because her watch was rather erratic that day and she consulted the large clock on a building across the square. She did not go straight in, for she had some tea in the cinema café, but that must have taken her only about a quarter of an hour to twenty minutes. She then sat through the whole programme and left the cinema about a quarter past eight and was back at home about a quarter of an hour later.

"But," Mooney asked, "you could not prove that you were at 'The Empire' all the time between ten to five and eight o'clock, could you?"

Miss Pritt seemed to be a little surprised at his question. Mooney's insistence on getting every movement of her checked to his entire satisfaction did not, indeed, seem to worry her, but wasn't he rather overdoing the thoroughness with which he wished to investigate her alibi? "As a matter of fact," she said, "I could prove it quite easily. You see, I had those records with me, and I naturally didn't want to take them inside the cinema with me, so I left them with one of the girls in the box office."

"And you took them back with you on your way home?"

"Yes," Miss Pritt replied, ending that absurd interrogation of his with a decisive nod of her head.

"Well," Mooney laughed, putting away his notebook, "if the rest of the office could supply me with so excellent an alibi, I should be entirely satisfied that Sir Robert's gun had not been replaced by any of the regular staff."

"I should think not!" Miss Pritt exclaimed with conviction. "And I believe," she added, having satisfied herself that Mooney was speaking sincerely, "that I could supply you with another piece of evidence so far as I am concerned, since you're so keen on direct evidence." She took her bag and began looking for something, but she shut it almost immediately. "How stupid of me," she said, "I forgot that I had my grey costume on on Friday. I believe," she explained to the superintendent, "that I still have the half of the cinema ticket that was returned to me by the attendant. I remember putting it into my bag, but, of course, it was my grey bag."

If Miss Pritt's already sufficiently perfect alibi had not made Mooney thoroughly suspicious, her last piece of information certainly did, and he began to wonder how he could fit in the half of the cinema ticket from "The Empire," which he had picked up near the second gorse bush where Beckett had found the cartridge. If Miss Pritt had merely entered the cinema in order to leave it at once by some side entrance and had later come back just in time to prove her alibi by emerging from the cinema at a quarter-past eight o'clock and claiming her records, she must have purchased another ticket in order to get into the cinema again. For it was inconceivable that with all her thoroughness, she would have simply walked up from the street and asked the cashier for her records.

There would have been no difficulty in her buying another ticket from a different girl without being observed by the one she had bought the first ticket from. There were usually two cashiers selling tickets at "The Empire," and the box office windows were, anyway, so small that it would have been quite possible for her to buy a ticket from the same girl without being recognised. But, surely, if that ticket he had picked up *was* dropped by Sir Robert's murderer, then Miss Pritt, if she had anything to do with the murder of her employer, would not have offered to show him the bit of her second ticket, for she must have realised that the second ticket she had bought, which must be the one she had kept, could be proved to have been issued at least two hours later than the time when she claimed to have bought it! And yet why should she have kept that bit of cinema ticket? Was she, perhaps, an accomplice of the murderer and was she simply anxious to establish an alibi for herself?

Ever since the thought of associating Miss Pritt with the murder of Sir Robert Boniface had occurred to Mooney, he had floundered in a morass of contradictory suppositions, for while each of the three suspects whose cases he had so carefully investigated had quite a reasonably strong motive for wishing to kill Sir Robert, Miss Pritt, so far as he could see, had no motive at all! And yet here she came along with a perfect alibi and wished to supply him even with the ticket which proved that at the crucial time when the murder must have been committed she was quietly amusing herself in a cinema!

But why had she kept that ticket? And why was she so careful to remember the times of her visits to the shops? And again, did not the fact that she had kept the ticket prove that the ticket he himself had picked up was valueless as evidence against her?

Mooney expressed his regret that Miss Pritt could not supply him with that final piece of evidence which confirmed her alibi and he suggested that she should send it on to him if she did find it in her bag. She readily agreed to do this, for her desire to be helpful to him appeared to be very great, even if she could not help showing that she thought he was merely wasting his time.

"There's just another matter," Mooney began a little hesitatingly, as though he did not really think it was of much importance, "I should like to clear up, even if only for the sake of form... I traced Sir Robert's movements till four o'clock on Friday. Now we know that he must have been shot somewhere between five and half-past six..."

"Between five and half-past six?" Miss Pritt exclaimed, unable to conceal her astonishment. "I thought it had been established that he had been killed about seven o'clock."

"That's very odd! I've never heard of that!"

"I mean," Miss Pritt hastened to correct herself, "that the general view in the newspapers is that Sir Robert was killed only about an hour before his murder was discovered."

"Quite," Mooney assented, looking at Miss Pritt with the air of a fellow-conspirator, "but the Press, you know, is merely the stepdaughter who gets the leavings. This applies to police matters as well as to politics and business. Unless we want the Press to help us, and we believe that by supplying the necessary information we shall get what we want, we are jolly careful that nothing of importance leaks out. Anyhow, I think I can safely let you know that it is the belief of the police that Sir Robert must have been killed between five and half-past six. Well, as I said, we know where Sir Robert was till four o'clock, but we can't trace his movements after that."

"But does it matter where Sir Robert was between four and five if he was killed somewhere else between five and half-past six?"

"I don't think myself it matters in the least," Mooney assented with a good show of conviction in his voice, "but the police must know where Sir Robert spent those two hours. Of course, we could probably get what we want by appealing for information through the Press, but we don't want to do that if we can help it."

"I don't quite see how *I* can help you," Miss Pritt said, looking at him very steadily, that second self of hers watching him very intently now.

"Now, Miss Pritt," Mooney was still trying to convey his entire trust in her readiness to help him, "you told me on Monday that you usually knew all about Sir Robert's business appointments. Are you sure that Sir Robert had no business appointments between four and five on Friday?"

"Even if I were sure, I shouldn't tell you!" Miss Pritt replied testily.

"Why?"

"Because, as I also told you on Monday, I'm quite certain that Sir Robert's murder had nothing to do with his business!"

"Would you be surprised to hear," Mooney persisted, "that the police have been informed that Sir Robert had two business conferences after four o'clock?"

"I shouldn't be surprised to hear anything," Miss Pritt replied without the slightest sign of agitation in her voice or manner, although from her eyes it was quite plain that that second personality of hers, which was watching him all the time, was beginning to feel apprehensive about his questions.

"Are you aware," Mooney tried as a last resort to intimidate her, although he knew perfectly well that it would be of no avail, "that you are purposely withholding information from the police which might be of the greatest importance for the tracing of the murderer of Sir Robert Boniface?"

"I am aware of nothing of the sort!" she replied with heat. "I merely refuse to satisfy your curiosity about matters which I know have not the slightest connection with Sir Robert's murder!"

"That remains to be seen," Mooney said, getting up and waiting to see if she would not change her mind after all.

But Miss Pritt merely pressed a button and asked a girl who answered her call to show the superintendent out. She did not conceal her great annoyance at Mooney's attempt to force the information out of her. But she was more than annoyed. Indeed, the impression Mooney carried away with him was of a very angry Miss Pritt, her black hair with the silver streaks carefully parted and everything about her neat and smooth, except the flush of anger on her face and the flame of hatred in her eyes.

Before entering his car Mooney stopped to admire the green, long-bodied car of the newly-appointed secretary of the Industrial Development Trust. His idea that it was quite new was right. The signs that it had only left the shop a few days ago could not be mistaken. It was, no doubt, a present from Miss Pritt to herself in recognition of the realisation of her ambition. As an accomplished motorist, her first thought would naturally have turned to acquiring a powerful car built for speed.

16

A WITNESS IN LEICESTER SQUARE

AT HIS FIRST INTERVIEW WITH MISS PRITT, MOONEY HAD gained the impression that the confidential secretary of Sir Robert Boniface might know more about the circumstances that led up to the murder of the millionaire industrialist and politician than she wished to disclose to the police. But that rather indefinite feeling had given place, after his second interview with her, to a suspicion, which, somehow, grew in strength the more perplexing it became, that Miss Pritt was directly concerned in Sir Robert's murder, and that the motive for the murder was in some way connected with the recent troubles on the board of directors of the Industrial Development Trust.

The broken barbed wire fence in Richmond Park no longer appeared to be so far off the map, especially as Lord Rollesborough's house practically adjoined it. But, if his suspicion was right, then Dr. Adams's theory must be wrong, for Miss Pritt could not be fitted into it. But whether Lord Rollesborough was the person Dr. Adams suspected to have been concerned in Sir Robert's death or not, Mooney felt that he held the key to the riddle of the murder.

It was, however, with Frank Littlewood that the superintendent was concerned now, and on his return to Scotland Yard from Lownds Square his first question was whether Sir Robert's nephew had been found. Inspector Beckett, who had been waiting for his superior, informed him that Frank Littlewood had been traced to the British

Museum. He had taken out books in the Reading Room, but he must have gone out somewhere, for he was not at his place in the library. He was bound to return, however, and the police were keeping a watch on the Reading Room and would detain him as soon as he came back to his numbered seat.

Inspector Beckett had also been down to the Vale of Health and had had a talk with Mrs. Littlewood. It seemed that Miss Pritt had rung her up about eleven o'clock on the Friday of the murder and had told her that Sir Robert wished to have a talk with her about Frank. Mrs. Littlewood had not seen her brother since her son's dismissal and she was naturally very hopeful that she might prevail on Sir Robert to reinstate her son to his former position in the office, or, at any rate, to persuade her brother to give him some sort of a job in Fleet Street. But Miss Pritt had warned her that Sir Robert was not at all in a conciliatory frame of mind and that it would be best if a meeting between the uncle and his nephew could be avoided, at least at present. Mrs. Littlewood assured her that it was extremely unlikely that her son would return home before seven o'clock. Miss Pritt then fixed the appointment for Sir Robert at six o'clock. Since Sir Robert's murder Miss Pritt had been in constant communication with Mrs. Littlewood, who did not share her son's views about her and who, on the contrary, thought that she was genuinely grieved at the tragic turn of events and that she was in reality well disposed towards Frank.

"It's very odd," Inspector Beckett concluded, "that Sir Robert never happened to let his sister know that he wanted to see her on Saturday, before he changed his mind to Friday, I mean!"

"We don't know that he did change his mind," Mooney, who looked rather pleased with the information brought by the inspector, said. "All we know is that Sir Robert had intended to see his sister on Saturday at six o'clock. He made a note of it in his diary and also told Mrs. Fuller about it. Sir Robert might conceivably have changed his mind about the day, but what I could never understand is why he fixed his call on Mrs. Littlewood at six o'clock when he already had an appointment with Fuller for that time. I could only suppose that he made a slip, his mind being preoccupied with his meeting with Fuller at six o'clock, and told Miss Pritt to fix the appointment with his sister at six o'clock instead of, as he really intended, at seven. Now I think a much simpler explanation than that is more likely to be the true one. But that I shall know for certain in a day or two. It wasn't at all necessary for Sir Robert to let his sister know beforehand, because he knew he could always find her in at six o'clock."

"But he did let her know in the end!"

"We don't know anything about that, either," Mooney remarked again rather cryptically. "All we know is that Miss Pritt arranged an interview between Sir Robert and his sister for six o'clock on Friday. And by the way, inspector," Mooney took out his notebook, "you'd better check Miss Pritt's alibi. I don't think you'll find anything wrong with it, but take good care to see that it is checked very thoroughly all the same!"

And, after giving Inspector Beckett all the details of Miss Pritt's movements on Friday afternoon, Mooney went off to have lunch. On returning to his office an hour later, he found Frank Littlewood waiting for him.

The three days that had passed since Mooney's first and only meeting with Frank Littlewood had evidently failed to compose the young man's agitation or repress his excitability. His face was even paler and more haggard than when Mooney had first seen him. His mind seemed to be plainly preoccupied with some thought which haunted and maddened him. He couldn't sit quietly in his chair, but got up and paced Mooney's room, at times hardly aware of the presence of the superintendent or of the inspector who was taking down his statement. He jumped up from his chair as soon as Mooney entered the room and addressed him with abrupt violence.

"Am I under arrest on suspicion of murder, or not? Will you tell me that!"

"No. I don't think so," Mooney replied, speaking slowly and trying vainly to make out the cause of Frank Littlewood's feverish excitement.

"Then I wish you would arrest me. I don't mind being under arrest. I wish you'd put me in a cell where I could be by myself!"

"Well," Mooney smiled, "if you can supply me with the necessary facts, I shall be glad to oblige you."

"I can't give you any facts, damn you!" Frank Littlewood exploded fiercely. "I didn't murder my uncle, but I almost wish I had! It would have saved me from all this unbearable torture."

"You'd better sit down," Mooney said calmly, pointing to the leather chair by his desk, "and try to compose yourself. I am not going to bother you about your movements on Friday. At least, not yet..."

"It won't make any difference whether you do or not," Frank Littlewood interrupted, sitting down in the chair, "I shan't tell you!"

"Very well." Mooney seemed to have resigned himself to the inevitable. "What I want you to tell me now is this: how do you explain the murder of your uncle? You must have thought of some sort of explanation, surely. Don't you suspect anybody?"

"Hundreds of people may have wished to kill Sir Robert, myself included. Anybody might have done it, but there's only I who live in the Vale of Health. That's the devil... But, of course," he exclaimed suddenly, as if the thought had only just struck him, "there's Caldwell! Caldwell sent him a pistol to blow his brains out with and he was knocking about the Heath all day..."

"Never mind Caldwell for the present," Mooney said, waving him back to his chair. "Tell me what do you know about the pistol? Did Sir Robert ever show it to you?"

"Of course he did. He showed it to everybody. He seemed very pleased about it, the swine! He even trotted out a Latin tag he must have picked up at some public function and later looked up in his dictionary of quotations to show off his oratorical polish: *'Timeo Danaos et dona ferentes!'* It pleased him very much. He thought it so very apt. But what he was really pleased about was that he had touched Caldwell on the raw by sending back his portrait to him. He wasn't sure how Caldwell would take it. It made him happy to think that he had succeeded in making Caldwell mad with fury!"

"Is that the gun?" Mooney asked, interrupting Frank Littlewood's flow of words and producing the small automatic pistol from one of the drawers of his desk.

At the sight of the gun Frank Littlewood sprang to his feet and looked at it in mute amazement for some time. "So it was Caldwell, after all..." he said at last in a whisper.

"How do you mean it was Caldwell, after all?" Mooney almost roared at him. "Didn't you just say that Sir Robert showed you the gun?"

"Yes... Of course..." Frank Littlewood stared at Mooney with the same blank amazement with which he had stared at the gun a moment earlier. "Of course, it was Sir Robert who had it last... It couldn't have been Caldwell, then... I just said Caldwell because it was his gun!"

"You weren't the only one to say it, but don't say it again unless you can prove it! Do you know where this gun was found?" And without waiting for a reply from Frank Littlewood, who was too bewildered to speak, Mooney answered his own question: "It was found in the Viaduct Pond! And do you know who threw it into the Viaduct Pond?"

"I'm sure I don't!" Frank Littlewood found words again to reply to Mooney.

"I quite believe you. I'll tell you, then: it was Fuller who threw it into the pond!"

"Fuller?" Frank Littlewood sprang to his feet again and stared at the superintendent in utter bewilderment. "But," he said, "why should Fuller wish to kill Sir Robert?"

"Well, there may be many reasons for that. Didn't you say yourself that there were hundreds of people who wanted to kill Sir Robert?"

"Yes, but not Fuller... It wasn't to his advantage to kill the goose who laid the golden eggs..."

"The goose may have refused to lay any more golden eggs. But never mind Fuller for the time being. Fuller says he didn't kill Sir Robert. He says *you* killed Sir Robert!"

"Me?" Frank Littlewood seemed to be rendered speechless again. The colour, which came into his pale face as his excitement grew with the entirely unexpected development his interrogation had taken, left it again as he suddenly realised that a new and undreamt of complication, the importance of which he only vaguely apprehended, had arisen and threatened to wrest his secret from him. "But does Fuller say I gave him the gun to throw into the pond for me?" he asked, grinning suddenly as the utter absurdity of the whole thing flashed upon his mind.

"Well, it does practically come to that! What he says is that you left the gun in the bottom drawer of the desk in your room in Lownds Square during your visit last Monday and that he found it there shortly after you'd gone."

"Why did he throw it into the pond, then?"

"He didn't think of throwing it into the pond, at first. He took the gun to Miss Pritt and together they decided that, since it was quite clear that you'd killed your uncle and since they did not want to be directly concerned in bringing any accusation against you, it would be best to return the gun to Hampstead Heath, where the police would eventually find it and draw their own conclusions."

"It's a damned plot!" Frank Littlewood shouted passionately, beginning to pace the room in his excitement. "I tell you, it's a plot they've concocted between them. It's the third time they've tried to get me, and I'm sure it's Miss Pritt who's behind it all."

"But why should Miss Pritt..."

"I told you she hates me! She'd do anything to get me out of her way."

"But you're no longer in her way! Now that Sir Robert is dead she needn't fear you any more."

"I'm not so sure about that! I may not have any proof of her dishonesty, but I'm sure I'm right. I could denounce her to the board of directors of the I.D.T. and they'd have to do something about it. She knows that and she's afraid of me!"

"Well, suppose it is a plot concocted, as you say, against you by Fuller and Miss Pritt. That would naturally mean that either Fuller or Miss Pritt had killed Sir Robert, wouldn't it? For there can be no doubt at all that Sir Robert was killed with this gun!" Mooney lifted up the gun from his desk and put it down again to emphasise his words. "Nor is there any doubt that both you and Fuller and Miss Pritt could have got hold of this gun from Sir Robert's room without anybody's knowledge. Leaving you and Fuller out of it at present, could you tell me why Miss Pritt should wish to kill Sir Robert?"

"Miss Pritt?" Frank Littlewood repeated, genuinely nonplussed by the question. "I don't know. I don't think she had anything to gain from Sir Robert's death."

"Nor anything to lose, either! For, as you know, she has been appointed secretary of the Industrial Development Trust, after all."

"That's true. I didn't expect that, I own. I suppose that must have been all arranged before Sir Robert's death."

"That I can't tell you, yet. But you didn't answer my question: why should Miss Pritt wish to kill Sir Robert?"

"I told you I don't know," Frank Littlewood replied a little petulantly, his nervous excitement beginning to get the better of him. He forced himself, however, to sit down in the leather chair and to answer Mooney's questions quietly.

"Now listen to me carefully," Mooney said, speaking very slowly and emphasising his words by hammering with the little gun on his desk. "You remember on Monday you said that by raising Miss Pritt from the position of a typist earning a few pounds a week to that of his confidential secretary with a salary running into four figures, Sir Robert had always reserved to himself the right to cast her down again (I'm using your own words) to where she started. You also said that Sir Robert knew all about Miss Pritt's dishonesty—I believe that was the word you used—and that he might wish to use his knowledge in order to keep her in her place. Well, do you think that such an occasion might have arisen quite recently? Or do you know of anything which might have given rise to such an occasion?"

But although Frank Littlewood was certainly listening very carefully, he could not think of anything that might confirm the superintendent's suspicions. He really knew nothing about what was happening behind the scenes of the Industrial Development Trust. He heard all sorts of rumours and made his own deductions, based chiefly on his knowledge of Sir Robert Boniface's character. He knew, for instance, that ever since the serious trouble, the nature of which he could only guess, three months ago, there were quite frequent rows between Sir Robert and Miss Pritt. But there was nothing unusual in that, for Sir Robert enjoyed having rows.

Mooney was disappointed that Frank Littlewood could not give him any more definite information. He turned to the more important part of the interrogation.

"You will realise," he said, "that your position has now become much worse than it has ever been before. You have two witnesses against you who are prepared to testify on oath that the gun with which Sir Robert was killed was found in the drawer of your desk after your visit on Monday to Lownds Square. They are also quite ready to testify that you could very easily have got the gun from your uncle's room shortly before your dismissal, and this even you would have to admit was quite possible. Taken together with the fact that Sir Robert's car was found only a few yards from your home and that you are known to have had a violent quarrel with your uncle, as a result of which you were dismissed from his service, and that a letter from you containing threats against him was found on his body, the case against you is about as strong as it can be. Unless, therefore, you are willing to prove an alibi, your arrest and trial for murder are quite inevitable. You can't say any more that the prosecution won't have sufficient evidence to convict you!"

"It doesn't matter to me," Frank Littlewood declared with great firmness. "Let them convict me!" And he brushed the hair from his high forehead a little theatrically. "I can't tell you where I was on Friday afternoon, because…"

"Because what?" Mooney rapped out, his irritation with Frank Littlewood suddenly breaking out in an outburst of anger. "Here you have your mother and your fiancée imploring you to tell them where you spent Friday afternoon, and you won't tell them, because you say it would mean something terrible to you. But, unless you did murder your uncle, it couldn't mean anything that you might not be able to put right again. You said yourself that it was nothing the police would take any objection to!"

But Frank Littlewood merely laughed scornfully. "You don't understand," he said, dismissing the subject with a gesture of utter resignation. "I don't mind being tried for murder. I don't even mind being convicted…"

"You're just talking about it because you don't realise the mess you're in. I tell you I shall have to arrest you on a charge of murder, if you persist in your refusal to give an account of your movements on Friday. Why are you so obstinate? If you've done anything you want to keep away from your mother or your fiancée, you needn't be afraid to tell me, because I shall do my best to keep it secret."

"But you can't promise, can you?" The question sounded more like a challenge than a request.

"No, I can't promise you anything!" Mooney lost his temper again. "If you really don't feel like saying anything, you'll have to take the consequences."

"You don't understand…" Frank Littlewood relapsed into his mood of utter dejection. Then he suddenly raised his voice and shouted: "I shan't tell you. Do what you damned well like! I'm not afraid to die. If I told you, it might mean more than death to me!"

But the superintendent had now recovered his temper and decided to make a last attempt: "We know," he said quietly, "that you spent the whole morning and part of the afternoon at the Reading Room of the British Museum. You were there till about three o'clock. Where did you go next?" And as Frank Littlewood refused to answer, Mooney went on with half-real, half-mocking despair: "You didn't by any chance go to 'The Empire' cinema in Leicester Square, did you?"

But the effect of his words was astonishing. Frank Littlewood leapt out of his chair and looked at the superintendent with panic-stricken eyes. "How did you find that out?" he almost screamed, with suppressed fury in his voice.

Mooney was even more surprised than Frank Littlewood. He stood up and faced the nervous, shaking young man with iron deter-mination. "Will you tell me," he asked, "the exact time you were at 'The Empire'?" And as he got no reply, he went on: "You went there straight from the British Museum, didn't you? You would be there, therefore, from about half-past three till six or half-past six, wouldn't you?"

"I left it," Frank replied, and the words seemed to have been forced out of him against his own will, "at a quarter to six."

"Can you prove it?" Mooney insisted on a reply with the same commanding emphasis in his voice.

"I can't prove it," Frank Littlewood burst out, no longer able to control himself. "How the hell do you expect me to prove it?" He sank back into his chair and buried his face in his hands.

"Very well. We shall try to get somebody to prove it," Mooney said, for again, as when on the way to Lownds Square earlier in the day, a possible explanation of Frank's refusal to prove his alibi occurred to him. "You'll come with me at once to 'The Empire.'" And he whispered a few directions to the officer who was taking down Frank Littlewood's statement.

On the way to Leicester Square in the superintendent's car, Frank Littlewood sat in gloomy silence, and he moved uneasily when Mooney began to speak.

"On Monday you told your mother," Mooney said without turning to his passenger, "that you didn't know Sir Robert was coming to see her. Don't you think she would have let you know if she had been expecting a visit from him?"

"I don't think she would," Frank replied quickly, looking up with revived interest. "You see, she seems to have been quite set on getting me back to work in Sir Robert's office and she realised that if I knew that Sir Robert was coming to see her I should insist on being there when he came, for I was absolutely determined not to go back unless I was given a responsible post which would be free from Miss Pritt's supervision."

"So that if you had by any chance learnt of Sir Robert's intention to see your mother on Friday, you would be sure to have hurried back home in time to intercept Sir Robert?"

Frank Littlewood, who didn't expect Mooney to turn round on him in this way, smiled wryly: he was forgetting he was talking to a policeman who was trying to trap him into unguarded admissions!

"I shouldn't have dreamt that Sir Robert intended to see my mother last Friday," he replied, "because I got a letter from him the same morning in reply to the letter you found on him, in which he said that he was absolutely finished with me and that I could do what I damn well liked, or words to that effect, and there was also the unexpressed, but plainly implied, threat that if I did try to expose him in the Press, he would not shrink from taking the necessary measures. And that was not all. I told you Sir Robert had an uncanny insight into human nature. He knew how to hit you in the most vulnerable place. You remember that story Fuller spread about my expectations as Sir Robert's heir. Well, in this letter to me my uncle made quite a lot of it. He taunted me with my poverty. He told me that, as I had proved myself to be an utter failure, I was now trying to get money from him by blackmail. Money was the whole world to him. Money was power, and power was what he worshipped most. But he knew perfectly well that it was not his money I wanted. I had demanded an apology for a personal insult and I was determined to get it! But that letter of his made me feel as if I had been thrown into a cesspool. It made me feel so foul that I could clean myself only by plunging even deeper in filth. I couldn't do my work at the British Museum. I went to a cinema to find distraction, but I could hardly follow the usual Hollywood mush on the screen. I…"

But here Frank Littlewood stopped abruptly, and no sympathetic prompting from Mooney could make him continue the story. They had now arrived at Leicester Square and Mooney parked his car in a side street. The police car, in which the inspector and two plain-clothes men had followed them, was also parked in the same place. Mooney and Frank Littlewood, followed closely by the three detectives, went into the cinema, where the superintendent demanded to see the manager. For the next hour a most rigorous examination in the manager's room of almost the entire staff employed by "The Empire" failed to produce any result. Not only was it quite impossible to establish the time when Frank Littlewood had left the cinema, but Mooney could not find anyone who could identify Frank Littlewood as having been to the cinema on Friday, although, according to him, he was quite a frequent visitor at "The Empire." But there was, of course, nothing unusual in that. Thousands of people visited the cinema in the course of the day, and on Fridays especially, when there was, as a rule, a change of programme, the place was crowded.

On emerging from the cinema, Mooney could not conceal his disappointment. He seemed undecided what to do, and he lingered at the entrance as if waiting for somebody to turn up. Frank Littlewood stood at his side, a little amused by the failure of the superintendent's efforts to display him as a sort of rare animal, and still absolutely determined to do nothing to help the superintendent to save him from a trial for murder. The three detectives kept unobtrusively in the background. Then Frank Littlewood must suddenly have seen somebody whom he was anxious to avoid, for a look of horror came into his eyes and he made a sudden dash across the road and disappeared behind the railings of the square. Some action of the kind must have been expected by the three plain-clothes men, for one of them detached himself at once from the group and followed Frank Littlewood. Mooney remained standing where he was, carefully surveying the crowd of passers-by, in search of the person from whom Frank Littlewood had made that sudden dash.

The woman was not difficult to spot, for she was standing quite close to Mooney, having stopped to watch Frank Littlewood dash across the road. She seemed to be hurt at the extraordinary way the young man had acknowledged her smile of recognition and invitation. In her eyes there was the cold, cruel look of contempt of one whose feelings have been outraged and whose expectations of easy gain have been deceived at the same time.

She was a fashionably dressed woman, but fashion in her dress was on the gay side and her make-up was just sufficiently emphasised to attract the necessary attention which might lead to an addition in the number of her clients. She was still quite young enough for youth to invest her figure with a certain glamour of romance, and she was very careful to conceal that mark of cynicism and greed which her profession often stamps on the faces of its followers. Mooney's attention did not escape her and, with the practised art of one whose emotions are strictly regulated by the demands of the hour, she changed her perplexed and contemptuous expression to one of intimate and eager willingness.

She could do it very well, without the crude, mercenary, knock-him-down smile of the woman of the streets. Her smile, if not innocent, was captivating and still quite fresh, her glad-eye had a twinkle of merriment and good sport, and her pretty face had a mischievous twist in it which gave rather a misleading impression of natural gaiety, but which kept some of its attractiveness even on closer acquaintance. It was true that the first impression of youth was apt to disappear suddenly on nearer approach, a fact which gave a disagreeable jolt, but by that time she had either caught her man or had failed to catch him, and, anyway, her charms were not quite deceptive and she usually kept her promise of "a good time," which she held out, in view of the rather high terms charged for her favours.

Mooney responded to her glance and walked with her to her flat, which was only a few yards away from the square. On the way there the strictly business part of their conversation occupied very little time, her terms having been accepted without haggling, a fact which surprised Miss Morrison (for that was the name of the lady who had so frightened Frank Littlewood), who was accustomed in these hard times to find her clients a little niggardly about their presents.

Mooney asked her if she had noticed the young man at his side who had sheered off at such a speed. She looked at him a little suspiciously, and asked him if he was his friend, and, on being assured by the superintendent that Frank Littlewood was not his friend, she admitted that she had met the young man before. He was not one of her regular clients, but he had paid her a visit recently and he had given her a lot of trouble. Yes, Miss Morrison with all her experience of men was still occasionally shocked by the deceptive appearance of some of her clients, and she seemed to be quite disgusted with Frank Littlewood, but she had her present client to attend to and she was not going to waste her time on complaints.

She stopped in a narrow passage, opened a door with her latch-key and invited Mooney to go in first, but, as he chivalrously stepped back, she went in before him without noticing the two other men, whose profession to her experienced eyes would have been as plain to her as hers was to them. When she turned round to see if Mooney was following her, she found the three men standing on the doorstep, and the hard, frightened look of a trapped animal suddenly appeared in her eyes. She would have banged the door on them in her impulsive rage of disappointment and fear, had they not entered quickly and shut the door behind them.

After a few minutes of angry protestations from Miss Morrison that she had not accosted anybody and that she did not think such a dirty trick would be played on her by a man who looked like a gentleman, Mooney succeeded in explaining to her that he was merely anxious to get a statement from her about that young man whom he had mentioned on the way to her flat and whose movements on Friday, June 23rd, the police were trying to trace. She seemed still very suspicious, but she led Mooney and the inspector into her flat on the third floor (the other plain-clothes policeman remaining in the hall downstairs), which consisted of a small, quite tastefully furnished room with a deep alcove occupied entirely by a bed.

Miss Morrison, whose hunted expression gave place to one of dumb acquiescence in a situation which she was quite helpless to control, watched Mooney with a look in which the primitive hatred of the hunted for the hunter was mingled with deep contempt for the trick he had played on her and with suspicion that he had not told her the truth about the object of his visit. Her suspicion deepened as the usual preliminaries about her identity were taken down by the inspector and, before Mooney could proceed with his interrogation, she burst out with an unexpected accusation.

"I know what you've come for," she said suddenly in a loud voice, unable to restrain her rage, "that young fool told you I'd stolen his money. But that's not true! He gave it to me himself. He stopped for over an hour here last Friday, crying like a baby and swearing like a trooper in one and the same breath. I didn't know what to do with him. Not that he was an innocent boy, either. He had been with many women before me. He told me so himself, and I could tell it, anyway. At first he was afraid for his health, but I told him he had nothing to fear, and that if he was so nervous about it, he shouldn't have anything to do with women, the nice sort being much more dangerous than those you pay. I'm not just any sort of woman. I have very decent clients and I take good care of everything. Then he began slobbering about a girl he was going to marry. But most of my clients are either married or are going to be married, and those who are going to be married come to me more often than the others. If I had known the sort of man he was I shouldn't have had anything to do with him. I am always trying to get quiet, decent clients. I couldn't have kept my place if I had taken any of the other sort. I am not a fool and I know what is best for my business. I never had any trouble with the police before about anything... That young fool gave me a shock. He nearly collapsed on my hands, crying and swearing and walking up and down the room. I had to make him tea and keep him here till he quietened down a bit. Then he went, and I could hardly believe my luck that I had got rid of him at last when he came back and threw all the money he had at me. Five pounds it was. I would not take it, because I wasn't sure that he mightn't come back for it when he'd thought better of it, but he made me keep the money because I had been so good to him and because he was afraid that if he kept the money he might go and spend it on somebody worse than me. I might have known better than to believe him. He didn't look like somebody who could afford to waste six quid in an hour. He wouldn't leave a tip for the maid, and then he comes and throws five pounds in my face. I tell you that's the honest truth! I didn't steal his money. I'm not that sort. I knew there was something fishy in him dashing away like that. He hadn't the pluck to face me with the lie. I tell you it is a lie! He can have his five pounds back, if he wants them, but I didn't steal them from him!"

Miss Morrison's rage seemed to have exhausted itself and she relapsed into silence, having plainly given up all hope of impressing the police with her story. She was not really very anxious to return Frank Littlewood's money, either, but the dread of being arrested for theft had overcome her greed. She looked resigned now and very quiet and rather pathetic in her make-up and gay clothes.

"I'm beginning to suspect, Miss Morrison," Mooney, who had listened to her outburst not without amusement at her strong prejudice in favour of decent clients, said, "that you wouldn't put me on the list of your clients. However, I'm not interested in them, and I'm not interested in your business except as it affects the young man whom you saw dashing across the street a few minutes ago. You needn't be afraid of being accused of theft. Nobody had brought such an accusation against you. The police, as I told you, are interested in the movements of that young man, and all I want to establish·is the exact time he spent with you a week ago to-day."

But it was impossible to persuade Miss Morrison that the visit of the police had such an innocent explanation. Still, she gave the details Mooney wanted. Frank Littlewood, there could be no doubt at all about it, was in the company of Miss Morrison from about six till half-past seven on Friday evening.

It was hardly necessary to have Miss Morrison identify Frank Littlewood, for there could be no doubt that she remembered him very well. She was warned, however, that she might be called upon to identify him and, much as she disliked being involved with the police, even in a case which did not really concern her, she consented quite willingly, now that the spectre of prison had disappeared and the five pounds were still left in her possession.

Mooney was well satisfied that he had at last eliminated Sir Robert's nephew as well as Matt Caldwell from the number of suspects. He never really believed that Frank Littlewood had committed the murder. Even if Frank had met Sir Robert, it was not at all certain that he would have dared to have it out with him, much as he liked to boast that he was not afraid of his uncle. His fear that June Gayford, who suspected his weakness of character, would discover his unfaithfulness, which might have meant an end to his engagement, had increased his genuine feeling of remorse and, together, they accounted for his distraught condition. By his violent death, Sir Robert seemed to have got in a final blow against his nephew!

Whether Frank Littlewood would really have preferred death to the loss of June Gayford, Mooney doubted very much. He probably would have revealed his unfaithfulness in the end, to the police, at any rate. He seemed already to be wavering.

But Superintendent Mooney could not afford to waste time on unnecessary arrests.

THE TESTIMONY OF THE UNSMOKED CIGAR

The Evening Courier, THE EVENING EDITION OF *The Daily Courier-Tribune*, the newspaper with positively the largest circulation in the world which owed its unrivalled success to the genius of Sir Robert Boniface, published on Friday, June 30th, a long article on the remarkable career of the new secretary of the Industrial Development Trust, under the headline of "One of Our Pioneer Business Women," the main points of which, together with a number of rather intimate details of Miss Pritt's views on fashions and on the bachelor business woman, were also reproduced on its woman's page.

The article was headed by a large photograph of Miss Pritt and it was signed by the cryptic mark: "—f—."

According to its author, Miss Pritt's great ability and sterling qualities of honesty and loyalty had at once been recognised by Sir Robert Boniface, whose violent death had so shocked the whole country. Sir Robert Boniface saw in her a worthy collaborator in his great schemes of industrial expansion on a scale undreamt of before his advent in the arena of modern capitalism. Indeed, it was not generally realised that the part played by Miss Pritt in bringing Sir Robert's vast schemes to fruition was as important as that played by Sir Robert himself, who fully recognised it and who had been chiefly responsible for Miss Pritt's appointment to her present post of great responsibility and authority.

A long disquisition on the significance of Miss Pritt's appointment for the women's movement of emancipation and equality with men, at a time when women were being deprived of their elementary political and economic rights in a number of civilised countries, was followed by a few biographical details and by a description of her hobbies, among which motoring and golf occupied the most prominent places.

Although most of the front page of *The Evening Courier* was occupied with a sensational account of a heavy lorry which had crashed into the parapet of Westminster Bridge at about two in the afternoon and had involved the deaths of one woman and three men, the news of the murder of Sir Robert Boniface was still apparently regarded as sufficiently "hot" to warrant the publication, in the centre of the page, of a short paragraph "from a special correspondent." This anonymous correspondent foretold the imminence of an arrest in connection with the murder of Sir Robert Boniface, "one of the most sensational murder cases of our time." The police, it appeared, had not been idle. Although there was from the very beginning a strong suspicion as to who the murderer of Sir Robert Boniface might be, nothing could be done until the chain of evidence against the suspected person was complete. It was not till that morning, however, that a most vital piece of evidence had been disclosed to the police, and it was now only a matter of hours before the murderer would be apprehended.

Superintendent Mooney found nothing to interest him in the article about Miss Pritt, but the story about the vital piece of evidence which would result in the arrest of the murderer of Sir Robert Boniface attracted his attention at once. The "special correspondent," he guessed, must be none other than the author of the article about Miss Pritt, and he could not help feeling that Fuller had sent neither the short news item nor the long article without first consulting the secretary of the Industrial Development Trust.

Mooney had just arranged an appointment with Lord Rollesborough at his Richmond home at eight o'clock. But he had yet to decide what to do with Frank Littlewood, who had been brought back to Scotland Yard by the detective who had gone in pursuit of him after his sudden dash across the road in Leicester Square. Mooney had not seen him and he realised that no useful purpose could be served in meeting him again. It would, perhaps, have been best to detain him and put him in a cell for a night to let his excitement work off. But the report in *The Evening Courier*, whose dreadful significance would not escape Frank Littlewood's mother and fiancée, made such action impossible. Nor would it be wise to let Frank Littlewood know that he had been cleared entirely of suspicion, for that, too, might reach Fuller and Miss Pritt. The best thing to do, Mooney decided, would be to get Frank Littlewood out of London for a few days, and he bethought himself of his small country cottage. If only he could persuade June Gayford to take her fiancé and, perhaps, also his mother away to his cottage for the week-end, the field would be clear for him to act without any unnecessary complications which might arise from Miss Pritt's frequent communications with Mrs. Littlewood!

It was not so easy to get hold of June Gayford, but a detective Mooney sent for her succeeded in bringing her to Scotland Yard before the superintendent was due to leave for Richmond. The girl seemed glad of his offer, but even more of his assurance that he was quite convinced that her fiancé had nothing to do with the murder and that the report in *The Evening Courier*, which she had seen, had no reference to him.

Mooney could see that June Gayford was anxious to find out if he had succeeded in tracing Frank Littlewood's movements last Friday and that the reasons for her curiosity were not altogether unconnected with the police investigations; but he left her in the dark about it, for it was now entirely a matter which would have to be settled between her and her fiancé. He did not doubt that June Gayford would make Frank Littlewood confess in the end, if she was really set on finding out whether the suspicion of his unfaithfulness which was quite evidently stirring in her mind, was justified. But would she really go so far as to break off her engagement to Frank Littlewood? Mooney doubted it now that he saw how anxious she was about the fate of her fiancé. Women were, on the whole, more reasonable about such aberrations from the path of virtue than men. They also derived much more comfort from forgiveness than men. Frank Littlewood was luckier than he deserved to be and a week-end in the country would certainly do him good.

June Gayford promised to get both her fiancé and his mother away to Mooney's cottage, and the superintendent made arrangements for a car to take the three of them there.

On his way to Richmond, Mooney again thought of the cigar found in the right-hand corner of the blue limousine, and of the part it might play in his attempt to get at the vital facts about Sir Robert Boniface's murder from the Earl of Rollesborough. He had already considered the possibility that Sir Robert had been to see Lord Rollesborough after his visit to Mrs. Fuller. That would account for *one* of Sir Robert's business conferences. What he wanted to find out was whom Sir Robert intended to see beside Lord Rollesborough and whether there was any connection between the two business conferences? What he was puzzled about was where the cigar (which he had taken with him) came in? Why, above all, should Dr. Adams, whose close association with Lord Rollesborough was quite beyond doubt, have been so anxious to find out whether the police had discovered a cigar in Sir Robert's car?

Mooney arrived at Steep Meadows about ten minutes past eight, and he was shown at once into Lord Rollesborough's study. The earl did not give the impression of a nervous man. On the contrary, he was the picture of health, a little short, but broad-shouldered, with the chest of an athlete and the arms of a pugilist. His broad face certainly showed great determination and will power. His lower jaw was firm and a little thrust forward and completed the impression of a fighter who was ready and eager to throw down a challenge and to rush into the battle irrespective of the strength of the enemy. There was, besides, about the new Chairman of the Industrial Development Trust a feeling of assurance, of success, of victorious accomplishment which, together with his combativeness, conveyed an impression which was so utterly different from what Mooney had expected, that for a moment he felt that all the hopes he had built on the meeting with Lord Rollesborough were destined to be disappointed, and that Dr. Adams's theory was a chimera constructed from the feverish imaginings of a lunatic. Was it possible that the Earl of Rollesborough was Dr. Adams's patient? And yet, no sooner had Lord Rollesborough inquired about what had brought the superintendent to seek an interview with him, than Mooney changed his opinion. There certainly was a strange hesitancy in Lord Rollesborough's voice and an apprehensive look in his eyes, which were all the more noticeable because they contrasted with the impression of moral and physical strength which his personality conveyed.

Mooney was not sure how to start. Sir Robert's murder, he said, had presented the police with a number of very difficult problems. One of these was the difficulty of tracing Sir Robert's movements prior to about six o'clock when the murder must in all probability have taken place. They knew that Sir Robert had two business conferences between four and six o'clock, but so far they had not succeeded in discovering either whom he had those conferences with or what the object of those conferences was. They had tried to get Miss Pritt to supply them with the necessary information, but without success.

Their only hope now was that Lord Rollesborough who, as Chairman of the Industrial Development Trust, was no doubt acquainted with the object of those conferences, would reveal them to the police.

It was plain that the subject Mooney had chosen as an opening was about the worst he could have hit on. Lord Rollesborough let him finish without interruption, but he was quite obviously uneasy and he made no attempt to conceal it.

"I don't see what all this has to do with Sir Robert's murder," he said irritably. "Haven't you all the facts now at your disposal? And what is this about, anyway?" he asked, pointing to an open copy of *The Evening Courier*, with the report from the "special correspondent" in the centre of its front page.

"I was wondering myself, my lord, what it is about," Mooney replied with great calmness, regarding the earl with a slightly baffled look. "I've been in charge of this case from the beginning, but I haven't heard anything of a most vital piece of evidence disclosed to the police this morning…"

"But, good Lord, don't you regard the finding of the gun as important evidence? Can't you see that the man who brought it to Lownds Square most probably committed the murder? And wasn't it evident from the very beginning who is most likely to have committed it?"

"It was not evident to me, my lord," Mooney said imperturbably, "and, if I may ask, how do you know all these facts?"

But the earl merely stared at him in blank amazement. "How do I know all these facts?" he repeated. "How should I know all these facts? Because they were reported to me!"

"By Miss Pritt?"

"Why, yes. By Miss Pritt…"

"So you, too, are of the opinion that the man who is said to have brought back the gun to Lownds Square is the murderer of Sir Robert Boniface?"

"What the devil are you beating about the bush for?" Lord Rollesborough suddenly flared up. "You know perfectly well who I mean. I mean Frank Littlewood, Sir Robert's nephew. An utterly unprincipled young man and, from what I hear of him, capable of anything... His article about his uncle in *The Call*, a paper I've never seen before, but which a dear friend of mine showed me, was singularly muddle-headed and thoroughly un-British in sentiment... And what do you mean by talking about the man *who is said to have brought back the gun*? Didn't Frank Littlewood bring it back?"

"The police didn't find the gun in Lownds Square. They found it in a pond on Hampstead Heath..."

"Yes, but what has that got to do with it? What the devil are you driving at? Are you suspecting anybody else?"

"All I can say at present, sir, is that the evidence against Frank Littlewood is not at all conclusive—it certainly is not conclusive enough to justify an arrest—and that, so far as I can see, I shall have first to clear up all the clues left in Sir Robert's car before making up my mind definitely."

"The clues left in Sir Robert's car?" Lord Rollesborough repeated a little unsteadily. "What clues are you referring to?"

"Well, there's one clue which has puzzled me all along," Mooney said in his confidential tone, without a note of suspicion in his voice, passing his hand over his scarred cheek. "It's a cigar found near the body of Sir Robert Boniface! It's this cigar!" And without appearing to have noticed the change which had come over Lord Rollesborough's face at the mention of the cigar, all colour having left it so suddenly that the superintendent feared the earl might drop in a faint, he took out the cigar from his breast pocket and unwrapped it.

"Well, what about this cigar?" Lord Rollesborough asked, taking the cigar a little gingerly and returning it almost immediately to the superintendent.

"Well, sir," Mooney went on in his confidential tone, "I've been trying to trace who this cigar belongs to. For, you see, Sir Robert did not smoke cigars, and the cigars he kept in his room to offer to his visitors are of a different brand."

"Yes, but what if you do trace the owner of this cigar? How would it help you to find Sir Robert's murderer?"

"Sir Robert was given this cigar at one of the business conferences he had between four and six o'clock. He had only just had time to light it. He then threw it away. Why? Well, one of the reasons why Sir Robert dropped the cigar might be because he was killed just after he had lighted it."

"Good Lord!" Lord Rollesborough said, raising his eyebrows in astonishment. He had now completely recovered his natural combativeness. "This is tommy rot!" he said firmly. "You must excuse me, superintendent, if I repeat my opinion of your theory again, it is tommy rot! And do you know why it is tommy rot? Because it is my cigar and because it wasn't Sir Robert at all who lighted it, but I! I lighted it and I threw it away!"

"So it was you, my lord, with whom Sir Robert had one of his business conferences on Friday?" Mooney asked, without showing the slightest sign of ill-feeling at Lord Rollesborough's candid view of his theory.

"Yes. It was me." Lord Rollesborough had now got over the worst of his shock and was making the best of the situation. "I tell you quite frankly," he said, "I didn't want you to know anything about it. And that cigar worried me. I knew I had thrown it down almost as soon as I had lighted it and that it was bound to excite the curiosity of the bright sparks at Scotland Yard. But I hoped that you wouldn't be able to trace it. I didn't want you to come prying about and trying to find out what it was Sir Robert and I were discussing. It isn't your affair. It has nothing to do with the murder and it is a matter of the utmost confidence, which, if it becomes known, might do untold harm, especially now that Sir Robert is dead."

"But I'm not at all sure that it has nothing to do with the murder!" Mooney said blandly.

"Good Lord!" Lord Rollesborough exclaimed, and he suddenly advanced on the superintendent as if he were going to challenge him for a fight on the spot. "Are you implying that I murdered Sir Robert?"

"I should like to know when your conference with Sir Robert was before replying to your question," Mooney replied with the same blandness as before, but his look told Lord Rollesborough that he meant it in earnest.

"If you must know," he said, giving Mooney up as a bad job, "it was between half-past four and a quarter-past five... Sir Robert was certainly gone at a quarter-past five. He didn't intend to stay so long, but our conference took rather an unexpected turn."

"That clears you completely of any suspicion, my lord," Mooney said with a touch of well-simulated gratification in his voice, which made Lord Rollesborough glare at him in incredulous astonishment: he could still not reconcile himself to the idea that the superintendent should really have suspected him of having murdered Sir Robert Boniface. "But there is still the second conference to clear up..."

"The second conference!" Lord Rollesborough repeated, looking now with real amusement at the superintendent and, seeing that Mooney seemed to be in dead earnest, he suddenly burst out in a loud guffaw.

"Ho-ho-ho!" he laughed, his short, but strong frame shaking and his throat emitting bursts of lusty sounds which ended in strange, high-pitched, nervous notes, which did not accord with the general sonority of his laughter. "You really must excuse me, superintendent," he said at last, wiping his eyes and forehead and sitting down at his desk, but still looking at Mooney with amused incredulity, "but you're so much like the Scotland Yard detectives a dear friend of mine puts in his stories, that I could not help laughing."

"I'm still waiting to hear who Sir Robert had his second conference with!" Mooney remarked, quite unruffled by Lord Rollesborough's laughter and keeping his imperturbably grave expression which had caused so much amusement.

"I'm sorry," Lord Rollesborough said, Mooney's grave face having recalled him to the seriousness of the detective's mission, "but, you see, if there had been the slightest likelihood of a murder at the second conference, it would be Sir Robert who would have committed it, for it was Sir Robert who left me vowing vengeance against the person he was presently to see."

"And that person was?"

"That person was Miss Pritt, his confidential secretary, whom he had accused quite absurdly and without the slightest foundation of having betrayed him to…" Lord Rollesborough stopped abruptly, having realised that he had already said too much.

"… his enemies!" Mooney completed the sentence. The superintendent still kept that mask of imperturbable gravity which screened his thoughts very effectively, but there now appeared in his eyes a hard, determined look in which his decision to probe the mystery of Sir Robert's murder to the very bottom could be quite plainly read. "His enemies," he repeated, "who had demanded his resignation from the board of directors of the Industrial Development Trust and who had agreed to a compromise which would have deprived him of his sole control of the Trust's affairs only after they had assured themselves that his confidential secretary, in whose loyalty he trusted and whom he insisted on being given an executive post with the Trust, was on their side!"

The last spark of merriment died out of Lord Rollesborough's eyes with a suddenness which was in itself sufficient to show the panic into which he was thrown. Those high-pitched notes in his laughter a few minutes ago, which seemed so out of tune with his general hale and hearty appearance, were symptomatic of the nervous tension under which he laboured. He looked at Mooney, half in terror and half in rage. His face, which had turned deadly pale at the mention of the demand for Sir Robert's resignation, almost at once recovered its colour, but his eyes narrowed and his lower jaw was thrust forward. His fighting nature reasserted itself over his weak nerves.

"You seem to know much more than you wanted me to believe," he said, "but I must warn you that your information, from whatever source you've got it, must remain secret. It isn't that we're afraid to reveal the fact that there were serious disagreements between Sir Robert Boniface and the board of directors of the Industrial Development Trust. These disagreements have been common knowledge in the City for the last five years. But we don't want anybody to know that things had gone so far as to force the directorate to demand Sir Robert's resignation. What we're afraid of is that, if this becomes generally known, the causes which compelled the directorate to take that very serious step might also leak out. If those leak out a crash will be inevitable, and the effect of this crash will be felt all over the world, although we have already succeeded in forestalling the more dangerous consequences of Sir Robert's recklessness. A crash will be inevitable!" Lord Rollesborough repeated, his voice raised warningly. "And if the Industrial Development Trust crashes, the whole world will be shaken!"

"You can rest assured," Mooney declared, "that so far as the police are concerned no unnecessary revelations will be made. But I'm not interested in Sir Robert's resignation, nor in the causes which forced the directorate to demand it. What I'm interested in is the disagreement between Sir Robert and his confidential secretary and the reason why Sir Robert left you 'vowing vengeance' against her!"

"You mustn't exaggerate what I said," Lord Rollesborough hastily corrected him, although the superintendent merely repeated his own words. "There certainly was a rather tempestuous scene between Sir Robert and myself before he left me on Friday and, as you've guessed, the reason was that he had discovered that Miss Pritt was on our side. He was very angry and he made a few rather reckless remarks about her, which in any ordinary way would undoubtedly have done considerable harm to her prospects with the Trust, but, of course, knowing Sir Robert as I did, I paid little attention to what he said. This seemed to have exasperated him even more and he drove off in a flaming rage promising to supply me with proof and what not. But Sir Robert was in a hole, in a hole into which I had driven him. He regarded me as his enemy, and he was quite right. I was his enemy. For the last five years I've been conducting a fight to a finish with him. He had become a danger not only to the Industrial Development Trust, but to the whole world. He took risks which no one, not even the most powerful dictator, would dream of taking. Even if he had been younger he would have been in danger of over-reaching himself. But he was getting old. He was only sixty-six, but he had had a very rough time, and age was beginning to tell early. He was getting more and more dependent on Miss Pritt, but she was no longer sure that he had the power to carry out his schemes. Indeed, some of them had made her very apprehensive and, as she told me herself, it was only her sense of loyalty which had kept her from revealing their nature to the board of directors. His last scheme, however, was so utterly fantastic that it would have brought every-thing down in ruins on his head. Miss Pritt had warned him again and again about the dangers he was running. But he wouldn't listen. The trouble was that it wasn't merely a commercial venture. It was chiefly a political adventure against a certain country, and I needn't tell you which country I mean. This would have brought about a war involving at least half a dozen countries. He had counted on the victorious outcome of the war for spreading the influence of the Industrial Development Trust into territories which are at present closed to it. He hoped to secure concessions, he hoped to lay claim to mines and oilfields which had formerly belonged to several of our subsidiary companies, he hoped to establish a government which would be entirely at his beck and call. And he was carrying it all out single-handed, without regard to the interests of the millions of the Trust's shareholders and without regard to the even more important fact that the governments with which he was conducting negotiations in secret were jealous of each other, and were merely using him for furthering their own interests. Things had gone so far that, with utter disregard to consequences, Sir Robert had pledged the Trust's entire resources for the carrying out of his scheme, and he had even gone through certain transactions of which the legal aspect was highly questionable. It was at that point that Miss Pritt thought it necessary to acquaint me with the position. I took measures at once to veto Sir Robert's plans. I had the power to do it," Lord Rollesborough raised his voice and thrust out his chin, as if the thought of his power over Sir Robert was still a matter of great pride to him, "because I was also supplied with certain facts by her which put Sir Robert in my power. Of course, there was no question of betraying the source of our information. We could have got to know about his latest scheme through different channels. His confederates, as I told you, were not trustworthy and, in fact, it wouldn't have been impossible for us to gather the chief points of Sir Robert's secret negotiations from some of the people he was negotiating with, if we had had any inkling of what was really at stake. Anyway, Sir Robert must have suspected quite a number of people of having, as he would have said, betrayed him, and he seems also to have suspected Miss Pritt, for she had warned me that very morning that he intended to find out from me who had given him away, and she also rang me up about three o'clock to tell me that Sir Robert had just tried to force her to confess that she had disclosed his plans to me. But Sir Robert did not show his suspicion till, quite inadvertently, I let him see that our objection to Miss Pritt's appointment was not really as strong as we had pretended when he first suggested it as the price of his surrender. Perhaps, while talking to him in his car, for he would not discuss anything with me except on 'his own territory,' I overdid it a little. For, when he first proposed that his confidential secretary should be appointed to an executive position with the Trust, there was quite strong opposition to it and I was rather against it myself, as I was not quite sure of Miss Pritt, who had been too long in Sir Robert's confidence to be quite safe when appointed to a position where she could easily throw her weight on his side. But at our last meeting I must have been provoked by something he said to me and I let him understand that we did not fear him any longer and that it really made no difference to us whether or not Miss Pritt was given the position he had asked for her. It was then that he suddenly snapped back at me and made me admit that Miss Pritt had supplied us with the information which had given us the power to control the affairs of the Trust in the interests of its shareholders. Of course, the effect of my admission was lamentable. I expected that, but I knew that he was quite helpless and that Miss Pritt had really nothing to fear from him. That was, indeed, why he had threatened to expose her and to put her in prison. It was the inevitable reaction of a man who knew he was defeated, although, I must confess, I felt so utterly disgusted with the way he took his defeat that I threw down the cigar I had only just lighted and stepped out of his car!" Lord Rollesborough's aristocratic nature even now recoiled at the recollection of the ungovernable passion of that great plebeian magnate of industry whom he had at last got the better of. "He followed me out, but I would have nothing to do with him. He then drove off at once to keep his appointment with Miss Pritt, with whom he had to discuss several things, as he was leaving for Ireland the next day. But, of course, I knew very well, as Miss Pritt must have also known, that the chief reason for his conference with her on Friday afternoon was to settle his account with her. I was not really sorry to have told Sir Robert about Miss Pritt, although I had no doubt that my admission might provide her with a disagreeable half-hour. For once Sir Robert realised that he could no longer rely on his former secretary it would be impossible for them to work together in the future and that was what I wanted to make absolutely sure of. There was no question of any bad faith on my part, for I was determined to keep my side of the bargain. Miss Pritt was not very sorry, either, for she rang me up the same evening..."

"When was that?" Mooney interrupted Lord Rollesborough for the first time during his long speech, of which he had made hurried notes.

"That must have been about half-past seven," Lord Rollesborough replied. "Yes, about half-past seven. She told me what had happened between her and Sir Robert and, as I had expected, Sir Robert cooled off quite soon and they parted amicably." He paused and examined the imperturbable face of the superintendent, as if trying to find out whether he had said enough to satisfy his curiosity. "Now, I've told you much more than I really intended to," he said, "and I hope you are quite satisfied. I wasn't going to tell you anything, but your absurd suspicions forced me to take you into my confidence. All I can do now is to impress on you the necessity of keeping all the facts which relate to Sir Robert's latest disagreement with the board of directors absolutely secret, until, at any rate, things quieten down a bit and the whole trouble, which the murder of Sir Robert has caused, blows over. I know that to people who have no knowledge of finance all this information seems quite harmless, as a dear and trusted friend of mine told me only yesterday. But, as I said to him, it is no use trying to construct all sorts of fanciful theories about Sir Robert's murder when these theories are based on the utterly unsound assumption that the murder had something to do with Sir Robert's business. It is a point which, I hope, you will now admit to be established. The fact, however, remains that all this talk even among friends helps to spread rumours, and there are quite enough rumours at present without additions from persons whose connections invest what they say with authority."

Lord Rollesborough seemed to be rather vexed with "his dear and trusted friend," and Mooney could not help wondering what his reaction would have been if he had been told that Dr. Adams half suspected him of having murdered Sir Robert Boniface himself. There was not much more the superintendent wanted to find out except a few details about the time and place of Sir Robert's confer- ence with Miss Pritt. These Lord Rollesborough could not give, but he did say that Sir Robert had left him to see her. It was quite plain that Sir Robert might have arranged to meet Miss Pritt somewhere near Lord Rollesborough's house and to a man like Sir Robert, who was used to discussing business in his car, Richmond Park was the most likely place for such an interview. There was, however, one thing Mooney did want to get Lord Rollesborough to promise him, and that was that he would keep his visit a secret from Miss Pritt.

He was conducting all sorts of inquiries, he explained, and it was absolutely essential to clear every person on whom the slightest suspicion might fall before the true murderer could be eliminated. Statements by different persons had to be checked and even the most innocent people were liable to modify their statements if they got to hear that the police were trying to trace their movements on a certain day. Lord Rollesborough, who found the placing of Miss Pritt among the suspects amusing rather than alarming, readily gave his consent to keep the superintendent's visit a close secret.

There was no exultation in Mooney's thoughts as he drove back from Richmond to Scotland Yard. He still had plenty of work to do. The case against Miss Pritt was complete. He felt quite certain that Lord Rollesborough's assumption that she was honest was wrong. Everything pointed to that. Frank Littlewood, however erratic and entirely subjective his account of Miss Pritt had been, was quite right in questioning her honesty. It was because of that that she was so anxious to involve him in his uncle's murder. Lord Rollesborough must have warned her also about Sir Robert's accusations and she must have realised that, if Frank Littlewood persisted in spreading damaging rumours about her, an investigation might be ordered by the board of directors, if, indeed, she herself might not be forced to take some sort of action.

Yes. The case against Miss Pritt was complete. Her motive for committing the murder was quite plain. She foresaw Sir Robert's reactions to the discovery of her treachery. She knew him better than Lord Rollesborough. She knew that he was in earnest about exposing her. He had reserved to himself the right to "cast her down," as Frank Littlewood so flamboyantly put it, and he was determined to do it. But not to where she had started. That was no longer possible; but he could cast her down even lower than that, much lower than that! He would put her behind prison bars!

Miss Pritt's motive, Mooney reflected, was clear beyond a doubt, but he still wanted to have that matter about the cinema ticket which she had promised to send on to him cleared up. It worried him. It couldn't be the second ticket she had bought after her return from the Vale of Health between half-past seven, when she had rung up Lord Rollesborough, and a quarter-past eight, when she got her gramophone records from the cashier; for, as he had told himself already, Miss Pritt must have realised that the time when that ticket was bought could be established. It must have been the first ticket she had bought about ten minutes to five. But, then, the ticket he had picked up near the second gorse bush must, after all, have been dropped by somebody who had no connection with the crime! The whole point was really of little consequence, but Mooney wished to clear it up all the same. Miss Pritt had promised to send him her ticket, and he had no doubt that he would get it in the morning. He therefore decided to let Miss Pritt's arrest wait till after he had examined her ticket.

Like an artist who resented the slightest flaw in his work, he wished his case against Miss Pritt to be absolutely complete.

Absolutely complete. Mooney, who had reached the Marble Arch, suddenly changed his mind and, instead of going on to Whitehall, he went down Oxford Street and up Regent Street into Great Portland Street on his way to Hampstead. For he suddenly remembered Samuel Halstead's confused story about seeing a woman at the wheel of the blue limousine the first time he had passed it on his way home, and it occurred to him that, now that he knew that it was a woman who killed Sir Robert Boniface, he might be able to clear up that point, too.

He found the window-cleaner's family assembled in the sitting-room of their basement flat listening to a variety programme on the wireless. Agnes, the window-cleaner's daughter, who had so disappointed the hopes of the police in their search for Matt Caldwell, sat in a corner of the room, away from her parents, in a very sullen temper, her eyes swollen with weeping and her nose very red with blowing. The visit of the superintendent evidently reminded her of something disagreeable, for she left the room almost at once.

Mooney still had his copy of *The Evening Courier* with him, but he was careful to tear out Miss Pritt's picture before showing it to

Samuel Halstead, who hadn't seen it, but who at once recognised it. Indeed, a sudden light seemed to burst in the window-cleaner's mind, for now his vague recollection of seeing a woman at the wheel of the blue limousine became more defined, and it appeared that it was not inside the car at all he had seen that woman (the wheel had really been suggested to him by the reporter of the Sunday newspaper), but on the path almost behind the first gorse bush beside which the car had been drawn up. He was made aware of her presence there because of a strange involuntary movement she had made, as if she wished to duck behind the bush and escape his notice. He hadn't thought anything of that incident at the time, although he could now plainly remember that the woman's face had seemed very excited and even frightened; for all sorts of queer things are liable to happen behind bushes on a summer evening even so near the road. Samuel Halstead had very nice feelings and he thought it was better not to embarrass people. But that curious action of the woman must have stuck in his mind and he later associated it in a rather vague way with the other much more important event of that evening.

There could be no doubt that Samuel Halstead's recollection was quite genuine. He even remembered the colour of the woman's dress which, he told the superintendent, was grey, and that she wore gloves of the same colour. Yes, now looking at her picture in the paper he remembered it all. Miss Pritt's general appearance was so obviously that of a "lady," that her strange behaviour on seeing him had impressed itself on his mind, although it needed the picture to bring it all back to him.

Mooney did not stop to satisfy the window-cleaner's curiosity. He merely told him that he might be wanted by the police to-morrow to identify the woman whose picture he had been shown. He then went across to Sycamore Cottage to satisfy himself that the Littlewoods had accepted the offer of spending the week-end at his country cottage. He found the house empty, a sign that June Gayford was successful in carrying out his instructions.

On his return to Scotland Yard, Mooney had a long telephone conversation with the Commissioner of Police and he remained quite late in his room that night completing his report.

18

T HE MYSTERY OF THE CINEMA TICKET WAS SOLVED MORE EASILY than Superintendent Mooney expected. It arrived by the first post, accompanied by a curt note from Miss Pritt, in which she expressed the hope that the superintendent was now satisfied, at any rate about her alibi, and that he would not trouble her any more as she was really very busy at present. Mooney handed the note to Inspector Beckett, who seemed to be fascinated by it, for he read it a few times and then smiled his good-humoured smile.

"The woman certainly has a nerve, sir," he remarked, handing the note back to his superior.

But Mooney said nothing. He looked at the enclosed green ticket and he smiled broadly. He opened a drawer and took out an album in which all the unsatisfactory clues of the crimes he had been recently investigating were preserved with explanatory notes and in which he had provisionally put the half of the cinema ticket he had found on Hampstead Heath. He placed the two halves of the tickets side by side and motioned to the inspector to examine them. The two tickets bore consecutive numbers; 68582 and 68583!

"She must have bought the two tickets at the same time!" Beckett said after a brief pause.

"Quite. I saw it at once, for I had memorised the number of the ticket I picked up. But in that case why did she *offer to* provide me with so damaging a piece of evidence?"

"In her anxiety to clear herself she must have overlooked the possibility that her other ticket would be found."

"I suppose she intended to keep the two halves of the tickets and, if necessary, provide me with one and destroy the other. But in her excitement at being seen by Samuel Halstead she must have dropped the used ticket when she was disposing of the cartridge. She must have had her doubts as to where she had dropped it and that was probably one of the reasons why she watched me so intently when I was taking down her alibi. I nearly gave myself away when she mentioned the cinema, but, if she had any suspicions, she seems to have dismissed them. Anyway"—the superintendent laughed, unable to conceal his satisfaction—"it's all quite cleared up now. The cinema ticket," he went on in a conciliatory tone, for he remembered the outspoken strictures passed on the torn bit of the cinema ticket by the inspector, "was a clue I just stumbled on in the utterly illogical, unreasonable way in which one often does in life. Miss Pritt might not even have suspected that she had dropped the cinema ticket when she was disposing of the cartridge, and even if she did suspect it, the possibility of anyone's picking up a small piece of a discarded cinema ticket on Hampstead Heath was so slight that she must have thought very little of it. A fatal slip, no doubt, but not so fatal as much more experienced criminals have made. It just completes the case against her in a way that leaves very little to circumstantial evidence. And it confirms Halstead's story, too."

"Yes. But what an utterly ridiculous yarn he told that reporter! He saw a woman at the wheel of the car!"

"Well, he most probably would have seen her at the wheel if he had come a little earlier, but I doubt if he would have remembered it. It was the extraordinary behaviour of an otherwise dignified middle-aged woman that stuck in his mind, but his thoughts must have been preoccupied with other things, for he had clean forgotten it. Very interesting psychologically."

But the inspector was not interested in strange psychological phenomena, for he was worried by the fact that they had failed to make anything of the clues he had found in the car. The cigar, no doubt, had proved an invaluable clue in the end, but it was by mere chance that the superintendent had stumbled on its owner. But for Marjorie Trevor they would hardly have been able to induce Lord Rollesborough to explain the circumstances that, unknown to him, had led to the murder of Sir Robert Boniface, and Marjorie Trevor would never have thought of coming to Scotland Yard but for the mess Matt Caldwell had got himself into. The inspector, who at the time could not forgive himself for having let Matt Caldwell slip through his fingers, now realised that it was just that fact which had helped the police to solve so expeditiously the mystery of Sir Robert Boniface's murder. And then there was the handkerchief, which led them straight to Miss Pritt, and which they never even suspected to have been a clue! The superintendent made light of it now, but Beckett could see that Mooney reproached himself for having thought so little of Miss Pritt's suspicious behaviour when he had shown it to her on his first visit to Lownds Square. And there was something else. What was that simple explanation the super-intendent had hinted at as to why Sir Robert had changed his mind about seeing his sister on Friday instead of on Saturday?

"There's still the difficulty about the visits Sir Robert wished to pay to Benjamin Fuller and Mrs. Littlewood at six o'clock on Friday…" Inspector Beckett ventured to remind his superior.

"But don't you see," Mooney exclaimed, "Sir Robert never intended to pay that call on Mrs. Littlewood at all! He intended to see Benjamin Fuller at six o'clock on Friday and Mrs. Littlewood at six o'clock on Saturday. It was Miss Pritt who made the appointment with Mrs. Littlewood, and she made it for her own purpose, for she was anxious to prepare everything in case Sir Robert forced her hand.

She was quite determined to kill him, if he proved as awkward as she suspected he would, and she was also prepared to get rid of Frank Littlewood by making suspicion fall on him for his uncle's murder..."

The telephone bell rang. The officer who had been detailed to follow Miss Pritt's movements reported that she had just arrived at the headquarters of the Industrial Development Trust in Leadenhall Street. It was only a quarter to nine, and Inspector Beckett looked up in surprise.

"Isn't she rather early at work?" he asked.

"Very eager to start on her new job, no doubt," Mooney surmised. He could not help feeling sad. "Don't forget," he said, "that she has at last realised the ambition of her lifetime..." For a moment it seemed that the superintendent was brooding over that thought, then he brushed it away: it was not for him to waste his sympathy on a murderer. "Let's go at once," he turned to the inspector. "The sooner it's over, the better for everybody."

About half an hour later, Superintendent Mooney, accompanied by Chief Detective-Inspector Beckett and Miss Simpson, a woman detective whom Mooney took with him in case her services should be required, parked his second-hand two-seater beside Miss Pritt's powerful new car in a little courtyard at the back of the offices of the Industrial Development Trust. Mooney pointed out Miss Pritt's car to Miss Simpson and Inspector Beckett: she must have bought it, he said, only a few days ago!

There was no reason to suspect that Miss Pritt would, even if she could, try to escape and no special steps were taken to guard the entrances to the offices.

The superintendent and his companions were shown into a sumptuously furnished waiting-room. The staff was only just beginning to arrive and for a time it was difficult to get hold of the right person to announce their arrival to Miss Pritt. But even when their presence was made known to her, she did not seem in a hurry to see them. She was clearly annoyed by their visit and sent a uniformed office-boy twice to ask them if they could not let her know what they had come about.

She received them at last, standing behind her desk, a very impressive and dignified figure, looking displeased and a little perturbed at the presence of the superintendent's companions, but also very anxious to impress Mooney with her fine new office and the wealth about her.

Her room was even larger than the one she had occupied in Lownds Square. Her desk was covered with documents and letters, and in front of her lay a copy of *The Daily Courier-Tribune*, of which most of the front page was given to a description of the accident on Westminster Bridge the day before. Miss Pritt must have been reading it before the detectives had entered the room, for the paper lay unfolded before her, showing across the whole width of the front page, a photograph of the damage done to the bridge and of the hoarding erected where part of the parapet had given way.

Behind the desk were two large windows, and on the wall opposite was a large portrait in oils of the founder of the Industrial Development Trust, Sir Robert Boniface.

"Didn't you receive my letter this morning?" Miss Pritt addressed the question to the superintendent, but no sooner had the words been spoken than the disturbed look in her eyes deepened and for a brief moment panic seemed to seize her.

But she recovered quickly and faced them squarely without a tremor of agitation. She sat down at her desk and invited the detectives to sit down, too, but only Mooney accepted her invitation. Inspector Beckett remained standing in front of the desk and prepared to take notes of the conversation, while Miss Simpson remained standing at the door.

"I hold a warrant for your arrest for the murder of Sir Robert Boniface," Mooney said in a level, emotionless voice, and he finished with the usual caution and with the usual advice about legal help.

Miss Pritt did not interrupt him. She must have been taken entirely by surprise, but the only sign she showed of the wave of terror which had swept over her was that she clutched the arms of her chair very tightly. She was trying to make up her mind quickly. She was entirely composed by the time Mooney had finished and her smoothly-brushed black hair with the silver streaks enhanced the composure of her face. She only made one attempt to find out whether Mooney had really discovered everything.

"Is this one of your jokes, superintendent?" she asked in a quiet, slightly ironic voice.

"You shot Sir Robert," Mooney said without replying to her question, "in his car about six o'clock, or a little later, on Friday, June the twenty-third, after a conference with him in Richmond Park near the house of Lord Rollesborough whom he had just left. You shot him with his own gun which you had taken out of his room, because he told you that he had found out that you had betrayed his plans to the board of directors of the Industrial Development Trust and that he was determined that you should never hold the position he had himself obtained for you. You shot him because he made it clear to you that he had sufficient proof of your dishonesty for private gain during the years you had been his confidential secretary to put you in prison. You shot him because you knew that he was not just threatening, but that he intended to bring about your downfall in the same way as you had contrived his!"

"That certainly sounds quite a plausible story," Miss Pritt said in her quiet, ironic tone, into which, however, there had now crept a distinct venomous note, "but can you prove any of your entirely ridiculous assertions?"

"I can prove that you killed Sir Robert. The rest will not be difficult to prove, either."

"But you can't even prove that I kept my appointment with Sir Robert on Friday afternoon! I gave you a detailed account of my movements on Friday. I was at 'The Empire' between five and eight o'clock. Isn't that sufficient proof that I had nothing to do with Sir Robert's murder?"

"You were not at 'The Empire' between five and eight o'clock on Friday! You were there about five o'clock when you bought two tickets, for you were anxious to return to the cinema unobserved later. You then entered the cinema and left it almost at once to keep your appointment with Sir Robert Boniface in Richmond Park at about half-past five. You shot Sir Robert about half an hour later, I believe, or just about six o'clock. He was late in keeping his appointment with you, for he had stayed longer than he intended with Lord Rollesborough. I have no doubt that you tried your best to dissuade him from the course he had decided to take and that you killed him only when you were quite certain that he would carry out his threats against you. But for you also it was getting very late. You were in a great hurry to leave because you were anxious to bring Sir Robert's car to the Vale of Health before Frank Littlewood was expected home. You knew that he would probably be home at about seven o'clock, for Mrs. Littlewood had told you that, when you made the appointment for Sir Robert to see her at six o'clock. And here you made your first mistake, for you didn't think it necessary to find out whether Sir Robert had not already made an appointment for that time. Or did you think that it was not likely that the police would find out about Sir Robert's intention to see Mr. Fuller at six o'clock? Anyway, it is quite clear that Sir Robert never instructed you to make the appointment with Mrs. Littlewood for Friday. In your hurry to leave Richmond Park you backed Sir Robert's car rather violently into the barbed-wire fence, which you broke, scratching the back of the car. Then you drove to the Vale of Health where you arrived at about a quarter to seven. You managed to leave the car unobserved, but you dropped your grey silk handkerchief as you were leaving it. As you were walking up the steep path by the gorse bush near the car, you saw a man, Samuel Halstead, a window-cleaner, coming along and you ducked instinctively behind the bush, wishing to avoid being seen. But that movement gave you away and Samuel Halstead identified your photograph in yesterday's *Evening Courier*. Later, when you read Samuel Halstead's confused story in the Sunday paper you must have thought very little of that incident, but at the time it excited you to such an extent that, when you came to take the cartridge from your handbag to throw it away, you did not notice that you had also dropped the returned half of one of the cinema tickets, which I picked up. The cinema ticket you sent me this morning is merely another confirmation of your movements on Friday, for the numbers of the two tickets are consecutive. Then on your way back to Leicester Square you telephoned to Lord Rollesborough, giving him an entirely false account of the issue of your conference with Sir Robert. Frank Littlewood's visit to Lownds Square on Monday gave you an excellent opportunity for disposing of Sir Robert's gun, which you were afraid to leave in the car because of the disastrous effect a rumour of Sir Robert's suicide might have had on the affairs of the Industrial Development Trust…"

"Exactly!" Miss Pritt exclaimed with an impulsiveness which seemed quite unnatural to her. She had been listening to Mooney without making any sign either of confirmation or of denial. But she was watching him with that intensity which he knew so well by now. At the mention of the Industrial Development Trust, however, her composure suddenly deserted her. Her face flushed. Her eyes shot a keen, triumphant glance at the portrait of Sir Robert Boniface on the wall opposite: she would escape his vengeance, after all! All her foresight had not availed her. The superintendent had been too clever for her. He had found out everything. But he had given her her chance now. She was not beaten yet! She wanted to live, to be free, to enjoy her success! "I'm glad you mentioned that, superintendent," she said, trying to keep out of her voice the feverish excitement by which she had been suddenly caught, "for it will help you to understand why I tried to make Sir Robert's suicide look like murder! He realised that he had lost his fight with the directorate, that his defeat was final, and he committed suicide. He knew he was played out!" she exclaimed, her voice becoming tense with sincere conviction. "Sir Robert Boniface," she repeated, turning for the first and only time to Inspector Beckett, as if she expected more sympathy from him than from the superintendent, "was played out! I knew it and I told him so. But he would not admit it. All he could do in future was just mischief. He was better out of the way. His last scheme would have meant untold suffering. I told him so. But he wouldn't admit that, either. Then he must suddenly have realised that I was right and he shot himself!"

"But why did you go to such lengths as to prepare an alibi for yourself?" Mooney asked. "Why did you go to the cinema only to leave it? Why did you buy two tickets?"

"I didn't prepare an alibi for myself! It isn't true! It's true I left the cinema to keep the appointment with Sir Robert, but that was not my intention when I went into the cinema. I don't know anything about the ticket you picked up on Hampstead Heath. It must have been dropped by somebody who bought it just before or after mine... I went into the cinema intending to stay there, for I knew perfectly well what it was Sir Robert wanted to discuss with me. He had already mentioned it to me when he took me to Harrods. But I came to the conclusion that I'd better go through with it. I knew

Sir Robert could do nothing against me. I had not betrayed him! I knew he couldn't carry through his scheme. I knew it could end only in disaster. But he wouldn't listen to me, and I decided to let Lord Rollesborough know about it. I repudiate emphatically your insinuation that I am dishonest. It's a lie! And I know who's spreading these slanders against me!"

"I'm quite confident that I shall be able to prove it!" Mooney interjected.

"It will be extremely difficult for you to prove anything of the sort," Miss Pritt exclaimed in a sudden outburst of anger, "because it is not true!" She continued more quietly, however, forcing herself to betray no emotion in her voice. "My conference with Sir Robert, whom I met, on his own suggestion, in Richmond Park, took its expected course, and when he realised his complete isolation and that I would never again consent to work with him against the board of directors, he shot himself... I was not even in the car then. Sir Robert was so angry with me that he would not drive me out of Richmond Park. I had already left him, when I heard a shot and, running back to the car, discovered the terrible thing that had happened. My first impulse was to inform the police. But, then, as you yourself so clearly realised, I saw what a disaster it would be if Sir Robert's suicide were to be known. I decided that the best thing would be to simulate murder. I thought of Sir Robert's quarrel with his nephew and it struck me that if I took the car with his body to the Vale of Health, the police might suspect Frank Littlewood of having murdered his uncle. I never really thought that they would have enough evidence to convict him..."

"But hadn't you taken care to find out already in the morning when Frank Littlewood would be likely to return home?"

"I'd done nothing of the sort! Sir Robert asked me to arrange the interview with his sister. He might have forgotten about his appointment with Fuller, or he might have decided not to see him. I don't know. I didn't know anything about his appointment with Fuller..."

"But you did put the gun in the drawer of Frank Littlewood's desk on Monday?"

"I admit it!" Miss Pritt made a tremendous effort to overcome the excitement which shook her with feverish intensity when she realised that she still had a chance of escaping the shadow of death which Sir Robert had thrown over her from his grave. She stood at her desk outwardly unruffled, but quite unexpectedly she would give in to the intense excitement within her. She would grasp the arms of her chair and her voice would assume a strange ringing tone which did not entirely accord with the words she was saying. "But then, it wasn't my fault that you found it out! It was Fuller's fault in going to Scotland Yard and confessing about having dropped the gun into the pond. For two days the police had been searching for the gun and couldn't find it. I told Fuller that he should drop the gun where it would be very difficult to find. I had to get rid of it somehow, and that seemed to me the best way. After all, I ran a terrible risk myself, and I took the risk because I was anxious to save the Industrial Development Trust from disaster!"

"That will be your defence, Miss Pritt," Mooney said, quite unimpressed by her story, "and you'd better discuss it with your lawyers..."

She shot a venomous look at him. His calm brought back to her that piercing agony of doubt which had seized her with such force when she first greeted the superintendent.

"May I ring up my solicitors now?" she asked.

Her face was still flushed from her excitement, but she did not believe any more that she would be able to escape. Hope had left her with the same suddenness as it had come, and despair now filled her thoughts. But it was most important to keep her head.

She realised that above everything else, and she kept her head remarkably well.

Mooney offered no objection to her request, and she rang up a well-known firm of solicitors and arranged for the head of the firm to meet her at Scotland Yard in half an hour. She put down the receiver and for a while she still kept her hand on it, as if uncertain whether to ring up someone else. Then she made a visible effort over herself and got up.

"I suppose," she said, "it's useless to ask you to believe that I'm innocent. But whether I'm acquitted or not, it will make no difference to me. My career is ruined, anyhow..."

She pressed her lips together tightly: she obviously had to make an effort to control her feelings. For a brief space of time her eyes remained fixed on the front page of *The Daily Courier-Tribune* on her desk with the picture of the hoarding on Westminster Bridge. Then she seemed to have made up her mind to accept the inevitable.

"You won't object to my putting on my hat and coat?" she asked.

Mooney offered no objection. "Miss Simpson," he said, "will accompany you!"

Miss Simpson, a young woman of thirty, of good physique but of smaller build than Miss Pritt, opened the door for her and followed her out of the room. As she passed out, Miss Pritt glanced for the second time at Sir Robert Boniface's portrait, but her glance was no longer triumphant. It was full of bitter, deep-seated, ineradicable hatred.

Mooney, who caught Miss Pritt's glance, remarked to Inspector Beckett on the extraordinary fact that, except for Lady Boniface and Mrs. Fuller and, possibly, Mrs. Littlewood, Sir Robert Boniface seemed to have made enemies of everybody with whom he had come into close contact. Miss Pritt's hatred, he said, was not of recent origin. It must have existed for a long time, for as long a time, perhaps, as Sir Robert had chosen her as the instrument of his will!

And the superintendent told the inspector of Miss Pritt's curious smile when she read the passage in Frank Littlewood's article about the need for getting rid of the modern Napoleons of industry by violence. She didn't, after all, think that passage fantastic! She must, in fact, have been amused to see her own secret idea expressed in print, and by Littlewood, of all people! Sir Robert Boniface, in the view of his trusted confidential secretary, was better out of the way, for he was no longer capable of any constructive efforts. He was capable of nothing but mischief! Miss Pritt and Frank Littlewood were, then, of the same opinion. Only while Sir Robert's nephew theorised, Miss Pritt put his theories into action!

But Inspector Beckett, who had not seen Miss Pritt's smile, could not compare notes with the superintendent. He wasn't, in any case, interested in subtle problems of that sort. What interested him at the moment was whether Lord Rollesborough would make any effort to come to Miss Pritt's assistance. It seemed to him, he said, that the new Chairman of the Industrial Development Trust would give anything to get her out of the country. Miss Pritt was, no doubt, quite aware of that.

"I'm afraid," Mooney said, "Lord Rollesborough's first and only concern will be to try to keep out of court anything that he may consider detrimental to the position of the Industrial Development Trust."

"Things have gone a little too far for that!" Inspector Beckett observed.

A sudden commotion outside the door put an end to the discussion. On rushing out, Mooney and Beckett recognised Miss Simpson's voice, which seemed to be coming from a room at the end of the corridor. She was shouting and banging on the door. A small crowd had already collected outside the room, consisting mostly of office-boys and typists. The caretaker appeared on the scene almost at once. He fumbled for some time with his bunch of keys till he found the one that fitted the door of Miss Pritt's small cloakroom. When the door was opened, Miss Simpson, who looked very distressed and red in the face from her recent exertions, was the only one to come out: Miss Pritt, she gasped out, had got away!

Inspector Beckett, having taken in the situation at a glance, dashed downstairs. Mooney motioned Miss Simpson to follow him to Miss Pritt's office, and shut the door unceremoniously on the curious crowd of boys and young women who were following them.

The woman detective's story was short: she had accompanied Miss Pritt to her small private cloakroom at the end of the corridor. Miss Pritt opened the door with her key, which she left in the lock. She then went in and was followed by Miss Simpson. Before putting on her hat and coat, she had a wash and powdered her face. She showed no sign that she had anything on her mind, and Miss Simpson was quite taken in by her sensible behaviour. When leaving the cloakroom, the woman detective opened the door and let Miss Pritt go first. But, as she was stepping over the threshold, the dignified, composed middle-aged woman turned round savagely on Miss Simpson and gave her a violent push. Before the woman detective could do anything, she found herself locked in the room. The whole thing was so unexpected that she still seemed to be amazed rather than angry.

While listening to Miss Simpson's story, Mooney found himself staring at the front page of *The Daily Courier-Tribune* on Miss Pritt's desk. He recalled how fixedly Miss Pritt had looked at the same page before she had left the room. Struck by a sudden thought, he went up to the windows behind the desk, which, as he rightly judged, looked out on the small courtyard where he had parked his car beside Miss Pritt's new car. His car was still standing where he had left it, but Miss Pritt's car had gone!

The superintendent made up his mind quickly. He ordered Miss Simpson to get through to Scotland Yard at once and tell them to have a fast car on the lookout for a green, long-bodied racing car which would probably pass the entrance of Scotland Yard on the way to Westminster Bridge in a few minutes. He himself would be following it. The green car with Miss Pritt, who was a first-class driver, at the wheel, was to be stopped at all costs. The police were to close Westminster Bridge till he arrived. A description of Miss Pritt and her car was also to be broadcast to all police stations.

On his way out of the room, the superintendent nearly collided with Lord Rollesborough. The earl had obviously been informed of the extraordinary happenings in Miss Pritt's office and there could be no doubt that he had guessed what the whole fuss was about, for he looked ghastly. His face was bloodless, and he had to support himself on his cane. He had evidently only just arrived at the offices of the Industrial Development Trust, for he still wore his hat which was tilted sideways, and which lent his massive, perturbed face a ludicrously rakish expression. He was followed by a small, stout, pompous, baldheaded man and a tall, well-built young woman, whose large face registered, as in a mirror, the earl's agitation, worry, shock and anxiety.

But Mooney did not wait to explain the situation to Lord Rollesborough. He waved him to Miss Simpson, who had already got on to Scotland Yard and was telephoning the superintendent's orders. In the entrance hall he found Inspector Beckett, who was just coming back from his investigation. The inspector had questioned the detective who had been detailed to shadow Miss Pritt and was keeping watch in the entrance hall, but he had not seen her. Nor had anyone else in the entrance hall seen her. Beckett thought that she might be still in the building, but Mooney told him that her car had gone. The two police officers went round to the courtyard, which they reached by way of a side street.

"How much start has she got of us, do you think?" Mooney asked, as Beckett sat down beside him in his car.

"Five minutes at least!" Beckett replied.

Mooney did not answer. He merely nodded and backed his car out of the courtyard.

"Where are we going?" the inspector asked, but the superintendent was too busy getting the car into Leadenhall Street to reply. "Well," Beckett went on, thinking they were going back to head-quarters, "I certainly shouldn't have expected her to give us all this trouble. But she *has* given us the slip this time and if she can get hold of Rollesborough before we get her, then it's ten to one we shan't see her again! He'd give a fortune to get her out of the country. He'll have no difficulty in believing her tale!"

Mooney, whose whole attention was given to getting ahead of the traffic which was pouring in an uninterrupted stream to the top of Cornhill, shouted to the inspector that there was no chance of that. But Beckett, who didn't know that the superintendent had met Lord Rollesborough a few minutes ago, was not convinced.

The superintendent was so intent on manœuvring the car across the road past the Mansion House into Queen Victoria Street that he did not take the trouble to reassure the inspector. But he did ask Beckett if he had seen this morning's front page of *The Daily Courier-Tribune*.

Beckett had seen it, but he didn't appear to know what Mooney was getting at, and as the superintendent had just accelerated and was speeding across the approach to Blackfriars Bridge on to the Embankment, he had no time to explain.

This was, in fact, no time for explanations, for Mooney was driving at the greatest speed his second-hand car was capable of and his whole attention was centred on the road ahead of him. On approaching Waterloo Bridge, he had to slow down.

"Look!" he shouted to Beckett. "There she goes!"

The inspector's eyes widened with amazement: sure enough, there was Miss Pritt driving her powerful sports car at a normal speed. She was evidently not expecting her pursuers to get so quickly on her track and she was not anxious to attract attention by reckless driving!

Mooney could only see the small, jade-green hat on the top of Miss Pritt's head, but when she presently turned round for a fraction of a second, he caught a glimpse of her face, which was very white and tense. What impressed itself on his mind was Miss Pritt's mouth, which was all puckered up like that of a child who finds himself lost in a crowd and begins to cry.

Mooney had no time to confirm his fleeting impression, for Miss Pritt, who had recognised her pursuers, tore forward at a terrific speed and narrowly missed knocking down a woman who was crossing the road by Cleopatra's Needle.

The cool precision with which Miss Pritt avoided the woman in the street reminded Mooney how he had admired her driving only the day before, and wrung an exclamation of admiration from Beckett.

"What a nerve that woman has!" The inspector repeated the tribute he had paid Miss Pritt a few hours ago, only now in a more awed voice. "Where's she going?" he asked, turning to the superintendent.

"Westminster Bridge!" Mooney replied cryptically, his attention being suddenly diverted to a row of stationary tramcars on the Embankment. His order to divert the traffic from Westminster Bridge had been carried out!

"Westminster Bridge?" Beckett echoed nonplussed. And then he remembered Mooney's question about the front page of *The Daily*

Courier-Tribune. "Good God!" he exclaimed. "You don't mean to say she's going to drive over the bridge through the gap in the parapet?"

"Yes!"

"But why on earth should she do it? Couldn't she think of some less spectacular and less dangerous way of committing suicide? She's sure to kill somebody in the attempt!"

But Mooney, who had already thought of that, was suddenly overcome with misgivings: wasn't it more likely that the only chance of preventing Miss Pritt from committing suicide would have been not to interfere with the traffic, but to overtake her when she reached Westminster Bridge, where she would have had to slow down on account of the traffic? Having seen Miss Pritt's face for that brief moment, Mooney somehow felt convinced that she would have done her utmost to avoid an accident which would have involved someone else's death! He contented himself, however, with replying to Beckett's question:

"Her car!" he shouted. "She feels safe in it!"

"Feels safe?" Beckett murmured in utter bewilderment. For a moment the inspector thought that Mooney had gone stark mad, but the next moment he persuaded himself that he must have misunderstood him.

As very frequently in their close association, Beckett refused to follow his superior's conclusions. He didn't believe that Miss Pritt intended to commit suicide. It was uncanny the way Mooney had guessed the route she was likely to take, but Beckett regarded it as nothing but a guess.

Miss Pritt's car was now almost opposite Scotland Yard, and Mooney sounded his horn in one continuous high-pitched blast. As he expected, Miss Pritt completely disregarded the signal to stop of the policemen who had been stationed near the end of the Embankment to examine and to divert the motor traffic. But in reply to his signal, a police car shot out from under the arches of Scotland Yard with two policemen on its running-board. It was a little ahead of Miss Pritt's car and it was obviously the intention of the police to let Miss Pritt pass while the police car kept close to the small island at the place where the road describes a bend a few yards on this side of the bridge. That would have enabled the policemen on the running-board to jump across into Miss Pritt's car the moment she came alongside their car, slowing down to turn on to the bridge. But the police had not counted on Miss Pritt's desperate resolution. She did not slow down, but drove furiously past and took the turning with ease, followed by the police car and Mooney's car in the rear.

A cordon of police cars and motor cycles was drawn up on the opposite end of the bridge, but, as Mooney realised, there was nothing now to prevent Miss Pritt from carrying out her plan. Her car gathered speed with a low roar and swerved towards the hoarding which concealed the gap in the bridge. It crashed through, missed the gap, but hit the edge of the broken parapet and turned over. Miss Pritt was shot, like a bullet, clean out of her car and fell into the river.

When Mooney and Beckett came up and pushed their way through the crowd of policemen, there was nothing to be seen. The tide was coming in rapidly and a great swirl was all there was to indicate the place where Miss Pritt's body had hit the water. The only reminder of Miss Pritt was her fashionable jade-green hat, which was being carried away swiftly towards Lambeth Bridge. Mooney could not help following it with his eyes, while his hand went involuntarily to his head, which he bared. The green hat soon became an indistinguishable spot, and in another moment it was gone with the other useless odds and ends which the river was carrying up with the tide.

"Feeling hot from the chase?" an excited young voice exclaimed at Mooney's elbow, and, on turning round, the superintendent, who hastily replaced his hat, recognised the boyish face of a young newspaper man well known to the police. The journalist modelled himself on the movie crime reporters. He wore his hat on the crown of his head and affected a Hollywood style of speech. "Oh, boy, oh, boy!" he addressed Inspector Beckett, who was a particular friend of his. "What a story! Murderess of Sir Robert Boniface Crashes Into Thames! Desperate Action To Evade Arrest! Police Trap For Runaway! Westminster Bridge In Another Daytime Drama!"

"What a collection of rotten headlines!" Chief Detective-Inspector Beckett, whose perplexed face lit up suddenly with his good-humoured smile, exclaimed, taking his young friend by the arm. "But you've hit the nail on the head! She crashed through the bridge because she found her escape cut off. The police were too quick for her! Come along," Mooney heard the inspector say as he walked off with the reporter, "I'll give you the full police version of the story!"

The superintendent, too, smiled: Beckett's version of Miss Pritt's suicide was good enough for the Press!

He remained on the bridge a little longer and he absent-mindedly watched the police remove Miss Pritt's smashed car, the workmen replace the broken hoarding, and the traffic resume its steady flow. He felt a twinge of conscience not only because he had bungled his own job, but also because he could not help feeling uneasy in his mind about his own part in Miss Pritt's suicide. He had been right in guessing her intention, and, once he had assumed that she was going to smash through the broken parapet of the bridge, he had to do all he could to prevent an accident, involving, maybe, the deaths of innocent people. The accident on Westminster Bridge the day before had plainly prompted his action in ordering the clearing of the bridge just as it had given Miss Pritt the idea of committing suicide in what was, perhaps, the only way in which she could summon sufficient pluck to do it. But Mooney could not forget his fleeting impression of

Miss Pritt's face in the car: was she losing her courage or was it merely a momentary spasm of terror which had overcome her? Would she have changed her mind had he not forced her hand? Would the traffic on the bridge have held her up and made her capture possible? Did he commit a blunder in clearing Westminster Bridge? Or would she have risked an accident in order to evade arrest and, improbable as the thought appeared, save the Industrial Development Trust?

No reply was possible to any of these questions. Even Miss Pritt, had she lived, would not be able to tell him.

A familiar sound roused Mooney from his thoughts and recalled him to his duties: it was Big Ben striking eleven...

ALSO AVAILABLE

Crime author Dick Markham is in love again; his fiancée is the mysterious newcomer to the village, Lesley Grant. When Grant accidentally shoots the fortune teller through the side of his tent at the local fair—following a very strange reaction to his predictions—Markham is reluctantly brought into a scheme to expose his betrothed as a suspected serial husband-poisoner.

That night the enigmatic fortune teller—and chief accuser—is found dead in an impossible locked-room setup, casting suspicion onto Grant and striking doubt into the heart of her lover. Lured by the scent of the impossible case, Dr Gideon Fell arrives from London to examine the perplexing evidence and match wits with a meticulous killer at large.

First published in 1944, *Till Death Do Us Part* remains a pacey and deeply satisfying impossible crime story, championed by Carr connoisseurs as one of the very best examples of his mystery writing talents.